Christmas Stitches

A HISTORICAL ROMANCE COLLECTION

3 Stories of Women Sewing Hope and Love Through the Holidays

Christmas Stitches

A HISTORICAL ROMANCE COLLECTION

Judith Miller, Nancy Moser
& Stephanie Grace Whitson

BARBOUR BOOKS
An Imprint of Barbour Publishing, Inc.

Print ISBN 978-1- 68322-715-1

eBook Editions:
Adobe Digital Edition (.epub) 978-1-68322-922-3
Kindle and MobiPocket Edition (.prc) 978-1-68322-923-0

All scripture quotations, unless otherwise noted, are taken from the King James Version of the Bible.

This book is a work of fiction. Names, characters, places, and incidents are either products of the author's imagination or used fictitiously. Any similarity to actual people, organizations, and/or events is purely coincidental.

Published by Barbour Books, an imprint of Barbour Publishing, Inc., 1810 Barbour Drive, Uhrichsville, Ohio 44683, www.barbourbooks.com

Our mission is to inspire the world with the life-changing message of the Bible.

Printed in Canada.

Contents

A Seamless Love

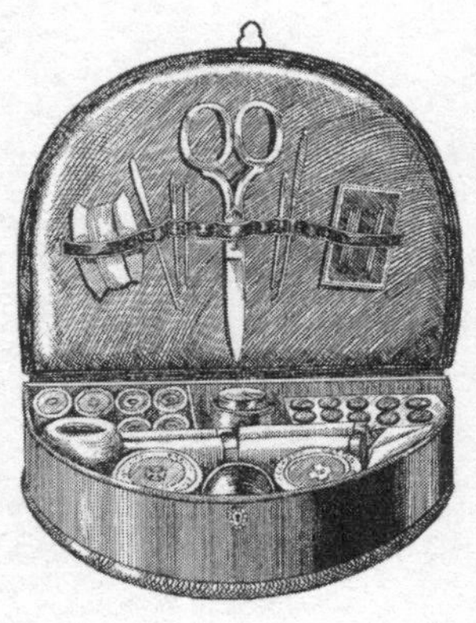

by Judith Miller

When I was a child, I talked like a child,
I thought like a child, I reasoned like a child.
When I became a man, I put the ways of childhood behind me. . . .
And now these three remain: faith, hope and love.
But the greatest of these is love.

1 CORINTHIANS 13:11, 13 NIV

Prologue

Pullman, Illinois
Christmas Eve 1883

Hannah Cooper's strategy to declare her love might have been considered a breach of proper comportment. But she wouldn't let such opinions stop her. She believed the Christmas Ball provided the perfect occasion to change her friendship with Daniel Price into a romance that would lead to engagement and marriage.

The party was a happy affair, yet one that she enjoyed with an extra dose of nervous knots in her stomach. Finally, the time arrived to implement her plan. She beckoned to Daniel as the guests prepared to depart. When he approached, his face was alight with pleasure. "Ready to go home?"

"Not quite yet. I have something to tell you. Why don't we step into the alcove, where it will be private?"

Once Hannah was certain they were alone, she reached into her pocket, withdrew a sprig of mistletoe, and lifted it above her head.

Anticipating his expected kiss, she held her breath and waited. For so long she had ached to feel his embrace and the soft fullness of his lips upon her own. A shiver coursed down her arms when he reached forward and lifted her chin. But when she opened her eyes, her heart plummeted. Rather than fervent desire, his eyes shone with distress.

He reached up and removed the mistletoe that she continued to hold above her mass of brown curls. "Listen carefully to what I'm going to say, Hannah. I would never do anything to intentionally hurt you because you are the best friend I've ever had." When she turned her head, he lightly touched her cheek and turned her head back toward him. "Please, Hannah. I don't want to ruin our friendship by entering into a deeper relationship that could eventually destroy the bond we've formed over the past twelve years. I watched what happened to Alfred and Nellie when he began to court her after years of friendship." He shook his head. "When it didn't work out, their friendship couldn't be restored and they remain bitter toward each other to this day."

She fought to hold back tears of pain and embarrassment. "But that doesn't mean. . ."

He touched his finger to her lips. "I know such an end isn't a certainty between us, but I'm unwilling to take that chance. Your friendship means far too much to me, and I pray what I've said won't change our bond." He smiled down at her. "Until you find the man of your dreams, I hope that you'll permit me to be your escort on special occasions and you'll continue to confide in me and permit me to do the same."

Though an aching heaviness settled in her chest, Hannah forced a weak smile. "Of course, Daniel. I never want anything to come between our friendship. Until some other man steps into my life, I'd be pleased to have you as my escort and confidant." She blinked back the tears that threatened, swallowed the lump in her throat, and looped her hand in his arm.

As he led her into the parlor to bid their farewells, the piece of mistletoe escaped his hand and dropped to the floor, and with it, Hannah's hopes fell.

Chapter One

September 1888

Hannah Cooper fumbled with the buttons of her gray wool jacket while making a rushed entry into the Pullman Arcade. The magnificent three-story edifice housed a variety of shops, the post office, bank, library, a splendid theater, and was the hub of activity in the company-owned town outside Chicago. By the time Hannah arrived at the Millinery and Dressmaking Shop, she'd removed her coat and tucked her sketch pad into the oversized cloth bag she clutched in one hand.

"Miss Cooper! Late again, I see."

Hannah jerked around as the wiry supervisor rounded a glass-fronted display case that featured an array of fancy lace trims.

The older woman pinned Hannah with a dark look. "Tardiness is a bad habit that must be corrected if you wish to succeed in your employment, Miss Cooper. You've been cautioned on previous occasions." Miss Hardelle's thin lips drooped into a frown. "What's your excuse today?"

Hannah's breath caught at the back of her throat. Instead of responding, she craned her neck and looked at the clock above the front door. What if Miss Hardelle terminated her? And if she did, would her termination reflect on her father's employment at the Pullman Palace Car Company? Could they be evicted from their home in Pullman? And even if they were permitted to remain, could her mother withstand the gossip that would spread from doorway to doorway? There were no secrets in Pullman. What happened to one person was soon known by everyone who lived and worked in this self-contained town created for the workers who constructed the luxurious railcars for the Pullman Palace Car Company.

"Well?" Miss Hardelle tapped the pointed toe of her black leather shoe on the wooden floor.

Hannah swallowed and gestured toward the clock. "I'm not really late. I stepped inside at the stroke of nine."

"That may be true, but you're expected to be at your workstation prepared to greet customers when the doors open. Instead, you're rushing in like a harried shopper eager to make a purchase before the train arrives." Miss Hardelle sighed and nodded toward the cloak room. "You test my patience. Put your belongings away and report to Mrs. Dunlap."

Hannah's stomach roiled. So she *was* being terminated. Mrs. Dunlap worked in personnel and had interviewed Hannah for her position at the shop last year. No doubt the woman was also charged with terminating employees who didn't arrive at work on time. Heart thumping, Hannah tightened her grasp on the woolen jacket, bowed her head, and hurried off to deposit her belongings.

Fastening her gaze on the floor, she rushed past several clerks who were dutifully standing at their assigned stations. How many of them already knew what lay in store for her this morning? No doubt they'd already guessed why she was going to the personnel office.

She couldn't blame Miss Hardelle for what was taking place. She had warned Hannah last week that her tardy behavior had to cease or she would speak to Mrs. Dunlap. If only she hadn't stopped to sketch that tree this morning—yet, she knew the design would be perfect on one of her beaded bags.

A dreadful realization washed over her as she hesitated outside Mrs. Dunlap's door: being punctual today would have made no difference. This meeting had to have been arranged yesterday or perhaps the day before. Miss Hardelle hadn't waited to see if Hannah's performance would improve. This morning's tardiness wasn't the cause of this looming catastrophe. Still, her late arrival could be used to affirm the decision made by her two superiors—and Hannah was now left without a leg to stand on.

Though she would accept her fate and could blame no one else, Hannah whispered a prayer for God's help. "If not for me, for my parents." Her long dark lashes brushed her cheeks with unexpected dampness, and she wiped away tears before straightening her shoulders. She couldn't stand here forever. Lifting her hand, she cupped her fingers into a fist and lightly rapped.

"Yes?" The voice was barely audible through the thick oak door. Hannah turned the brass knob and opened the door a mere crack.

"Do come in." The voice was stronger now, and Hannah pushed the door wide but entered only far enough to clear the threshold. Mrs. Dunlap sat at a large desk that dwarfed her diminutive stature. Had the circumstances not been so dire, Hannah would have grinned at the gray-haired woman sitting behind the oversized desk. If not for her wrinkles and graying hair, Mrs. Dunlap would have looked like a schoolgirl sitting at her teacher's desk.

Hannah nodded to the woman. "Miss Hardelle said you wish to speak with me."

Before entering the room, Hannah had contemplated arguing against her termination but decided it wouldn't be prudent. After all, she truly had no defense. She'd been late three times this month.

"Please have a seat, Miss Cooper." She smiled and gestured to a nearby chair.

Hannah would have preferred a swift end to their meeting—something akin to a beheading—quick and clean. However, she wasn't in charge, so she forced a half smile, and decided upon a chair near the door rather than the one beside Mrs. Dunlap.

Her skirt had barely brushed the seat when Mrs. Dunlap shook her head. "No, no. Come over here." She patted the arm of a chair she'd positioned next to her own. "I can't have a proper conversation with you when you're sitting so far away." This time her smile was so broad her cheeks plumped until her eyes disappeared into two slits. With a sigh, Hannah stood, crossed the room, and sat down beside Mrs. Dunlap. The older woman rotated her chair. "Much better."

Hannah squeezed backward until her spine protested the

undue pressure. Mrs. Dunlap might be comfortable, but Hannah had never been so uneasy. Why didn't the older woman hand her an envelope with her final pay and be done with it?

Mrs. Dunlap folded her hands and rested them in her lap. "I'm sure you're curious why I summoned you to my office, so I won't keep you in suspense any longer." Her voice bore a happy singsong tone that seemed curiously out of place. Evidently Mrs. Dunlap wasn't the sweet lady who had hired Hannah. Did she enjoy terminating employees?

"Thank you," Hannah murmured, keeping her eyes focused upon the folds in her navy-blue skirt.

Mrs. Dunlap turned her chair only far enough to reach an envelope on her desk. Hannah inhaled a halting breath. *Here it comes. My termination letter and final pay.* Her palms were suddenly damp and her cheeks flamed with heat.

The older woman's mouth curved in a generous smile. How could she be so insensitive? Hannah longed to run from the room, but she remained as still as a statue. Her mind was willing, but her body wouldn't cooperate.

"The letter is from Mrs. Pullman. She has already discussed the contents with me, and I have given my full approval."

Hannah jerked to attention. "Mrs. Pullman? Th–th–the Mrs. Pullman?" She pushed the strangled words around the lump in her throat. Why had Mrs. Dunlap discussed her termination with the owner's wife? Her breath came in short bursts as Mrs. Dunlap rattled the envelope. Hannah sighed and reached for the unwelcome missive.

There was no doubt now. Her father would lose his job. And so would she. It was the way of things in Pullman. Employees and their families were expected to follow the company rules. Hannah wasn't certain it was true, but she'd been told that termination of one family member could lead to problems for the entire family. The thought that her parents might suffer because of her tardy behavior caused Hannah's stomach to lurch.

Her hands trembled as she stared at the envelope. Her name had been written with a flourish rivaling that of any expert calligrapher. She traced her finger over each letter. With her love of design, she could appreciate the swirls and flourishes captured in the letters of her name.

Mrs. Dunlap cleared her throat and gestured to the letter. "You should open it, Miss Cooper."

The woman's urgent voice intruded upon Hannah's moment of peace and returned her to the present. Obliging the directive, she slid her finger beneath the flap, released the seal, and removed the folded sheet of cream-colored stationery. Her eyes fixed upon the initials embossed at the top of the page. *HSP.* Harriet Sanger Pullman. Every employee in the store knew the names of the Pullmans, but Hannah had never met or even seen Mrs. Pullman.

Mrs. Dunlap leaned forward and gestured toward the letter. "Hurry and read it."

Hannah returned her attention to the letter, expecting to discover she'd been terminated effective immediately. Her gaze flitted across the lines. "I'm not sure I understand. Does this mean I'm *not* being terminated?"

Mrs. Dunlap's forehead creased into a multitude of undulating fine lines. "Of course not. Why would you think you were being terminated?"

She momentarily considered withholding the truth, but that wouldn't be proper. After all, she knew better. "I've been late to work on several occasions." She bowed her head. "Today was one of those instances, so when Miss Hardelle told me to report to your office, I. . ." her voice faltered.

"You assumed I was going to terminate you?"

Hannah bobbed her head. "Yes, so this is quite unexpected." She offered the older woman a fleeting smile. "And quite wonderful."

Mrs. Dunlap nodded. "Indeed, it is. I hope you won't disappoint me. I gave Mrs. Pullman my personal recommendation."

"The letter says she wants me to design and stitch gifts for guests attending a party she's hosting." Hannah reread the letter. "A Fall Soiree for twelve of her lady friends." She looked at Mrs. Dunlap. "Have you any idea what kind of gifts she has in mind? If it's a party celebrating the fall season, there isn't much time."

"I did mention that to her and she was quite understanding. She's going to meet with you this afternoon. She's arriving on the two o'clock train and wants to go over her ideas with you at the hotel. You should be there promptly at two thirty. Given the time constraints, I'm sure she won't expect anything extravagant."

Hannah's heart pounded beneath the rows of lace that centered the bodice of her white shirtwaist. What if she couldn't meet Mrs. Pullman's expectations? Would this new assignment mean she could lose her job? If Mrs. Pullman was unhappy with her work, would there still be a position waiting at the shop? The thoughts raced through her mind like horses sprinting for the finish line. While she was flattered by the offer, this change could be disastrous.

Mrs. Dunlap patted her hand. "Mrs. Pullman was in town with her husband one evening last week. They stopped in the Millinery and Dressmaking Shop, and Mrs. Pullman noticed the unusual embroidered beading on one of the evening gowns. She wanted to know the name of the seamstress." Mrs. Dunlap chuckled. "In truth, she wanted to know who had designed the fancywork on the gown—the plum silk you adorned with tiny pearls and glass beads."

Hannah massaged her forehead. "Oh yes. That was a special order from a guest who'd stayed at the hotel earlier in the year. The wife of Mr. Allen, I believe."

Mrs. Dunlap nodded. "So I've been told. After learning that you had both designed and completed the beadwork, Mrs. Pullman was convinced you were the perfect person to design gifts for her upcoming event."

Thoughts of being unable to meet Mrs. Pullman's expectations continued to plague her. "I'm sure there's been some mistake. With her variety of acquaintances and unlimited financial means, there are so many excellent designers who could assist her." Hannah tugged at her collar. "Doesn't it seem odd to you that she would choose me?"

"Not entirely. She was very impressed with your work. In addition, I'm guessing she wants to spread the word that there are fine goods to be purchased in Pullman. After all, the offerings in our stores are as fine as any in Chicago."

Hannah considered the older woman's response. Perhaps Mrs. Pullman did want to prove the Arcade shops had fine goods hanging on their racks and lining their shelves. However, Hannah didn't agree the offerings in Pullman were as fine as those that could be purchased in Chicago. After all, she'd walked the aisles of Marshall Field's on several occasions. But she wouldn't dare argue with Mrs. Dunlap.

"I want you to know that you'll be relieved of your regular duties while you're working on your assignment from Mrs. Pullman. Of course, you'll report to the store each morning, but you can immediately go to the sewing room and work where you won't be interrupted."

"Is Miss Hardelle agreeable to this new arrangement?" She certainly didn't want to suffer the ire of her supervisor.

"I will be discussing it with her. No need to worry. She'll offer no objection. In fact, I'm sure she'll be delighted that Mrs. Pullman is pleased with your work." Mrs. Dunlap leaned her head close. "Miss Hardelle has no choice. She wouldn't dare object to a request from Mrs. Pullman." She straightened her shoulders. "Besides, you'll no longer report to Miss Hardelle."

Hannah arched her brows. She'd been reporting to Miss Hardelle ever since she'd begun work in the shop. Granted, Miss Hardelle wasn't in charge of the sewing and fitting area, but because Hannah had initially been trained to wait on customers and keep the accessory shelves filled with lace, ribbons, hat pins, evening bags, handkerchiefs, and the like, she'd been assigned to Miss Hardelle.

However, once Mrs. Langham, the sewing room supervisor, learned of Hannah's sewing talents, she'd pulled her away from the front of the store whenever possible. Since then, the two supervisors had waged a rivalry about where Hannah would work.

"Will I now report to Mrs. Langham?" Hannah was sure such an arrangement would result in a hue and cry from Miss Hardelle. Not because she wanted to keep Hannah but because it would mean one less girl to work the floor. And it would mean she would supervise one less employee than Mrs. Langham. No small matter to Miss Hardelle.

Mrs. Dunlap shook her head. "Since neither Miss Hardelle nor Mrs. Langham will be assigning your duties, you will report to me—and to Mrs. Pullman, of course. I believe this plan will provide the best outcome for all concerned." She beamed at Hannah. "Until it's time for your appointment, you should return to your regular duties with Miss Hardelle. Please remember to put your best foot forward, and make certain you're not late." She looked over the top of the spectacles that rested on her nose.

Mrs. Dunlap's parting words rang in Hannah's ears. If ever she needed to be on time, today was the day. She was still reeling when she returned to the accessories department. Miss Hardelle met her with a hard stare. "There are empty shelves in your area, Miss Cooper. I expect them to be filled before your lunch break. And do see to the two customers over there." She pointed toward two middle-aged ladies perusing the bolts of fabric in the dressmaking section.

"They're in Miss Fitzgerald's section. I don't think she would. . ."

Miss Hardelle's lips tightened into a thin line. "I don't believe I need you to tell me who is assigned to the various sections of the store, Miss Cooper. However, if I find myself in need of direction, I'll be sure to ask you." Sarcasm dripped from the woman's voice.

Soon after her employment, Hannah realized Miss Hardelle disliked being challenged or corrected. However, she'd also discovered the employees were angered when another salesperson entered their workstation. Hannah mentally weighed her options and decided upon the lesser of the evils. She'd rather be subjected to Lizzy Fitzgerald's momentary irritation than the fury of Miss Hardelle.

As Hannah turned toward the fabric section, Mrs. Dunlap rounded the corner and gestured to her. Hannah came to a halt and glanced toward Miss Hardelle. The supervisor tapped her leather-clad shoe on the wooden floor and screwed her features into a tight knot.

When she caught sight of the personnel director, she folded her arms across her chest. "It appears Mrs. Dunlap wishes to inform me what transpired in your meeting." Triumph shone in her dark eyes. "I hope you're prepared for any punishment she plans to mete out, Miss Cooper."

Before Hannah could respond, Mrs. Dunlap closed the distance and came to a halt alongside Miss Hardelle. "I wanted to speak to you regarding Miss Cooper."

Miss Hardelle directed a sideways glance at Hannah and

tightened her lips into a thin line. "I expected as much."

The personnel director glanced at Hannah. Her lips lifted into a wide smile before she returned her attention to Miss Hardelle. "I'm sure she has told you of her new assignment, but. . ."

Hannah shook her head, and Miss Hardelle arched her brows. "New assignment? Is she to be demoted and retrained for her sales duties?"

Mrs. Dunlap chuckled. "No, of course not. She's being assigned to work directly with Mrs. Pullman on special projects."

The supervisor's mouth opened in a wide oval and her arms dropped to her sides. "Surely there's been some mistake. Why would Mrs. Pullman want *her*?"

The disdain in the woman's voice caused Hannah to flinch. Mrs. Dunlap frowned at the supervisor. "Miss Cooper has been chosen because she possesses great talent. Mrs. Pullman is very impressed with Hannah's designs and beadwork, and she wishes to put Hannah's creativity to good use."

Miss Hardelle sucked in a breath. "Well, I'll be pleased to meet with Mrs. Pullman and point out some of Hannah's abilities as well as her imperfections. I know—"

"The arrangements have already been made, Miss Hardelle. Mrs. Pullman requested a private meeting with Hannah at two thirty this afternoon at the hotel. I'm telling you because I'll hold you personally responsible if she's late to the meeting."

"Me?" The woman's voice quivered with a mixture of anger and humiliation.

Mrs. Dunlap nodded. "Once you've delivered her to the front

of the hotel, your duties as Miss Cooper's supervisor will cease. She will report directly to me or to Mrs. Pullman."

Miss Hardelle paled, and Hannah thought her supervisor might swoon in the middle of the accessories section, but Mrs. Dunlap appeared not to notice. "Carry on, ladies. I'm confident in your excellent skills."

Before Miss Hardelle could regain her composure, Hannah rushed toward the fabric section. Hopefully she'd have time to gather her thoughts before Miss Hardelle followed and assailed her with questions.

Chapter Two

At exactly ten minutes past two, Miss Hardelle appeared at Hannah's side, clad in a black wool coat with a fur collar and black hat embellished with two large feathers. "Gather your belongings, Miss Cooper. It's time to depart. I'll accompany you as far as the front doors of the hotel."

Being escorted by Miss Hardelle seemed ridiculous. Although many of the town's residents had never crossed the threshold of the Hotel Florence, anyone who lived in Pullman could locate it. In addition, anyone who lived in Pullman knew the hotel had been named for George Pullman's daughter, Florence. Some said he favored the child above all else, but Hannah wasn't so sure. Florence might be his favored child, but it appeared Mr. Pullman favored money even more.

Hannah didn't reveal she'd been inside and had dined in the hotel dining room on many occasions. Such a disclosure would mean she'd need to divulge her relationship with Louis Nicholson, and Hannah had no desire to discuss Louis with her supervisor.

Hannah's thoughts momentarily lingered upon the man who had been courting her over the past year. Louis lived in Chicago and she saw him only when he came to Pullman on business or for a special visit, so it didn't seem possible a year had passed since he first stepped into the shop to purchase a gift for his mother. Certain he would be pleased and proud of her promotion, she would be delighted to share her news with him—at least if all went well. Unlike many men, Louis thought women should be permitted to use their talents and find fulfillment in work outside the home.

"Come along." Miss Hardelle's command pulled Hannah from her thoughts, and she hurried to the closet with Miss Hardelle close on her heels. While Hannah donned her coat, Miss Hardelle issued final orders to any clerk who came within earshot then pointed Hannah toward the entrance.

Sunlight shimmered through the leaves of the perfectly aligned trees on each side of the street. As if to herald the impending change of season, the rich green foliage now revealed hints of burnt orange, muted red, and pale yellow. Colorful mums dotted the green spaces that had been strategically placed throughout the town. The three-story, ninety-foot-tall shopping Arcade cast a mammoth shadow that stretched from the flagstone sidewalk to the perfectly manicured grounds of the Arcade Park across the street.

As they neared the Hotel Florence, Hannah's palms turned damp within her gloves. She longed to remove them. Had she been alone, she would have yanked them off and shoved them in her pockets. But not today. Miss Hardelle would not approve. A train whistled in the distance and several folks on the opposite side of the street immediately hastened their step. Their bags bounced against their legs with each hurried movement. Hannah stared at them, wondering where they were going and what exciting things they would see.

"We've arrived, Miss Cooper." Miss Hardelle's tone was harsh. "I have delivered you to the front door in a timely fashion. Make certain you announce yourself to the clerk at the front desk. I'm certain he will have directions for you." She gave Hannah's arm a slight shove. "Go on. Don't be late or I'll receive a reprimand from Mrs. Dunlap, and I don't intend for that to happen." Her eyes pinched together until they were mere slits.

"Yes, ma'am." Hannah ascended the hotel steps. She crossed the wide front porch that wrapped around the hotel and glanced over her shoulder before opening the front door. Miss Hardelle hadn't moved an inch. Hannah lifted a gloved hand and waved. Without acknowledging Hannah's gesture, Miss Hardelle quickly turned on her heel and marched off.

Hannah inhaled a deep breath. She'd been distracted on the walk from the Arcade, but now that the meeting with Mrs. Pullman would soon transpire, she'd begun to shake like a wet dog coming in from the rain. She turned the brass doorknob and pushed open the front door. The desk clerk turned in her direction. His eyebrows knit together at the sight of an unescorted woman entering the hotel.

Hoping to lessen his worries, Hannah forced a smile as she strode toward the oak desk that encircled the man. Rows of keys hung from a nearby wood board, and a large guest registry lay open on the desk. He tapped the registry as if expecting her to request a room. "May I help you?"

She dipped her head in a slight nod. "I am here to meet with Mrs. Pullman. I believe she's expecting me, but I'm uncertain where we're to meet."

"Your name?"

"Hannah. Hannah Cooper."

He withdrew a paper from beneath the desk, traced his finger down the page, then nodded his head. "The Pullman Suite is located on the second floor." He glanced toward the gleaming stairway to his left. "Up the stairs, turn right, first door on the left. You'll see the engraved nameplate on the door."

Hannah's heart pounded a new beat when the door to the Pullman Suite opened. A servant led her into a sitting room appointed with gilded mirrors and a brocade-upholstered settee and matching chair. A mahogany writing desk and chair had been arranged near a corner window overlooking the park across the wide driveway that fronted the hotel.

Mrs. Pullman turned from the window. A few gray strands peppered her dark hair and delicate creases lined the contours of her pale complexion. She greeted Hannah with a bright smile. "Miss Cooper. I'm so pleased you could meet with me." She gestured to the settee. "Do sit down." The older woman settled into the chair opposite Hannah then motioned to the servant. "Please have the kitchen send up a tea tray, Mildred." She returned her attention to Hannah. "I am delighted you agreed to work with me, Miss Cooper."

"It's my honor. I was pleased to hear that you are fond of my handwork." Did Mrs. Pullman truly believe she was given a choice? Not that Hannah would have turned down the opportunity, but she couldn't help but wonder if anyone had ever refused one of the woman's requests.

"After seeing your beading and designs, I'm sure I'll want you to do more than make a few gifts. Truth be told, I'm certain I'll be keeping you busy most of the time." She leaned forward in her chair. "I believe our future meetings and work sessions should take place in Chicago since I'm not frequently in Pullman. I hope you won't find it inconvenient taking the train, but with my social obligations, it's difficult for me to get away. Even though it's only a thirty-minute train ride, there's the time getting to and from the station in Chicago and then more time getting settled at the hotel in Pullman." She sighed as though simply relating the details was exhausting. "I'm sure you understand." She didn't wait for an answer. "Now, tell me what you've come up with that I might use as gifts."

Hannah swallowed hard. She didn't know she had been expected to arrive with ideas. Even if she'd been told, her time had been consumed stocking shelves with lace and hat pins. Her mind raced as the maid arrived with tea and Mrs. Pullman poured the steaming brew into two cups. When Mrs. Pullman lifted her cup, she arched her brows in obvious anticipation.

"I don't have a clear idea of when you'll need the gifts." She looked down as she stirred a lump of sugar into her tea. "I would need to know the number of guests, and it would also be helpful to know the nature of the gathering and how much you wish to spend on each item."

Mrs. Pullman touched her fingers to the perfectly coiffed curls atop her head and offered an indulgent smile. "Cost isn't an issue, my dear, so you may set aside that worry. My list includes twelve ladies for a Fall Soiree at my residence the first week in October. I believe that gives you almost a month." She tipped her head to the side. "Will that be sufficient?"

"I believe I could complete some uniquely embellished handkerchiefs within three weeks."

Mrs. Pullman gave a slight shake of her head. "No, not handkerchiefs—too common." She sighed and glanced at the clock. "I have another appointment, but I know you'll create something that will astonish me. Why don't you prepare a sample and bring it for my review on Tuesday? You can meet with me at my home. Say four o'clock? You can board the three-fifteen train and I'll have my carriage meet you at the station."

Rather than awaiting a reply, Mrs. Pullman stood. A thousand unanswered questions swirled in Hannah's mind as she walked toward the door.

final work bell sounded. Once the snow began to fly, the walk home would be far less pleasant. Daniel had hoped to end his apprenticeship before winter arrived, but much depended upon his new supervisor, John McNulty.

"How well do you know Mr. McNulty?" Daniel pulled the folded woolen cap from his back pocket and yanked it atop his unruly light brown hair. "I'm hoping once he examines my work, he'll agree that I've fulfilled my apprenticeship."

"You know McNulty will want a promise you'll stay with the company before he signs off that you've completed your apprenticeship, don't ya?" Joe glanced at him. "I hear tell that's what he did to the apprentices at his old job. Of course, most of us aren't like you. The other fellows pray they'll be offered a job once they complete their apprenticeship."

Daniel frowned. "That doesn't mean he'll do the same thing in the embossing department. It wouldn't be fair. If I can perform the work and pass each of the inspections, he has to sign the papers that prove I've successfully completed my apprenticeship." He hesitated. "Doesn't he?"

Joe shrugged. "If he knows you want to go elsewhere, I figure he'll find little flaws in your glass embossing and say it wasn't fine enough to pass you. You know how it is—one inspector will pass a piece if a bit of the embossing is outside a pattern line while another will mark it defective. If I was you, I'd keep quiet about wanting to find work in Pullman."

Daniel nodded. He'd told only Joe and one other fellow that he didn't plan to remain in Chicago. Besides, if there weren't any openings in Pullman, he wouldn't be going anywhere.

When their paths parted, Joe gave him a mock salute. "I'll see you on Monday morning. Have a nice visit, and be sure you spend a little time with your aunt and uncle. Otherwise, they'll get jealous of Hannah." He strode off, with his lighthearted guffaw echoing in the early evening breeze.

Daniel strode inside the boardinghouse and up the stairway to his room. He tossed his leather case onto the bed. While he folded and packed a few belongings, Joe's cautionary warning replayed in his mind. He couldn't ignore the possibility that Mr. McNulty might want a commitment to remain with the company. Still, it wasn't as though the company would be losing a man with long years of experience. After all, he'd been there only two years, and like the other apprentices, Daniel's work still had to be checked and approved by the permanent embossers.

He washed up, changed his clothes, and picked up his case before returning downstairs. After dropping his bag near the front door, he took his place at the dining room table beside Mr. Hanson. The older man nodded toward the kitchen. "Mrs. Garbert's running a bit late tonight."

One of the other men grunted. "She runs late every night. We're supposed to eat at six o'clock, but it's never on the table until ten minutes past. He pointed at the clock sitting on the buffet. "Mark my words, you won't see any food for five more minutes."

Daniel grinned at the man seated across from him. "It smells good enough to wait an extra ten minutes, don't you think?" The scent of beef stew and biscuits wafted from the kitchen, and his mouth watered in anticipation.

"If I was ten minutes late to my job each day, I'd be fired." The boarder sitting across from Daniel shifted around in his seat. "Trouble is, we can't fire Mrs. Garbert."

Just then the boardinghouse keeper bustled into the room, carrying two large platters filled with biscuits. She handed them to Mr. Wilson before she returned to the kitchen. Moments later she reappeared, carrying a large porcelain tureen. She ladled a serving of stew into each man's dish. When she offered it to Mr. Wilson, she pinned him with a defiant look. "If you're unhappy with me, you can find another boardinghouse, Mr. Wilson. There's no one forcing you to keep your room or eat my food, though I'd challenge you to find better food and board at a less expensive rate."

"My apologies, Mrs. Garbert. I had a difficult day today."

She gave a slight nod. "Apology accepted." Once they'd all been served, she looked at Daniel. "I believe it's your day to offer thanks for our meal."

Mrs. Garbert and the men bowed their heads while Daniel offered a brief prayer. Had he been alone in his room, his prayer would have been longer and less formal, but praying in front of others had always been difficult for him. He had already paid a week's room and board before he learned the men were expected to take turns offering the mealtime prayers. Otherwise, he might have looked for another boardinghouse.

The first time had been the most difficult. He'd stuttered and stammered his way through only a few words before saying "amen." Now, he no longer stammered, and he could manage at least two sentences before ending the prayer. And they came from his heart—which was far more important than pretty words—at least that's what his aunt had taught him when he was growing up. Warmth spread through his chest as he recalled the kindness of both his aunt and uncle and how they'd opened their arms, their hearts, and their home when his parents had died.

"Thank you, Daniel." Mrs. Garbert's voice pulled Daniel from his thoughts and he offered a slight nod. She snapped open her cotton napkin, arranged it on her lap, and waited for each of the men to follow her lead before picking up her fork, the signal they could begin their meal. She set her gaze on Daniel. "What time does your train depart?"

He swallowed a bite of stew. "Seven o'clock, so I'll need to hurry." If the train was on time, he'd arrive in Pullman by seven thirty. The miles between Chicago and Pullman weren't many, yet his visits to the town had been few during the past year. He'd told his aunt it was because he needed to study new embossing techniques. While that was partially true, the primary reason was the blossoming romance between Louis and Hannah.

Mrs. Garbert tapped her fork on the edge of her plate. "Don't rush. It isn't good for the digestion. Mr. Wilson can use my carriage and take you to the station." She passed the biscuits to her right. "Can't you, Mr. Wilson?"

"Be glad to. Always enjoy driving your carriage, Mrs. Garbert."

She nodded. "When you return, you can unhitch Bessie and put her in her stall. Her feed is in the usual place, and if you'd give her a good brushing, I know she'd be thankful for that as well."

Daniel looked at Mr. Wilson and hiked a shoulder. No doubt the older man would grouse on the way to the station. While Mr. Wilson enjoyed driving the carriage, caring for old Bessie gave him no great pleasure.

The boardinghouse keeper engaged the men in conversation for the remainder of the meal but excused Daniel and Mr. Wilson from the table earlier than the others. After bidding the others goodbye, the two of them hurried out back to the carriage.

Once settled, Mr. Wilson lightly slapped the reins on Bessie's backside. "She enjoys doing that to me, you know? She likes to take advantage of us, but she never gives an inch herself."

"She's a widow trying to do her best to get by. I'm sure she appreciates your help."

"Easy enough for you to say. You'll be riding on the train while I'm out back caring for the old nag—and I don't mean Mrs. Garbert—though sometimes she fits the description too." The older man laughed. "When you coming back to Chicago? Sunday evening?"

Daniel gave a nod. He hadn't decided what time he'd return. Much would depend upon Hannah and any plans she might have. He hoped she'd have some time for him, but if Louis was in town, she'd likely be busy.

His Uncle Henry had promised to ask a supervisor in the Pullman Embossing Department if he might be needing an embosser within the next few months, and Daniel was eager to discover what he'd learned, but that wouldn't take long. Of course, he could see about filling out an application. After he passed his apprenticeship tests, an unexpected opening could occur at any time. And who could say what might happen with Hannah if he could return and work in Pullman?

Mr. Wilson nudged Daniel. "Ya know, I lost a girl once. A girl I loved more than anything."

Daniel wasn't certain why Mr. Wilson wanted to talk about his lost love, but he gave the older man an encouraging nod. "That's too bad."

"I bring it up only to say that's the one regret I have in life. If I would have worked a little harder at keeping our love intact, you wouldn't find me living in any boardinghouse, and that's for sure."

The older man's words seeped into Daniel's consciousness. If he didn't want to end up like Mr. Wilson, perhaps he shouldn't give up so easily. Maybe, just maybe, he should fight for Hannah's love.

Daniel glanced at the huge clock tower as they neared the granite and brownstone station. Six forty-five. His heart picked up a beat. If he missed this train, he'd have to wait until morning.

"Here we are." Mr. Wilson pulled back on the reins and brought the carriage to a halt inside the arched carriage court. "Better hurry."

"Thanks, Mr. Wilson. I'll see you Sunday evening." Daniel grabbed his bag, jumped down, and ran inside the station.

After navigating his way through the marble-floored waiting room and out to the train shed, he hesitated. A porter stood a short distance away and Daniel gestured toward the multitude of tracks jammed with hissing trains. He cupped his hand to his mouth and shouted over the deafening noise. "Which one's going to Pullman?"

The porter waved farther down the platform. "Number three."

Daniel ran at breakneck speed. With each step, his leather case beat against his leg with a bruising insistence. When he finally arrived at the proper car, he bent double, his chest burning and his breathing labored.

"All aboard!"

He jerked to attention, climbed the few steps into the car, and fell onto one of the seats. Next time he wouldn't attempt to eat supper before leaving town. His breathing steadied after a short time and he sat back and relaxed, his thoughts jumping between Hannah and the possibility of a permanent return to Pullman.

He closed his eyes and pictured her waiting for him when he arrived. Seeing her at the station would be worth every second of the tumultuous rush to the train. If only. . .

The train slowed a short time later, and the conductor announced their arrival in Pullman. Daniel scooted close to the window and peered through the glass. The station lights glowed, and he thought he saw Hannah stepping onto the platform. His heart raced. Even though he'd written to tell her of his arrival, he wasn't certain she'd appear.

He squinted, and then he was sure. It was Hannah. She'd come to meet him. His lips curved into a generous smile that evaporated almost as quickly as it had arrived.

Hannah's hand rested in the crook of Louis Nicholson's arm.

Chapter Four

Daniel shifted to look out the window as he recalled the letter Hannah had sent him several months ago—the one in which she'd written Louis Nicholson had requested permission to call on her. He felt a stab of pain, a familiar pain that occurred each time he thought of them together.

Daniel's friendship with Hannah ran deep, and there was something about Louis that didn't ring true. Then again, perhaps it was his own feelings of losing Hannah's friendship that had colored his opinion. He didn't want to admit jealousy was the cause, since he'd been the one who had insisted a romantic relationship could ruin the enduring friendship they'd developed through the years. But now that she appeared to be falling in love with Louis, Daniel questioned whether his thinking had been sound. Especially since he'd been the one to delay telling her how he truly felt. He'd wanted to be certain he could provide for a wife and family before declaring his love. But now, seeing her holding Louis's arm, memories of what Mr. Wilson had said about regrets flooded Daniel's mind. Ever since Louis had come into Hannah's life, she'd often been too busy to see Daniel when he came to Pullman. He had hoped this visit would be different, but the moment he saw Louis, his expectations dissolved like snow on a warm day.

Clutching the handles of his small valise, he stepped down from the train and wended his way through the crowd of passengers. Hannah stood on tiptoe and waved in his direction with a smile curving her lips, but Louis turned to look in the opposite direction.

Despite the cool weather, Daniel felt perspiration form on his upper lip as he approached the couple. He came to a halt beside Hannah and smiled. "It's good to see you." Determined to remain cordial, Daniel extended his hand to Louis. "Nice to see you again, Louis."

Louis ignored Daniel's outstretched hand. Instead, he leaned close to Hannah, whispered in her ear, and strode toward the train without acknowledging Daniel's presence. Hannah's eyes remained fixed upon Louis until he boarded the train.

She waved and blew out a long sigh as she turned to face Daniel. "He's in a wretched mood. He was supposed to remain until Monday, but he received a call at the hotel last night and must return to Chicago. Something to do with his work and several orders being incorrect or some such thing." Her lips tightened. "I don't know what he can accomplish by returning to Chicago, but he was unyielding when I tried to dissuade him. This seems to happen at the most inopportune times."

"I'm sorry you're sad." That much was true. He didn't want to see Hannah unhappy. Still, he was glad Louis wouldn't be around.

His absence would mean Hannah would be free to spend time with Daniel.

She turned toward the depot. "Shall we go?"

He offered his arm. She slipped her hand into the crook of his elbow, and Daniel wondered if Louis was watching from the train window. If so, was he feeling that same sharp pain Daniel had experienced only moments ago?

"I'm glad you're here, Daniel. Any chance you could escort me to the opening of a new play at the theater tonight?" She hesitated only a moment. "If you don't already have other plans. Perhaps your aunt and uncle are planning to attend and have already purchased a ticket for you."

"They didn't mention attending a play. Besides, except for attending a free tour of the theater when it first opened, they've never set foot inside. They think it's frivolous to spend money on such things."

She nodded. "Perhaps it is. I'd like for you to act as my escort, but I don't want to infringe upon their time with you. They could have other plans."

"So I'd be taking Louis's place?" He arched his brows.

"In a way. At least for the duration of the play." She looked up at him and a glint of gold shimmered in her brown eyes.

"You know there's nothing I enjoy more than being with you."

"So, have you found anyone special in Chicago?" Her lashes fluttered as she gave him a sideways glance.

"No, but I'm not looking. In fact, once I finish with my apprenticeship, I'm hoping I can move to Pullman."

She stopped short, nearly causing a collision of several passengers inside the depot. "Truly? You want to return to Pullman after living in Chicago? I can hardly believe my ears. Is it because of your aunt and uncle? Is one of them ill?"

He shook his head. "They are both fine, but you know how much I've always enjoyed my time in Pullman. After the death of my mother, coming here to live with my aunt and uncle was the best thing that could have happened to me. Life in Pullman was so different from our tenement in Chicago. If I'd had to remain in Chicago, I don't know if I would have ever gotten over her death. Besides, I couldn't have survived on my own."

They waited for a passing carriage before crossing the street and continuing toward Watt Street. "I know it was hard when you were young, but after several years in a nicer area of a big city, I wouldn't think you'd find Pullman as enchanting as you did when you left. It has to be boring by comparison."

"It isn't boring," Daniel protested. "It's peaceful. Clean. Welcoming. "As for missing the city, I won't miss the noise or the crowds." He didn't want to tell her about the sewage in the streets, the rats as big as small dogs that ran through neighborhoods, or the tenements teaming with hungry children. She believed in an idyllic Chicago, and he wouldn't destroy her vision.

"And all the rules we must follow as residents—do you not feel them unreasonable? Do you want to put on a suit jacket each time you step out the door, or have every theater production chosen for you, or pay fees for using the library? And what about that beautiful church Mr. Pullman had constructed in the middle of town?

It sits empty on Sunday mornings because no congregation can afford the exorbitant rent he requires."

"I don't find the rules unreasonable, though I disagree with the high rent he's asking for the church building. As for the rules, I think they are in place so that Pullman remains clean and safe for employees to live—nothing more and nothing less."

Her lips turned downward. "Of course, most can't afford the library fee, so I suppose it doesn't matter what books are available." She inhaled a quick breath. "More importantly, don't you want to own your own home one day? We both know that could never happen in Pullman."

"If I ever decide to purchase a home, I could do so in Roseland, where some of the Pullman employees already live."

"Perhaps, but I'm told those who live outside of the town are the first to receive notice when there's a slowdown."

"The town was built to house the company employees, so I can understand that policy. Besides, if I remain in Chicago, I'll continue living in a boardinghouse or a tenement. In Pullman, I'd have a front and back yard, a lake where I could row and fish or ice skate in winter. There's much to be said for the town." He chuckled. "If I didn't know better, I'd think you didn't want me around."

She shook her head. "That's not true. Perhaps we have differing views because I've never lived in the city. Still, I don't know that there are as many opportunities for job advancement here."

He shrugged. "I'm seeking a permanent position that pays a decent wage. I don't have any desire to become the manager or own a business."

"Yes, of course." She nodded. "It's just that your desire to move here comes as a surprise since I don't recall you mentioning you planned to leave Chicago."

Memories of his mother momentarily flooded Daniel's thoughts, and he cleared his throat before speaking. "I'll soon complete my apprenticeship. With that, there's no reason to remain in Chicago." As they approached one of the small parks, Daniel leaned down and picked a blooming purple mum. He held it out to Hannah. "I long to have extended time with family again."

"How insensitive of me, Daniel. I can understand you'd much prefer to be near your aunt and uncle." She took the flower from his hand and smiled up at him. "In case you haven't been told, picking flowers from public parks isn't permitted. Another one of those rules." She glanced about with a furtive look in her eye. "But I promise I won't tell."

He joined in her laughter, pleased she'd lightened the mood. He longed to tell her that while his relatives played a small part in his decision, she was the primary reason he wanted to make his home in Pullman. "Since Louis has returned to Chicago, why don't you join us for lunch tomorrow? I know Aunt Jane would enjoy having you join us."

"That would be lovely." Her eyes widened and shone with excitement. "I forgot to tell you my news." She directed him to one of the benches that surrounded the walkways in the park. "Sit down while I tell you." She quickly detailed her assignment with Mrs. Pullman then placed a hand atop his arm. "Isn't it wonderful, Daniel? And, if all goes well between Louis and me, it would mean

I could continue my employment with Mrs. Pullman and live in Chicago."

Daniel inhaled a sharp breath. How had Hannah and Louis progressed to talk of marriage so soon?

Chapter Five

The following Tuesday, Hannah carefully folded the beautifully embroidered satin fan bag and elastic belt, both embellished with beads and colored stones, and placed them in the small valise Mrs. Dunlap had provided, still worried Mrs. Pullman wouldn't like either.

She glanced at Mrs. Dunlap. "I hope she chooses the belts. I'm not certain I can complete the fan bags in time."

The belts wouldn't require as much work since the colored stones could be attached more quickly than the tiny beadwork she'd embroidered on the fan bags. Still, the belts were lovely. She'd embroidered enough beading and goldwork to make them quite beautiful—at least that's what Mrs. Dunlap had told her.

"You need to cease your fretting, Hannah. Your handwork is exquisite. Mrs. Pullman is going to have a difficult time with her decision. Either way, you'll complete them on time. If need be, I'll have one of the other seamstresses help you with the simple embroidery. Now hurry along or you'll miss the train. I'll be eager to hear your report tomorrow morning."

After a quick goodbye, Hannah hurried out of the Arcade and made her way to the train station. Mrs. Dunlap had been correct about the train. Passengers were already waiting on the platform when she arrived. Quickening her pace, she rushed out of the depot and stepped on board the train.

She edged down the aisle while brushing unwelcome dust from her Byzantine blue jacket. She'd chosen a suit, thinking it would prove appropriate for both her meeting with Mrs. Pullman as well as her dinner engagement. She had hoped to meet Louis, but when she'd mentioned her appointment in Chicago, he'd seemed annoyed by her request to meet him afterward. When Hannah expressed her surprise at his tone, he'd apologized and said only that she'd misinterpreted his attitude. Rather than being annoyed, he was sorely disappointed that he would miss her visit to the city.

She'd been cheered, however, when Daniel had offered to escort her to dinner. He'd agreed to meet her in the accessories department of Marshall Field's after work. His ready acceptance had salved her wounded feelings. Her heart picked up a beat as she anticipated showing him what she'd accomplished since his departure. His support made her feel she could achieve anything.

As promised, Mrs. Pullman's carriage was waiting outside the station. Never before had she been treated with such regard. The driver behaved as though she were visiting royalty. She leaned back on the cushioned seat and attempted to calm her nerves. They passed several grand houses. Finally, the carriage came to a halt under the portico of the Pullman home on Prairie Avenue.

A maid took Hannah's coat and directed her into a formal sitting room furnished with velvet-upholstered settees and gilded mirrors. She remained standing as she studied the intricate friezes surrounding the door frames. She was silently admiring the damask draperies of pale blue and fawn when Mrs. Pullman entered the room.

"Do sit down, my dear. I've ordered tea." The older woman directed Hannah to the nearby settee before choosing a fawn button-backed ladies' chair positioned nearby. "I'm eager to see what you've brought for me."

Mrs. Dunlap had been correct. Mrs. Pullman was pleased with both items, but she waited until they'd finished their tea before reexamining each. She stretched the belt several times then gave a slight nod. "I believe the belts will be quite suitable for this group." A slight smile played at her lips. "While the elastic stretches quite admirably, I have some acquaintances who might have a little difficulty with the fit. Thankfully none of them are among this group. I think we'll save the fan bags for another time when some of those ladies might be included."

Hannah didn't offer comment. Even though she was certain the belts would fit most any woman, she didn't want to discourage Mrs. Pullman's choice. "I'm pleased you like them both."

Mrs. Pullman leaned back in her chair and traced her fingers over the delicate beading on the fan bag. "How could I not like them? They're exquisite." She exhaled a long sigh. "I believe I'd like ten of the fan bags for Christmas gifts. Could you make each one a bit different?" Before Hannah could answer, she continued.

"And we'll be hosting a formal dinner on New Year's Day for family and close friends. Perhaps you could design a gift for each of those guests as well."

Hannah gasped. "I'm sorry to say that I don't think there is enough time for me to create so many gifts, Mrs. Pullman. Perhaps we should first decide what is most important and I can give you an estimate of how much time it will take me."

Although Mrs. Pullman looked disappointed, she nodded and said, "Of course."

When the meeting had finally ended, Hannah's thoughts were spinning like an autumn leaf blowing in the wind. Mrs. Pullman stood and led the way into the entrance hall. "Shall my driver return you to the train station?"

"No, I'm meeting a friend for dinner before I return, but if he could take me. . ." She hesitated, uncertain whether she should tell Mrs. Pullman of her wish to peruse the aisles of Marshall Field's fine store.

Mrs. Pullman arched her brows.

"We're meeting in front of Marshall Field's. It's a location known to both of us."

"Of course, but be sure you don't line Marshall Field's pockets with your hard-earned wages." She offered a tight smile before giving the driver instructions. "Keep me advised should any problems arise. Why don't you plan on personally delivering the belts a few days before the party? That way you can make any changes or repairs I might believe necessary."

Being away from work would only slow progress on the other

projects Mrs. Pullman had requested, but Hannah couldn't refuse. She gave a nod and was soon on her way to Marshall Field's. Though the meeting with Mrs. Pullman had taken longer than anticipated, Hannah still would have sufficient time to examine the offerings in the ladies' accessories department.

The moment she entered the store, her senses alerted to the sights and smells surrounding her. The scent of fine perfume lingered in the air as she studied the scarves, gloves, belts, and every other imaginable accessory. She made her way through the displays of lace and was considering a visit to the dress department when Daniel lightly grasped her arm.

"I hope I haven't kept you waiting too long, but I wanted to take time to clean up. I didn't think you'd want me escorting you in my work clothes." He smiled down at her. "Do you want to look around a little longer, or would you like to go to dinner?"

"I'd love to spend several days in this store, but if I'm going to accomplish all the stitching Mrs. Pullman has assigned, I'll need to be at work early tomorrow morning, so we'd better go."

While they dined on spaghetti and meat sauce at Madame Galli's, Hannah related all that had happened earlier in the afternoon. She was pleased when Daniel asked several questions and appeared to take an interest in what Mrs. Pullman had requested. She took a sip of water and met his gaze. "Now, tell me what has happened with you since we visited on Sunday?"

He grinned and leaned back in his chair. "My supervisor told me that he would test my skills beginning on Thursday. I should know by next week if I've successfully completed my apprenticeship."

He inhaled a quick breath. "If so, I'm hopeful I'll receive one of the positions in the Pullman Embossing Department."

"That's wonderful, Daniel. I know your aunt and uncle would be delighted to have you living in Pullman."

He considered asking if she would be pleased to have him living nearby but decided this wasn't the time. After all, if he didn't receive a job offer, he wouldn't be moving.

Chapter Six

Hannah poked her needle through the elasticized belt and yelped when the sharp point pricked her finger. After shoving her finger between her lips, she checked to make certain no blood had stained her work. The long hours of carefully stitching the exact beads or sequins into place had taken a toll. Her back ached from sitting hunched over her worktable. She'd taken to standing for brief intervals, but then she would drop beads and make more mistakes. Any seamstress could attest that bleeding fingers, aching backs, and blurring eyes were mishaps to be expected after working long hours.

After tightly wrapping a strip of cloth around her finger, she picked up the pair of reading glasses Mrs. Dunlap had loaned her and tucked the metal earpieces into place. While she didn't want to become dependent upon the spectacles, she couldn't deny the clarity they provided, especially as the evening hours wore on.

She sighed and glanced at the clock. The other workers had departed for home two hours ago, but she would be here far into the night. After carefully placing the belt on her worktable, she made her way through the darkened store, thankful for the illumination from the gaslights in the hallway. She smiled when she caught sight of her mother outside the door.

Hannah turned the lock and opened the door. Her gaze settled on the basket her mother carried. "What would I do without you, Mama?"

Her mother smiled. "I'm not sure. Perhaps you would walk down the hallway to the café."

"Your food is much better than what they serve in the café." Hannah glanced down the hallway. Though many of the shops were closed for the night, many of the Pullman residents were in the Arcade for meetings in the club rooms, or visiting the library. "Where's Papa?"

"He's already gone up to the library. One of the men told him there's a new magazine that has an article about Pullman. He wants to read it if one of the members hasn't already borrowed it."

She lifted the cloth napkin and peeked in the basket. "Mmm, chicken and dumplings. Thank you, Mama."

"I worry you're going to become sick working these long hours." She cupped Hannah's cheek in her palm. "At least you'll be away from this place tomorrow evening."

Hannah's mouth dropped open. "What do you mean?" Before her mother could respond, Hannah gasped. "Oh no! Louis and I are supposed to go to dinner and attend the play at the Arcade Theater. I'd completely forgotten." She shook her head. "Although we missed going to the last play together, I simply can't go. He'll have to understand."

Her mother sighed. "I believe it would do you good to go, but the decision is yours. I won't say any more about the subject."

"If I had a little more time to complete all the belts, I'd go, but Mrs. Pullman's order is my first step toward success."

Her mother leaned close to her ear. "*This* job was your first step. You should not forget that."

"You're right, Mama. I wouldn't have received the order from Mrs. Pullman if she hadn't seen my work here in the shop." Hannah glanced over her shoulder toward the workroom. "I need to get back to work if I'm going to get home before midnight."

Her mother *tsked* as she handed the basket to Hannah. "You need to come home no later than eleven o'clock. Without sleep, you'll be of no use tomorrow."

Hannah didn't argue. Like every other night, her parents would be asleep when she returned tonight. They had no idea she'd not been home before midnight for more than a week.

"Thank you again for my supper." She remained until her mother turned and walked toward the wide staircase leading to the library. Hannah took a deep breath and made her way back to the workroom, determined to complete one more belt before midnight.

"Welcome, Mr. Nicholson. We're pleased to have you back with us." The hotel clerk gestured to a boy on the other side of the foyer.

The boy rushed forward with an expectant look in his eyes.

"Take your bag up for you, sir?"

Louis gave the boy a quick glance and nodded before signing the register.

The hotel clerk reached over the counter and handed a key to the boy. "Mr. Nicholson's usual room." Louis replaced the pen into the bronze holder and turned, but before he'd arrived at the stairs, the hotel clerk called him back. "I almost forgot." He reached beneath the desk and retrieved an envelope. "A young lady asked that I give this to you upon your arrival."

"Thank you." Noting the interest that shone in the clerk's eyes, Louis shoved the envelope into his pocket without further comment. Taking the stairs at a quick pace, he arrived at his room just as the boy was unlocking the door. He handed him a coin. "No need to come in. I can manage on my own."

Louis crossed the room, dropped into an overstuffed chair near windows overlooking a well-manicured park, and removed the envelope from his pocket. After withdrawing the single sheet of paper and reading the brief paragraph, he clenched his teeth until his jaw ached. In one quick motion he flung the paper toward the floor and jumped up from the chair. With a determined step, he crossed the room and yanked open the door. He cared little that the wooden door banged and reverberated behind him as he bounded down the stairs.

Eyes wide, the clerk stared at him. "Is there a problem with your accommodations, Mr. Nicholson?"

"The room is fine." He ground out the answer from between gritted teeth and glanced toward the hotel bar. A quick drink might diminish his anger. Then again, it could heighten his rage even further. Best to keep moving. He continued out the front doors, turned, and strode at a quick pace toward the Arcade. How dare she cancel their plans on such short notice?

The brisk walk and cool air hadn't been sufficient to calm his anger before he entered the front door of the Millinery and Dressmaking Shop in the Arcade, but a disapproving look from an approaching matron when he knocked over a glove display was enough to adjust his attitude. He stooped down, gathered the gloves together, and splayed them atop the table with a final pat.

"No, no, no!" The woman wagged her finger back and forth. "I'll reorganize the display." She sighed and forced a smile. "How may I help you?"

Glancing over the woman's head, Louis attempted to gain sight of Hannah but to no avail. He knew the clerks weren't permitted personal visitors during work hours, so he doubted the saleswoman would be willing to help him. Especially since he'd ruined her glove display.

He cleared his throat and smiled. "Some time ago, I purchased a beautiful beaded collar in your shop. I was hoping to find something similar while I'm in town. I believe one of the shop employees designed and made the collar."

The woman nodded. "That would be Hannah Cooper. We have some of her items over here." She waved him forward. "If you'll just follow me."

While keeping watch for Hannah, he trailed behind the woman and nearly knocked into her when she came to an unexpected halt.

She gestured to the glass case. "All of these accessories are quite beautiful. If you're looking for an embellished gown, that would require a special order and fitting, of course."

Louis leaned down and peered through the glass case then looked up at the saleswoman. "I was hoping to match the piece I've already purchased with a pair of gloves. Would it be possible to speak with the designer?"

The saleswoman caught her lower lip between her teeth and shook her head. "I don't believe so. She's working on a special project, and we have instructions that she's not to be disturbed."

He leaned in and forced what he hoped was a charming smile. "My aging mother is going to be terribly disappointed. Won't you at least ask Miss Cooper if she'll spare me a moment?"

"Well, I suppose it wouldn't hurt to ask." The color in her cheeks heightened as she fluttered from behind the counter and waved. "I'll be right back."

The moment her back was turned, the smile slid from Louis's lips. He paced in front of the counter and could feel his anger mounting when the saleswoman reappeared by herself. She came to a stop in front of him and offered a demure smile. "I failed to ask your name, sir."

He forced himself to remain calm. "Louis Nicholson." He reached into his jacket, retrieved one of his calling cards, and handed it to the woman. "Perhaps this will help her recall my earlier purchase."

"Oh, I'm sure it will. Thank you."

Once again, he watched the woman disappear. Moments later,

she returned with Hannah following close on her heels. She turned toward Hannah as they approached. "This is Mr. Nicholson, Hannah. He's hoping you can reproduce a pattern on a pair of gloves for his mother."

Louis directed a hard stare at the woman. "Thank you for your help. If you'll excuse us, I believe I can explain to Miss Cooper."

The woman gave him a wounded look before she turned and walked back toward the jumbled glove display.

Hannah stepped behind the counter, reached behind the glass case and removed a beaded bag. She placed it atop the counter and pushed it toward Louis. "Have you been to the hotel? I left a note for you."

He leaned forward as if to examine the bag. "Of course, I've been there. I got your note and that's why I'm here. Why would you permit me to come to town if you knew you weren't going to spend time with me? Do you think it's easy for me to schedule my time in Pullman?"

Her eyes widened as he spoke. "I called your office and tried to speak with you, but they said you were out of town. I was afraid you'd get in trouble for receiving a personal call, so I didn't leave my name or a message. What else was I to do?"

"You're supposed to keep our plans. That's what you're supposed to do. What's so important that you can't go out?"

She quietly reminded him she needed to complete the order for Mrs. Pullman. "You know this is important, Louis. If I'm able to impress those Chicago ladies, I may be able to secure employment at Marshall Field's and move to Chicago."

"Moving to Chicago isn't going to help us at all. I travel extensively." He folded his arms across his chest. "Are you going to change your mind and go out with me tonight?"

"I've told you—I can't. I've been working every night, and I'm still not sure I'm going to have all the belts completed on time." She tugged on his arm and looked at him with pleading eyes. "Please say you understand, Louis."

"I don't understand, so I can't tell you that I do. If you'd rather spend your time sewing beads than going out to supper with me, so be it. But don't expect to see me anytime soon."

"What about the Harvest Ball? You'll be back for that, won't you? You promised we'd attend."

A flash of resentment shone in his deep blue eyes. "You promised to go out to supper tonight, but you're not. I guess you'll have to wait and see if I keep my promise."

Chapter Seven

Hannah exhaled a sigh of relief. The completed belts had been delivered to an appreciative Mrs. Pullman. Now Hannah could enjoy lunch in the city before returning home. Mrs. Dunlap had rewarded Hannah with the remainder of the day off work, and she had hoped Louis could meet her. Instead, he'd declined. His work schedule was too busy, he'd told her. She wondered if it was true or if he was punishing her because she'd remained at work when he was in Pullman.

However, she'd taken heart when Daniel had agreed to meet her at Kohlsaat's Dairy Lunch Room on Madison Street, yet she remained uncertain how he'd get away from work for the noonday meal. She stepped inside the restaurant, with wooden tables and benches lining the walls and a row of tables and chairs down the center of the room. A pathway remained open on either side for the customers and waitresses to make their way through—but only if they turned sideways. Chairs scraped on the wooden floor as workers scurried to be seated and order a meal. Hannah scanned the crowd for a moment before she caught sight of Daniel. He stood and waved from his position near the rear of the restaurant.

After being seated, she touched the lapel of her jacket. "I'm surprised to see you in a suit instead of your work clothes."

He grinned. "I could have told you before now, but I wanted to surprise you with my news."

She tipped her head back and met his eyes. "And what news is that? You've been promoted to foreman?"

He shook his head. "No, even better. Beginning next Monday, I'm an employee of the Pullman Palace Car Company in the etching and embossing department. I ended my old job yesterday, and I'll be moving from the boardinghouse tomorrow. I can spend the entire day with you, if you're going to remain in town." He pushed a menu across the table.

She stared at him, momentarily stunned into silence. "This is all so sudden." Her voice cracked. "It's difficult for me to grasp that you've taken your tests, quit your job, accepted a new position—and you'll be moving to Pullman, but I'm truly proud of you."

"I didn't think it would happen as quickly either, but I've been praying the Lord would do whatever He believes is best for my future." He smiled. "Looks like maybe He agrees Pullman is the best place for me." He folded his hands atop the table.

"Maybe I should begin praying the same thing as you. Perhaps the Lord will agree that Chicago is the best place for me." She sighed. "If my handwork designs are going to become sought after, I'll need to live somewhere other than Pullman."

They placed their orders, and then he leaned forward, his chest touching the table. "I don't know why you think you need to leave Pullman. Thanks to Mrs. Pullman, your name will become well known here in Chicago. I'm sure all her friends will be interested in your designs."

"Possibly." She bit her tongue before saying anything more. She didn't want to argue.

He swallowed a bite of his roast beef sandwich. "You haven't told me what Mrs. Pullman thought of the belts. Did she think the designs the best she'd ever seen?"

"Well, of course." She grinned. "She did like them and has asked me to complete other orders for her. Some are to be Christmas gifts and some for New Year's Day guests, but at least this first order met with her satisfaction. Unfortunately, she doesn't seem to understand the amount of time necessary to complete the hand-beading and she wants each gift to be a little different, so it takes even longer. And I haven't even begun the beadwork on the gown I plan to wear to the Harvest Ball." She clapped her hand to her bodice. "I just now realized you'll be in Pullman for the Harvest Ball."

He grinned. "You're right. I will. So if you need an escort, just let me know."

She shifted in the chair, sorry she'd mentioned the ball. "Louis has promised he'll be in town. Otherwise, I'd be pleased to have you by my side, but you'll recall that lots of folks attend by themselves."

"I do recall." His lips curved in a weak smile. "I didn't expect you to accept my invitation, but a fellow can still hope, can't he?"

She didn't answer. Hope? Her chest squeezed. Why would he

ask such a question? After all, he was the one who had insisted they could never let their feelings go beyond friendship. Lately, however, it seemed he was sending her mixed messages. Perhaps it was his way of joking with her now that she had a beau. He likely thought he could tease her and his words would carry no more import than if they'd been spoken by one of her lady friends. But he'd be wrong. Each teasing remark was a reminder of that Christmas party nearly five years ago, and the feelings for him that she'd had to ignore. She'd now moved on. With Louis. Didn't he realize that?

She'd been sure he would change his mind about that night, so for several years she'd rejected any offers from a possible beau. Not until Louis came into the Millinery and Dressmaking Shop to purchase a gift for his mother had she been swayed from her decision. His dashing good looks and praise for her handwork had been too hard to resist. Granted, she'd been taken aback when she learned he was thirty-five years old, but by then he'd already received her father's permission to call on her. Besides, his appearance belied his age, and after nearly a year, she'd become accustomed to a man who was far more sophisticated than the young men who worked and lived in Pullman.

At first, Hannah had been unhappy when Louis wasn't as attentive as she'd originally hoped. However, she'd gained insight over the passing months and eventually understood Louis had to be away for extended periods. His work as a salesman necessitated travel, and his schedule could change at a moment's notice. She'd learned to accept his fluctuating plans with a smile—at least most of the time.

While Hannah no longer expressed frustration in front of her father, her mother continued to provide a listening ear whenever Louis didn't arrive when expected. Her father said a good man must keep his priorities in order. When she'd asked her father where he thought she should rank on Louis's list, he'd been clear. A man's first priority is to the Lord, second is to the employer, and the third is to family. She'd attempted to argue that he had numbers two and three out of order, but her father hadn't relented.

Instead, he'd said, "If a man doesn't give his employer priority over his family, he can lose his job. If he is unemployed and can't support his family, has he done well by placing them above his employer?"

She'd had no answer to his question, though she still wasn't certain she agreed. And she wasn't sure God would agree either.

Daniel leaned across the table. "A penny for your thoughts, my lady."

She jerked to attention. "I'm sorry. I didn't mean to let my mind wander, but since you've asked about my thoughts, let me pose a question."

"I didn't bring my thinking cap with me, so I hope I'll be able to answer."

She grinned. "This isn't a question that requires book knowledge. Rather, it's an inquiry regarding personal judgment."

He nodded. "Go on."

She placed her hands in her lap and fussed with the edge of her linen napkin. "If you were given the three priorities of God, employer, and family, in what order would you place them?"

He blew out a long breath and pretended to wipe perspiration from his brow. "I'm glad you were true to your word and the question wasn't too difficult." A glint of humor shone in his eyes. "I think the answer would vary from person to person. Much would depend upon their love of God, their love of family, and respect for their employer."

"I'm not asking about other people, just you. How would you prioritize your list?"

"God, family, employer." His gaze didn't waver. "Did I pass the test?"

"It wasn't a test, but I do like the way you answered. My father believes an employer should come before family, but I disagree. He was so adamant about his belief that I wondered if anyone would agree with me, so I'm glad you feel the same."

He tipped his head to the side. "I'm sure you asked that question because you feel Louis doesn't put you before his work, but the same would be true for a working woman, don't you think?" He didn't wait for an answer. "If you cancel plans because of your duties at work, then you can't fault Louis when his work necessitates a change, can you?"

"I suppose not." She pushed away from the table. "If I'm going to catch my train, we'd best be on our way."

Daniel hailed a hansom cab, insisted upon escorting her to the depot, and then waited with her until she safely boarded the train. Their chatter about his move to Pullman had filled the few minutes before the train had arrived, but once settled on the cushioned seat, her thoughts returned to Daniel's earlier remark concerning her own priorities. While his comment made sense, she'd canceled her plans with Louis on only one occasion. On the other hand, Louis had been changing and canceling plans only days after he received permission to court her.

In addition, he'd made it clear that she should readily accept and not question his behavior. Until now, she'd done her best. When they had parted at the Pullman Depot last week, his response to her question about the Harvest Ball had sounded retaliatory. Was Louis a man who would make a habit of such behavior? Though he hadn't said he was breaking his promise to escort her, he hadn't said he would keep it either.

And since he'd refused her offer to meet today, there would be no further opportunity to see him before the ball.

Gaining an answer would be akin to chasing a carrot dangling from a stick. If only Louis were as attentive as Daniel. He'd been willing to give up his entire afternoon to do whatever might please her. Would Louis ever make her feel like she was the most important thing in his life? It was a question that deserved a well-thought-out answer.

Chapter Eight

At the clang of the final bell, Daniel and the other men employed by the Pullman Palace Car Company gathered their lunch pails, all of them eager to depart for home. He'd settled into his new position, and his fellow workers had proved both kind and helpful, especially Edward Milligan, the man who'd been assigned to oversee Daniel's work during his probationary two months. Although Edward was only five years older than Daniel, he'd started work as an apprentice in the embossing department when he was sixteen and was now considered one of the best in the department. Daniel had to agree. Edward's work was as good as or better than any he'd seen while working in Chicago.

Over the past weeks, Edward had proved a friend as well as a fellow worker, and on several occasions, he'd invited Daniel to his home for dinner. His wife had been as friendly and welcoming as Edward and they were a good match, both enjoying life in Pullman. It was during one of those dinners at their home that Daniel met Edward's sister, Ida, a lovely young woman his own age.

Edward clasped his hand on Daniel's shoulder. "Gertrude says you should join us for supper tomorrow evening."

Daniel gave a firm nod. "Your wife is very kind. Just tell me what time and I'll be there."

"Six thirty work for you? She thought we could visit the library afterward. There's a new magazine she and Ida want to look at." Edward chuckled. "Probably filled with all the latest fashions."

Daniel didn't miss the reference to Ida. Upon their first meeting, Daniel had wondered if Edward was attempting to find a beau for his sister, but he'd soon learned Ida was already spoken for. Though not formally betrothed, James Danfield, a supervisor in Mr. Pullman's Allen Paper Wheel Works, had already made his intentions clear, which was fine with Daniel. Although he should open himself up to love, he couldn't stop thinking about Hannah. Who loved Louis. Oh, what a twisted situation.

"Six thirty is fine. Any word when Ida's beau will return from Cleveland?"

Edward hiked a shoulder. "She had a letter yesterday. Seems they're having some trouble bargaining for the new lathes. He's attempting to negotiate the price and specifications, but from what he wrote, the owner of the company is on a ship returning from Europe and nobody else has the authority to lower prices. He telegraphed Mr. Pullman but was told to remain in Cleveland until he had an agreement." He leaned closer to Daniel's ear. "I don't think James is happy with Mr. Pullman's answer. And neither is Ida."

A gust of wind whipped countless colorful leaves around their feet and threatened to send Daniel's cap flying. He tugged on the brim and pulled it forward. "I'm sure she's eager for his return."

Edward chuckled. "That's a fact. Especially with all the parties and dances that take place from now until after the New Year." He slowed his step as they neared the home of Daniel's aunt and uncle. "I'll see you at work tomorrow. And don't forget to tell your aunt she shouldn't expect you for supper tomorrow evening. I'm sure she'll be disappointed to have only your uncle to feed."

"Quite the opposite, I'm sure." Daniel laughed as he mounted the front steps.

Tomorrow evening was sure to be entertaining. While he enjoyed his aunt and uncle, time with folks his own age was a genuine pleasure, and he was thankful Edward occasionally invited him for visits. In truth, he had hoped some of his free time would be filled by Hannah, but so far that hadn't happened. Each time he'd stopped by her home, Mrs. Cooper told him the same thing: Hannah wouldn't be home until bedtime as she needed to continue working on Mrs. Pullman's latest order. He prayed Hannah wasn't putting her work before taking care of herself.

Daniel and Edward followed the two ladies toward the Arcade. They'd finished supper and decided the library visit could wait no longer.

Edward slowed his pace as they passed the park. "I was wondering if you've invited anyone to the Harvest Ball?"

Daniel grinned. "Are you inviting me?"

Edward jabbed a light punch to Daniel's upper arm. "No.

Fortunately, I am a permanent escort for the lady walking in front of me, but I was hoping you would consider escorting Ida. She doesn't want to attend unescorted. Even though she could attend with Gertrude and me, she refuses. She says that's the same as attending without an escort." He tipped his head to the side. "I'd count it a real favor, Daniel, and I believe James would thank you as well. We could all go together."

There was no reason to refuse the request. Ida was good company, and the evening would be far more pleasurable than attending on his own. He had never enjoyed standing among a group of men at these events.

"I would be pleased to act as Ida's escort. Am I to invite her, or do you prefer to ask on my behalf?"

"Why don't we do it together?" Edward didn't wait for an answer. Instead, he hurried forward and grasped his wife's elbow. When the two ladies came to a halt, he turned to Daniel. "I believe Daniel has something he'd like to ask you, Ida."

A light wind swayed the overhead branches and cast a jagged pattern in the moonlight. Daniel cleared his throat and looked at Ida. "I wondered if I could escort you to the Harvest Ball? We can attend as a foursome with Edward and Gertrude. Edward has assured me James wouldn't object, but I understand if you think it would appear improper."

Her lips curved in a generous smile. "I don't see why it would be improper. We're not formally engaged, and James knows how much I want to attend the ball. He'll be delighted. Especially when he learns we'll be chaperoned by my brother and Gertrude." She giggled as they continued toward the Arcade. "I'm just joking with you, Daniel. James trusts me and would never believe I was in need of a chaperone."

"That's good to know. I don't want him to return and punch me in the nose."

The four of them were laughing as they walked past the Millinery and Dressmaking Shop inside the Arcade and continued to the library housed on the second floor.

Hannah glanced at the workroom clock then stood and stretched her back. Her mother had promised to deliver supper at seven thirty, and Hannah didn't want to keep her waiting in the Arcade hallway. She massaged the back of her neck while wending her way toward the front door of the shop. She'd neared the glove display when she glanced out the front window and stopped short. Was that Daniel? She squinted her eyes against the dim light in the store. It was Daniel, but who was that with him? They were laughing as though something had struck them as quite humorous. She took another step closer and furrowed her brows. He was with Edward and Gertrude Milligan, and that was Ida Milligan walking at Daniel's side.

Her breath caught. Was Daniel courting Ida? The thought caused a sharp pang. She should be pleased for Daniel. After all, he had every right to court Ida or any other woman he chose. Yet an inexplicable sense of loss wrapped around her like a burial shroud.

Her mother's rap on the glass window jarred her back to the

present. She forced a smile and hurried to unlock the door. "Come in, Mama."

Carrying a basket on one arm, her mother stepped inside. "You appeared to be in a daze. I waved several times but finally decided I would need to knock if I was going to gain your attention."

"I'm sorry. I suppose I was in a bit of a stupor. I saw Daniel and Ida Milligan pass by the shop, and I was taken aback. I shouldn't be, of course. Daniel has every right to escort Ida or any other woman he chooses."

Eager to end further talk of Daniel and Ida, Hannah reached for the basket, but her mother moved her arm. "That's strange. I thought Ida had a suitor." A frown creased her forehead. "You know, I don't recall seeing her with that young man lately. Perhaps they've had a parting of the ways and Daniel received permission to court Ida. They'd make a fine-looking couple. Not as good as you and Daniel, but since that isn't in the offing, I hope things will work in their favor."

Her mother's words did little to ease Hannah's sense of loss. She gestured toward the basket. "I think I smell beef stew. Am I right?"

"Yes." Her mother extended the basket. "Were they alone?"

"What?"

"Were they alone? Daniel and Ida?"

Hannah shook her head. "No. They were with her brother and his wife. She lives with them, doesn't she?"

"Yes. She took a position over in the laundry a few years ago. At least that's what Janet Harvey told me. I believe Ida is a supervisor, but I can't be sure. If I recall, the family lives on Erickson Street. I spoke with Mrs. Milligan at the library on one occasion, and she seemed quite nice." Her mother gestured toward the basket. "You had better eat before your dinner gets cold." She turned to leave and then stopped. "Oh wait. I almost forgot. I put my library book in the basket and I must return it today, or I'll owe a fine and your father won't be happy. It was difficult enough to get him to pay for the library membership."

Hannah watched as her mother lifted the basket lid and removed a copy of *Ben-Hur: A Tale of the Christ* and tucked it in the crook of her arm. "This is a fine book, although portions were a bit difficult to read." She shuddered. "Very gory in places but unfortunately true to the times, I suppose." She smiled at Hannah. "Well, I'm off. Do come home earlier this evening. I worry about you, my dear."

Hannah followed her mother to the door. "Give my regards to Daniel."

Mrs. Cooper tipped her head to the side and looked at Hannah for a moment. "If there isn't something special you need to tell him, such a greeting might cause discomfort for both Daniel and Ida." She hesitated a minute. "Don't you think?"

"You're right. And I don't want to be the cause of embarrassment to either of them."

Hannah offered a fleeting smile as her mother departed then locked the door and hurried back to the workroom. Why had she even considered such a thing? Deep within, she knew the answer: though she had no right, she was jealous—jealous that

Daniel was enjoying the company of another woman. Jealous that Ida was free to be courted by him. And jealous that she was alone in a workroom long after everyone else had gone home for the night.

Chapter Nine

A single tear slipped down Hannah's cheek and splattered onto the forest-green satin fabric draped across her lap. She stared at the dark splotch on the bodice. What difference if her tear caused a stain? She wouldn't be wearing the dress.

She crumpled the note her mother had delivered only minutes ago. The message from Louis stung. His words had been brief: "*I won't be in Pullman for the Harvest Ball.*" His missive contained no explanation and had been posted to ensure she'd receive it only one day prior to the ball. No doubt he thought his behavior a justified retaliation because she'd canceled their plans for dinner. Ever since his remark at the train depot, she'd continued to wonder if he would keep his promise to escort her.

Now she regretted the extra hours she'd worked on beading the gown. She could have been using that time to complete the fan bags for Mrs. Pullman. She stood, placed the gown on the dress form, and then looked upon her creation. Her tear had already dried, leaving no evidence of a stain.

A wave of sadness washed over her as she threaded her needle, dipped the point into a blue crystal bead, and carefully stitched it to a black silk fan bag. Her thoughts wandered as she attached the colorful beads to her carefully drawn pattern. Since moving to Pullman, she'd attended every Harvest Ball. During her younger years, her parents had taken her, and she'd danced around the gaily lit room with her father patiently guiding her steps. As she'd grown older, she'd been escorted by a fellow who worked in the paint shop and later another who'd worked in the hammer shop. But on most occasions, she'd been escorted by Daniel.

She caught her lower lip between her teeth. Maybe Daniel could escort her this year. From what her mother had told her, Daniel and Ida hadn't been together in the library. Mrs. Milligan and Ida had been in the magazine section while Daniel and Mr. Milligan had been visiting in another section of the library. Perhaps he wasn't courting Ida. If not, he'd be the perfect escort for the ball, but she'd need to find an opportunity to see him today. If she left now, it wouldn't be too late to stop at his aunt and uncle's house.

A glimmer of hope seemed to light her way as she hurried along the brick sidewalk toward home. When she finally arrived, she stopped in front of her house. Should she go in and discuss her plan with her mother, or should she go directly next door and speak to Daniel? Before she could come to a decision, Daniel stepped onto the porch of his uncle's apartment.

"Hannah! Why are you standing outside? Are you locked out?"

She grinned. "No. My parents are at home, but I wanted to speak with you and I couldn't decide whether I should go home first."

He descended the steps at a jaunty clip and drew near. "I'm glad you didn't wait. You wouldn't have found me at home."

"Oh? Something important? I wouldn't want you to be late because of me."

"Nothing is more important than a few minutes with you. Haven't I always had time enough for you?"

She grinned. "Yes, you have." His words created a tinge of guilt, for she couldn't say the same to him.

"So what did you want to talk about?" He tipped his head to one side and waited.

"The Harvest Ball." She swallowed hard. "I thought you might agree to escort me."

His jaw tightened, and he shifted his gaze to the sidewalk. "I'm sorry, Hannah, but I've already agreed to escort someone else. I'm sorry. If I had known—"

She shook her head to interrupt his apology. "No, it's fine. I was sure you'd be attending, but I thought I'd ask—just to be sure." In spite of the cool autumn breeze, heat warmed her cheeks and she turned away. "I better go inside. I don't want to keep my father waiting on supper."

Before she could go, Daniel stayed her with a light touch to her arm. "Is Louis out of town?"

She swallowed hard and forced back tears. "I'm not sure

where he is. I received a note from him in today's mail. He said he couldn't be in Pullman tomorrow, but he didn't explain the reason."

"I'm sorry, Hannah. If I would have known sooner. . ."

"I understand. Believe me, if I'd known before today, I would have asked you much earlier." Her voice trembled, and she rubbed her hands together, pretending to ward off the cold. "It's getting chilly out here. I'd better go inside." She moved toward the steps, hoping the evening shadows had hidden her disappointment.

"Just remember what you told me when I was preparing to move to Pullman."

Her eyebrows pulled together. "What was that?"

"Lots of folks attend without an escort. Ask one of the women you work with to go along with you. I promise I'll ask for a dance."

Tears pricked her eyes. His offer of a dance wasn't enough to lighten her mood, but it appeared as if agreeing with him might be the only way to end their conversation. "I'll give it some thought."

"Promise?"

She gave a slight nod and pushed open the door. "I'm home, Mama."

"Hannah? I wasn't expecting you." Her mother stepped to the kitchen doorway. "This is a pleasant surprise. Did you bring your gown home to finish the beading?"

"No need to finish the gown. I won't be attending the Harvest Ball."

Her mother's brows knit together. "Is that what was in the letter from Louis? He isn't coming to Pullman to escort you?"

"Yes." Hannah shrugged, hoping to look nonchalant. "Is there anything I can help with?"

Her mother gestured toward the other side of the room. "You can set the table. Your father will be downstairs in a few minutes." Hannah was gathering the dishes from the sideboard when her mother turned from the stove. "Well, if Louis isn't going to escort you, why not ask Daniel? I'm sure he'd be—"

"I've already asked him. He's escorting someone else."

"He is?" Her mother arched her brows. "Who?"

Hannah hesitated. "I didn't ask. If I were to venture a guess, I would say Ida Milligan." She placed a fork beside one of the plates then looked at her mother. "Is he seeing someone other than Ida?"

"I don't know. I haven't talked to his aunt recently. Since the weather has turned cooler, I don't see her outdoors. And with her poor health, I'm never sure when she's resting." Her mother lifted the roasting pan from the oven. "I saw Flora Kohl the other day. Her husband is friendly with Daniel and his uncle Henry. Flora said her daughter, Mildred, was hoping Daniel would ask permission to court her, but he doesn't seem to be taking the hint. From what Flora told me, Mildred did her best to wrangle an invitation to the Harvest Ball, but Daniel didn't invite her."

"Then he must be escorting Ida. I believe she and Daniel would be a better match. Mildred is a sweet girl, but I've always considered her a bit flighty. Perhaps it's her age. I believe she'd be seven years younger than Daniel." Hannah carried a pitcher of water to the table and filled the three glasses. "Will Papa want coffee now or only after dinner?"

Her mother finished carving the chicken then handed the oval platter to Hannah. "Has it been so long since you've eaten with us that you've forgotten he never drinks coffee until after his meals?"

"Well, it has been a while, but we all change our routines from time to time."

"True enough. You've certainly changed your routine since you began working for Mrs. Pullman." After spooning the potatoes and carrots from the roasting pan into a china serving bowl, her mother placed it on the table. "What about going to the ball with some of your friends? I'm sure there are other single young women attending alone." She didn't wait for an answer before hurrying down the hallway to the bottom of the stairs. "Frank! Supper is on the table." She returned to the kitchen without waiting for an answer.

She strode to the table and gestured for Hannah to sit down. Moments later, her father stepped into the kitchen. "This is a surprise. Our daughter eating a meal with us. What's the occasion? Did Mrs. Pullman cancel her orders?"

"No, but I think that meeting her expectations is taking a greater toll on my life than I anticipated."

Her father gave thanks for their meal. For the remainder of the dinner, Hannah attempted to focus upon her parents' conversation but to no avail. Her thoughts skittered from Louis's untimely cancellation to Daniel and his unavailability. Her father had said she needed to understand Louis was a company man and his time was not his own, and that all successful men understood sacrifice was essential. Would becoming successful in *her* profession mean she must sacrifice plans for marriage and a family? If so, she feared the cost of success might be too dear.

Chapter Ten

Two days after the ball, Hannah penned a letter to Louis and invited him to join her family for Thanksgiving dinner. She wanted to provide him with ample time to either accept or reject her offer. In response, he declined the invitation a few days later, stating he had a conflicting obligation. However, he invited her to join him for dinner when he was in Pullman on the twenty-sixth of October. At that time, he promised to explain his inability to join her for the upcoming holiday. He hadn't asked if she was free on that date, but he likely surmised she would make herself available if she wanted to restore their relationship—and he was correct.

Her dress of pale blue cashmere was one that accented her fair complexion and never failed to garner compliments. She wove an ivory ribbon into her upswept brown curls and carried a small reticule embroidered with tiny pearl beads. The design of intertwined hearts had been one of her first items to sell at the Arcade shop, and though much less intricate than her current work, it remained one of her favorites.

Her father gave an approving smile as she stepped into the parlor. He withdrew his pipe from between his teeth and nodded toward the front door. "What time is Louis expected?"

"I'm meeting him at the Hotel Florence in fifteen minutes, so I must be on my way." She turned toward the hallway to retrieve her coat.

"He's not calling for you? If he wants to court my daughter, the least he can do is arrive at the front door and escort her. I'm surprised you agreed to such an arrangement." He shook his head. "I don't know what the world is coming to. Back in my day. . ."

"Now, Frank. This isn't the time to get into a discussion of how things were done years ago." Her mother waved Hannah toward the hallway. "Hannah will be late. When Hannah meets with Louis she can tell him you don't approve of this arrangement." She glanced toward Hannah who was donning her coat.

"I'll be sure to relay your disapproval, Papa." She graced him with a bright smile, waved to her mother, and hurried out the door.

She nodded to several acquaintances along the way, but her heart plummeted when she caught sight of Daniel in the distance. Ida Milligan was holding his arm, and they were following behind Ida's brother and his wife. As they turned and entered the Arcade, she wondered if the four of them were going to dinner and then attending the play at the theater on the upper floor. Why did she feel a sense of betrayal each time she saw Daniel with Ida? Did she truly want to deny him the pleasure of keeping company with another woman? She silently scoffed at the idea. Daniel was her friend, nothing more. She was pleased for him—and for Ida. At least that's what she told herself as she entered the foyer of the hotel.

Louis was standing near the front desk and stepped forward to meet her. After removing her coat, Louis checked it in the hotel coatroom and escorted her into the dining room. "You look quite lovely this evening, Hannah." The waiter pulled out her chair, and Louis sat down opposite her. He nodded toward her reticule. "I particularly like the design on your bag. Were you thinking of me when you beaded those hearts?"

She let her eyes linger on the intertwined hearts for a moment, before looking up at him. "I can't say that I was, Louis. You see, I created that design long before we ever met."

"I do believe my mother would like something similar. Could you find time in your busy schedule to make one for her?"

"No need. There are several for sale in the shop. What color do you think she would like? Something in a neutral shade so she could carry it with most anything she chooses to wear?"

He shrugged. "It doesn't matter. She'll find something to match it, no matter the color."

"Then I'll be certain to put one aside for her."

"Or we could stop by the Arcade after dinner. I'm sure you must have a key to the shop since you keep such long hours."

She hesitated. "I do have a key, but I'm not certain it would be proper to actually shop at that time. I could get in trouble."

His features tightened into a frown. "Her birthday is tomorrow, and I've forgotten to purchase a gift. I see little difference whether you're at the shop late at night stitching beads on fabric or if you're selling one of the items that's been placed on the shelves for sale. I don't believe George Pullman would want his staff to turn away a customer."

She wanted to tell him that George Pullman might own the Arcade, but he wasn't her boss. Instead, she'd have to explain the nighttime purchase to Miss Hardelle or Mrs. Dunlap. No doubt, there would be questions asked, and Hannah didn't care to discuss her personal life with either of the ladies. Still, how could she refuse Louis? Certainly a refusal would further fracture their somewhat tenuous relationship. He'd started the evening on a flattering note. She didn't want to lose that mood.

"You're right. We can make a quick stop at the Arcade after dinner, and you can choose a bag for your mother." She tipped her head to the side. "You said you'd explain why you couldn't accept my Thanksgiving invitation, and I'd be pleased to know why you couldn't escort me to the Harvest Ball as well."

He cleared his throat. "You certainly move from one topic to another without a breath, but you're right. I did say I'd explain." He leaned back in his chair and wiped the corner of his lips with his napkin. "I was unexpectedly required to go out of town the day of the Harvest Ball. Of all people, you should understand that I must keep my employer happy." His words bore a mocking tone. "As for Thanksgiving, Mother has invited a group of close friends and relatives and asked that I be in attendance—to act as her stand-in host, of sorts."

"Did she believe I wouldn't be comfortable attending since

you'll be acting as the host? Because if that's the case, you can assure her I wouldn't feel slighted while you helped entertain the other guests." She shot him a bright smile. "And once I explained the circumstances, I'm sure my parents would understand my desire to be with you on Thanksgiving."

His jaw tightened. "That would be lovely, but. . ." He coughed and then downed a gulp of water and cleared his throat. "As I was saying, if circumstances were different, I'm sure Mother would be pleased to have you attend. However, space is limited in her apartment and she can seat only twelve. The invitations have gone out and all of the invited guests have responded that they will attend."

Hannah arched her brows. "So early in the month?"

"Mother has always been one to plan far in advance."

"It would appear all of her friends and relatives do the same." Hannah took a sip of coffee. "Except you, of course." She tapped her fingers atop her bag. "I'm sure your mother would be aghast that you've not even purchased her birthday present."

"She understands that my days are very busy."

"Yes, of course she does. Mothers are most forgiving." She forced a weak smile. "Has your mother indicated any desire to meet me?" Hannah inched her shoulders forward. "She does know you're courting me, doesn't she?"

Louis gave a slight nod. "Certainly. However, Mother told me long ago that she didn't want to meet any young lady until I was engaged." Rather than look at her, he remained focused upon the green beans on his plate. "Mother becomes easily attached to people. She believes she would be devastated if, after forming a friendship with a woman I was courting, we then ended our relationship." He finally looked up. "I'm sure you can understand."

Hannah's mind whirred at the response. Granted, Louis was older, but he'd never indicated a history of serious relationships with other women. "Does she feel this way because you've ended courtships with several ladies that she's met in the past?"

"Perhaps." He blew out a long breath. "I've already explained that she becomes easily attached to people."

"But she does know that I'm the one who made the beaded collar? And you'll tell her I designed and beaded the bag you plan to give her for her birthday, won't you?"

"Yes, of course." Irritation punctuated his curt response.

Though his revelations begged a deeper explanation, it was evident any further queries would be met with more irritation and meager responses, so she remained silent. The remainder of their time in the gilded dining room was strained, and by the time they departed for the Arcade, Hannah's dinner had settled like a rock. Perhaps if Louis had ordered something a bit lighter than the stuffed pork loin, or if his explanations hadn't been so strange, or if he hadn't been so disagreeable each time she attempted to converse, maybe she wouldn't be suffering indigestion now. His behavior was troubling. He'd offered no genuine apology for sending regrets only one day before the ball, and their discussion regarding Thanksgiving had ended in disaster.

They walked side by side without a word. Given his disposition this evening, Hannah decided against any further attempts at conversation. He'd been defensive one moment and aggressive the next. In truth, she preferred the silence over his ever-changing temperament.

While he held open the ornate Arcade door, she proceeded a few steps in front of him until they arrived at the shop. After removing the key from her reticule, she slipped it into the lock and opened the door. She glanced over her shoulder, her nerves taut. "The shop will appear open if I turn on any of the lights. We'll have to rely upon the light from the Arcade, but I think you'll be able to see well enough to make a choice."

When he didn't respond, she gestured for him to follow her down the second aisle. The Arcade lights reflected off the glass cases and cast shadows across the aisle. Hannah stepped around one of the counters, removed four beaded reticules, and placed them atop the glass case.

She pointed at the blue one. "This is exactly like mine, but she might like the rose beige. I think it's quite lovely. Or this one in chestnut could be carried with most any color."

He shook his head. "No. I believe she'd be fond of the one just like yours."

Though she thought a woman of his mother's age would prefer the chestnut color, Hannah didn't attempt to dissuade him. In truth, she would have chosen an entirely different bag. The entwined hearts seemed an odd choice, but Hannah was pleased his mother was fond of her designs and beadwork.

He counted and placed payment on the counter while Hannah wrapped the bag. She picked up the money and gestured toward the rear of the store. "Wait here while I take the money to Mrs.

Dunlap's office. I'll only be a minute."

He nodded. "I'll stand by the front door."

Hannah sighed. He even had to overrule her simple request to remain at the counter. She decided against remaining there to argue with him. Given the progression of the evening, it would do little good. But then, as she hurried to Mrs. Dunlap's office, Hannah further considered the possibility of a confrontation with Louis. After all, what difference would it make? He was already in a foul mood. Even if he didn't believe he had wronged her, she'd done nothing to deserve his thoughtless conduct. Airing their differences might be for the best.

She arched her brows as she strode toward the front door to meet him. "Ready?" He nodded, and she leaned forward to unlock the door. When they were in the hallway of the Arcade, she turned toward him. "If you haven't made any further plans for this evening, perhaps we could go down the hall to Thurman's Ice Cream Parlor, where we could talk."

"Haven't we been talking?" He flipped a hand. "However, if that's what you'd like."

They began to walk. "I do hope your mother will enjoy the gift. Tell her to feel free to spread the word that we sell them at the shop. Of course, I hope that one day soon I'll be working at Marshall Field's and we'll be selling them in his store."

His smile immediately vanished. "I thought I'd made it clear that I don't think your moving to Chicago is a good idea. You do recall that conversation, don't you?"

"I do, but if my designs are going to become recognized, I need to be employed in a larger city. If my designs are well received in Chicago, Mr. Field has connections in the fashion industry that could propel my designs all over the world."

"All over the world? I doubt that." His words were laced with sarcasm. "You don't need to live in Chicago to have your work recognized. If you are good enough, buyers will come here to seek you out. I know you believe I'll have more time with you if you're living in Chicago, but I've made it clear that won't happen. Besides, your parents want you nearby. Your father has already told me he has reservations about such a move."

Once inside the ice-cream parlor, she sat down at one of the small round tables while Louis stepped to the counter to place their order. Louis turned toward her then gazed above her head. He nodded at someone, and she looked up. "Daniel." She hesitated as she locked eyes with Ida Milligan. "And it's Ida, isn't it? How nice to see both of you."

Edward and Gertrude circled around the table and offered their greetings, but it was Daniel who remained by her side. "The four of us went to the theater to see Callender's Minstrels." Daniel glanced at Louis. "I believe they appeared in Chicago before coming to Pullman. Did you happen to see their show?"

Louis appeared, carrying two dishes of ice cream. He'd obviously overheard and curled his lip. "I much prefer more serious offerings when I attend the theater. I've never found minstrel shows particularly entertaining."

Edward chuckled. "We working fellows need to enjoy a good laugh when we go out for an evening of entertainment." He slapped

Daniel on the shoulder. "Isn't that right, Daniel?"

Daniel nodded. "You know what the Good Book says, Louis. 'A merry heart doeth good like a medicine.'" He settled his gaze on Louis. "And I couldn't agree more. Just look at us." He extended his arm in a sweeping motion. "You can't deny the four of us appear very happy."

Louis tightened his lips into a thin line. "Did you come in to make a purchase or merely to instruct us on how to be happy?"

Hannah reared back in her chair and Daniel looked as though Louis had struck him, yet he maintained a feeble smile. "We're going to enjoy a soda. Please forgive us for intruding."

The foursome hurried away, all of them wide-eyed. As soon as they were out of earshot, Hannah leaned forward. "You were rude and insulting, Louis. You owe them an apology."

Louis shrugged. "I don't intend to apologize for stating my opinion, and there was no reason for them to circle the table like a pack of hungry wolves." He pushed his ice cream away and stood. "I'm ready to leave."

He didn't ask if she wanted to depart. Instead, he assumed she would leave whenever he was ready. And she did, but not because she wanted to please Louis. Rather, she wanted to escape the sidelong glances from Daniel and the Milligans.

Chapter Eleven

The following week, Mrs. Pullman sent word she'd like to examine any completed fan bags. The request came as a surprise since Mrs. Pullman had approved the designs before Hannah set to work on them. While she didn't mind having her work scrutinized, Mrs. Pullman didn't seem to understand that a day away from the shop was a day that could be put to better use stitching the designs. However, when Mrs. Pullman requested one's presence, one didn't send regrets. Instead, one arrived at the time and place of her bidding.

Hannah's mother fluttered through the kitchen preparing breakfast, her complexion flush with excitement. "Why didn't you tell me last night that you were going to Chicago again? I would have had your breakfast prepared earlier."

"There's plenty of time. Today is like any other day. I'm just going to work at a different location." Hannah sat at the kitchen table.

An unexpected frown creased her mother's face. "Visiting

the Pullman home isn't work, Hannah. Do you know how many employees would consider it a privilege to have a peek inside that mansion? You've been given a rare opportunity."

Hannah didn't argue, though she didn't view her visits to the Pullman home in the same light as her mother. While Hannah was certain the remainder of the home was quite elegant, her visits so far had been limited to the small sitting room off the foyer.

"My appointments with Mrs. Pullman aren't social visits, so I didn't receive a grand tour of their home. I'm no different than her maid who serves tea or the butler who opens the front door when guests arrive."

Her mother swiped her hands down the front of her apron. "It's still an honor to have someone like Mrs. Pullman invite you into her home."

Hannah sighed. "It's simply more convenient for her. Nothing more and nothing less." Seeing the glimmer fade from her mother's eyes, Hannah immediately regretted her negative response. She reached for her mother's hand and gave it a gentle squeeze. "I'm sorry. You're right. Working directly with Mrs. Pullman is a privilege. I'm just a bit out of sorts this morning. Traveling into Chicago takes away time I planned to use beading one of her fan bags."

Her mother patted her shoulder and smiled down at her. "I know you, Hannah Cooper. You'll complete every last one of those bags, even if it requires working around the clock."

After finishing her breakfast, Hannah kissed her mother on the cheek, tied her velvet bonnet, and donned her thick woolen coat. "I don't want to miss the train. I'll see you this evening, Mama."

She pulled on her gloves while descending the front steps. Had they not stepped aside, she would have plowed into a couple of schoolboys. One of them glared and pointed at her. "You should watch where you're going, miss."

Hannah's face flamed with embarrassment. She mumbled a hurried apology before continuing down the street. She desperately hoped the remainder of her day would go better than the first few hours. Otherwise, the meeting with Mrs. Pullman could be disastrous.

The hoot of an approaching train sounded in the distance and she quickened her step. The last thing she needed to do was miss the train. Dodging a carriage, she crossed the street and stepped inside the station while the train hissed to a stop near the platform. After flashing her train pass at the trainman, she boarded and settled into her seat. A loud "All Aboard!" echoed through the car, and soon the train lurched and chugged forward.

She held tightly to the satchel containing the fan bags and let her thoughts wander. How she wished there had been an opportunity to let Louis know she'd be in the city today. Perhaps he would have joined her for a late lunch or asked her to remain in town for dinner. Though she needed to return to Pullman and work, she would have stayed this one time and taken a late train home. A strain lingered in their relationship. If not mended, the fracture between them would deepen and time apart was not a solution.

In truth, she thought he would have already let her know whether his mother liked the birthday gift, but there hadn't been a word from him. Then again, she'd also expected him to come by the shop before he departed town to make certain she hadn't suffered any repercussions for permitting his late-night purchase of the beaded bag. He'd failed on that account as well. She told herself he was busy with his work. Surely, she should understand that reason, since she offered the same excuse to him from time to time. Or perhaps he no longer cared for her. The thought passed through her mind like a flash of lightning in a midnight sky, but she silently refuted the idea. Louis loved her. He'd told her so. Yet his actions no longer reflected love. Not as they had when they'd first met. She tried to remember when things had begun to change between them, but before she could arrive at a tangible conclusion, the train pulled into the Chicago station.

Once inside the terminal, Hannah moved through the crowd but abruptly stopped short. Her gaze settled on an elegant pin that adorned the coat of a woman seated nearby. She was certain the pin's design could be enlarged into a perfect motif for a future project. Without giving thought to the time, Hannah yanked the drawing pad from her bag, sat down opposite the woman, and sketched the pin from several angles. When she was finally pleased with the results, she stood and glanced at the clock. A gasp escaped her lips. If she was late and Mrs. Pullman reported the incident, there could be terrible consequences. Wouldn't Miss Hardelle be pleased to know her predictions had come true! Hannah was going to be late for her meeting with Mrs. Pullman.

She raced through the terminal, her thoughts whirring. Why had she stopped? Hadn't her impetuous behavior gotten her into enough trouble in the past? She continued to condemn herself until she finally reached the front doors of the terminal and caught sight of Mrs. Pullman's driver. As he assisted her into the carriage, she offered a silent prayer of thanks that he'd waited.

Grateful the ride didn't take long, she rushed up the front steps and lifted the heavy knocker. Before it could clank more than once, the butler pulled open the door. He ushered her inside, took her coat, and directed her into Mrs. Pullman's office, where the older woman was already seated with a tea tray in front of her.

Mrs. Pullman's gaze traveled toward the bronze mantle clock. "I do wish one could depend upon trains arriving on schedule." She sighed and gestured to the chair next to her own. "Well, no matter. You're here now. Do sit down. I'm eager to see what you've accomplished."

Hannah opened the satchel and withdrew a muslin-wrapped package. She placed the packet atop the table in front of Mrs. Pullman, untied the string, and pulled back the cloth. Pearls and transparent beads twinkled on a midnight-blue silk bag. Mrs. Pullman sighed with pleasure and lifted the bag, her fingers tracing the beadwork as she examined the stitching. "It's exquisite." She placed it aside then continued to examine each of the bags with the same attention to detail. "I am more than delighted with these. Your handwork is beyond reproach, and your eye for color is truly magnificent. I know the recipients will consider themselves very fortunate to receive such a gift." She graced Hannah with a bright smile. "You will have them all completed on time, won't you?"

"Yes, of course. You have my word."

The older woman arched her brows. "I also want your word that the handwork on the last one will be as flawless as it is on these since I'll be gifting family members and close friends with these."

"Of course. I pride myself on presenting the very best of my talent with each piece, Mrs. Pullman."

"Yes, I'm sure you do." She poured tea into a cup and offered it to Hannah. "Do you recall that at one of our previous meetings I mentioned a gift for guests who come to call on New Year's Day?"

Hannah's heart lurched. She had no idea how many guests might call on the Pullmans on New Year's Day, but she was certain she wouldn't have sufficient time to complete a gift for all of them. She attempted a weak smile. "I vaguely recall you mentioning New Year's Day, but I don't believe we agreed upon a gift."

"No, we didn't. That's one of the reasons I wanted you to come today. I've been thinking about that possibility, and I thought perhaps we could give each visitor a small velvet bag with a gold cord. You could embellish the bags with the letter *P* along with a sprig of holly and some red beads. What do you think?"

She hadn't said what she was going to put inside the bag, how large they would be, or how many she would need. And, no matter the number, Hannah didn't know how she could possibly achieve such a feat. "I don't believe there's sufficient time, Mrs. Pullman. If you would like me to prepare what you've suggested for next year, I'd be pleased to do so. Right now, I need to devote my time to completing the fan bags."

Mrs. Pullman leaned against the back of her chair and sighed. "I was afraid that was what you'd tell me. My daughter tells me my expectations frequently exceed possibilities." She stared out the window. "Now, what am I to do? I dislike handing out the same small tokens each year."

Hannah inched forward on her chair. "If you would agree the bags could be made by machine, I think they could be produced in the upholstery department. I could create a design if you gave me the dimensions. The letter *P* could be done using the embroidery machines in the upholstery shop and possibly the holly leaves as well. The girls in the dress shop could stitch the red beads in place and thread the gold cord through the casing at the top of the bag. I would oversee the project if you like."

A smile began to tug at Mrs. Pullman's lips, and she bobbed her head. "I do believe that would work quite well. Of course, I'll need to get my husband's approval to have the bags made in the upholstery shop, but that shouldn't be a problem." She pushed up from her chair, stepped to her desk, and retrieved a paper and pen. "Why don't you draw something I can show George so he'll have an idea what is needed, and then he can speak to the foreman in the upholstery department?"

Hannah hesitated. "How large a bag?"

"Hmm. Only large enough to hold some sugared almonds and a few other sweet treats." Using the thumb and forefinger of each hand, she held them aloft to resemble a small bag.

Hannah nodded and set to work drawing the design. When she'd complete the task, she handed the drawing to Mrs. Pullman. "What do you think?"

She beamed. "I think it's perfect. I'll speak to my husband this evening, and once I've gained his approval, I'll send you a note or call the dress shop and speak to you."

Hannah took the older woman's cue. Their meeting had come to an end. She folded the muslin over the bags and placed them in her satchel, before standing. "It has been a pleasure to meet with you, Mrs. Pullman. I look forward to receiving your final decision regarding the New Year's gifts."

Mrs. Pullman walked her to the office door. "Thank you for your hard work, Hannah. I do appreciate your willingness to assist me."

Hannah strode toward the waiting carriage driver who smiled as she approached. "Shall it be the train depot or Marshall Field's, miss?"

There wouldn't be another train to Pullman for several hours, and she certainly didn't want to wait at the train depot when she could survey the delights that awaited at Marshall Field's. "I believe I'd like to enjoy some time at Marshall Field's."

The driver nodded and assisted her into the carriage. In no time, they arrived at the store. The doorman greeted her with a cheery smile and bid her "good day" as he held open the door. She walked along the first aisle of accessories, her fingers tracing the glass-topped cases as she surveyed the variety of gloves, scarves, hat pins, and bangles.

A clerk stepped forward, but Hannah shook her head. She wouldn't be purchasing anything from their well-filled cases. When she approached the handbags, she stopped and admired several. She was leaning over one of the cases when someone said, "That's particularly serviceable, isn't it?"

Hannah turned and looked up at a beautifully coiffed woman who was staring at the same bag. "It appears to be alligator, don't you think? Nice for everyday use. I'm told it wears quite well, but I prefer beauty over utility."

The woman looked down at her own handbag and Hannah followed her gaze. Her breath caught and she swayed before grasping the counter and forcing down a gulp of air.

"Are you ill? Your complexion is suddenly quite pasty. Do you need to sit down?" The woman waved a glove toward one of the clerks. "Bring a chair for this young lady before she swoons and hits her head on the floor."

"No, no. I'm fine. I don't need a chair." Hannah gestured to the woman's bag. "May I ask where you purchased your handbag?"

The woman straightened her shoulders and her eyes beamed with delight. "My husband gave it to me as a birthday gift. He had it made especially for me." She extended the bag. "The beadwork is exquisite, don't you think?"

"Your husband?" The words croaked from Hannah's dry throat. Her mind reeled. There had to be some explanation. Had Louis sold the bag to someone rather than giving it to his mother? Perhaps he'd left it on the train and someone had found it.

The woman smiled and nodded. "He travels a great deal, but he's quite generous with his gifts."

"How nice of him." Hannah longed to ask the woman her husband's name, but such a question would go beyond proper etiquette. "I'd love to know where he purchased such a lovely bag."

"He didn't mention the store, but I thought he'd purchased it here. However, I've seen nothing like it in the store. I have a beautiful beaded collar that I'm sure was purchased in the same shop. The beadwork on the collar exceeds anything I've seen in Marshall Field's—or anywhere else for that matter."

Hannah hadn't completely digested her remarks before the woman offered a fleeting smile. "If you're certain you're all right, I must be on my way. Louis will be home for supper, and I have a list of errands to complete before five o'clock." That said, she rushed off, with the scent of her heavy perfume lingering in the air.

Hannah's stomach roiled. All the regrets Louis had sent, the sudden changes in schedule, the strange Thanksgiving plans—it all fell into place. What a fool she'd been.

Chapter Twelve

Unable to propel herself toward the door, Hannah continued to clutch the edge of the counter. Had that been nothing more than a bad dream? That's what she wanted to believe, but she knew every word and action had been real. She straightened her spine and lifted her head. She would not let this pass. She would find out the truth about Louis today. After inhaling a deep, cleansing breath, she made her way to the front door of the store and hailed a hansom cab.

She removed a paper from her bag and read the address before looking up at the driver. "The offices of Carney and Barnes, on West 14th Street." She handed him the paper; he nodded and handed it back to her. "How far is it?"

He shrugged. "Too far to walk."

If the driver had taken the most direct route, he'd been correct about the distance. The office was too far for her to walk, especially since she didn't know her way around Chicago.

When she stepped out of the carriage and handed him payment, he nodded toward the building. "Want me to wait or you gonna be in there a long time?"

"I won't be long."

He gave a slight nod before he jumped down. After strapping a bag of feed on the horse, he leaned against the carriage and shoved a wad of tobacco into his mouth. "I'll be waiting right here."

Hannah's hands shook and her mouth turned dry as she opened the door and entered the front office. A clerk sat at a desk surrounded by a high circular counter that reminded Hannah of the front desk at the Hotel Florence. He looked up when she drew near, though he made no move toward the counter.

"Help you?"

"Yes. I'd like to speak with Louis Nicholson, please."

The man traced his finger down a list then looked at her. "Do you have an appointment?"

"No, but I'm sure he'll see me. It's urgent."

The man rolled his eyes and tightened his lips in a grimace. "Of course it is."

He pushed a button on his desk, and moments later Louis appeared in the foyer. His attention was focused upon the clerk until the gentleman nodded in Hannah's direction. Louis glanced her way and then jerked to attention.

Eyes burning with anger, he took two giant steps, grasped her upper arm in his hand, and propelled her toward the front door. Unable to free her arm, she moved alongside him, almost skipping to keep pace.

When they were near the door, he leaned close to her ear.

"What are you doing at my office?"

He opened the door with his free hand and pushed her toward the opening. Anger rushed over her like a gale and she jerked loose of his hold. "I stopped by to tell you that I met your wife today."

He followed her out the door. "What are you talking about? Is this some sort of foolish prank?"

She didn't miss the tick in his jaw. "No, Louis. We met in Marshall Field's. She was carrying the purse you purchased as a birthday gift for your mother—except your wife told me that you had purchased it for *her* birthday. She also mentioned you'd purchased a beautiful hand-beaded collar for her—the one you told me was also for your mother. Furthermore, she said you travel a good deal but you're quite generous with your gifts, and that you have excellent taste." Hannah glared at him. "How dare you, Louis? You've done nothing but lie and deceive me since the day I met you. Did the Harvest Ball conflict with your wedding anniversary perchance? Is that why you couldn't attend with me?"

"Don't be ridiculous. I don't know who you met in the store—"

"Stop it! Please don't make a fool of yourself by trying to lie your way out of this. The fact that you've deceived me for all this time is bad enough. Don't insult me further with more of your lies."

Despite the chill in the air, perspiration beaded his forehead. "I think it may have been my sister that you saw in the store. She frequently borrows jewelry and handbags from Mother. I'm sure she—"

Hannah thrust her hand forward. "Stop! We both know that isn't true. So much has become clear to me since speaking to your wife today. Your inability to share holiday meals with my family, your last-minute cancellation of plans, your inability to meet me when I'm in Chicago, the warning never to come to your office and never to give my name if I called you at work, and seeing the young woman carrying the handbag you purchased at the store—it doesn't require a genius to know you're married! The truth is, I feel foolish I didn't realize you had a wife before today."

"Let me explain, Hannah. I didn't intend to deceive you. Our marriage was failing before I met you, and. . ."

She shook her head. "Don't embarrass yourself with far-fetched excuses. You came to my home and asked my father for permission to court me. How does a married man do such a thing with no compunction? I don't ever want to see you again. You should confess your dreadful behavior to your wife and beg her forgiveness. She deserves better, Louis—and so do I."

Tears rimmed her eyes as she turned and hurried out the front door. How had she been so blind? Keeping her head bowed to hide her tears, she grasped the carriage handle. "Train station, please."

"As ya wish." The driver's gravelly voice drifted from his perch.

The moment she closed the door, the carriage moved forward with a jolt that thrust her toward the window. She locked eyes with Louis who appeared frozen in place. Had he truly believed she would never find out? Or that his wife never would? Or had he planned to end their so-called courtship when he feared one of them might discover the truth? Had that been the cause of his recent sullen behavior? Had he planned to end things because she'd indicated a desire to meet his mother and be invited to her home?

Her thoughts swirled like leaves in a windstorm. And what would her parents think when she revealed the truth to them?

By the time she returned to Pullman, her head was throbbing with pain and her stomach had tightened in knots. Her emotions switched like boxcars on a siding. One minute anger surged through her veins, the next guilt, only to be followed by deep sadness. How could Louis profess his love when his heart belonged to another? Did he have girls in every city he visited as a salesman? And his poor wife. Would he ever tell her the truth?

The dress shop would still be open, but instead of turning toward the Arcade, she walked directly home. She needed to speak to her mother, and she needed to cry. Perhaps then she could experience some semblance of peace. More than anything, she longed for a return to normalcy, yet she wasn't certain what that looked like anymore.

She trudged up the front steps and entered the small foyer. "I'm home, Mama." She tugged off her coat and hung it on the hall tree before unpinning and removing her hat. "Mama! Where are you?"

Her mother appeared at the top of the steps holding a dust rag in one hand and a broom in the other. "You surprised me, Hannah. I didn't expect you home this early, but I'm pleased to see you. I'm eager to hear how things went with Mrs. Pullman." After placing the cleaning supplies against the bannister, her mother hurried downstairs. The anticipation that shone in her eyes immediately changed to concern when she looked at Hannah. "Whatever is wrong, dear? Come to the kitchen and I'll set the kettle to boil."

Hannah moved down the hallway like one of the mechanical

soldiers she'd seen in the Arcade Toy Shop earlier in the month. She dropped onto one of the wooden chairs while her mother pumped water into the kettle then set it on the stove. Her mother drew near and gathered Hannah's hands between her own. "Tell me what has happened."

While massaging her temples, Hannah related the details of the day. She swallowed a sob. "Then the woman said she was his wife. I could barely believe what I heard. And the way he behaved! Trying to make me believe his wife was his sister then telling me they were planning a divorce. He's a man who doesn't care who he hurts as long as he gets what he wants. Even worse, he has no morals." She shuddered. "I've been trying to make sense of it, but I simply don't know how." She wrapped her arms around her waist and rocked back and forth. "I was such a fool."

Horror shone in her mother's eyes. "Oh Hannah! You weren't a fool. He deceived all of us, and how awful for you to come face-to-face with his wife. It's a wonder you didn't faint on the spot."

"I came close." She dabbed at her eyes. "How could he do this?"

"It's difficult to believe he lied to all of us—and his poor wife has no idea what kind of man she has for a husband." Her mother inhaled a deep breath. "But I truly believe meeting her today was God's plan to protect you."

Hannah offered a weak smile. "Perhaps, Mama, but it would have been much better if this had happened when I first met him. I've planned my future around him. I thought we would be married. I wanted to work in Chicago so I could be close to him and we would have more time together. I was willing to change my whole life for him. Even knowing all of that, he continued with his charade."

Her mother poured water into the teapot and returned to the table. She pulled her chair close to Hannah. "You must remember that moving to Chicago wasn't entirely because of Louis. You wanted to further your career. If I recall, he wasn't in favor of the move."

"That was another warning I should have seen. What man who loves a woman doesn't want her to live nearby? I feel so foolish for blindly believing whatever he said."

"Don't be so hard on yourself, my dear. Even though at first I objected due to his age, I eventually thought Louis a fine man—and so did your father. You trusted Louis, and you mustn't let his behavior cause you to lose trust in others." Her mother took a sip of tea. "Painful as it is, I'm thankful you now know the truth. You need to forget the past and look to the future. I tell you all the time that God has a plan for each of us. His plan for you didn't include Louis Nicholson, but you still have your work, your family, and good friends."

Her head still throbbing, Hannah once again massaged her temples. "I know you're right, but it's difficult to put things in a positive light right now. My life has turned upside down, and I believe it's going to take a little time to set it aright."

"It will take some time, but with the love of friends, family, and God, you're going to be just fine. I can feel it in my heart." She cupped Hannah's cheek in her hand. "Why don't you go upstairs and rest until time for supper? I think a short nap will ease your headache. When you awaken, you may even have a different perspective on all that has happened."

Hannah pushed up from the table and strode down the hallway to the stairs. The nap might ease her headache, but it would take much more than an hour of rest to ease the ache and anger in her heart.

The following days passed in a haze. In an attempt to forget Louis and his many lies, Hannah returned to her long hours in the dress shop. On several occasions, Mrs. Dunlap inquired about Hannah's reserved countenance, but Hannah insisted that all was fine. Thankfully, the older woman soon ceased her inquiries, and Hannah was left to her beadwork and the quietude of the small workroom.

Though it had taken longer than Mrs. Pullman had projected, word finally arrived that Mr. Pullman had agreed the upholstery shop could assist with the velvet gift bags Mrs. Pullman wanted for her New Year's Day Open House.

Mrs. Dunlap waved the missive she held in her hand. "This says you're to meet with Albert Johnson, the foreman of the upholstery shop."

Hannah looked up from her sewing. "Does it say when or if I am to contact him?"

Mrs. Dunlap lifted the page and read farther down. "He'll contact you when he has time to meet."

"Let's hope he doesn't wait too long. Once he completes his work, we'll need to finish the bags here in the shop."

Mrs. Dunlap sighed. "True enough, and I doubt Mr. Johnson is going to put velvet gift bags before the work orders he needs to complete for the railcars."

Hannah shrugged. "If Mrs. Pullman doesn't hear from me that work has proceeded, I'm certain she'll speak to her husband. And if Mr. Pullman desires a happy wife, I'm certain he'll speak to Mr. Johnson."

Mrs. Dunlap grinned. "I'm sure you're right. What man doesn't desire a happy wife?"

A vision of Louis's wife flashed before her, and Hannah wondered if he was striving to make his wife happy. But since the woman likely had no knowledge of her husband's unacceptable conduct, perhaps she'd always been happy. Isn't that what Thomas Gray had alluded to in his ode when he'd penned, "Where ignorance is bliss, 'tis folly to be wise." Hannah had been happy until she'd learned the truth. Whether Louis ever shared the truth with his wife was his decision. Yet she now believed that knowing the truth was far better than continuing in blissful ignorance—at least for her.

As the days marched on, the pain inflicted upon Hannah diminished to a dull ache and was then overtaken by a sense of deep embarrassment. Now that Louis was no longer a part of her life, it seemed every conversation with friends and coworkers turned to one of suitors and social engagements—guest lists for Thanksgiving gatherings, escorts to the upcoming Christmas Ball, and invitations to New Year's Day receptions were all discussed in detail. Though she did her best to take her leave when such topics arose, Hannah couldn't completely avoid questions about Louis's recent exit from her life.

She'd discovered no easy way to reveal she'd been duped. That a man had convinced her of his love and it had taken her months to learn he already had a wife, that she'd believed his lies and had hoped to build a future with him, that he'd exited her life without concern for the wounds he'd inflicted upon her. How did one explain such horror?

While she tiptoed around explanations with coworkers, her father had been an entirely different story. He wanted, and deserved, a full explanation. Amid tears and bouts of hiccups, she'd recounted the ugly story. Her father had remained grim and stoic, angered that he'd permitted Louis to court his only daughter.

Though he'd berated Louis's behavior, her father had soon picked up his well-worn Bible and patted the leather cover. "The answer lies within these pages," he'd said. "We must forgive before we can heal." He'd fixed his gaze on Hannah. "You, most of all, my dear. Don't let Louis's shoddy actions destroy your trust in others. The only way your heart will mend is if you forgive him. God blessed you with a sweet and gentle spirit, but bitterness will change who you are. I pray you won't allow that to happen."

Hannah had taken her father's words to heart and she'd continued to fervently pray for the power to forgive. In truth, it hadn't been as hard as she'd anticipated. The possibility of seeing Louis again was unlikely. On his trips to Pullman, there would be no need for him to leave the hotel except to visit the Administration Building to conduct business. No doubt Louis wanted to avoid her just as much as she wanted to avoid him. And while she'd forgiven him, embarrassment continued to plague her like an endless nightmare.

In the evenings after the other clerks and seamstresses had departed and she was alone in the workshop, Hannah's thoughts had begun to wander down another path. As she stitched and beaded, she wondered what would have happened if she'd never met Louis. Possibly her friendship with Daniel would have blossomed into something more. He'd given some indication that he cared for her as more than a dear friend, but back then she'd had Louis. And now Daniel had moved on with his life. No doubt he and Ida Milligan would court for several more months and then announce their wedding plans. She envisioned Ida breezing into the shop with a request that Hannah design and fit her gown. The first time that thought arose, Hannah had shouted her refusal aloud. Since then, she'd done her best to push such thoughts aside. In truth, Hannah simply could not imagine Daniel married to Ida—or anyone else for that matter—except maybe her.

Chapter Thirteen

The noon whistle sounded as Hannah exited the upholstery shop. Her meeting with Albert Johnson had gone well today. He hadn't been pleased when she pointed out flaws in some of the velvet pouches produced in his shop, but he'd finally agreed the faulty pouches would be replaced with new ones. There was little doubt he considered the task an inconvenience that slowed production of the ornate interiors of the railcars. His job depended upon excellent craftsmanship and meeting deadlines, but so did Hannah's. While she'd been sympathetic to his argument, she'd pointed out the fault didn't lie with her. Hannah departed with a promise to collect the pouches the following Monday. Mr. Johnson's sullen countenance didn't change, but his mumbled agreement was enough to lift Hannah's spirits.

Hannah strode down the walkway in front of the Administration Building with an air of purpose in her step. This afternoon she would meet with the four ladies assigned to help with the embroidery work. Mrs. Dunlap had assigned shop clerks rather than seamstresses from the dressmaking department, a fact that concerned Hannah. However, when she'd voiced her apprehensions to Mrs. Dunlap, the older woman assured Hannah each of the ladies declared advanced stitchery abilities. Hannah could only hope they hadn't overstated their qualifications. Today she would put their skills to the test.

"Hannah! Wait up!"

At the sound of her name, she turned to see Daniel loping toward her with his lunch tin pail dangling from one hand. With surprising deftness, he wove his way through the crowd of men and came to a halt beside her, a broad grin spread across his face.

Pulling her scarf tight around her neck, Hannah met his gaze. "Hello, Daniel. I didn't expect to see you over here. Isn't the glass etching and embossing done in another area?"

"Yes, but I had to speak with the foreman who oversees interior installation on the private railcars—seems the schedule in his shop and the embossing shop aren't properly coordinated. I think we solved the problem." He grinned. "How are you? It's been so long since I've seen you. Your mother tells me you're working all the time."

"I wouldn't say all the time, but Mrs. Pullman's orders and my other duties at the shop have been keeping me quite busy. What about you? The last time I saw you I believe you and Ida Milligan had attended the theater."

"Then it's been even longer than I imagined since I've seen you. We'll have a great deal to talk about on Thanksgiving, don't you think?"

At a complete loss to understand his question, she shrugged her shoulders. "Thanksgiving?"

"Yes. Didn't your mother tell you that she invited Aunt Jane, Uncle Henry, and me for dinner?" Before she could respond, he continued. "I think your mother knows Aunt Jane doesn't feel up to preparing a large meal. She's been unable to regain her strength since being ill last month."

"Mama did mention your aunt hadn't been feeling well, but she didn't tell me about the Thanksgiving invitation. Then again, we're like ships passing in the night. When I get home, my parents are in bed, and I seldom take time to join them for breakfast in the morning."

"Well I do hope you're going to take the day off to enjoy dinner with all of us." He matched her stride as they continued past the small park. "Some time ago, you asked me to list my personal priorities for you. I said that my order of my priorities would be God, family, and work, and you said you agreed with me. Have you now changed your mind?"

"No, of course not. Why would you think I've changed my opinion?"

He tipped his head to the side. "I don't know how much time you dedicate to prayer and reading God's Word, but your mother indicates you devote little time to family. And from what you tell me, it sounds as though your every waking hour is occupied with your work."

His comments knifed through her. Though there had been kindness in his tone, his observation cut to the quick. She had needed time alone to sort out her thoughts, to regain the poise and self-confidence that had wounded her spirit, and to forgive and move on with a renewed strength.

She met his eyes. “You’re right, Daniel. My time is filled with work, but I believe that will change once I’ve completed my orders for Mrs. Pullman.”

“But what if she continues to place more orders? What then, Hannah? Will you then make more time for God and family?” He hesitated a moment. “And possibly me?” A glimmer shone in his eyes.

Was he teasing her? Why would he want more of her time when Ida Milligan could satisfy his need for companionship? If this was a game, she didn’t like it—not one bit.

She nodded toward the Arcade. “I do plan to make more time for God and family in the New Year. But, for now, I must return to work. We can talk about it on Thanksgiving.” She hurried off, longing to ask why he wasn’t spending the holiday with Ida and her family. But there would be time enough for questions on Thanksgiving.

Daniel looked across the table as he leaned back in his chair. “That was a fine Thanksgiving dinner, Mrs. Cooper.”

Hannah’s mother beamed. “Well, I do hope you have room for a piece of pumpkin pie.”

Daniel sighed and shook his head. “As tempting as that sounds, I believe I’m going to need a long walk before I can partake.” He turned toward Hannah. “What about you, Hannah? Would you like to take a walk before dessert?”

"A walk sounds lovely, but I need to help Mama clear the dishes."

Her mother flicked her hand. "Go on and enjoy yourselves. I can manage just fine without your help."

Hannah hesitated a moment. "Only if you promise to leave them for me to wash when I return."

Mrs. Cooper nodded. "I promise. Now, go on and enjoy yourselves, before it gets dark outdoors."

They donned their coats and Daniel grasped Hannah's elbow as they descended the front steps. "Seems like old times, being with you again." He gave her a sideways glance. "Has something happened between you and Louis, or was he out of town on business today?"

"I would think you already know the answer to that question. Are you seeking more of the painful details?"

He stopped short. How could she think such a thing about him? "If I knew the answer, I wouldn't have asked." He didn't miss the pained look in her eyes. "I would never want to hurt you, Hannah. I hope you know that."

"I'm sorry, Daniel. All the ladies who work in the Arcade know that Louis and I have parted ways, so it feels as though the entire town must know."

"I'm sorry. I truly didn't know."

She glanced at him then nodded. "I learned that Louis had been courting me in Pullman while he had a wife waiting for him in Chicago."

Daniel stopped mid-step and gasped. His hands clenched into

tight fists and anger burned deep in his chest. He pushed his feelings aside. Right now, Hannah needed him. "Go on."

A cloak of sadness seemed to envelop her as she revealed the details of her broken relationship with Louis. Yet when she neared the end of the account, she brightened. "I know now he never truly loved me, and my life is better without him. I have prayed fervently, and God has provided me with the grace to forgive him—though I never want to see him again." She gestured toward the park and he followed her lead. "And what about Ida? Why aren't you with her on Thanksgiving?"

His brows knit in confusion. "Why would I be with Ida?"

"Because you've been courting her since you arrived in Pullman."

"That's not true."

"All right. Not since the very day you arrived but soon after you moved in with your aunt and uncle."

"That's not true either." His stomach knotted at her accusation. Did she think he was no different than Louis? That he would court a woman who was already betrothed to another?

She stood and turned toward him. "Daniel, I saw you with her at the Arcade. You escorted her to the Harvest Ball, and I'm sure you've been in her company at every possible opportunity. You don't need to hide your attraction to her. She's a beautiful young woman."

Understanding dawned on him. He stood and grasped her hands. "You're right. She is a beautiful woman. A woman who has plans to wed James Danfield. James has already made his intentions known to Ida's brother, Edward."

Hannah gaped at him. "But, but you. . ."

He touched his finger to her lips. "I have helped a friend, nothing more. Edward works with me and we've become well acquainted. You likely know that Ida lives with Edward and his wife." He moved his finger from her lips. "Being a caring brother, Edward didn't want Ida to sit at home alone when he and Gertrude attended social events, so he asked me to act as her escort. I objected to the idea at first, but he promised we would always be in their company and he'd vouch for the propriety of the arrangement with James or anyone else who inquired." The shadow of doubt clouding her eyes began to diminish. But he had to be certain she believed him, or he'd never regain her trust. "If you have any doubts, please speak to Edward or Gertrude—or Ida. Any of them can confirm what I've told you." He offered a gentle smile. "I wouldn't be offended if you confirmed what I've told you by speaking with them."

She shook her head and sighed deeply. "That won't be necessary. I believe you, though I must admit I'm embarrassed and feel somewhat foolish for my thoughts. I shouldn't have jumped to conclusions."

He shrugged. "I'm sorry you didn't come and talk to me after you first saw me with Ida." He grinned. "I hope this means you were jealous." When she didn't immediately respond, he tipped his head to the side and met her eyes. "Tell me, Hannah. Were you a tiny bit jealous?"

A smile tipped the corners of her mouth. "Maybe a little, but

I tried to tell myself that it was only because I feared losing your friendship."

"Really? Is that all?" He longed to hear her say that seeing him with another woman had rekindled her feelings from five years ago and she now realized he was the only man she could ever love.

Her eyebrows shot high on her forehead. "What does that mean? Is our friendship not important to you?"

"Of course it is, but. . .but I had hoped for more."

Hannah's thoughts remained a jumble as they returned home. Didn't Daniel understand what effect his spontaneous remarks might have upon her? Did he truly want more than friendship? Lately, he'd given her numerous opportunities to believe he did. Yet, she'd thought he wanted more than friendship several years ago before he'd rebuffed her. Back then, he hadn't voiced an interest in anything more than friendship, but she'd convinced herself that he desired a romantic relationship as much as she did—only to be proven wrong.

Five years ago, she'd misjudged Daniel's intent. Later, she'd misjudged Louis's character as well as his intent. She wanted to believe Daniel wanted more than friendship and that he truly cared for her, but dare she take another chance? Could her heart withstand the pain of being rejected yet again?

Once they stepped inside the house and Daniel helped Hannah off with her coat, they joined their families in the parlor. Hannah's mother patted the seat beside her on the sofa. "Come sit and chat with us, Hannah. Jane was just asking about how you'd been chosen to sew for Mrs. Pullman." Her mother smiled. "I told her it was your happy story to tell."

Hannah sat down beside her mother. As she was offering details of her employment to Daniel's aunt, Hannah's gaze frequently settled on the three men. Daniel's uncle appeared relaxed, but her father and Daniel had hunched toward each other deep in conversation. Strange that Daniel's uncle appeared totally disinterested in the discussion.

A short time later, Jane gestured to her husband. "I think it's time for us to go home, Henry." She turned toward Hannah's mother. "I do wish we could stay longer, but I need to lie down and rest. The doctor says it's the only way I'm going to finally regain my strength." Her lips formed a half smile as she slipped her arms into the wool coat her husband held for her.

"Now, now, my dear. You've made great strides. By this time next month, I'm sure you're going to be good as new." Daniel's uncle buttoned his coat then glanced toward Daniel. "We'll see you at home later, Daniel."

Daniel gave a slight nod then crossed the room to speak to Hannah. "If you have time, I'd like to talk to you." He glanced toward the door then leaned closed to her ear. "Alone."

"I have an idea." She curved her lips in a mischievous grin. "Mama and Papa, Daniel would like to speak to me in private. May we be alone in the parlor, please?"

Her father laughed aloud and gave a nod. "By all means. I'll go out to the kitchen and help your mother with the dishes."

"In that case, I agree with your father." Hannah's mother retrieved a dish towel and presented it to her father with a broad smile and a wave. "Follow me, my dear."

Once her parents stepped out of the room, Hannah glanced at Daniel. She felt as though a kaleidoscope of butterflies had taken up residence in her stomach. Exactly what did Daniel want to discuss? Her emotions fluctuated from elated to fearful to distressed. She moved toward the couch.

Daniel sat down beside her. He cleared his throat several times and picked at a nonexistent piece of lint on his suit pants before he finally found his voice. "You may have noticed that your father and I were having a discussion after we returned from our walk."

Hannah folded her hands in her lap and nodded. There was only one reason Daniel would be so nervous—and she now knew what it was—at least she hoped she knew. "I did." She tipped her head forward and waited. "What. . .what did you talk about?"

He fumbled with his necktie. "I didn't think this would be so difficult."

She fixed her eyes on him and waited, her own nerves taking hold. She offered an encouraging smile, but when he remained silent, she reached forward and covered his hand with her own. "Talk to me, Daniel."

He drew in a deep breath. "I've asked your father for permission to court you. I know you have the final say, but I wanted to gain his permission before I asked you. I didn't know if you'd told him about the, the time five years ago. . .the. . ."

"Mistletoe incident?" She clapped her hand over her mouth.

"I'm sorry. I promise I won't interrupt again."

He grinned and nodded. "Yes, the mistletoe incident. I thought he might be hesitant to give his approval if you'd expressed any ill feelings toward me after that Christmas party five years ago."

She wanted to ease his concerns, but she'd promised to remain quiet, so she gestured for him to continue.

"Thankfully, neither your father nor I mentioned mistletoe, but he did give me his permission. However, he added that it depended upon whether you had any desire to be courted. He had some reservations and thought you might want to wait awhile before you accepted another suitor." He looked down at her hands. "I hope that isn't true, but if it is—I understand—but I hope that you won't let what happened five years ago influence your decision. I've had a change of heart and now fully believe that friendship is a strong foundation for courtship and a happy marriage." He met her gaze. "In truth, my feelings for you have already deepened beyond friendship. Hannah, I love you."

At the mention of love and marriage, a rush of heat warmed Hannah's neck and face. No doubt her cheeks were as red as two freshly picked apples.

His eyes shone with anticipation. "Tell me what you think. Do I stand a chance of winning your affection? Will you allow me to court you?"

Her breathing turned shallow as she weighed her answer. Through the years, her strong feelings for Daniel had remained, but she'd tempered them when Louis had stepped into her life. While their friendship had always been strong, there were differences that might prove to be stumbling blocks.

His fingers trembled as he reached for her hand. "I wanted to believe you'd be quick to accept my offer, but if you need time to consider, I'm willing to wait."

"Aren't you worried that I'll put work before our relationship?"

He shook his head. "If we both are growing closer to the Lord, I know He will direct our paths." He brought her hand to his lips and pressed a kiss to the back of it. "If God leads you to Chicago or New York or even Paris, I will be beside you."

Overwhelmed by his generous spirit, she leaned close and touched his hand. "I now realize the only reason I wanted to leave Pullman was because of Louis. If my designs and beadwork are destined to become well known, I believe it will happen no matter where we live. However, if we could save enough for a house in Roseland, I wouldn't object. But you must promise that you'll never allow me to become obsessed with my work for Mrs. Pullman or anyone else."

Daniel smiled. "The only obsession I want you to have is with me—and I with you."

She beamed. "Then, I would be more than pleased to accept your offer of courtship."

"Shall we seal that with a kiss?"

Hannah leaned back and placed her hand on her heart and curved her lips in an impish grin. "Why, Mr. Price, I believe it's far too soon for a kiss. We've not even begun our courtship."

Daniel nodded. "Quite right, Miss Cooper. I'm a bit rusty in my courting etiquette. Flowers, candy, and a lengthy courtship must always come before a kiss, isn't that so?"

She smiled and gave a prim nod. "Yes, though I'm not certain how lengthy the courtship must be when two people already know each other as we do. I believe that's a matter to be decided in the future. However, the flowers, candy, and an evening out are always an excellent beginning."

Chapter Fourteen

Hannah smiled instinctively when she caught sight of Daniel waiting outside the shop in the Arcade hallway. At the *clink* of the metal door handle, he turned and came to attention, extending his hand to take the key and lock the door for her. Thus far, he'd been good to his word. Each evening Hannah had expected to hear a complaint about her late hours at work. Instead, Daniel appeared in the Arcade and patiently waited to escort her home.

"I keep telling you that you don't need to come and wait for me every night." Hannah pulled her blue wool scarf tight around her neck. She looked up at him. "But I won't go so far as to say I don't enjoy your company." She pulled on her gloves and glanced toward the Arcade doors at the end of the hallway, where the moon was casting a glow on frosted tree limbs. "It looks cold out there."

"You're right, but I promise I'll do my best to keep you warm." He extended his arm and waited as she placed her hand in the crook of his elbow.

She moved closer to his side and gave his arm a gentle squeeze. "Have your aunt and uncle been missing you since we've begun courting? I'm sure your aunt Jane misses your company in the evening."

"They're both quite pleased about our courtship, so I've heard no complaints. Besides, by the time I leave the house in the evening, Aunt Jane is about ready for bed. Her strength still isn't what it used to be."

"I'm sorry to hear that. I thought the doctor expected her to be better by now. And I saw their names listed as greeters for the Christmas Ball."

Daniel nodded. "You did, but Aunt Jane signed them up before she took sick. She's still hoping she'll be well enough to attend, but only time will tell." He looked down at her as they waited for an oncoming carriage before crossing the street. "Speaking of the Christmas Ball, have you had time to consider what you'll wear?"

She chuckled and nodded. "I'm planning to wear the dress I fashioned for the Harvest Ball. It's far too lovely to remain hanging in my wardrobe, and the forest-green color will be perfect for the Christmas Ball. I removed some of the fall-colored beading and used red and pearl replacements. I hope you'll like it."

"I'm sure I will, but you're beautiful in whatever you wear." Daniel's sweet words and kind actions over the past weeks had been a balm for her wounded spirit. After being courted by Daniel, she recognized how a man who truly cared for a woman conducted himself. Daniel didn't hesitate to put her wants and needs before his own or to listen and consider her concerns and worries. He didn't push her to agree with his every thought or action. Instead, he encouraged her to express her thoughts and desires. Though she'd been too eager years ago, their years of friendship had truly worked in their favor. They remained best friends, yet so much more.

Daniel grasped the cuffs of his suit jacket as he slipped his right arm and then his left into the heavy overcoat Aunt Jane insisted he wear. The freezing December temperatures called for added warmth, but he'd wanted to look dapper in his new suit when he called for Hannah. Instead, he'd appear in his worn overcoat that fit tightly across his chest and would likely crease his suit in all the wrong places.

Aunt Jane fussed with the knot in his tie before buttoning the top closure on his coat. "You need to keep warm. I don't want you getting sick." She patted his arm. "You're certain you and Hannah don't mind acting as greeters at the ball?"

He kissed her cheek. "I've told you that we're both happy to stand in for you and Uncle Henry."

"I don't want to be the cause of you two not having a good time." She looked toward the parlor. "I think I'm well enough to attend, but your uncle won't hear of it."

"Uncle Henry has made a wise choice. Standing for a half hour or more to check names off a list and greet the attendees would sap all your strength." He placed his hand on the doorknob. "I better be on my way. While Hannah is happy to act as a greeter, she might not be pleased if I don't arrive at her house on time."

He hurried out the door before his aunt could further delay him and ran the short distance to the Coopers' flat.

"Good evening, Daniel." Mrs. Cooper pulled open the front door and ushered him in. "Hannah will be down in just a minute."

"I'm coming, Mama."

Daniel's voice caught at the sight of her. Thin green and red ribbons adorned her dark brown curls, and a belt embellished with beads of red, green, and ivory encircled the waist of her forest green dress. He could scarcely believe such a sweet and beautiful woman could love him. Daniel was certain God had smiled on him the day Hannah entered his life.

He extended his hand as she descended the steps. "You look beautiful. Every man at the ball will envy me."

"Thank you, Daniel."

A short time later, his heart soared as they entered the Arcade and ascended the steps to the gaily decorated ballroom. After hanging their coats, he returned to her side near the entrance and reached for her hand.

"I was going to wait until the end of the evening, but I'm far too impatient." He nodded toward the small alcove. "Why don't we step over there where it will be private."

Once they'd entered the arched nook, she looked up at him, her eyes alight with curiosity. He reached into his pocket and withdrew a sprig of mistletoe, waiting only long enough for her to see it before lifting it above her head. "May I kiss you, my dearest Hannah?"

Hannah glanced toward the doorway before nodding her approval. "I've been waiting a long time for this."

She leaned into him as he pulled her close and covered her soft lips in a lingering kiss. He continued to hold her waist with one arm while he withdrew a small black box from his pocket. Using his thumb, he flipped back the lid. "I thought this was the perfect time and place to declare my desire to marry you, Hannah. Will you be my wife?" His heart hammered in his chest. Until this moment, he'd not given thought to whether she might reject his proposal.

Her lips curved in a sensual smile. "I would be delighted to become your wife but only if you place that mistletoe over my head one more time." She winked. "For old time's sake."

Judith Miller is an award-winning author whose avid research and love for history are reflected in her novels, many of which have appeared on the CBA bestseller lists. Judy makes her home in Kansas. Visit her website at www.judithmccoymiller.com.

Pin's Promise

by Nancy Moser

Prologue

Summerfield, England
New Year's Eve 1899

Penelope Billings yanked the love of her life away from the crowd in the village square.

Jonathan resisted. "I want to stay and see the fireworks."

"We'll be back in time. I promise." She squeezed his hand harder and ran through the crowd, dragging him with her.

Her mother saw them. "Pin? Where are you going? The fireworks…"

Yes, yes, the fireworks. "We'll be back. I promise."

Mama gave her a familiar look that said she didn't necessarily doubt what Pin said, but she did *not* agree with it. Another sort of mother would have insisted fifteen-year-old Pin remain in the square with the rest of Summerfield. After all, it was the eve of a new century. Pin recognized the immensity of the moment. To draw in a breath in 1899 and let the same breath out in the new twentieth century? She was certain everyone in the square would remember this evening, this celebration.

So would Pin. But not for the same reasons—which would *not* occur if she didn't get Jonathan away, and to herself.

She felt him reluctantly give way to her will and hurry alongside. If Jonathan had his way, he would remain in the place that he had determined would give them the best view of the fireworks, and be content to remain there throughout the festivities. Sometimes she gave into his need for order and planning. But tonight she needed to insist on her way. At least for a short time.

Pin drew him into her father's carpentry shop, the familiar aroma of sawn wood eliciting a sense of safety and encouragement.

Just what she needed.

She closed the door against the winter air.

"We need light. I'll light a lamp," Jonathan said.

She put a hand on his. "Don't." The moonlight was enough.

He grinned and began to put his hands around her waist.

She took them captive and stepped back. "I have a present for you."

"We've already had Christmas."

She wasn't surprised he didn't understand. "It's a promise present, perfect for the new century."

"Meaning?"

She drew him toward the window and the moonlight it provided. Then she took the present out of her skirt pocket. "Here."

Jonathan studied it as though he had never seen a handkerchief before.

"Unfold it. It's special." *At least I hope you think it's special.*

He held it toward the light and read the words Pin had embroidered. "Penelope and Jonathan Forever. 1900." He looked at her. "Who's Penelope?"

"That's me, silly."

"You're Pin."

She was stunned. "You thought Pin was my real name?"

He shrugged. "I had no reason to think otherwise. Even your parents call you that."

"*They* were the ones who gave me the nickname. I was rambunctious and kept them on 'pins and needles.' Plus, the only thing that would make me sit still and focus was pinning fabric together at the sewing workshop."

"So it follows you're good at sewing."

It was her turn to shrug.

He pinched her chin. "And you're still rambunctious."

"It's not a bad thing."

"It's not, for you offset my serious nature."

Fight against it, most of the time. She pointed at the stitches in green and blue. "Do you like it?"

He kissed her cheek. "Of course I do. Though it is much too pretty to use."

The thought of him actually using it had never entered her mind. "It's a keepsake." Did boys understand "keepsake"?

"Speaking of. . . I have a gift for you too."

She grinned at him. "We've already had Christmas."

He took up her part. "It's a promise present, perfect for the new century. Hold out your hand."

He pulled something out of his pocket and placed it on her palm.

It was a carved female figure about three inches tall. Pin held it to the light and saw that it had long hair and a pensive smile. "Is this me?"

"It is." He took the carving and upended it. The year 1900 was carved in the bottom.

"This is beautiful," Pin said.

"As are you."

She kissed his cheek. "You have a real talent."

"Father taught me. He says it helps to have something to do at the bedside of his patients. He's warned me that doctoring involves a lot of waiting."

The mention of Jonathan's chosen profession made Pin step close and lower her head beneath his chin. "I'm going to miss you horribly while you're off at school."

"I can't learn to be a proper doctor here. My parents want me to take over one day."

She leaned back to see him. "What do *you* want?"

He hesitated then smiled down at her. "You."

His words could not have been more perfect if she had told him what to say. "Which leads me to the promise part of the present."

"I can guess."

"Then say it so I don't have to. It's not like we haven't talked about it."

He led her to a bench and sat at an angle so their knees touched.

"Will you promise to say yes when I ask you to marry me someday, Penelope Billings?"

She smiled. "A promise of a promise?"

"Our parents would be sorely upset if we told them we were betrothed now. Even though we're both fifteen they still think of us as children."

He was right. Although both families knew she and Jonathan were good friends, they didn't know love had blossomed. They would never approve of any promise, especially with Jonathan on the verge of a long college education away from Summerfield. Pin could imagine her parents saying they were too young to know what true love entailed and that a lot could happen in the six years Jonathan would be away at university, with more years spent honing his skills in a hospital.

Nonsense. Pin knew she loved Jonathan more than the stars and the moon, and would still love him in six years. In sixty.

"I accept your promise of a promise, Jonathan Evers. And I will hold you to it."

They sealed the moment with a kiss just as they heard the boom of fireworks.

The crowd dispersed, and the villagers of Summerfield headed home to begin the new century.

Pin held back, needing to be one of the last to leave the square. Once again Mama called to her, and once again she said she wouldn't be long.

"I'll see you tomorrow." Jonathan turned to leave.

"Just one minute more." She slipped her arm through his and led him toward the low stone wall that circled the communal water pump. "Let's put our gifts in our hiding place for safekeeping."

He didn't argue. If found by her parents, her carving could be explained away. Not so, with the "Penelope and Jonathan Forever" handkerchief.

"Keep watch," Pin said.

Jonathan stood in front of the wall as she sat upon it. Using her skirt as a shield, she pulled out the stone that guarded their secret hideaway—a hideaway they'd created five years earlier by replacing a loose thick stone with a stone that had less depth, thus creating a niche for their notes and treasures.

"Hurry!" he whispered. "People are going to walk by."

She stuffed the handkerchief-wrapped figure inside, replacing the stone just in time to stand by his side and say good night to the couple strolling by.

"That was close," he said.

"When we're officially engaged, we can remove our treasures with great ceremony, showing everyone how long we've loved each other."

Until then. . .

They stole a kiss and bade each other good night.

And good century.

Chapter One

December 1906

The screech of the train's brakes yanked Jonathan out of his sleep. A man sitting across from him said, "You wanted off at Summerfield, didn't ya?"

"I did. Thank you." He grabbed his carpetbag and bowler hat and rushed to the door wanting to be the first one off.

The rushing proved unnecessary. He was the only one to disembark in tiny Summerfield.

Only one off, with none getting on. Quite the change from the train station in London.

The stationmaster greeted him. "Jonathan. I didn't expect to see you. Do your parents know you're coming?"

"They don't." He stepped to the platform and nodded toward the baggage car. "I have a trunk."

"I'll get it."

"I'll help."

Together, Jonathan and Mr. Brodnick moved the trunk from

train car to platform. It winded the older man and he suffered a fit of coughing.

"Are you all right?"

He used a handkerchief then stuffed it in his pocket. "Just a bit under the weather."

It could be bronchitis or pleurisy. "If it persists, come into the office and I'll have a look at you."

Mr. Brodnick beamed. "Your parents told us you were a full-fledged doctor now. Home to become the third generation in your family's practice?"

"Home to help."

He slapped Jonathan on the back. "We all knew you could do it. Summerfield may be small, but we can always use another healer. Your father was run ragged last week dealing with a toppled wagon where Mr. Whipple broke his arm and his farmhand gashed his leg something awful. All while Mrs. Cumberson was having her fourth. Your mother had to deal with the birthin'—though she *has* done that a time or two."

Or twenty. Since the beginning of his parents' marriage, his mother had assisted in all things medical—and learned through the doing.

"I will be glad to be busy."

"And glad to be home?"

It was a more difficult question to answer than it should have been. Jonathan had received an offer to practice medicine elsewhere, but the lure of home. . . He gave Mr. Brodnick the short answer. "I am glad to be here."

They set the trunk in the terminal, and Jonathan said he'd come get it later.

First things first.

Pin studied the stitches of the hem Mrs. Dudley had been working on in the sewing workshop.

"I'm impressed. Your stitches are small and consistent. Much improved over a week ago."

"Thank you, miss. I do hopes to get this dress done for our visit to me mister's brother in Devonshire next month. Me husband will think I'm dressed for a dog's dinner when he sees how pretty I look. I've worn the same best-frock for six years."

"Then you deserve something new. And how special that you've sewn it yourself."

The older woman laughed. "He'll be shocked to sitting by that one. As am I." She took the dress back and returned to her hemming.

The next sewing student wasn't due for her lesson for an hour, so Pin had a choice: she could work on the lovely linen shirt she was sewing for Jonathan for Christmas, or peruse the pile of *La Mode Illustree* and other fashion magazines. The latter was more inviting, as she didn't just look at the illustrations of Paris fashion, she absorbed them. The Summerfield Sewing Workshop had dozens of issues, spanning twenty years. Not that the women who came to learn how to sew had need of fancy flounces and layers of lace, but Pin had seen more than one woman peruse the pages with a look of utter pleasure on her face.

Although Christmas was less than two weeks away—and the shirt needed finishing—Pin chose her favorite magazine from last summer. From her many viewings, the publication naturally turned to page six, to a wedding photo of Princess Victoria Eugenie, Queen Victoria's granddaughter. Ena had become the queen consort of Spain the previous May and Pin had followed every detail. That a bomb had been thrown upon the happy couple's carriage procession after the ceremony—killing twenty-three yet not injuring King Alfonso or his bride—was tragic, yet added to Pin's interest. To be married in Madrid and be made a queen. . . The latest news was that the bride was with child. To wed a dashing man, wear a gorgeous dress, have a family, and live happily ever after. . .

Yet Pin knew the princess's dress was far too fancy for Summerfield. The white duchesse satin embroidered with silver roses and orange blossoms was accented by Brussels lace. It was a dress fit for a princess.

Pin herself had aristocratic ties. Her mother was closely related to the two most prestigious families in the county. Mama's cousins were the earl of Summerfield on the Weston side and the viscountess Newley on the Kidd side. Both families were the least showy toffs Pin knew—not that she knew that many.

Her mother, Clarissa Weston Billings, had married below her station by becoming the wife of the village carpenter—or so whispered rude people. Although this made Pin's heritage unconventional, she rather liked it, for it placed her in a comfortable spot between posh and plain. The real advantage was that she could choose whichever side best suited her needs at each moment of each day. Right now she admired a luscious wedding dress and dreamed of a huge fete to celebrate her marriage to Jonathan Evers.

If he ever got home from London. If he ever officially proposed.

She held tightly to the promise they'd made on the eve of this century. One day they would be officially engaged and would shout it to the rooftops. In truth, Pin had never thought Jonathan would make her wait six years. She knew he was doing important work. But couldn't they be betrothed *while* he was immersed in his studies?

Apparently not. Yet since he'd just completed his degree and practice, he would soon be home and their life could finally begin.

She ran her fingers over the photo of Ena, imagining how it would feel to wear such lavish silk, to hear the swish of it as she walked down the aisle at church and feel the slight pull of the lengthy veil as it trailed behind her. She and Jonathan would marry in the spring, surrounded by the heady scent of peonies, and have a wedding breakfast and serve—

The door to the workshop opened, drawing Pin out of her reverie.

She froze. But only for a moment.

The magazine slipped to the floor as she rushed into the arms of her beloved.

Jonathan spun her around. *I don't ever want to land!*

After a twice-go-round, he gently set her feet upon the floor and with a quick glance and hello to Mrs. Dudley, gave Pin a kiss.

It wasn't a full kiss like the ones in Pin's daydreams, but it was a start.

It was a new beginning.

She took hold of his hands and peered up at him. "You're home now? For good?"

"I am."

Which meant. . .

Pin wanted privacy, so led him to the door. "Excuse us, Mrs. Dudley?"

"No need for excusing that," the woman said with a laugh. "Go on now."

Pin pulled him outside, drawing him around the side of the workshop. Once fully alone, he opened his coat to offer her some warmth. She leaned in, fiddling with the buttons on his shirt. "I've missed you utterly, fully, and with extreme exasperation."

He laughed. "All that."

She leaned her head against him. "Did you miss me?"

"Very much so."

Pin stepped back and slapped his arm. " 'Very much so'? Against my utterly, fully, and extreme exasperation?"

He pulled her close again and whispered, "Unreservedly, wholly, and with acute aggravation."

She smiled. "Better."

"No, this is better." He kissed her utterly and fully, and all the years of waiting fell away.

As they neared the house of his family, Jonathan held back—enough so, that Pin noticed. "Why are you hesitating? They'll be thrilled to see you."

He nodded. "I want to see them too."

"Then why are you acting like you're going to the gallows?"

He stepped behind a bush, not wanting his parents to look out the window and catch him unprepared.

Which, of course, was preposterous. He'd been gone six years becoming the doctor his parents had wanted him to be.

"What's wrong?" Pin asked.

He didn't answer but pinched a wilted leaf, tossing it to the ground.

"You have to answer me. It's a set rule between us."

So it was. Since childhood full honesty had cemented their bond.

She crossed her arms and gave him that look, the one that declared there was no way out but to bend to her will. "Tell me."

He expelled the breath he'd been saving. "Once I walk through those doors, my life here is fixed. Permanent."

Her mouth turned into a pout. "As it will be when we marry."

He pulled her close, relishing her familiar scent of honeysuckle. "*That* is a permanent fix I long for."

"When will you make it official?"

This was a question she'd asked each time he'd returned home for a visit. "Christmas?"

"That long?"

"Just a few weeks more. Let me get settled. I have so many ideas for the practice, so many plans to set in place. I want to excel, not just follow how things have been done for two generations."

Her nod was half-hearted. "Plans. Yes. I have plans too. There is much to do to prepare for marriage. We'll need to plan the wedding, find a place to live. . . ."

These enormous to-dos fell heavily upon his shoulders. "I will leave you to that planning."

Her eyes brightened. "Really?"

"When the time comes." He touched her cheek. She was the loveliest of lovelies, her skin as smooth as the finest ivory, her hair a raven's black. And her brown eyes were deep enough to swim in. "I'm returning after years of intense work, Pin. Not just book-learning but learning with real patients in hospital. To live in London so long is like living on the moon compared to the pastoral world of Summerfield."

"You grew up in Summerfield. It's home. You know everything about it."

Perhaps that was part of his hesitation. He'd grown used to the loud and populous world of London, had even thrived in it. Although he loved Summerfield with all his heart, he juggled a fear that it wouldn't be enough for him. Or that he would be too much for Summerfield.

"It's complicated, m'love. Part of it involves the true fact that studying to be a doctor is far different than *being* a doctor."

"You worry too much. You'll be a fine doctor. And it's not like you'll be alone."

"But will I be a good doctor *with* my father? Our temperaments are vastly different. He is easygoing, and I am. . ."

"Tightly wound?"

He laughed. "You peg me."

"You'll do fine." She took his hand. "Come now. Greet your parents—and your destiny."

Her words should have helped but didn't.

Jonathan's family reunion went as he expected. His mother gasped and drew him into an embrace, and his father beamed and pat him on the back. "Well done. We're so glad you're finally home for good."

They sat in the parlor looking at each other and shared an unnerving silence. Finally his mother asked, "Are you hungry?"

Although he wasn't, he said he was. The activity of food would lessen the awkwardness.

Only it didn't work that way, because Pin got up to help his mother, leaving Jonathan alone with his father.

"Well then," Father said, rocking up and back in his favorite chair. He repeated what he'd said earlier. "We're so very proud of you and so glad you're—"

"Home," Jonathan said.

Father blushed and fidgeted then said, "Mrs. Cumberson had her fourth child. Another boy."

"When I left for school, the first one was barely born."

Father shrugged. "She lost one in between three and four."

"How is Mr. Cumberson faring?"

His father gave him a questioning look. "You don't ask after the baby or the mother?"

"I assume they are fine or you would have said something. I ask after the father because he's the one who has another mouth to feed."

His father smiled slightly. "Are such realities on your mind?"

It was Jonathan's turn to blush. "Eventually."

Father stopped rocking and leaned closer, causing the chair's runners to point upward. "Pin has been waiting a long time."

"*You've* told me to wait."

He held up a hand. "And you have. But now that you are fully home. . ." He began rocking again, and looked in the direction of the women as they poured tea. "Pin's a good one, she is. A sweet and pretty girl, lively and smart. And—"

"I'm twenty-one," Pin said as she carried a tray of biscuits into the parlor. "Hardly a girl—though I thank you for the compliments."

Father nodded at Jonathan and gave him an I-told-you-so look. To add to his silent communication, he mouthed the word *soon*.

What a frightening word.

Annie Wood grabbed her little brother's arm and ducked behind the pile of cut logs.

And just in time too, as their mother stepped out of their shack in the Summerfield woods. "Annie! Alfred! If yer not back here in one-two-three, yer in fer it!"

Alfie giggled. "I got out."

"Yes, you did," Annie whispered.

"Ma doesn't like me out."

"No, she doesn't."

Annie sat on the ground, using the logs as a backrest. This would not end well, yet grabbing this few moments of peace kept her sane.

Alfie picked up a stray stick and slapped it against his clubfoot. "Bad, Alfie. Bad. Bad."

Annie took it away from him. "Stop that."

He mimicked Ma's voice. "You no-good idgit!" He looked at Annie. "I got out. Ma's goin' to wail on us."

"She'll wail on us either way. When Pa's under-it she takes it out on us. Remember the trickle down."

He nodded. "Trickle down, trickle down. Slap. Slap. Ouch. Ouch." He touched his left arm that Ma had twisted because he'd stumbled against a chair, causing it to fall and wake their father.

Nobody wanted Rufus Wood awake more than necessary, though Annie had a hard time noting *any* time that was necessary for her father to be awake. He worked little, always finding some reason to quit a job or getting let go for pilfering or laziness. Work and Pa sat together like a bottom on a sharp rock. Yet when he did venture out in public, he always smiled and bemoaned a sickly nature, often getting people to give him a coin or two. If it weren't for the money he made selling moonshine from his still in the woods, the family would totally depend on Annie's money, earned selling eggs. Actually, she *was* the main source of income as Pa usually drank more than he sold.

The only time there was peace in the house was when he passed out. Yet that was the calm before the storm. He was an angry bear when he drank and a crazed bear when he was awakened after sleeping it off, moaning about his head hurting and wanting the rest of them to shut it and leave him alone.

Leaving Pa alone was Annie's preference. And not just a preference but the best way to avoid getting hurt.

She glanced at ten-year-old Alfie as he stacked small pieces of bark into a tower. He took up a twig like a tiny sword. "Poke, poke, poke!"

"No poking right now. We must be quiet."

Suddenly Ma appeared from behind the woodpile and smacked each one on a leg. "There you are, you dossers! Get inside or I'll sic yer father on ya." She reached for Alfie's sore arm, but Annie stepped between them and took a slap to the side of her head for her trouble.

Alfie skipped back to the house, singing a fa-la-la song Annie had taught him. She rushed after him. If he annoyed Pa. . .

Long ago she'd taken on the role of his protector. Somehow saving one of them from extra hurt and harm made her own pain easier to bear.

Pin pointed at the bright December sky. "I know that the three stars in a row is the belt of someone, but. . ."

"It's Orion's belt," Jonathan said, leaning his head close to hers.

"I remember now. He's a hunter."

"His father was Poseidon, the Greek god of the sea."

She turned her gaze away from the skies and snuggled against the warmth of his chest. "Tell me the story of him and Artemis."

"I've told you many times."

"I know. But I like it."

He sighed deeply. "Artemis had a twin brother, Apollo. They were the children of Zeus."

"The king of the gods."

She felt him nod. "Artemis and Orion were both hunters and spent time together. But Apollo didn't want his sister to risk losing her virtue, so he killed Orion by having him stung on the heel by a scorpion."

Pin finished the story. "She was mad. To honor Orion she flung him into the sky as a constellation and flung the scorpion into another constellation on the far side of the sky."

Jonathan let go and flicked her on the arm. "Why do you ask, if you have the answer?"

"Because I like hearing you tell it. I never would have known anything about Greek mythology if it weren't for you."

He studied the sky. "I will miss learning new things."

"You can learn new things here."

"Like what? Name one thing."

He'd led her into an impossible corner. "I know things you don't know, Jonathan Evers."

He drew her into his arms. "I know I love you. We both know that."

She didn't like how he changed the subject, yet how could she argue against his words? "I know that," she said. "And I love you too. But what I'd really like to know is when—"

"You do know I'm going to have to spend tomorrow with my father, yes? He needs to tell me about the practice and our patients. I've dabbled in the work when I've been home, yet now that I'm to be a real part of it. . ."

Pin played with a button on his jacket. "But you just arrived."

He kissed her forehead. "It's late. I need to get you home."

Pin was tempted to stand her ground and press the issue, yet discretion prevailed.

It was only his first night home. She'd know the details of his proposal soon enough.

He could count on it.

Chapter Two

Pin awakened with a single plan that satisfied two goals. Goal number one: she would prove to Jonathan that he wasn't the only one who knew things. Goal number two: she would do her best to maneuver their situation toward marriage, sooner rather than later. Since Jonathan had a lot to think about as he took on medical responsibilities, she would take the initiative.

The task for today was to find them a place to live. A cottage.

At breakfast with her parents, she initiated her plan. "May I borrow the carriage today?"

Her mother's right eyebrow rose. "Toward what end?"

"I want to go out and about with Etta."

"To where?" Her father split a scone as a footman waited close by with a pot of blackberry preserves.

"I feel the need for fresh air."

Mama's other eyebrow rose. "You were out last evening until after dark. I would think your fresh air quotient has been fulfilled."

Papa nodded. "We're pleased Jonathan is home, but—"

Mama finished his thought. "You must be watchful of your reputation."

This was ridiculous. "I'm twenty-one years old. Everyone knows Jonathan and I will marry someday."

"Has he proposed?"

"Well. . .no." They had strayed from the point. "May I have the carriage?"

Her parents exchanged a look, then her mother flipped a hand. "Go on with you. But don't be gone all day."

Pin pulled into the drive leading to the home of her second cousin, Henrietta Kidd. Etta to family. Crompton Hall stood like an aged but stately matron, dressed in her best finery, awaiting all guests with open arms. It was adorned with turrets, gables, and chimneys galore, with stone balustrades marking its edges, and an assemblage of leaded windows turning beams of sunlight into dancing rays. Its permanence bespoke of a long history—though Pin knew it had been greatly destroyed by a fire before she was born. That it had been repaired in ways that embraced the centuries of its history while modernizing it, was largely due to her mother and father. Before they were married, a very creative Clarissa Weston had made the renovation her cause, and Pin's father, Timothy, had used his carpentry skills to make the Hall better than it was before.

Pin was proud of their abilities, yet felt envious of the end result. Although her mother had an aristocratic lineage, and though Pin's parents had been invited to live in either Summerfield

Manor or Crompton Hall when they were wed, they had declined. Instead, they had chosen to live in a house they'd built together, a respectable—but rather bland—brick structure in the village, with only a few chimneys, no exterior balustrades, plain glass windows, and far fewer servants.

Pin admired her mother's independent nature, which had revealed itself most tellingly in the fact she had *not* married some titled colt of a man, but the love of her life. And yet, every time Pin visited the Manor or the Hall she was assailed by the fact that these mansions could have been *her* place of residence if only her mother had *not* owned that independent attribute.

The notion that on this very day Pin might find her own home in which to start her life with Jonathan gave her extreme satisfaction. It might not be a grand home in mass or decor, but it *would* be grand because it would be theirs, a place they could escape from all others, where it wouldn't matter how late they stayed out—or up—and Pin could eat all the blackberry preserves she wanted without fear of a scolding for being greedy with it.

She pulled in front of the Hall and a footman appeared to help her down. "Good morning, Miss Billings."

The butler let her inside, saying Miss Henrietta would be down presently and Pin could wait in the drawing room. Out of habit she crossed the large foyer by stepping only on the black squares of the checkerboard floor. The wider gait this pattern necessitated was a bit unladylike, but Pin felt enough at home here that she didn't much care.

Also, as usual, she peered up at the massive portrait of Etta's grandmother that held court over the fireplace. Etta had told her the sad story of the young bride who'd died soon after the birth of her son—Etta's father. How tragic to have her life snatched away when it was just beginning.

She felt a presence behind her and saw Lady Newley enter the room. "Good morning, Cousin Lila," Pin said.

"Good morning to you, dear." She held out a key.

Pin put the key in her skirt pocket.

"Make sure you lock up when you leave."

"I will."

"When do you think you and Jonathan will make a decision?"

Considering he knows nothing of my plan. . . "I'm not sure."

"The sooner the better. We don't like properties to sit idle lest they attract mischief."

"I understand."

They both heard feet on the stairs and turned toward Etta. The butler helped her on with her cape.

"Hood up," her mother said. "We don't want you to catch a chill."

Etta raised the hood. "We won't be gone too awfully long."

"Best not be. We have the meeting this afternoon about upcoming Christmas services," her mother said.

"We'll be back in time." Etta took Pin by the hand and whispered, "Let's be off!"

They scrambled down the exterior steps and climbed into the small two-wheeled carriage. They tucked their skirts and coats around them and Etta threw back her hood. "I need to breathe!"

Pin laughed and took the reins. She waited until they were near the end of the drive to let the horse take off.

Etta held on to the seat. "Slow down! We're not in a race."

"But we are," Pin said, even though she *did* slow down. "A race toward my future."

"You never did tell me what we were going to do today."

"You'll see."

Pin drove to a side road off the main, halfway between Crompton Hall and the village.

"Doesn't this lead to the Horton place?"

Pin couldn't help but smile. "I believe it does."

"But Mrs. Horton died."

"I know."

"But—"

"Patience, Etta." Pin pulled in front of the cottage and got down, giving her cousin a hand. As she took out the key, she felt emboldened, as though merely holding the object made her older and more grown up.

"Where did you get that?"

"Your mother gave it to me."

"What for?"

"Let's go in."

Etta peered at the house as though it were haunted. "Are you sure?"

"It's all right. I asked to see inside."

"But why?"

Pin sighed and dug her hands into her hips. "Because I want

Jonathan and I to lease the place, as our own."

Etta's eyes widened. "Has he proposed?"

Did everyone need to remind her of this deficiency? "Not yet. But when he does, I want to be ready to begin our life straightaway."

"Why the rush?" Etta put a hand to her mouth. "You're not...?"

Pin swatted her hand down. "Gracious. What kind of girl do you think I am?"

"An impatient one."

Point taken. Pin unlocked the door and they stepped inside. It took a moment for their eyes to adjust to the dim.

"It smells bad," Etta said. "Didn't Mrs. Horton die in here?"

"That's a pleasant thought." In spite of the chill outside, Pin left the door ajar because there *was* a pungent smell to the place. "It's just been closed up too long." She strolled through the main part of the cottage that was populated with two chairs by the fireplace, an odd shelf or two, and a table big enough for four.

She ran a hand along the back of an upholstered chair. "This will be Jonathan's chair."

"Leaving you the hard oak one?"

"I can sew a cushion or two." She peered at the fireplace and imagined it blazing on a cold winter night, as she and Jonathan shared the warmth from chairs set close together. Pin would read Dickens or Jane Austen aloud. When a new chapter was finished, Jonathan would say, "Come to bed, my love" and they would retire for the night under cozy covers, wrapped in each other's arms.

"The kitchen is a wee one," Etta said.

Pin was forced to set the tender images aside for more practical considerations. She was relieved to see faucets, meaning there was running water. There was an oak icebox and a small cast-iron stove. One lone cupboard held mismatched dishes, cooking bowls, and a variety of utensils. Surely they would receive wedding presents enough to fill the gaps.

"You're used to much more," Etta said.

"Not as much as you."

Etta shrugged. "My parents will insist I marry some horribly boring but titled acquaintance with a good income. He'll have no sense of humor whatsoever but will be a good dancer, smell of boot polish and cigars, and provide me with some old manse that's been in his family for centuries."

"And you'll love him."

"I will love him for the sake of love. And he will love me because I will give him children and be a female on his arm at parties."

"That sounds dreadful."

Etta removed a plate from the cupboard, ran a finger over its chipped edge, and put it back. "Not all of us can marry the love of our lives."

Pin agreed but didn't say more lest it add to Etta's romantic resignation.

They went into the larger of the two bedrooms. The thought that old Mrs. Horton might have expired in the bed made Pin vow to get a new one. But there were bureaus enough, and the second bedroom held a child-sized bed. Pin could easily imagine having a child. Or three. But she needed to secure a husband first.

Etta studied a painting over the main bureau. "It's nice—if you like sheep and hills."

Pin remembered Jonathan's comment about Summerfield's "pastoral" setting. If they let the house, she would see the painting removed so as not to feed into his view. Needing to replace a picture here and there were small details, unimportant to the whole.

But then she noticed something that *was* important. "The bath is minimal and needs a good scrubbing."

"At least it has one." Etta peeked inside and squished up her nose. "The county still has cottages aplenty that don't."

Pin returned to the parlor and gave it one last look. It had possibilities. But what would Jonathan think about it? They'd never talked about his income—that he would be splitting with his father. Could they afford it? Surely, it wouldn't be that expensive. Yet what did she know about such things?

"Are you going to rent it?" Etta asked.

With a final look, Pin headed outside. "I want to. But I haven't even told Jonathan I'm looking."

"That's pouring the tea without a cup." Etta climbed into the carriage.

"We *will* need a place to live." Pin climbed in beside her. "He told me it would be up to me to arrange it."

"Between your parents and his, there are rooms aplenty."

"I will not live with our parents!"

"Don't get your quiff all aquiver. I'm just being practical."

"Practical" did not come easily for Pin.

Jonathan stood behind his father as he examined Mrs. Cosgrove who complained about fatigue and headaches.

"When did you start to feel poorly?" his father asked after taking her pulse.

"A few weeks ago. But otherwise I feel fine."

Her husband stood at the foot of the bed. "She's not fine. She's acting barmy, wanting to eat paper and dirt."

"I—"

"Don't deny it, Esther. I caught you, more than once."

Esther covered her face with her hands. "I must be going wonkers. Why do I crave those things?"

"Pica," Jonathan said.

His father looked over his shoulder at him. "Pica?"

"What's that?" Mr. Cosgrove asked.

"In your wife's case, it's probably a symptom of iron deficiency."

"Iron, as in metal?" she asked.

Jonathan remembered this particular lesson at university. "It's a mineral our body needs. It's found in the red cells of our blood and in the hemoglobin that is needed to move oxygen from the lungs to the rest of the body, the tissues and organs, and—"

"It makes you strong. Without it, you are weak," his father said.

"Not having it is causing me to eat strange things?"

Jonathan nodded. "Your body is instinctively seeking something to relieve its craving."

"There's iron in paper?" Mr. Cosgrove asked.

Father put a hand on Mrs. Cosgrove's arm. "Some things are a mystery. But if you'll soak some nails in warm water for half a day and then drink the water, the iron from the nails will get you fixed up in no time."

Jonathan scoffed. "Really?"

His father glared at him. "Really."

Jonathan couldn't believe the arcane instruction. "I heard a lecture by Sir Gowland Hopkins, a fellow from Cambridge. He thinks there are elements in food that are important to health. There is iron in food. In meat especially."

"We don't eat much meat," Mrs. Cosgrove said. "We need our cows and chickens. Hank says we need the milk and eggs more than the meat."

Father stood and closed his medical bag with a snap. "Jonathan is right. Eating meat will also help."

Mr. Cosgrove shook the elder doctor's hand. "I'll bring you some fresh cheese and milk for your visit today."

"That would be nice."

Father didn't speak to Jonathan until they were in the wagon, on their way home. "Don't belittle our established cures."

"Nails in water?"

"It works and costs little. Much better than telling them to eat meat when meat is a luxury."

Jonathan felt his pride shift. "I didn't think of that."

"I appreciate that you have just come from London and know about the latest advances, but I went to school too. Though it's been twenty-some years, most of what I learned still applies."

Jonathan hadn't meant to discredit him. "I apologize."

Father shrugged. "Next time let's see if you can listen as much as you talk."

"I was only trying to help."

"As was I."

Annie tucked the towel into her basket—her empty basket. "Thank you, Mrs. Keening."

"Take care of yourself, girl. I hope your parents feel better soon."

Annie left the bakery, finding comfort in the woman's usual parting words. Annie had heard her say goodbye to other customers, sharing the usual "Good day to you" or "I hope you like the bread"—or whatever item they'd purchased from the bakery. Yet hearing Mrs. Keening add a show of concern for her parents—whom Annie was forced to portray as perpetually under the weather, *and* adding kind words to Annie—made Annie feel better. It was silly, for how could mere words ease the situation at home? Yet the possibility that Mrs. Keening was aware that all was not buttercups and roses gave Annie hope.

It proved she was not alone.

Not completely.

She tightened the knot of her shawl against the December chill and rested a moment on the bench outside the bakery. Annie liked this time of year when the streetlamps on the village square were adorned with pine boughs, red ribbons, and pine cones. Christmas was a time of gaiety and hope. Or so she'd heard. Although presents weren't exchanged in the Wood household, Annie always managed to give Alfie something special. This year. . .maybe a pad of paper and a new pencil? He liked to draw. Scribble mostly. She had taught him to write a few letters. He would never learn to read, but she was proud of him anyway. Annie knew the basics because the local schoolteacher had given her a primer book to study on her own. Although Miss Tilda wanted her in school, she understood that Annie needed to work. On many a night Annie practiced reading and numbers after everyone was asleep. She enjoyed that peaceful time she had to herself.

Annie leaned down to tie her right shoe. The lace had broken twice. The knots made it too short, forcing her to use one less pair of eyelets, which made the back of the shoe rub against her ankles. She checked the shoelaces on her other foot and found them tied, but the lace was in much the same condition. She peered at the mercantile. Surely a pair of shoelaces wouldn't cost that much. She *had* sold every egg and had a pocketful of coins.

She walked across the square before common sense could change her mind. She liked the elderly Mrs. Hayward who would always smile as if Annie was just as important as the next customer. And sometimes she'd give her a piece of hard candy—that Annie would give to Alfie. Annie was sure if Mrs. Hayward knew about Alfie, she'd offer an extra piece. But no one knew about her brother. With his clubfoot, crooked smile, and odd ways, their parents wanted little to do with him. The deal Annie had made with Ma and Pa was that he could stay if Annie earned enough money to pay for his keep, *and* if she didn't tell anyone about him. If not, they'd send him away. Beyond their disinterest in Alfie, Ma and Pa didn't want anyone snooping around the shack lest they find Pa's still. Plus—though it had been a few years—Pa always worried about the London law finding him and putting him in jail for robbing the wrong toff and beating him bloody. So Annie kept the secret safe.

She went inside the mercantile, closing the door quickly against the winter air. Mrs. Hayward was there but was not alone. She was having a discussion with her granddaughter, Miss Henrietta.

"I know Pin shouldn't be looking for houses, but how could I keep her from it?"

"She's headstrong like her mother," Mrs. Hayward said. "Clarissa. . ." She looked up and saw Annie. "Annie, dear girl. It's so nice to see you. Does your mother need more flour?"

Annie shook her head and pointed to her shoes. "I need laces, please."

Both women looked down then nodded. "Much overdo, I'd say." Mrs. Hayward—who at a pronounced age rarely got up from her chair near the counter—pointed to a shelf on the left. "Etta, go fetch a pair. The medium length, I'd say."

Miss Henrietta retrieved a pair of black laces. "Would you like me to put them in for you, Annie?"

The thought of either of them dirtying their hands on shoes that had trudged through dirt and dung. . .

"Here," Miss Henrietta said. "Have a seat over there and take them off."

"You don't have to put them in, miss."

"It's part of the price."

"Go on, girl," Mrs. Hayward said.

Annie did as they asked, handing over her boots. She quickly thrust her feet back under the chair to hide the numerous holes in her stockings. She'd been meaning to stitch them up but hadn't had the time. Nor the thread. She'd used the last of it repairing a rip in the knee of Alfie's britches. Nothing she could do about it now. She didn't dare spend another penny on thread or Ma would notice.

"Are your parents still feeling poorly?" Mrs. Hayward asked.

Annie was tired of lying but didn't have a choice. "They liked the soup you sent home with me last time. We all appreciate it."

"You're welcome," Mrs. Hayward said.

Miss Henrietta set the shoes on a newspaper on the counter. "Go fetch a peppermint stick for yourself."

"Thank you," Annie said. "But I'll wait until I get my shoes."

After their removal, Miss Henrietta let the old laces hang loose. "These have a story to tell. They've been through a lot."

I've been through a lot.

"Get the polish, Etta."

Miss Henrietta nodded and gathered two cloths and a white tin of something. She took one of the cloths and wiped the filthy shoes.

Annie stood. "You don't have to do that."

"Might as well give you the full treatment." Miss Henrietta held up the tin. "Cherry Blossom Shoe Polish. It's our favorite brand."

Annie had never heard of such a thing.

The can was opened and the clean cloth dipped in the black paste. It was smoothed over the leather of her shoes, making the color rich and fine.

"We have to let it dry a few minutes," Miss Henrietta said. "Then we'll shine them."

Shiny shoes?

"They'll be so shiny you could wear them to church," Mrs. Hayward said.

Annie nodded, though she knew that was never going to happen. Sometimes she snuck off to church on Sundays when both her parents were sloshed and sleeping it off. She made sure Alfie had something to eat to keep him occupied, and she would hurry toward the church. She never went in, but she sat behind the bushes outside, listening through the open door in the summertime. She'd peek in and see most of the village of Summerfield sitting neatly in pews, staring ahead, soaking in the pastor's words about God and Jesus. Love and forgiveness. When they prayed, she prayed. She knew the Our Father prayer by heart. Periodically, the people would stand and share books that must have had music in them, for they all sang together. Just by listening a time or two, Annie thought she could hold her own with most of the singing.

If she ever really went to church. Which she wouldn't. For to do so would surely spur people to talk to her, and they'd ask after her parents beyond a polite question. Then, being such good Christian people, they'd likely come visit, and then. . .

She couldn't go to church and risk losing Alfie.

"It's time to buff them out," Miss Henrietta said. She took a brush with short bristles, put her hand inside Annie's shoe, and brushed at the polish.

"Crikey," Annie said. "Look at it shine!"

Miss Henrietta laughed and handed the buffed shoe to her grandmother who began lacing it. Together, they finished the pair. "There you go," she said. "Good as new."

"Better than new. They never was new to me. I found them in a ditch a year ago."

The two women exchanged a look, then Mrs. Hayward pointed to another shelf. "Shiny shoes deserve new stockings."

Miss Henrietta handed a pair of black stockings to Annie.

So they'd noticed. "Thank you kindly, but I can't. I just need the laces, please. How much do I owe you?"

"A penny."

Annie got a coin out of her pocket then feeling blessed and happy asked, "I would like to buy a pad of paper and a new pencil, please." She couldn't say they were for her brother.

"Of course." Miss Henrietta handed them to Annie and she stuck them in her pocket. "That will be another penny."

Annie added another coin, ignoring the consequences that would fall on her at home. Alfie hadn't had anything new for ages. She wanted him to have something special on Christmas. She began putting her shoes on.

Miss Henrietta held the stockings close. "No charge for the stockings."

Annie looked up at her, wanting to take them, needing them very badly, yet. . .

"Please, Annie. It's cold outside. Holey stockings make for cold feet."

She wasn't too proud for charity, and yet. . . "I could sweep the floor for 'em, miss. Or wash the window?"

"A swept floor would be a good trade," Mrs. Hayward said.

The stockings slid on like butter. And somehow her shoes felt more comfortable. It was a silly notion, but a true one.

"Where's the broom, ma'am?"

Annie ran home. Taking time at the mercantile had made her later than usual. Ma kept track of Annie's time away like a possessive suitor, afraid they'd lose the object of their affection if it were out of their control too long. Only Mama wasn't concerned with affection but did thrive on control. In her defense—when Annie felt generous—Annie knew Ma got as much as she gave, meaning there was a reason for Ma's meanness. Or maybe just an excuse.

Annie stopped and caught her breath, her heart pounding in her ears. She couldn't come running up to the house. Announcing her tardiness in such a way guaranteed a licking. Walking in as if nothing was amiss offered Annie a slim chance Ma wouldn't notice the time. Annie often felt like one of the jugglers she'd seen in a traveling carnival, always keeping multiple balls in the air, doing her best not to let one fall.

She walked toward the front door, her hand in her pocket, her fingers around the payment she'd received for the eggs. Money talked.

She entered quietly because she never knew if Pa was dozing. Ma was rolling out dough on the table and immediately put a finger to her lips. Annie could hear Pa snoring in the bedroom. Alfie was lining marbles on the seams in a rag rug. She'd give him his present later. She couldn't wait until Christmas.

Annie put the coins on the table, hoping Ma wouldn't notice the two pennies missing.

Ma gave a glance and didn't even have to stop rolling the dough. "Yer short."

Annie's stomach clenched. "I needed shoelaces." She lifted one foot slightly to show her.

It was a mistake. Ma stopped rolling and came around the table, using the rolling pin as a pointer. "Lift up yer skirt."

Annie raised her skirt a few inches. If only Ma hadn't seen.

"Ya got new shoes."

"I didn't," Annie said. "Miss Henrietta shined them for me, made them look new." She dropped her hem, but Ma lifted it again with the rolling pin.

"New stockings? Did ya pinch 'em? If so, I's proud of ya."

"I didn't pinch them," Annie said. "They were a gift."

Suddenly Pa appeared in the doorway. "How do you rate?"

Annie stepped away from him. "Actually, I earned them. I swept the floor for them."

"Ya shoulda gotten more for yer work," he boomed.

Even from a distance, Annie could smell the liquor on his breath, mixed with the stench of his rotting teeth and unwashed body.

"So it's all right if I stole them but not all right if they're earned?" Even as she said the words, she knew there would be consequences for the saying.

Pa crossed the space between them in one long stride and grabbed hold of her upper arms, lifting her up until her toes skimmed the floor. "You talkin' back to me? Are you really talkin' back to me?"

Alfie stood and danced a little jig. "Socks, socks, I want socks. Sweep, sweep, I want sweep."

Pa let Annie down, none too gently. "Nobody's getting nothing." He looked at her shoes. "And no child of mine is going to walk 'round town with shoes as shiny and uppity as the toffs."

"I won't have you taking on airs," Ma said.

The notion made Annie snicker.

Which was not a good choice.

Pa grabbed her by the arm and pulled her outside to the edge of the muddy pigpen. "Go on. Take a stroll."

Annie pushed back against him. "There's no reason to muck 'em up. I'm not putting on airs, Pa. I promise."

In one movement Pa picked her up and tossed her over the fence where she landed on her back. "Now they won't even let you step inside the mercantile."

He stormed back to the house. The pigs kept their distance, except for the babies who came looking for something to eat. With difficulty, Annie stood and climbed over the fence. There was no question of her boots being dirty. There was muck *inside* her boots, all over her dress, and in her hair. She pulled her old stockings from one skirt pocket and tried to get the pencil and pad out of her other pocket without getting them muddy, but some of the pages were ruined.

She made her way to the water pump. In spite of the cold, she stripped down to her drawers and camisole—which were not untainted—and proceeded to wash herself, her dress, stockings, and boots. Her skin bit with the cold of it.

Shivering, she strung her clothes on a line and hung her boots from a branch. With every task her anger steamed and threatened to overflow. She wanted to grab her clothes—wet or not—and run away from home, and even from Summerfield. Somewhere she could start fresh.

But what then of Alfie? She couldn't leave him behind.

She saw her mother approaching. Was she bringing her a blanket to give her some semblance of modesty, to warm her before she caught her death?

Ma's hands were empty, her face stern. She didn't say anything but stormed to the clothesline and swiped the new stockings from it. "These are mine now." She turned back to the house. "Stay out here until you're decent."

Annie wrapped herself in an old tarp, hunkered down in her usual hiding place behind the woodpile. And cried.

Chilled to the bone, Annie slipped into the house after dark, tiptoeing to the room she shared with Alfie. He looked up from his bed. As usual his hands were tied to its legs. "Annie cold."

"Annie is very cold." She wrapped her blanket around herself. Then she untied his hands. "I have something for you, but you have to be quiet."

Once free he sat upright, and she gave him the pad of paper and pencil. She'd thrown the first few pages away, and the edges were stained with mud, but there were still plenty of pages for him to use. "Draw me a circle."

His eyes glimmered in the moonlight as he took the pencil and awkwardly drew a circle, biting his tongue in concentration. "There!"

"Shh," she reminded him. "That's very nice. But you have to—"

Annie heard movement in her parents' bedroom and quickly slipped the pad and paper under her straw mattress. Alfie lay down and put his hands up, ready for her to retie him.

But then Ma came in.

"What's this?"

"I untied him so he could use the pot," Annie said.

Ma walked the narrow aisle between the beds and picked up the chamber pot. Which was empty.

"He was going to use it."

Ma shook her head, disgusted. "Lay down, boy."

Alfie did as he was told, and Ma tied the strips around his wrists and checked the ties that were attached to the legs of the bed. "Extra tight this time." Then she turned toward Annie and with all her strength, hit her on the side of the head. "Do we need to tie you up too?"

Annie quickly got under the covers. "No, Ma."

After Ma left, Annie reached out and touched her brother's cheek. "Sorry, Alfie."

He just smiled at her. "Annie good."

She didn't feel good. Not in any way.

Chapter Three

Jonathan needed more sleep. His father had run him ragged the last few days, traveling all over the countryside, visiting patients. Today his mind and body could use a respite—which probably wouldn't happen. A big lesson in doctoring was that illness and injury never took a day off.

While his mother cooked breakfast, Jonathan inspected his father's medical office that was attached to the main house. There wasn't much to inspect.

It was just one room. There were two chairs for consultations, an examination table for the patient, and a water basin and pitcher with clean towels. A small desk was heavy with ancient medical books and notations on slips of paper. Jonathan opened one of the books and was appalled to find it was written in 1860. A cupboard held bandages and bottles of medicines and herbs, some familiar and some not.

Jonathan took up a bottle of a yellow oily substance marked "Calendula," unstoppered it, and held it under his nose. It had a woodsy, almost rotten smell.

"Marigolds," said Father from the doorway. "Used for rashes and bed sores. It soothes the skin and makes it less itchy."

"It smells awful."

"As do marigolds, yes?"

Jonathan chose another bottle. "Hawthorn?"

"It's good for the heart, gets the blood flowing. Good for gout too."

Jonathan was skeptical and chose another. "Blackberry?"

"Sore throat. I treated you with it." His father sighed. "You know these remedies. Unless you've completely forgotten them in your time away."

"You're behind the times, Father." He pointed at the medical book. "1860? We've made a few improvements since then."

"A few."

"I suppose it details the finer points of bloodletting."

"It does not. I do not. You know that." He sat in a chair and pat the arm of its neighbor. "Come tell me what's really bothering you."

Jonathan took a seat but found it hard to pinpoint the cause of his unease.

Father did it for him. "You are filled with the exuberance of fresh knowledge."

He nodded. "I am eager to use what I've learned." He nodded toward the cupboard. "But if you are using old methods. . ."

"Just because they are old does not mean they are outdated."

"Just because they are old does not mean they are right."

"Touché." Father cocked his head. "One large point you must

embrace: having a good bedside manner is never old-fashioned."

Jonathan nodded, but he was distracted by the notes on the desk. "Do you have papers I could read regarding your patients?"

Father pointed at his head. "I'm afraid the details are mostly in here."

"How can I treat them when I don't know their history?"

"You ask me. You ask them."

"You expect them to remember all those details?"

"Between the two of us, yes. Most people are very aware of their past aches and pains. They are intimate with the memories."

Talk about behind the times. Jonathan tried to calm himself. He'd spent part of his education at the Guy's Teaching Hospital, gaining experience but also learning how to chronicle it.

"You may write things down, if you prefer," Father said. "And I will do the same. Since we are sharing a practice, it's the least I can do." He smiled. "Anything else strike you as old-fashioned?"

Jonathan knew he'd come on too strong—especially in view of his faux pas regarding the iron deficiency. He decided to avoid the question. "What's our schedule today?"

"We wait for someone to need us."

"That will get tiresome very fast."

"You *want* people to need our services?" Again, a smile.

"Of course not. But I do need something to do. I want to be useful."

"You could go with your mother to bring stew and bread to the Cumberson family as Mrs. Cumberson heals from childbirth."

That was not what he had in mind.

"Or, you can come with me to check on Mr. Brodnick."

At the train station. That was better. "I noticed he has a bad cough."

"He has a cancer of the lungs."

Jonathan remembered the man helping him with his luggage—something he shouldn't have done in his condition. "He didn't say anything to me—and I mentioned that he should stop by because of his cough."

Father stood. "He wouldn't mention it. He's a proud man who's doing his best to deal with a serious illness."

"He's dying then?"

"He's dying sometime. Probably sooner rather than later."

Jonathan sighed. "I've always liked him."

"There is much to like. Will you come then?"

"I will."

"But Jonathan? Don't mention the word *cancer*."

"Doesn't he know?"

"He does not."

"Shouldn't the patient be told?"

"Some patients. Not Mr. Brodnick."

"But why?"

"Trust me."

With their two days of forced absence over, Pin was just about to knock on the door of Jonathan's house when he and his father came out.

"Good morning, Pin," Dr. Evers said.

"Good morning. Is. . .is there an emergency?"

"Not at all," he said. "Jonathan would love a visit from you." He looked at Jonathan. "A short visit?"

Jonathan nodded and strolled to a bench near an arbor. They sat close and exchanged a kiss. "I'm glad to see you. As expected, my time has been extremely busy. We saw five patients, and—"

"Would you like to know how I spent my days apart?"

"Of course. How did you spend your days?"

"First off, before I forget, Mother has asked you for dinner tonight. Can you come?"

"Of course. I would love to see them."

"Good." Then she took his hands in hers, her excitement demanding release. "You asked what I've been doing? I found us a place to live."

He blinked. "What?"

"A cottage. To live in after we're married. It's the Horton place. You may not know, but Mrs. Horton died recently, and Lady Newley has it for rent, and Etta and I went to see it, and—"

"This is what you did?"

"You asked me to."

"I did not."

Desperation took hold. "You did. I mentioned there would be things to do with the planning of the wedding and finding a place to live. You told me these were my tasks to handle. So that's what I did. The cottage isn't fancy, but I know we could be very happy there."

He stood, took two steps away, and ran a hand through his hair. "You shouldn't have done that."

Pin was glad she was sitting down. "But you said—"

He returned to her side and took her hand. "I did. I remember now, but. . .you're moving faster than I expected. I just returned. I'm getting settled into the practice, and—"

She pulled her hand away. "So you don't want to marry me?"

"Of course I do. Please don't think otherwise. Just. . .just give me some time."

"I've already done that. Six years' time." She stormed off, leaving him on the bench.

"Pin!"

She heard his footsteps behind her, so stopped and faced him, raising a hand. "Leave me alone, Jonathan Evers."

"But I—"

"I don't want to hear your excuses. Leave me be."

Pin hurried toward the town square. She realized she was acting childish, yet she was unable to stop herself. Jonathan had made her feel foolish for looking at the cottage, and implied it would never be *their* cottage.

What did he want from her?

She turned the corner at the sewing workshop and nearly ran into Annie Wood.

"Sorry, Miss Pin," Annie said.

The girl didn't move on. "Can I help you with something?"

"I need to learn how to fix my stockings. They have holes in them and we don't have any thread at home."

"Of course." Helping Annie would be a good distraction.

They went inside and Pin told Annie to sit. She then got out a wooden darning egg and black thread, and sat beside her. She opened the egg and retrieved a needle from a pincushion inside.

"That's clever," Annie said.

Pin closed the egg and asked, "Do you know how to thread a needle?"

"I do."

Once that was done, Pin turned the stocking inside out and put the egg inside. "Stretch the area of the hole smoothly over the egg." She showed Annie how to sew a weft pattern across the hole and then weave the thread through in the other direction.

"Look at you," Pin said, as Annie did the work. "You catch on quickly."

Annie beamed and started fixing the next hole, which gave Pin a chance to really look at her. Annie had been delivering eggs for years. Yet, in truth, she was nearly invisible. There, then not there. Pin felt bad for this revelation. Summerfield was a small village. Everyone should be *seen*.

Upon inspection she found the girl quite pretty. She was thirteen or fourteen. Her brown hair needed a good clean and comb. She was too skinny, yet had a toughness about her as if she was the kind of person who would do whatever needed to be done.

But then, when Annie pushed her sleeves up, Pin saw red and purple bruises.

"What happened there?"

Annie quickly covered her arms. "It's hard work keeping animals. I get hurt sometimes."

Doubt entered Pin's thoughts. The girl's parents had a reputation for being elusive, if not difficult. Often ill. Rarely working. Surely they wouldn't add cruelty to their attributes.

"I'm all right," Annie said. "I just bruise easy."

The fact she hadn't let the subject slide made Pin's fears intensify. Yet how could she help? To suddenly show interest, to interfere. . .

But then she thought of a way to get Annie among caring people. "Come to church tomorrow. You, and your parents too."

"I don't have Sunday clothes."

Pin had never seen Annie in any skirt and blouse other than the one she was wearing. It was worn and ripped, and the once blue color was now a dingy gray. "You don't need to dress up. I'll wait for you outside the church at nine. You can sit with me."

"Really?"

Her hope was almost pathetic. "Really."

"That would be real nice, Miss Pin. If I can get away, I'll be there."

Why wouldn't she be able to get away?

Annie sat by the window in the workshop. She'd finished her darning but delayed removing the wooden egg from the last hole in the stocking. She didn't want to leave yet but knew she needed to get home.

The sewing workshop fascinated her. To think she'd walked past it many times a day as she made her egg deliveries, yet had never gone inside—she wasn't sure why.

She'd heard women in Summerfield speak fondly of the place and had seen the dresses they'd made for themselves or clothes made for their children. Having no money to pay for fabric or thread and no time to spend in the sewing, Annie had resigned herself to peering in the front windows when no one was looking. She'd long ago learned that thinking too much about what she couldn't have didn't do a whit of good.

But now. . .she watched Miss Pin help Mrs. Collins sew some sleeves into a shirt—on a sewing machine, no less. And Mrs. Dulling sat nearby, ripping out a seam, telling the other two about her sister coming to visit in the coming week. The friendly chatter was a balm, and only with difficulty did Annie keep her eyes open. She could have easily closed them and let the hum of their voices weave a cocoon of warmth and safety around her.

Pin turned in her direction. "How are you doing, Annie?"

"I just finished the last of them."

Pin came to examine her work. "Well done."

Annie looked toward the sewing machines.

Miss Pin saw the direction of her gaze. "Would you like to learn to sew?"

"I would. Very much. But. . .I don't have the time. Once the eggs are delivered I need to hurry home. Ma always has chores for me to do." She hated the look of disappointment on Miss Pin's face. "But if I ever do find the time, I will be here."

"I look forward to it," Miss Pin said. "Will I see you at church?"

Annie pulled on her mended stockings. "I will try." She hurried home, sending a quick prayer heavenward, hoping God would provide a way.

Jonathan stared at the train schedule tacked to the wall of the depot. The page was old and curled upward at the bottom. Was it even valid anymore? Everyone in Summerfield knew when the train came and went. There was no need for—

Jonathan's father nudged him. "Are you with us?"

"Sorry." Jonathan tried to concentrate. After Pin left him in a huff, he'd gone to the train station to catch up with his father as he checked on Mr. Brodnick. He'd heard them chatting but had been so preoccupied with what he should have said to Pin that he hadn't heard a thing.

"Mr. Brodnick, would you repeat what you said for my son's sake?"

"The cough's getting worse, and I'm losing weight."

Jonathan nodded once. "That means the cancer is getting worse."

He received stares. *Oops.* Father had told him not to say the word aloud.

"Cancer?" Mr. Brodnick turned to the elder Dr. Evers. "I have cancer?"

Jonathan stopped breathing. "I'm so sorry."

The two men gave Jonathan very different looks. Mr. Brodnick's face crumpled in despair, while Jonathan's father glared at him in anger.

The anger would have to wait. Father sat next to his patient and put an arm around his shoulder. "I'm sorry, George."

"I knew I wasn't getting better, but I thought. . ." He peered at his doctor. "How much time do I have?"

"There's no way to tell."

"Can I keep working? I need to keep working for my family."

"You choose how long you work according to how you feel."

He suffered a fit of coughing and Jonathan brought him a glass of water.

It was the very least he could do. The very least.

Jonathan and his father walked home.

"Say something," Jonathan said after a length of silence.

"It's 'saying something' in front of Mr. Brodnick that got you in trouble."

Jonathan felt horrible about it. And yet, "Isn't it better for a patient to know the facts? Isn't that the most compassionate thing?"

His father stopped walking. "There's a time for total honesty and a time when the most compassionate thing you can do is to leave people their hope. Each patient is different."

Jonathan felt his own hope seep away. "I keep making mistakes."

"Experience, son. Learn from every experience."

"But I wanted to come home and. . .and. . ."

"Save the people of Summerfield from disease and peril?"

He had to smile. "Something like that." He remembered the other offer he'd received. "I *was* offered a position in Dover."

"Dover?"

He shrugged. "A well-paid position."

His father blinked. "Why didn't you take it?"

Pin, the known versus the unknown, the lure of home... "Money isn't everything."

"At least you're wise about that." Jonathan was thankful when his father put an arm around his shoulders as they walked.

Annie returned home with new hope in her heart. Miss Pin was going to teach her how to sew. Annie wasn't sure what good would come of it, but learning something beyond the tedium of chores lit a bright light within.

Coming around the last bend to home, she felt the light fade and its warmth withdraw, causing her to shiver. She wasn't *that* late, but it wouldn't matter. She could arrive early and her parents would find a reason to condemn her. She shook her head, trying to expel the thought. At the moment she was happy. She needed to hold on to that.

But then she spotted Pa turning from the trail that led to their shack onto the road. He was walking in her direction fast and hard, his head down. It was his mad walk so Annie rushed behind a tree and waited until he passed by. He mumbled under his breath, and she caught the words "stupid" and "give 'em what for." Since Annie had heard those words applied to all three of the remaining

Wood family members, she couldn't guess who was in trouble now. Someone was always in trouble.

As soon as Pa disappeared around the bend, she ran ahead, just in case the subject of her father's mumbles was Alfie.

As soon as she neared the house, she heard a moan. She ran inside and found Alfie lying on the floor, his knees brought close to his chest. She fell beside him. "I'm here, I'm here."

He barely opened his eyes. "My middle hurts."

Ma came out of the bedroom. "He's a whiner."

"What happened?"

Ma shrugged and tucked her blouse in her skirt. "He's too loud, that's what he is."

"Help me get him to bed."

Ma half-heartedly helped, and Alfie rolled onto his narrow cot, drawing his legs up tight. His moans filled the small room.

"He needs a doctor," Annie said.

"He just needs to toot," Ma said.

Alfie grimaced. "No toot."

"Then it's from eating some of my bread dough that was rising," Ma said. She pointed to her cheek. "See what your pa just did to me?" Her cheek was red.

Annie was incredulous that Ma compared a slap to whatever was sending her brother into agony. She put a hand on his forehead. "He has a fever."

Ma backed away.

"I'll get a rag and a bowl of water."

Annie came back and handed the supplies to her mother. "Put

the cool cloth on his head. I'm going to get Dr. Evers."

Ma grabbed her arm. "You can't do that. You know you can't bring anyone here."

"It's time, Ma. Alfie's getting bigger. You can't keep him hidden forever."

Ma pointed a finger at Annie's face. "You'se the one wanted to keep him in the first place. We wanted to send him away."

This was no time for the old argument. "Send him to a place where no one would love him? Where he's put in a cage?"

"Pfft. He's a hardship to us, plain and simple."

"He's sweet, and—" Alfie's moan spurred Annie to move. "I'm going to fetch the doctor."

Annie hated leaving Alfie in their mother's questionable care, but she had no choice.

After the day he'd had, Jonathan didn't feel like going to dinner at Pin's house. He would have rather gone to bed early and maybe read a book that had nothing to do with medicine or doctoring.

Yet as he walked to the Billingses' he knew that choice wasn't possible, not after he'd made her storm away this morning. He hadn't meant to be so blunt, but couldn't she see it was far too soon to be thinking about letting a house? What he *should* have told her was that—as the husband—it was his responsibility to earn a living. There couldn't be a house if he didn't earn money to pay for it. She was putting the cart before the horse. A mile ahead of the horse.

But he also knew that was Pin's way. She was eager for something new and special. He'd lived in London, while Pin had remained among the same people she'd known all her life, having the same experiences one day as she'd had a hundred days before that. He felt like he'd grown up, but had Pin?

In so many ways she was still the Pin who'd made a promise to get engaged one day. He loved that girl. It's not that Jonathan didn't want to fulfill that promise, but a part of him was wary of her simpler view of life. Were they compatible anymore?

He stood at the front door of Pin's house, smoothed his coat, took a fresh breath, and knocked.

Pin opened the door, her usually bright smile subdued. *She's still mad at me.*

"Come in," she said, stepping aside so he couldn't kiss her cheek. "My parents are in the parlor."

Actually, with Pin acting this way, Jonathan preferred their company. He went to greet them and was welcomed back to Summerfield. After some small talk they moved to the dining table, with Jonathan sitting across from Pin.

During the meal they asked about his schooling experiences, and he was quite willing to let the conversation flow to talk of London, university, and his medical studies. He glanced at Pin often, trying to gauge her mood. Was she finding such talk tedious? She didn't ask any questions, nor react, even when he told a funny story about a chicken that wandered into anatomy class.

Mrs. Billings sat back as the butler spooned more carrots onto her plate. "I spent a good deal of time in London myself when I was your age. I went as a rebellious young woman, determined to make a name for myself on the stage."

"I've heard about that," Jonathan said.

"I hope you haven't heard too much," she said with a chuckle. "I was not a success."

"But you tried." Mr. Billings winked at her and gave her a nod of approval.

The obvious love between them spurred Jonathan to move his foot under the table until it touched Pin's. She looked at him. And almost smiled.

Just that small gesture lifted a weight from his soul. And suddenly, Jonathan knew firsthand what his father was talking about in regard to hope. Hope gave life. The lack of hope. . .

There was a loud knocking on the door and the butler left to answer it. He reappeared at the dining room. "A young woman named Annie is here. She appears quite upset."

Pin stood. "Annie? Bring her in immediately."

Annie entered the dining room, her face drawn with worry. "Sorry to disturb, but. . ." Her words came out in a rush. "My brother is moaning with pain and—"

"Brother?" Pin asked. "You have a brother?"

Annie hesitated just a moment. "Alfie's ten, and he's hurting bad. I went to Dr. Evers's, but there's a note saying they've gone to the Smythes' to help birth a baby. That's in the opposite direction of home, so. . ." She took a breath. "I came to find you, Miss Pin."

Jonathan stood. "I'm Jonathan Evers. I'm a doctor too," he said. "Maybe I can help?"

Relief flowed over the girl's face. "Oh yes. Please."

Pin took up her coat. "I'll come with you."

A brother?

"Stop here!" Annie said.

Jonathan stopped the carriage but saw no house. "Here?"

"Our house is through the woods."

They entered the forest on foot, utilizing a narrow dirt trail over fallen leaves. Annie led the way, walking quickly, holding a lantern as their only light.

"I didn't know there was a house back here," Pin said.

Annie spoke over her shoulder. "No one does."

A few minutes later they spotted some light from the windows of a small house. *Shack* was a better description. The door opened on weak hinges. Smells assailed them: earth, old food, unwashed bodies, and worse. But Jonathan didn't have time to take it in. Annie showed him into a tiny bedroom where a skinny boy lay on a narrow cot. Jonathan sat inches away on the other cot and offered a smile. "Hi, Alfie. I'm Jonathan. I'm a doctor. May I take a look?"

The boy grimaced but nodded.

Jonathan peeled back the boy's ragged blanket and felt Alfie's abdomen. It was tender on the lower right side, with the boy wincing at his touch.

"He ate my bread dough," the mother said from the doorway. "I've told him not to, but he's probably got an entire loaf rising up in his stomach."

"Can that happen?" Pin asked.

"It can," Jonathan said. "The yeast continues to rise." He looked at Alfie's abdomen. It *was* enlarged.

He felt his pulse but wished he had a stethoscope to listen to the boy's heart and lungs. He hadn't thought of stopping at the office to get his medical bag—a grave mistake. His father had made the strong suggestion he always carry it with him.

"Perhaps chamomile tea?" Pin asked. "Mama gives me that when my stomach is queasy."

"We don't have none of that," Mrs. Wood said.

"I could go home and get—"

Alfie let out a moan and doubled in on himself.

With a start, Jonathan knew what it was. "It's appendicitis," he said.

"What's that?" Annie asked.

"The appendix is a small organ that can become inflamed. If it's not removed, it can burst and spill poison into the abdomen."

"Poison?" Annie asked.

"Removed?" Pin said. "As in cut it out?"

Jonathan's heart skipped a beat. Although he'd witnessed surgeries and had even assisted in two, he had never completed one on his own. "I don't have my tools."

"What do you need?" Annie asked.

"A scalpel."

"What's that?"

"A very sharp, precise knife."

"We have a knife."

Jonathan looked around the filthy house. Who knew how clean or sharp the knife was? He also needed clean towels, soap, water, bandages, good light, a needle, suture. . .and ether. He couldn't cut into this boy while he was awake. It would be inhumane.

He had to make a quick decision. "We need to get him back to the office where I can operate. Help me get him to the carriage."

"Yer taking him?" the mother asked.

"I have to."

She began to hem and haw, but he focused on the task at hand. They wrapped the blanket around the boy, and Jonathan carried him through the woods. The weight of him coupled with the uneven terrain made Jonathan nearly fall more than once. Annie climbed into the forward-facing seat and held out her hands for Alfie. Jonathan placed him next to her, tucked under her arm. Pin sat across from them, and Jonathan shut the carriage door and climbed onto the driver's perch. "Heya!"

With each bump in the road, Alfie wailed.

Please, God, help me save him!

But as they turned into the town square, Pin and Annie began to scream. "Alfie, wake up! Wake up!"

Jonathan made the horses go faster. They were almost there.

Before the carriage was fully stopped, he jumped down and opened the door. "Let me get him inside."

But the girls just sat there, sobbing. "He's gone," Pin said.

Annie had her brother's head on her lap, stroking his hair. "I'm so sorry, Alfie. So sorry. . ."

Although the truth was obvious, Jonathan took the seat

beside Pin and felt for a pulse.

There was none.

He put an ear to the boy's chest.

And heard nothing.

Nothing?

Alfie was dead?

He sat back, staring at the boy. He listened to Annie's sobs. He endured Pin's questioning eyes.

He had no words for them, and only one for the Father who looked down upon them all: *Why?*

The heavens wept silent tears.

Jonathan and Pin moved Alfie to the examination table. Then he gently held one of the boy's hands. *I'm so sorry, Alfie. So sorry.*

"We need to get Annie home and tell their parents," Pin said.

The thought of the Woods, weeping and falling to the floor in grief. . .

Blaming me?

Should I be blamed?

"Jonathan?"

He wished his parents were home. They'd know what to do. "I. . .I need to stay here with Alfie."

Pin's perplexed look turned to one of aggravation. "You need to come—"

"I'm staying here." He avoided her gaze.

"Can I say goodbye?" Annie asked.

Jonathan stepped back and let Annie move beside her brother. She stroked his hair, murmured soft words, and kissed his cheek. Then with a heavy sigh, she turned away. "You'll take good care of him, won't you? Until my parents and I can come back?"

"Of course." Yet Jonathan's words clashed with the knowledge that he *hadn't* taken good care.

A few minutes later the sound of the carriage faded, as did any semblance of control.

He fell upon a chair near the boy. "I wish I could have saved you. I'm so—"

Jonathan heard the front door open.

"Jonathan?" his mother called. "We're back."

He stood on wobbly legs. "In. . .in here."

They came in the examination room but stopped short. Jonathan's father ran toward Alfie. "Who is this?"

"Alfie—Alfred Wood. Annie's brother."

"A brother?"

Father pressed a hand to his forehead while his mother shook her head. "What happened to him?"

Jonathan shared the entire story. "I think it was his appendix. I couldn't operate in their house. I didn't have any tools."

His father put a tender hand on Alfie's head. "I can't say I'd have done anything differently."

"I couldn't help him. I wanted to, but. . .he died!"

His mother put a comforting arm around his shoulders. "It's something we never get used to."

"Nor should we," his father said. "Have you told the parents?"

"Pin and Annie went to do it."

"You should have gone with them."

"I. . ." He knew his reasoning was flawed. And cowardly? "I thought I should stay with Alfie."

"The dead don't need a doctor. The living do."

Jonathan could only nod.

Father pointed toward the door. "Go."

"Go?"

"Run and catch up with them. Act like a doctor."

"Alfie's parents will hate me."

He shrugged. "Probably. But you need to think beyond yourself. Do the right thing even if it's hard."

Jonathan looked to his mother, hoping to be saved from the awful task.

"Go on now," she said. "We'll say a prayer for them. And for you."

As he ran, Jonathan said a prayer of his own. A prayer for forgiveness, courage. . .and the right words.

There was no need to hurry.

Where just a short time before the carriage had sped through Summerfield on the way to Annie's house to help Alfie, now the two girls sat side by side in the driver's seat, while Pin let the horses choose their own speed.

They didn't talk. And Annie didn't cry. Clouds covered the stars and the moon, as if God had dimmed their light in respect for the death of a child.

Yet where *was* God? How could He let Alfie die?

As they reached the trail that led to the Woods' home, Annie clasped her hands to her chest. "What will I tell them? How can I—?"

Pin took her hand. "That's why I'm here. To help with the telling."

They heard a commotion down the road. "Wait!" Jonathan ran toward them.

So he came after all.

Jonathan stumbled the last few yards, gasping. Winded.

"It's nice you could join us," Pin said. She still couldn't believe he'd stayed behind.

"I'm sorry. I should have come." He pointed toward the house. "I'm here now."

They walked single file into the dark woods.

As they approached the shack, Annie's mother appeared in the doorway. "Where's Alfie?"

Annie stepped toward her. "He's gone, Ma. He died."

Mrs. Wood shook her head *no* twice. Then she lunged at Annie and grabbed hold of her wrists. "This is your fault! You're the one supposed to watch after him. What we gonna do now? Didn't have money for a doctor to begin with, and now we got a funeral to pay for too? Did you ever think of that, you stupid girl? What're we gonna to do now?" She began slapping Annie's head.

Jonathan rushed forward, pulling Annie to safety. "I'm so sorry, Mrs. Wood. It's not Annie's fault."

She pointed a finger at him. "Don't you dare go blaming me.

Alfie's the one ate the dough."

"It had nothing to do with dough. It was his appendix."

The woman glared at him. "So you're to blame then. You take him away and he dies?"

Blame being tossed around like a hot potato made Pin speak up. "It wasn't anyone's fault."

Suddenly, Mr. Wood appeared out of the forest. He carried two bottles, swigging out of one. "What's going on?"

Mrs. Wood pointed at Jonathan. Then Annie. "They killed our boy."

"Killed?"

"He's dead, Rufus! Dead!"

Mr. Wood took another swig from the bottle and wiped his mouth with his sleeve. "Who killed him?"

"He did!" His wife pointed at Jonathan.

Mr. Wood stepped in front of him. He was a full head taller and four stone heavier. "What're you going to do to make up for what you did?"

Jonathan took a step back, and Pin linked her arm in his. "It's no one's fault," she said. "It was Alfie's appendix. It burst. That's what killed him."

Pin shivered when Mr. Wood looked in her direction. "Someone's gotta pay."

Annie pushed her father toward the door of the shack. "No one's paying anything, Pa. Go inside."

The man stumbled, clearly drunk. Annie's mother took his arm and the two females led him inside.

"Let's go," Jonathan said.

Pin shook her head. "I don't want to leave Annie alone with him." She remembered the bruises she'd seen on Annie's arms. She strode to the door and knocked. Mr. Wood could be heard, railing and yelling.

Annie came to the door. "Go home, Miss Pin."

"Come stay at my house tonight," she said. *You'll be safe there.*

She closed the door enough to cover her words. "I need to stay here. Pa will pass out soon enough. You and Dr. Jonathan go home. I'll come tomorrow"—her face crumpled—"to see Alfie."

She closed the door.

"I feel so helpless," Pin said.

"As do I," Jonathan added as they walked toward the road. "I couldn't help Alfie, and now we can't help Annie either."

The sounds of yelling stopped. Maybe Annie was right. Maybe Mr. Wood had passed out from the drink.

She hoped so.

Pin and Jonathan stood at her front door. "I'm glad you came after us, to tell Alfie's parents," she said.

"Little good it did. They blame me for Alfie's death."

"They'd blame the moon if it would do any good."

"Nothing will do any good." He pulled her close and whispered into her hair. "The boy died in my care. I should have had my bag with me. I couldn't even relieve his pain. I was of no use at all. I've been acting like I know so much, but. . . Father wouldn't have forgotten his bag."

She wasn't sure what to say to him, for he spoke the truth.

He didn't wait for her to respond but kissed her forehead and opened the door for her.

"It will be all right," she said, stepping inside.

Pin's mother met her at the door. "What happened?"

Too much.

When Jonathan came in the house, his parents looked up from their chairs by the fire. "How did it go at the Woods'?"

"It's all my fault."

"They said that?"

He didn't want to discuss it, so he turned to go in his room. But then he remembered Alfie. He looked in the direction of the examination room. "What happens now? To him?"

"We took care of the boy. He's been washed and made ready."

Jonathan held back tears. "Thank you. For doing that for me."

His mother stood and drew him into an embrace. "It will be all right, Jonathan. Don't hide away. Death is a part of life." She leaned back and looked into his eyes. Her blue eyes matched his own. "Talk to us, or better yet, talk to the Almighty."

Jonathan nodded, retreated to his room, and fell into bed. He tried to pray, but the words wouldn't come. There *were* no words.

The house was quiet but for the snores of Annie's parents. After her father passed out, her mother had drunk herself into her own stupor. Only then could Annie try to sleep.

She went into the small bedroom she'd shared with Alfie and undressed. She slipped onto her narrow bed and turned on her side.

The moonlight fell across the floor and upon her brother's empty place.

She threw back the covers and climbed onto the bed where Alfie had lain just hours before. She pulled her knees to her chest and smelled the scent of him.

It was all she had left.

Chapter Four

It had been sixteen hours since Annie had lost her little brother—the longest hours of her life. It had taken all that was left of her energy to stay with her parents as they ranted, drank, and argued over nothing and everything.

Oddly, Annie found herself glad that Alfie wasn't there to see it.

Alfie. She missed him with an ache that threatened to gnaw through her soul.

More than anything she wanted to get away from this house of bad memories. She smiled when she remembered her brother's way of stating it when he managed to escape: "I got out."

She wanted out. But every time she moved to the door. . . "Where do you think you're going?"

Finally, she thought of an answer that might set her free. "I'm going to church, to pray for Alfie." She patted her pocket where she'd hidden a lace collar she'd borrowed from her mother.

"Why you want to go there? They never cared about us.

Preacher's never so much as come by this place."

"Would you have let him come in if he had?"

Pa shook the question away. "God don't care about us, so we don't care about 'im." Pa pulled his suspenders over his shoulders. "God let our boy die. I'll ne'er forgive 'im for that."

Annie couldn't believe her ears. "You. . . ? Once you saw the kind of boy he'd be, you didn't want him. When we left London, you wanted to leave him behind!"

"Watch yerself, girl," Pa growled.

"We had to leave," Ma said. "You know that."

"We had to leave because the law was after Pa. I know that. I know that's why we're living in the woods, lying low. Hiding out. It's why we can't have a normal life."

"Girl. . ." Pa drew out the word and took a step closer.

She knew there would be consequences to her words but had to say them. "You threatened to put Alfie in an asylum almost every day. I've heard about those places. They'd keep him in a cage and treat him like an animal. But did you treat him better? You tied him up! You hit him!"

Pa reached for her, but she slid out of his way. She grabbed her coat and ran out the door.

His words followed her. "Git back here, girl! How dare you talk to me like that!"

Sobbing, Annie stumbled along the trail, low branches grabbing at her hair, scratching her face.

It served her right. She'd botched her one job to keep Alfie safe.

Pin waited outside the church.

Her parents were ready to enter. "Did Jonathan say he was coming?" her mother asked.

"I assumed he was."

"Come inside, Pin," Papa said. "He'll slip in when he arrives."

Yet Pin couldn't do that. For there was someone else she was waiting for. "Just a few minutes more."

They went inside, leaving her to look for Jonathan *and* Annie. She expected the first more than the second but hoped they'd both turn up. Sitting in church among their neighbors, praying together, hearing words of comfort would help everyone. *Please, draw us close, Lord.*

Then she spotted Jonathan's parents walking toward the church. She rushed to greet them. "Where's Jonathan?"

The two exchanged a look. "He's not feeling well this morning," his mother said.

"Hmmph," was his father's reply.

"Come by later," Mrs. Evers said. "I'm sure he'd be glad for the company."

They went inside. Pin's mood was heavy with disappointment. Alfie's death wasn't Jonathan's fault. But as such, wouldn't it have been wise to show his face? People might take his absence as guilt.

Pin heard running feet and saw Annie racing toward the church. She came to a stop in front of Pin, out of breath. "I'm not too late, am I?"

"Just in time." Pin noticed Annie was wearing a pretty lace collar on her raggedy dress. It seemed very incongruous, but Pin appreciated the effort. "You look very nice."

"It's Ma's. She doesn't know I borrowed it."

"I'm sure she'd approve," Pin said, though she wasn't sure at all. She held out her arms, drawing Annie into an embrace. "How were things last night with your parents?"

"They were sick with grief. They passed out from crying."

"I'm so sorry."

Annie shrugged. "Actually, it was for the best."

Best? Pin let it go. "I'm so glad you came."

"I needed to." She looked at the church. "I also need to ask the pastor about the funeral. I don't know what to do. Will he agree to say something?"

"Of course he will. I'll make sure there's a very nice service for your brother."

"We don't have. . ." She looked down.

"No worries. Just this morning my father instructed his workers to build a nice coffin for Alfie. Gratis."

"Gratis?"

"Free."

Annie's eyes filled with tears.

Pin put a hand on her back. "My mother said she'd have a reception at our house afterward. And she's also put together a meal for your family that's in a basket. I was going to bring it over after church if you didn't come."

"You're so kind to me. To us. I just wish. . ."

Inside, the congregation began singing.

"Don't we need to go in?" Annie asked.

With one last look for Jonathan, Pin nodded and took the girl inside.

As Pin and Annie slipped into the pew, Pin's parents showed surprise—but only for a moment. Mama reached over and put a hand on the girl's arm. "I'm so sorry for your loss, Annie."

The girl nodded then surprised Pin by singing along without even looking at the hymnbook. She had a lovely, pure voice.

When the song was over, Annie whispered, "I may not have come inside, but I sat outside and listened. And I taught Alfie some of the songs too."

That Alfie had known something of the Word of God offered a bit of comfort.

I am not alone.

Looking around the church, with Miss Pin sitting on one side of her and a stranger sitting on the other, Annie felt a part of something much larger than herself.

She closed her eyes and let the songs sung, the words said, and the prayers prayed wrap around her like loving arms holding her close. It was such a foreign feeling that she began to cry.

Miss Pin's mother handed her a handkerchief, and Pin held her hand. Was this what love felt like?

The service ended, and Annie filed out with the others. She

received so many kind words that she wished she could collect them all in a basket so she'd have them forever.

The pastor even took both her hands in his. "We're so glad you're here with us today, Annie. Please know that you have the entire village praying for you and your family. Would you like the service to be tomorrow? At ten perhaps?"

"I. . . Yes. Please."

"Your parents. . ." He looked uncomfortable. "Will they approve? I would be happy to go see them, and—"

"No," Annie said. "No, thank you. Whatever you have planned is much appreciated."

"Good. We have a place for Alfie in the cemetery, a special place for children."

Miss Pin's father stepped forward. "I'll get a headstone made. If you give me his full name and birthday?"

Annie felt light-headed.

Miss Pin spoke for her. "I'll get you the information, Papa. And, Pastor Davies, whatever you put together will be welcomed. But I think I need to get Annie home. Mama made a meal for her family."

Annie let Miss Pin lead her away but quickly called over her shoulder, "Thank you. All of you."

The two girls walked toward home, but it was the last place Annie wanted to go. After experiencing the warmth of the church people and the service, returning to the house where her brother was absent, the house that had tension wrapped around it like a tightly bound rope, strangling her. . .

Tears began to flow.

"Would you like to stop and sit somewhere?" Miss Pin asked.

"No, no. I'll be fine. It's just. . .I miss him so."

Miss Pin put an arm around Annie's waist and held her hand. "Of course you do."

"I wish he could have felt the love I felt today from all of you. Sitting there in church, it's like I was being hugged tight."

"Alfie is being hugged tight too, up in heaven. He's probably sitting on Jesus' lap right now, listening to all sorts of wonderful stories."

"He liked stories." As they walked in silence the rest of the way, Annie embraced the image of Alfie being loved. When they reached the trail to Annie's home, she hesitated.

"Would you like me to come in with you?" Miss Pin asked.

Yes, but. . . "No, thank you." *They're always in a foul mood after a good drunk. Especially after I yelled at them. Actually, they might not even let* me *in.*

"I could tell them about the funeral. Certainly knowing their son will get a fine service will please them."

The fact it is free will please them.

"It's best I go by myself."

Miss Pin nodded, but her face was drawn with concern.

Annie was concerned too. But the basket of food might ease the situation. A bit.

And God would help her. He would be with her. All the hymns said so.

"Annie?"

For a moment she'd forgotten Pin was still there. "I need to go. I never collected today's eggs. I may see you tomorrow on my deliveries."

"With the funeral and all. . . We could arrange for someone else to—"

Annie shook her head. "It's my job."

Miss Pin put a hand upon her arm. "Of course. And I will also see you at the funeral."

"You will?"

"Of course."

The thought of it offered a ray of hope.

Annie approached her house quietly, gauging if her parents were asleep or arguing. Sadly those were the most likely options.

She stood outside and was heartened to hear voices—speaking, not shouting. With a deep breath and a quick *Help me, God*, she opened the door, holding the basket from Pin front and center. Maybe they would take the food as her peace offering.

Her parents stopped in mid-sentence and stared at her as if she were from the moon.

She set the basket on the table. "I brought food from the Billings family."

"Whatever for?"

"It's a kindness. Because Alfie died."

Her father peeled back the napkin suspiciously. "That's something anyway." He plucked out an apple. "An apple? I coulda picked this myself."

But you didn't. And you wouldn't because it would be too much work. Besides, it's winter, so there are no apples to be picked, meaning the Billingses took these from their winter stores. Did you ever think ahead and save, Pa? Ever?

Annie wished she could speak all these thoughts but knew it would cause more harm than satisfaction. Instead she got out three bowls and spoons. "I thanked Miss Pin for their kindness."

"Hmmph," Ma said. "We'll see how much to thank them after we see how good it tastes." She took out a tin. "Stew. But it's cold."

"They put it together before church, so it's been sitting," Annie said. "I'll heat it."

Pa grabbed her arm. "You have a lot of gall, coming back here after the way you spoke to me."

"I. . .I'm sorry, Pa. I was upset." *Surely you understand upset.*

He leaned his face close, his breath putrid. "You better watch yerself, girlie, or you'll join yer little brother."

Annie tried to step back, but the table was in the way. She managed to turn sideways and slide out of his reach.

"So you went to church, did ya?" Ma said. "Did God tell you why He killed Alfie?"

"God didn't kill Alfie."

"Somebody did." Ma cut a thick slice of bread. "It was that doctor. Coming in here and dragging our poor little Alfie off like he was a sack of potatoes. Killed him, he did."

"He did the best he could, Ma. It was simply too late."

"Too late?" Pa stepped close again and stabbed a finger into her chest. "Maybe if you'd run faster to fetch help, my boy would still be alive."

My boy? Since when have you ever claimed him?

Yet her father's words added to an existing guilt. *Could* she have run faster? Should she have known there was something seriously wrong sooner?

Annie hated to bring it up but had to. "The service is tomorrow at ten o'clock. Mr. Billings is building a coffin, and I'm guessing I need to bring some clothes for Alfie to wear. He was only wearing his nightclothes."

"Take what you need," her mother said. "But maybe not his boots. Would they fit you?"

Annie was appalled. "No, they wouldn't." And even if they would have fit. . .

Annie went into the bedroom and retrieved her brother's boots, his only pair of pants, and a shirt.

"Who's paying fer all this?" her father asked.

His greed was expected but made her keep the kindnesses of others to herself. "I suppose we are."

"I'm not paying," Pa said.

His wife touched his arm. "We'll get it paid for. Make another batch of moonshine—and this time don't drink it yerself."

After a brief moment, Pa nodded. "And perhaps we can get a bit from the situation. As the grieving parents?"

Ma's eyes brightened. "If we play it right we can."

Annie came out of the bedroom, stunned. "You're thinking of what you can *get* from Alfie's funeral?"

"Why shouldn't we?" Ma said.

Annie set the clothes near the door. Then she poured the stew into a pot on the stove and lit the wood in the firebox, glad all could be done with her back to her parents. They didn't respond well to tears.

"Don't go sniveling in the stew," Ma said.

Her words burst through the dike of Annie's patience, and she faced them. She opened her mouth to tell them off, while her mind raced ahead, warning her of the consequences. But before she could make the final choice to confront them or remain silent. . .

Ma's eyes fell upon Annie's dress. "That's my collar! You stole my collar?"

Annie had forgotten she was wearing it. "I didn't steal it. I borrowed it. I wanted to look nice for church."

Ma grabbed it, ripping it from the pins that held its edges. She stared at it. "Now it's ruined!"

You ruined it! "I can fix it," Annie said, hoping it was true. "I'm sorry for wearing it without asking."

"You ungrateful girl."

"I'm very grateful, I—"

Pa's hand swooshed through the air and slapped the side of her head. She faltered under its power and sting, landing on her knees. "Get out of our sight, you worthless girl."

Ma tossed the torn collar at her. "Don't come back till it's fixed."

Annie grabbed her brother's clothes and stumbled out of the house. Ma slammed the door behind her.

Forget what Annie had felt while in church. She *was* alone. Very alone.

Jonathan's mother came into his bedroom after church. "Still in bed?"

"I told you I wasn't feeling well."

Her left eyebrow rose. "We saw Pin at church—and Annie Wood too."

"Annie was there?"

"She's a brave girl, she is. And Pin said she'd stop over here later."

"I don't want to see her. Or anyone."

Mother put her hands on her hips. "Sulking is very unbecoming."

"I'm not sulking. I told you, I don't feel well."

She sighed. "Can I get you anything?"

"No, thank you."

She left him alone, which all in all, did not put him in good company.

Pin slammed the door of her house, causing the teacups on the wall shelf to rattle.

"Gracious," her father said. "What's that about?"

"Jonathan. I just came from there. He won't see me."

"He feels badly."

Pin tossed her hands in the air. "We all feel badly. But that doesn't mean we can hide away and pout about it."

"I'm sure he's not pouting."

"Then what's he doing?"

Papa didn't have an answer.

"Even Annie came to church."

"I'm impressed by her strength."

"I wish Jonathan had a bit of it."

"Now, now, Pin. Extend him a little grace."

She slumped onto a chair. "I don't feel graceful."

Her father smiled. "Or grateful, from the sounds of things. Hold fast to what you two have. Be there for him."

"That's a little difficult considering he won't even see me."

He pulled her to her feet. "When you see Annie. . . I know it's delicate, but tell her we need some clothes for her brother to be buried in."

Pin let out a sigh. "Something else she needs to deal with."

"Would you like me to go out there and ask the parents?"

"No," Pin said. "I'll get it done."

"You're a good young lady, Pin, and a good friend to both Annie and Jonathan."

"This isn't the kind of friendship I had in mind."

"Grace, daughter." He flicked the tip of her nose.

"Take the pie to Jonathan," Pin's mother said. "No man can resist mincemeat pie."

Although Pin wasn't eager to be rejected a second time in one day, she had to try. As she left the house, she prayed for patience and the elusive grace her father spoke about. If their positions were reversed, wouldn't she want Jonathan to keep trying to see *her*?

Yet the truth was, she would never hole up in her room. When Pin was upset she made sure everyone knew about it. She understood Jonathan enjoyed solitude over company, but to use it as a wall between them? If the pie didn't break down that wall, she didn't know what would.

As she walked through the square, she spotted Annie peering in the windows of the sewing workshop. "Annie?"

The girl turned toward her, her cheeks tracked with tears, her eyes swollen, as was the left side of her face.

As if she'd been slapped.

"What happened?"

Annie pressed some clothes into Pin's hands. "I don't know who to take these to. But I want Alfie to wear something presentable for his burial."

"I'll make sure it's taken care of." Yet the clothes and her brother's memory didn't seem to be the reason for her tears.

Annie took a lace collar from her pocket. "Then there's this. It tore. I need to fix it right away."

Pin pointed to her red cheek. "You've been hit."

Annie angled her left cheek away. "Can you help me mend it?"

"Of course I can, but tell me what happened."

"I'd rather not."

"Annie you need help. Let me help you."

She shook her head. "Just help me fix the collar, please."

They went inside and Pin examined the collar. Using the darning ball was the best option. "Would you like to learn how to fix lace?"

Annie shook her head. "Not today. Could you. . . ?"

"Of course." Pin tried to get Annie to talk, but after receiving one-word answers, she let their conversation die. Annie stared at the sewing as Pin did the mending, yet she didn't seem to see it.

Suddenly she piped up. "Thank you for the food. It was delicious and much appreciated."

"You're welcome. If there's anything else you need, just—"

"No. We're fine."

You are not fine. Pin glanced at the bin in the corner, to the place where people brought clothes they didn't want anymore. "Would you like a new skirt and blouse to wear to the funeral? Help yourself from the basket over there. They're all in good shape. People grew out of them or made something new."

Annie eyed the basket.

"Go have a look." She thought to add, "Just yesterday Mrs. Cumberson came in and took a new skirt for their oldest girl."

The fact others in town had taken clothes seemed to convince her. Annie chose a blouse and a skirt and stepped behind the wooden trifold screen that served as their fitting room.

When she emerged, she was beaming. "They fit!"

"That they do. You look very pretty."

Annie smoothed the skirt over her slender hips and looked in a full-length mirror. "Are you sure it's all right that I take them?"

"Absolutely. We like to find new homes for gently used clothes."

Pin was just about to tell Annie she would be happy to discard her old ones, but the girl folded them up neatly even though they deserved the dustbin.

Pin finished the work. "There. It's nearly good as new. Nearly."

"Thank you for this, and for these." Annie was still beaming about the clothes.

But then she eyed the stack of her brother's garments. "I wish they were nicer."

Pin hadn't unwrapped them but expected they were comparable to Annie's ragged clothes—if not worse since the parents had kept Alfie hidden away.

Suddenly, she got an idea. She looked at the shirt she was making Jonathan for Christmas and made a decision. "Leave the clothes here. I'll make sure Alfie looks nice. I promise."

"Thank you for everything you've done, Miss Pin." Annie laid the lace collar on top of her folded clothes. "I need to go. But. . .if you see Dr. Jonathan, can you tell him thank you for me?"

"Thank you?"

"I know he did his best."

Annie's words were steeped with grace. "That's very generous of you, Annie."

She shook her head. "Nobody ever cared about Alfie except me. But Dr. Jonathan cared. It wasn't his fault what happened next."

The thought of Annie returning home to whichever parent had slapped her was like sending a sheep into a lion's den. Pin remembered the pie. "I was bringing a pie to Jonathan and his family. Would you like to go with me? Then you can thank him yourself. He's been feeling very sad about Alfie."

With a glance in the direction of her home, Annie nodded. "I would like that very much."

Pin noticed Annie hang back as they approached the Evers household.

"What's wrong?"

Annie stopped walking. "Is Alfie still in there?"

Pin gave herself a mental slap. "Yes. They're watching over him."

"I. . .I want to see him one more time."

Pin was taken aback, but she said, "We can ask."

When they reached the door, Mrs. Evers answered their knock. "Pin. Annie. How nice to see you."

"I've brought a pie for Jonathan," Pin said. "His favorite." She handed it over, suddenly feeling very foolish. What was a pie or seeing Jonathan in relation to what Annie was going through?

"Thank you, Pin. Come in."

Mrs. Evers set the pie on the table. "How are you doing, Annie?"

The girl held out the boots. "These are for my brother."

Mrs. Evers's forehead tightened. "It's good of you to think of it."

Pin interjected. "I'm bringing the rest of his clothes over later."

Mrs. Evers cocked her head, obviously curious. "All right."

Annie fidgeted. "Can I. . . ?"

"Would you like to see him?"

There was a moment's hesitation. "I think so."

"Come with me." Mrs. Evers put an arm around Annie's shoulders and led her toward the examination room. Pin stood in the doorway, unsure she wanted to see.

Yet Alfie looked very peaceful, with a white sheet drawn up to his chin. Mrs. Evers let go of Annie, and the girl walked toward him, her eyes focused on his face. She reached out to touch him then looked to Mrs. Evers for permission. "Can I?"

"Of course."

Annie tentatively touched her brother's cheek then ran a hand over his hair. "I went to church today, Alfie. I even went inside. It was nice being with the others and not sitting in the bushes. God was there. I felt Him. Have you met Him yet? Tell Him I'm going to be talking to Him more." She leaned down and kissed his forehead. "I miss you so much."

Pin held in a sob. Witnessing the pain of Annie's loss was almost too much to bear.

The girl took a deep breath and turned her back on her brother. "Do you have any boot polish and a cloth? I'd like his shoes to be cleaned up. I probably should have cleaned them while you were fixing the collar."

"No worries. We'll do it now." The boots were caked with dried dirt.

"It's not too chilly out," Mrs. Evers said. "Why don't you take them outside on the bench. I'll get you a cloth to cover your skirt."

Annie and Pin sat on the bench beneath the front window. Mrs. Evers brought out a box containing boot polish supplies, and a cloth for Annie's lap.

"And here's a damp cloth to get them cleaned first."

"Thank you." Annie opened the box of supplies and took up the first boot.

"I'll help," Pin said, reaching for the other boot.

"You should go see Dr. Jonathan. Bring him his pie."

Pin shook her head. "This is more important."

Jonathan was confused. He'd heard Pin's voice and her mention of a pie. Then Annie's voice, and his mother's. He'd even decided he would agree to see Pin. Yet after a brief silence, he heard some commotion, then the door closing and the dim sound of voices, as if speaking from outside.

He put his ear to the bedroom door and listened, straining to hear more. But when he heard footsteps coming close he stepped back toward the bed.

His mother opened the door. "You're up. Are you feeling better?"

"Somewhat."

"Pin brought you a pie—a mincemeat pie."

"That's nice of her."

"Yes, it is."

"Where is she?"

His mother's left eyebrow rose. "So you'll see her?"

"Perhaps."

She gave him a look of disgust. "She's outside helping Annie polish her brother's boots."

"That's nice of her," he said again.

"Yes, it is." She gave him a sideways glance. "Would you like me to get her?"

"Let her finish."

Mother studied him a moment then flipped a hand at him. "I thought you were a man."

"What?"

"You heard me."

His throat was dry. "I am a man."

"Then act like it." She left him.

Jonathan got back into bed even though he knew he shouldn't. He felt an inner battle between playing the martyr or being a man. But knowing what he should do didn't make him do it. *Lord, please help me.*

A few minutes later he heard voices outside his window. Pin's voice. He bolted to the window and saw her walking away with Annie. Away from the house.

Why hadn't she come in to see him?

Because you'd told her to go away. Because you're a coward.

He returned to bed, feeling a new kind of sickness.

Annie and Pin stood in the square, both heading home.

"Thank you for everything you've done for me, Miss Pin."

"I'm glad to help."

Annie's stomach growled loudly. "Pardon me."

With a blink, Pin looked past Annie toward the road that would lead her home. "Would you like to come to Sunday meal at my house?"

Annie wasn't sure what to say. She'd never been invited to dinner—anywhere. Her stomach growled because she hadn't had anything to eat since a stale roll for breakfast. Although she'd brought the gifted meal home from church, her parents had kicked her out to fix the collar before she could eat any of it.

Miss Pin didn't wait for a verbal answer but took Annie's arm. "It's settled then."

One huge question loomed in Annie's mind. Did she know the right manners to eat such a meal among refined people like the Billings?

She'd soon find out.

Annie was overwhelmed. Mrs. Billings had been the epitome of graciousness, making Annie feel very welcome. "We always have plenty of food for special guests."

Annie was used to "not enough." To eat until she was full was a new experience.

The table was set with bowl after bowl of food: chicken, potatoes, squash, and bread. A grace was said by Mr. Billings, with a special prayer for Annie: "Please be with Annie and her poor parents tomorrow as they put little Alfie to rest. And thank You for letting us share this meal with her. Amen."

"Amen," Annie said. "I've never had anyone pray about me."

"That you know of," Mr. Billings said.

"Really?"

"Of course, dear," Mrs. Billings said. "The people of Summerfield are very good about praying for each other." She let a man wearing a black suit and white gloves spoon potatoes onto her plate. "When I was young, on my adventure as an actress in London, their prayers kept me safe. I know it."

But I'm not safe. And Alfie was never safe.

"I wish we'd known about your brother sooner," Mr. Billings said.

"How did you manage the secret?" Miss Pin asked.

Annie wasn't sure how much to say. "Ma never goes anywhere except to. . ." She was going to say "steal," then thought she'd better not, then decided just to say it. "Except to steal apples or the vegetables from other people's gardens."

"Oh dear," Mrs. Billings said.

"Pa kept himself scarce too. He speaks to men who buy his moonshine, and occasionally does fieldwork." *Until he gets tired of the effort.* It was lucky he'd only been arrested once for poaching on the land of the earl.

"You're the only one we see when you come by with your eggs," Mrs. Billings said.

"I was told not to tell. Never to tell."

"Why?"

"Because. . ." She wanted to be kind but needed them to know the full of it. "Because Alfie wasn't smart. At all. He acted strange. And he had a clubfoot. Pa and Ma were embarrassed by him." She didn't share their threats to send him away.

Mrs. Billings looked uneasy. "I'm sorry for the situation. But people in Summerfield would have helped. I know it."

Annie shrugged. "I did my best to protect him. But. . . I guess it wasn't enough."

"You're a good sister," Mr. Billings said.

"A good daughter," Mrs. Billings added.

At the moment she didn't feel she was a good anything.

"Are you all right, Annie?" Miss Pin asked.

She realized she'd been holding an empty fork over her plate without taking a bite. She needed to change the subject. "Sorry. I'm just very thankful. For this meal, and the one you gave us at church." *Even though I didn't get to eat any of it.* "You're a very good cook, Mrs. Billings."

The woman laughed. "Our cook Sophie is a very good cook. I have no such talent."

Annie felt her face redden. Of course the Billings would have many servants. Mr. Billings ran a successful carpentry shop. And Mrs. Billings was the cousin of the earl *and* the viscountess Newley. She grew up at the grand Summerfield Manor.

"Eat, dear," Mrs. Billings said. "*Bon appétit.*"

Annie's plate was filled to overflowing. She speared a piece of squash and studied how the others used their knives and forks. Her stomach greedily accepted the food—the best she'd ever eaten. If only Alfie were here to share it with her.

"So, Pin," Mrs. Billings said, "did Jonathan like the pie?"

"I wouldn't know."

"What does that mean?"

"I didn't see him."

"He refused a visit, again?"

Pin shrugged. "I made no attempt to see him."

Her father responded. "You shouldn't sound so smug about it. You shouldn't give up on him."

Pin shrugged again.

Annie set down her fork. "It's my fault Miss Pin didn't see her beau. I wanted to see. . .see my brother, and we ended up polishing his boots."

"*You* polished boots?" Mr. Billings said, looking at his daughter.

Miss Pin shrugged. "Just because I let my boots be shined for me doesn't mean I can't do it, Papa."

"I apologize." He grinned. "But my question stands."

Annie enjoyed the easy banter of the family. There was no happy talk during meals back home. Accusations, complaints, and silence accompanied their meager fare as Pa chomped and slurped and belched. Even Alfie had learned not to play with his food or sing or talk at the table.

As her stomach filled, so did her heart. Between the meal and eating a large slice of pumpkin cake, Annie slipped in a prayer for her parents. *I hope you find happiness like this someday.*

She assumed God heard but was not confident He would answer. Some prayers were impossible, even for the Lord God Almighty.

Pin took the carriage and dropped Annie near home. It was dark out, but Annie negotiated the trail to her house from memory. Yet once she reached the door she hesitated. She'd been gone a long,

long time. With any luck her parents were sleeping.

She slipped inside as quietly as possible.

Her mother stood with her hands on her hips and asked with a whisper, "Where have you been?"

The whisper was a good indication the man of the house was sleeping. Although she wanted to point out that her mother had kicked her out of the house eight hours earlier, she wisely chose to retrieve the mended collar from her pocket and lay it on the table. "It's fixed."

Ma lifted it up, gave it a passing glance, then tossed it down again. "The mend is too good to wear to the funeral. If it looked torn we coulda used it to our advantage. Maybe someone would see it and feel sorry for me and offer a new one."

A response came to mind, but Annie held it in.

Then her mother eyed Annie from top to bottom. "Where did you get those clothes?"

"Miss Pin. They're secondhand."

"What did ya have to do fer 'em?"

"Nothing. She gave them to me. She's kind that way."

Ma fingered the fabric of the skirt then shook her head. "You wear yer old ones to the funeral. The poorer you look, the more people will give us."

"But I want to look nice for Alfie."

Ma drilled a finger into her chest. "You wear the old ones. Look pathetic."

Her mother was pathetic.

Pin was exhausted, yet she couldn't retire for the night. Not when she'd made a promise.

Telling her parents she had sewing to do at the workshop and would be late getting home, she took up the beautiful shirt of white linen she was making for Jonathan. Linen she'd ordered special from the mercantile.

She shook the thoughts away. Now was not the time to second-guess. Now was the time to act.

She took up the dingy shirt Annie had brought for Alfie to wear, and cut it apart to use as a pattern. Then she set to work.

Three hours later, in the cold, wee hours of the morning, Pin carefully folded up the shirt and the newly patched trousers and set a green tie on top of the pile. It would look nice in a bow at Alfie's neck. She added a note that said, *For Alfie*.

Then she ran through the cold night to the Everses' home and laid them on the doorstep. As she passed the window to Jonathan's room, she kissed her fingers and touched a pane of glass. *Sleep well, my love. Everything will be better soon.*

It felt good to offer grace.

Chapter Five

When Annie awakened, the first thing she saw was Alfie's empty bed. The first thought she had was that today was his funeral. A child's funeral. A tragedy.

She startled when she heard pottery breaking. Then her mother's voice. "Get up and go with us, you drunken lout. You's the one came up with the plan to make use of it. So hop to. And put a sad face on it so everyone can feel sorry for us."

Her father groaned, but Annie heard him get out of bed. "I don't have to sob, do I?"

"As if you could. I'll do the sobbing. You pretend to comfort me."

They were despicable. Annie couldn't wait for the day to be over.

Jonathan got out of bed with a new determination. The memory of yesterday when Pin left his house without even attempting to see him, galled him to motion. He was losing Pin's attention. Was he losing her affection?

His mother's admonition to be a man had troubled him all through the night. A real man didn't hide away but stood up when times were tough. Wallowing in self-pity was the antithesis of who he wanted to be—who God wanted him to be.

He dressed quickly then paused at the bedroom door to pray. *Give me the strength to be the man I'm supposed to be. Today is the funeral of little Alfie. Be with us, and hold Alfie close.*

Jonathan opened the door just as his father let in Mr. Billings who handed a stack of clothes to Jonathan's mother. "These were on the doorstep. The note says, 'For Alfie.'"

She unfurled the clothes. "These must be Pin's doing. What a lovely shirt. And mended pants and a new tie too."

"She *was* late at the workshop," Mr. Billings said. "We didn't know what she was doing, but I approve of the results."

Pin had worked hard doing good things for Alfie. While Jonathan had slept and pouted.

No more.

"The coffin is ready," Mr. Billings said. "It's in the wagon."

"I'll help you get it," Father said.

Mother turned to Jonathan. "I'm glad you're up. Come help me get Alfie dressed."

He stepped into the examination room. His insides stirred as he faced the full reality of the day.

His mother pulled back the sheet that covered the boy's torso. "Get the shirt read—" She stopped in mid-sentence. "Oh my. Look at this."

Jonathan stepped forward. There was a large bruise on the boy's abdomen. "What would cause that?"

"Someone hit him," Mother said. "Hard."

The men came in the room, carrying the coffin, which they set on the floor nearby.

"Look at this," Jonathan said.

His father gently touched the bruised skin. "This is from a blow. More than one blow from the looks of it." Father sighed and ran a hand across his forehead. "I saw old bruises too." He gently leaned Alfie on his side where faded bruises could be seen on his back and shoulders.

"I. . .I didn't see any bruises when I first examined him," Jonathan said.

"They can take some time to appear."

Jonathan's thoughts raced to a conclusion. "His father hit him. He's a violent man."

Mr. Billings shook his head. "I wish we'd known. But they kept to themselves."

"Hiding the boy completely," Mother said.

"Did the blow kill him?" Jonathan asked.

His father gently returned Alfie to his back. "I'm not saying Alfie died from being hit, but if his appendix was inflamed, a blow would make it worse."

So I couldn't have saved him?

"It's a disgrace," Mr. Billings said.

Mother unfurled the shirt. "It's a disgrace it took this boy's death to get us to realize what's been going on. I wouldn't be surprised if

Annie has endured her share of blows."

"She has," Jonathan said. "When we told the parents about Alfie's death, both parents slapped her more than once."

"Why didn't you say something?" Father asked.

Why indeed? He'd been so caught up thinking of himself. . . "I should have. I'm sorry. I should have."

"You should have," his father said quietly.

Jonathan was thoroughly chastened, yet he had to move on. "We can't change the past, but we can make sure Annie doesn't suffer the way her brother did."

"Agreed," Father said.

Mother stroked Alfie's hair. "I'm so sorry, little one. I wish we would have known."

They shared a moment of silence.

Then Jonathan said, "What should we do about what we've discovered?"

"Nothing today," Father said. "The funeral is today. Get through that."

"Should we call the constable?"

"There's no time before the funeral," Mr. Billings said.

"Will he believe us—without seeing for himself?" Jonathan asked. "I can go get him right now."

His father put a hand on his shoulder. "We've known Constable Hawkins for years. He'll believe us. Four sets of eyes have seen what Alfie endured."

Jonathan's thoughts sped forward. "What about Annie?"

"We *will* make sure she's safe," Father said. "But later. First, let's get this boy buried."

Later seemed a long time away.

Jonathan was on a mission for justice. Although he initially had every intention of going to the funeral, as he headed toward the church he pulled up short when he saw the Woods arriving. What if they railed at him again?

Then you endure it.

Yet it was more than the possibility of his own humiliation that spurred him toward another destination. Justice drove him.

He thought about going to the constable, but telling Alfie's story would take time. Since the Woods were currently occupied, the best option was to go to their house in hopes of finding something else that could be used as proof against them. Proof that the parents had abused both Alfie and Annie.

It was odd approaching the empty shack. Last time he was here he'd told the parents their son was dead. Now, he was determined to prove they were responsible.

There was no lock on the door, so Jonathan entered. He strolled through the three rooms, not sure of what he was looking for. If the constable would take action because of living conditions, this home would qualify, but he knew he needed something more.

One bedroom clearly belonged to the parents, while the other where Alfie had lain was so small its two beds held only a foot's space between them. Jonathan had sat upon the one bed to check on Alfie, in his.

He did so now, remembering the poor little boy, writhing in pain. He bowed his head. *Lord, I couldn't help him then, but let me help him now. Help Annie now.*

When he opened his eyes, he noticed something next to his left foot. He reached down for it and found a narrow strip of cloth. He pulled on it and found it was tied to a leg of the bed. It was about a yard long and was wrinkled, frayed, and crimped as if it had been. . .

"Tied?" He shoved aside the dirty covers and found another cloth tie attached to the far leg of the bed.

He stood, shaking with the knowledge that little Alfie's hands had been bound. Every night? More than just at night?

Either way, he'd been held prisoner. And knowing he was a crippled boy, and a bit odd and simple, made it all the worse. It made Jonathan wonder how many hours a day Alfie had been restrained.

He was faced with a decision. If he left the restraints in place and told the constable about them but the official didn't act straightaway, there was the chance the Woods would remove them. His only choice was to take one of them as evidence and hope the other remained when the constable came to investigate.

Jonathan untied the restraint next to the wall and shoved the other one under the bed. Then he hurried away.

"Ashes to ashes, dust to dust. . ."

Pin took hold of Annie's arm, trying to hold back tears. There were many who were softly crying: Etta and Mrs. Hayward, her own parents, a few other villagers, and Jonathan's family. Minus Jonathan.

Pin felt her ire rise against him but pressed it down. She'd give him what-for later. Now was the time for mourning.

As the pastor finished his words, Mrs. Wood let out a primal wail, falling into her husband's arms. His face was oddly contorted, as though he were trying unsuccessfully to match his wife's show of grief.

For it *was* a show. Pin didn't believe a bit of it. Although she hadn't been to many funerals, she had never seen such histrionics. She saw that her opinion was shared. Everyone looked upon Mr. and Mrs. Wood with studied suspicion.

But Pin's attention was drawn elsewhere as Annie said, "I love you, Alfie. I always will."

With the final prayer and amen from Pastor Davies, Mrs. Wood threw herself to the ground. Annie went to her side, trying to comfort her. Mr. Wood brushed her away. "I'll do it."

Pin was glad when her own mother took charge. "Please, come to our home for a reception in honor of little Alfred."

When Mr. Wood looked up his grief was gone. "Come, Agatha. Get yer wits about you. There's refreshment."

His wife quickly got to her feet, took his arm, and headed off. Leaving Annie standing at the grave. Pin went to her side, as did Pastor Davies.

"Are you all right?" Pin asked.

"I have to be."

"No, you don't," the pastor said. "It's all right to grieve, Annie.

But it's also important to remember the good times you had with your brother."

"I should have done more for him."

"I'm sure you did all you could. I'll stop by your house in a couple days and check on—"

"No!" Annie calmed. "Please, don't. It won't do any good and will only stir them up."

He studied her a moment. "I'm so sorry we didn't know about Alfie. I knew of your family, but I neglected my Christian duty to seek you out. Do you forgive me?"

"We didn't want visitors."

"That shouldn't have mattered." He put a hand upon her shoulder. "I'm truly sorry. Come to me if you need someone to talk to. My door is always open to you—and so is God's. We're both here for you, Annie."

She nodded and he walked away.

"Do you want to go to the reception?" Pin asked.

Annie peered at the grave. "He'll be all right, won't he?"

Pin had no experience talking about heaven but shared what she knew: "God has a special place in heaven for boys like Alfie. He's probably running through some gorgeous meadow, trying to catch a butterfly, and playing with other children."

Her eyes lit up. "Running free?"

It was an apt choice of words. "As if he had wings."

Annie nodded once. "Let's go to your house. I need to keep a watch on my parents."

Poor Annie. Always having to keep a watch on someone.

Annie sat with a plate on her lap and watched in horror as her father went through the buffet line and filled his plate to overflowing, while stuffing his face at the same time. Ma did the same, adding some rolls to her skirt pockets.

Why couldn't they accept a kindness without taking advantage?

Mrs. Hayward from the mercantile sat beside her on a settee. "I'm so sorry about Alfie. If I'd known about him. . ."

"He liked the pad of paper."

"Could he write?"

Annie shook her head. "He liked to draw. Circles mostly."

"He sounds like a sweet boy."

"The sweetest. Never did any harm to nobody." *Only had harm done against him.*

She spotted her father sliding some silverware into a pocket. "If you'll excuse me?"

"Of course."

Annie took a seat beside her father and reached into his pocket to retrieve a knife and fork. "No," she said.

"They's a souvenir of the day."

Annie stood and deposited the silver on a tray of used dishes. She wondered what he had pilfered before she'd caught him in the act.

"Annie?" Miss Pin stood nearby with her mother and Miss Henrietta from Crompton Hall. She motioned her over.

Annie was glad to join them because she had something to say. "Thank you for the lovely feast, Mrs. Billings. I really appreciate it, and so do my parents."

The woman put a hand on Annie's. "I did it for you, dear. And Alfie."

Then Miss Pin looked at her mother, as if confirming something previously discussed. "Mother says you are welcome to stay here, Annie."

Really? More than anything she wanted to accept, and yet she heard herself saying, "I thank you for the invitation, but I need to stay at home." *Do I? Why didn't I say yes?*

"Surely your mother could handle the chicken eggs."

Mrs. Hayward spoke up. "We could send someone to gather the eggs and get them deli—"

Mrs. Billings raised a hand. "Only Annie knows what must be done. Just know the invitation stands."

Annie embraced their kindness. The invitation shone like a bright light of hope.

For the second time Jonathan pointed at the restraint he'd placed on Constable Hawkins's desk. "They tied him up."

The constable stroked his beard. "That's unfortunate."

"Unfortunate?" Jonathan couldn't believe his ears. "A child is not an animal. They held him prisoner and kept him hidden from everyone in Summerfield."

"*That's* unfortunate."

"There's more."

The man raised his right eyebrow.

"Alfie died of a ruptured appendix, but there were bruises. He was hit hard in the abdomen, more than once, which most likely caused the appendix to burst."

"Burst?" He made a face.

"Burst. Sending poison throughout his system. It killed him."

"Do you have proof of these bruises?"

"I saw them, as did my mother, father, and Mr. Billings. Four reputable witnesses."

"Maybe he fell."

Jonathan shook his head vehemently. "He was slugged in the gut. And upon further examination we saw evidence of older bruises, all over his body."

"That's un—"

"This boy suffered for years, perhaps his entire life. The Woods have another child at home. They need to be brought to justice so they don't hurt Annie."

"Has she been beaten and tied up?"

"I've seen them hit her. Slap her. Ask her about it."

"Perhaps I should."

"Perhaps you *must*. I'll go with you, and—"

Constable Hawkins stood. "Thank you for the information, Jonathan. I will take it from here."

"So you'll arrest them?"

"I will do what's necessary."

"Soon? Today?"

He looked reluctant. "Yes. Today."

As the day wore on, Pin found herself incensed that Jonathan had missed the funeral and reception. She had to confront him about it or burst from anger.

She stormed through the town square, knowing she was getting people's attention. She heard an old man at the water pump say to another, "I wouldn't want to be on the receiving end of that mood."

She agreed. Jonathan would not like what she had to say.

She reached the Evers residence and knocked just three times, though her fist yearned for more.

Mrs. Evers answered. "Good afternoon, Pin. Tell your mother the reception for Alfie was very nice."

Pin forced her ire down—for now. "I will. But I need to speak to Jonathan. Must speak to him. Now. Please tell him I'm not leaving until I do."

"Oh. Well then. I'll go get him."

The thought of having this discussion in their home suddenly offended. "Please tell him to meet me outside."

"It's a bit chilly."

You have no idea. "Outside, please." She left the house and paced in front of the window, turning up and back so quickly, the condensation from her breath repeatedly hit her in the face. What if he didn't come out? She'd throw a wobbly if she couldn't say what she had to say.

But then the door opened and he joined her. "Hello, Pin."

His nonchalant greeting riled her all the more. She put her hands on her hips. "I haven't talked to you in two days—though not for lack of trying—and when you do grace me with your presence, all you can say is, 'hello'?"

"I—"

She took his hand and led him down the road to the edge of a thicket. She walked through fallen leaves until they had the privacy she craved. She faced him.

"Pin. . . I—"

She raised a hand, stopping his words. "Let me say what I need to say."

He waved a by-your-leave. Suddenly faced with his listening ears, she wasn't sure where to begin. "You weren't at the funeral, which was a huge disappointment. Don't you understand this is not about you? Not one person at the funeral was thinking of Jonathan Evers. They were thinking about little Alfie and Annie."

"I know, and I'm sorry."

His apology made her blink, but she couldn't be distracted. "And your treatment of me. . .not seeing me? Not meeting me at church as we always do on Sundays when you're home? Not letting me help you through this? Of course you're upset about Alfie's death. But I'm sure it won't be the last crisis you handle. You can't hide away from the world, and especially from me. I. . ." She took a new breath. "I won't stand for it. I won't be ignored."

With that, she dashed back the way she'd come.

"Pin! Stop!"

But she didn't stop, and ran all the way home.

Her mother was startled when she burst through the front door. "Gracious. What's wrong?"

Pin's heart beat in her throat, and her legs demanded a chair. "I. . .I just yelled at Jonathan. Gave him the whole spit and wad."

"Don't be crude, Pin."

"Sorry."

"What did you say to him?"

Couldn't she guess? She began counting the points on her fingers. "That I was upset he wasn't at church *or* the funeral, and that it wasn't all about him, and he can't hide away from me every time he's upset and. . .and that's about it."

"What did he say?"

Oh. "I didn't let him say anything. I ran home."

Her mother pulled a chair close. "Which *was* the mature thing to do."

Mature?

She put a hand on Pin's knee. "I'm not denying he has issues to deal with, but so do you. It is also not 'all about you,' daughter. It's about you and Jonathan, together. As a couple. You've been distracted too."

"I've been busy helping Annie."

"I commend you for it. But love, and especially marriage, is for better or worse, in sickness and in health. You can't abandon Jonathan in this 'worse' time."

Pin felt the fight flow out of her. "I tried to help. I went to visit him over and over and he wouldn't see me."

"He saw you today. Maybe he's climbed out of his dark place, or is in the process. If so, he needs to know you'll be there on the other side."

Pin sighed deeply. "I cut up his Christmas present to make a shirt for Alfie."

Mother chuckled, cupped Pin's chin in her hand, and looked in her eyes. "Was this an act of revenge or generosity?"

Pin shrugged.

"I'll assume the latter. You *are* a good person, Penelope Billings. Share some of that goodness with Jonathan."

"I need to make him a new shirt."

"Yes, you do."

"But. . ." The lingering doubt that hid in the corners of her heart surfaced. "What if we don't ever get married?"

Mother cocked her head. "Has he said. . . ?"

"No. But he wants more time."

She looked relieved. "Then give it to him."

"But I *have* given him time. Six years."

"Then a few more months won't matter. True love is patient and kind."

Pin pondered her words and found sudden clarity. "I've been patient and kind to Annie but not to Jonathan."

"Sometimes it's easier to do right by a stranger than to do right by those we love the most."

Suddenly, Pin knew what she needed to do. She stood. "I have to go."

"To see Jonathan?"

"I'll be back soon."

Once outside, Pin walked in the opposite direction of Jonathan's, up a lane, to the cottage she'd wanted to rent once they married. She went up to the door and put a flat hand upon it. "I thought you would be ours, but it's not to be. Mother says I have to wait." She dropped her hand and looked to the heavens. "Help me in the waiting, please?"

Annie sat on the cold ground behind the woodpile and cried. Alfie was gone and all her parents did was argue. How could they fight with such ferocity on the day they buried their child?

She closed her eyes and remembered the gracious invitation from Miss Pin and Mrs. Billings. It was hard to imagine staying with a family who loved each other, where peace reigned. She'd given the excuse that she needed to be at home. But did she? What good was she doing here? She'd tried to speak words of sense and calm to her parents but had been yelled down. And what good was there in a household where she would suffer the brunt of their whims of anger? *Help me know what I should do.*

Annie was drawn out of her thoughts and prayers by the sound of a vehicle on the road. She peeked out from behind the wood and saw Dr. Jonathan and the constable coming up the trail. What were they doing here?

She made her presence known.

Dr. Jonathan held out a hand. "Annie. Come here."

She did as she was told. "What are you doing here?"

"We're arresting your father."

"For what?"

"For abusing Alfie, for contributing to his death."

"Contributing. . . ?"

"Alfie had bruises on his abdomen—and other places. A blow caused his appendix to rupture."

She tried to think back to the day of her brother's death. She hadn't witnessed any blows, but that didn't mean they hadn't happened. Many a time she'd come home from her deliveries to find Alfie in pain from some punishment.

The constable pounded on the front door. "Rufus Wood. I need to speak to you."

"Go away!" came her father's reply.

"We will not. I am here to arrest you for the death of your son. And for keeping him tied up against his will."

Suddenly, Ma opened the door. "The boy agreed to the tying. It were for his own good."

It was a ridiculous statement. Annie stepped forward. "She's lying."

"Shut up, you!" Ma lunged out the door toward Annie but was stopped by Dr. Jonathan.

Then her father pushed his wife into the constable and ran out toward the back of the house and into the woods.

Jonathan ran after him. Annie saw the constable had her mother in check, so joined in the chase. She was no match for her father's longer legs, but on she ran, needing to be a part of his capture.

Luckily, Pa was more brawn than grace, and tripped and fell.

During his attempt to stand Jonathan tackled him.

"Get off me!"

Jonathan straddled his back, pressing his shoulders into the ground. "Annie, go back to the wagon and get a length of rope!"

Annie didn't have to be told to hurry. Jonathan was younger than her father, but Annie had witnessed the power behind his anger. He'd be like a caged animal in his ferocious desire to be free.

When she got back to the road, the constable was lifting her mother into the bed of a wagon. Her hands were tied behind her back, and she was hurling her entire repertoire of curse words at him.

It was obvious she had not been an easy catch, for the constable's hat was missing, his hair was mussed, and the sleeve of his coat was torn from its seam. "Did Jonathan get him?"

"He did. He needs help. I came for rope." She pointed in the right direction.

"Stay here. Guard your mother." He grabbed some rope and closed the tailgate.

The idea of watching Ma was disconcerting yet was also steeped in satisfaction. To be in her mother's presence and *not* be in danger?

As soon as the constable ran off, Ma stood in the wagon bed. "Help me down."

Annie took two steps back.

"Get over here, you ungrateful girl. Help me jump down!"

Annie shook her head. "You hurt Alfie. You killed him."

"Yer father did that. Didn't mean the killing part, but the boy kept moaning something awful. You know how he gets when something keeps him from sleep."

The absurdity of her excuse pressed on Annie's emotions, forcing release. She took a step toward the wagon. "You hurt me too for no reason at all. Over and over you hit and screamed at me. Nothing I ever did was good enough."

"Can't a mother correct her child?"

Annie scoffed. "You kept Alfie tied in his bed! He was a good boy, and you tied him up like an animal."

"He got out of control. Calling out. Breaking things."

"He just needed to be loved."

Ma shrugged. "We shoulda left him in London when we had the chance. No good came from bringing 'im here."

"No good came from keeping him a secret. People would have helped. I know it."

Annie heard the men coming back. They had her father tied at the hands and the feet and were carrying him as he squirmed and added his own litany of curse words. Annie was glad for the extra restraints.

With grunts of effort they put him in the wagon and the constable climbed in to drive. "Annie, do you have some place to go? I don't want you out here by yourself."

Actually. . . "Mrs. Billings invited me to stay with them."

Her father called out, "You stay here and guard the house, Annie Wood. You do not leave."

She didn't answer him. There was nothing to guard. In fact, the entire place could do with a good burning.

The constable spoke to Dr. Jonathan. "You'll see that Annie gets to the Billingses'?"

"I will."

As the constable took up the reins, Annie had a question. "What's going to happen to them?"

"Justice." He clucked at the horses and the wagon pulled away, accompanied by the shouts and curses of her parents.

When their noise faded, Annie found her legs weak and began to falter.

"I've got you," Dr. Jonathan said, taking her arm.

"This all happened so fast."

"Not fast enough," he said. "Gather your things and let's get you out of here."

Once in the house she took the skirt and blouse Pin had given her from the workshop, but other than that. . . Standing in the room she'd shared with her brother, there was nothing else she wanted to take. Except. . .

She retrieved the pencil and the pad of paper with the circle drawn on a page. It was all she had left of him. The only thing that mattered from this before-life.

Pin opened the door to a burst of cold air and was shocked to see Jonathan. And Annie.

"Can Annie stay with you?"

It took Pin a moment to grasp what was happening. "Of course. Come in."

She led them to the parlor where they sat down, Annie beside Jonathan.

"You are very welcome here, Annie. But what made you change your mind?"

"My parents have been arrested."

"Arrested?"

Between Annie and Jonathan, Pin heard the story.

She drew Annie into an embrace. "I'm so sorry for all you've been through. You must be exhausted."

Annie's forehead furrowed as though she was on the verge of tears.

"Come with me and I'll get you settled in."

Jonathan moved to leave.

"Thank you for bringing her," Pin said.

He held his hat in his hands. "You'll be all right now," he said to Annie.

"I know I will. Thank you for all you've done, Dr. Jonathan."

Pin wished she had time to speak with him, to apologize for her previous tirade. To see that he hadn't been thinking of himself but had been thinking about Annie chastened her. And he hadn't just been *thinking* about the girl but had taken action to help her.

The apology would have to wait until tomorrow.

A bath!

Annie had never had a bath in a real tub. The fact it was accomplished by simply turning a spigot for hot water and cold. . . A maid had brought her soft towels and bottles of hair soap, body soap, and a comb. A toothbrush and tooth cream sat on the sink.

She sank into the water and groaned with the ecstasy of it. She'd taken an occasional dip in the river, but other than cooling herself off, it had never given her the feeling of being clean. And more than clean, pampered.

She found herself smiling and giggled with happiness. "Thank You, God," she whispered.

She soaked until the water began to turn cool. Then she got dressed in a beautiful white nightgown with pink tatting at the edges. Back in her room were more gifts from Miss Pin: some new bloomers, a camisole, slip, stockings, a pretty navy skirt, and a white blouse with tiny tucks.

Annie looked in the mirror above the sink and studied herself. She'd rarely seen her reflection. The only mirror back home was cracked and was her mother's, which meant it was unavailable for Annie's use. She touched her cheeks. "I'm sort of pretty." Did happiness make a girl pretty?

She took the comb and—with work—managed to smooth out the tangles. She gathered the ragged clothes her mother had made her wear to the funeral to take back to her room. Then she had a different thought and detoured down the hall to the chute where she'd seen the maid discard some rubbish. Down to the fire they went.

Back in her room, she turned out the light and got into bed.

It was like lying on a cloud. It smelled of fresh air and soap, and the thick covers wrapped her in a cozy embrace. Annie didn't want to go to sleep even though her body craved it. She spread her limbs and arms to the four corners, marveling at the space.

Even though the cause of her being here was full of sorrow, she couldn't help but smile at the end result. For the first time in her life she was safe from all harm. She was among people who cared after her. They would be her protectors just as she had tried—unsuccessfully—to protect Alfie.

Yet Alfie was in a happy place now. A perfect place. Sitting outside the church time and again, Annie had overheard the pastor's sermons about God sending His Son to earth, and Jesus dying for our sins so we could spend forever in heaven. Alfie was there in that forever. Safe, and like Pin said, probably running with the other children, laughing, full of delight. Her sorrow was nothing compared to his joy.

She looked at the moonlight seeping around the edges of the curtains and listened to the crackle of the fire in her very own fireplace. She stared at the flickering of its dancing light.

Her heart overflowed with thanksgiving. She remembered praying just a few hours earlier: *Help me know what I should do.*

She giggled at the knowledge that God had answered her prayer beyond her wildest imaginings. And now—what she should do—was go to sleep and dream happy dreams, wrapped in safety and joy.

Chapter Six

Annie awakened and realized one very important fact: she was well rested. Completely rested. Rejuvenated. Almost new.

She couldn't be fully new because of her grief, but the knowledge that her parents were being held accountable for their awful deeds made the day bright, the air fresh, and her mood enthusiastic.

When was the last time she'd felt enthusiasm for anything?

Then she remembered one such time: when Miss Pin had promised to teach her to sew. Did she finally have time for that?

She bolted upright. The chickens! The eggs! She needed to get home and care for them.

She quickly dressed and noticed her shoes set just inside the bedroom door. They had been cleaned and polished. *You think of everything, Miss Pin.*

Annie combed her hair, which looked uncharacteristically smooth and shiny. Then she made her bed. Hopefully someone was awake so she could tell them where she'd gone. She didn't want them to think she'd run away without a word.

Annie hurried downstairs but stopped halfway as she heard Miss Pin speaking with her mother in the parlor below. It wasn't polite to eavesdrop, yet she couldn't help herself. They were talking about her.

"I'm glad to know Jonathan is out and about," Mrs. Billings said. "Now you can spend time together."

"I'm glad too," Miss Pin said. "But I'm focusing on Annie right now."

"Perhaps you can focus on her together."

"Perhaps. If he'll ever speak to me again. I was so mean to him about Annie."

"You *will* make amends. Today. This morning. Do not let the hours pass."

Annie was appalled to know that she had come between Miss Pin and Dr. Jonathan. She would have to do something about that.

Without warning Miss Pin came out of the parlor and looked up the stairs. "Annie. You're up."

"I am."

"How did you sleep, my dear?" Mrs. Billings said, joining them in the foyer.

"Better than I ever have. Ever."

"That's good to hear. Breakfast will be served shortly."

Breakfast sounded wonderful, but her chores beckoned. "I have to go home to feed the chickens and collect the eggs."

"No need," Pin said. "We sent a boy to do it for you. He said he's familiar with chickens so you needn't worry. He's to bring the eggs back here."

Annie was overwhelmed by their kindness. "That's so nice of you. Let me know when he's returned and I'll make my deliveries."

"If you wish."

She nodded. She needed to do something to earn her keep.

Even though Annie had traveled her delivery route daily for years, today her task seemed easier and was filled with an odd joy. She hadn't realized how much her home life had weighed on her, always a burden, always promising tension and fear—even when she wasn't there.

She found herself skipping to her last delivery at Crompton Hall and stopped herself with a laugh. She was too old to skip. With another laugh she took it up again, unable to stop herself. The bite of the brisk winter air only added to her delight.

"Annie!"

She turned around and saw Miss Pin riding up in an open carriage. "I'm going to visit Etta. Climb in. It's too cold to walk."

Annie handed Miss Pin the basket of eggs and climbed in, adjusting the lap blanket around the two of them. The horse took off in a fast trot, the steam from his nostrils floating toward them.

Upon reaching Crompton Hall, Annie expected Miss Pin to drop her off at the kitchen entrance and go around to the front.

Instead, she accompanied Annie inside.

"Come in, Annie," said Mrs. Dermott, the cook. When she saw Pin she stood straighter. "Well, well, Miss Billings. I never expected to see you at this door."

"I'm helping Annie today."

The cook looked skeptical. "How nice of you."

The eggs were brought in and counted. Coins changed hands.

"Care for a morning roll, ladies?" Mrs. Dermott asked.

Annie grinned and put a hand to her stomach. "I couldn't eat another bite."

"Eh?"

Annie began to tell them about the change in her situation—but stopped, thinking that she'd better get home or Ma would yell at her. But then she relaxed as she remembered Ma wasn't there. She could take her time and tell the tale of her escape, of her saving, and of God's amazing provision.

"She's staying with us now," Miss Pin said at the end of Annie's story.

"We didn't know you had a brother," Mrs. Dermott said. "I wish we had. Maybe we could have helped somehow."

"It's not your fault," Annie said. "My parents wanted him kept secret."

"I'd best go find Etta," Miss Pin said to Annie. "She's coming home with me, so we will come fetch you shortly."

"Thank you, Miss Pin."

As soon as she left, Mrs. Dermott got busy instructing a kitchen maid who was rolling out a piecrust.

Two sculleries came close. "You've got the ups now, don't ya," a scullery said. "Living in a fine house like the Billingses'."

The other scullery added, "It's nice enough but not as nice as the Hall."

"Wasn't saying it was," the girl said. "It's just nice for Annie."

One of the sculleries nabbed an extra roll for herself. "But ya can't stay there forever, can ya? They'll send you on your way soon enough."

The other scullery nodded. "You ain't one of them."

"You's one of us. Or near—"

They all stood at attention when the housekeeper, Mrs. Halsing, entered the kitchen. Annie knew of her but had rarely seen her. "What's going on here? Is there no work to do?"

The sculleries scurried away. Annie began to leave. "I'll wait outside."

Mrs. Dermott raised a hand. "Hold on, girl." She turned toward the housekeeper. "Mrs. Halsing. Didn't you say we're in need of another housemaid?"

Housemaid? There was a position open?

Mrs. Halsing looked at Annie, then back at the cook, then at Annie again. She looked confused.

Mrs. Dermott moved to explain. "Annie's parents have been arrested for abusing the children, and perhaps causing their son's death."

Mrs. Halsing turned kind eyes on Annie. "Have you been hurt, dear?"

"Well, yes. Me and my brother."

Mrs. Halsing shuddered. "How horrible for you. And for the boy, of course. I am very sorry for your loss."

"Thank you, ma'am."

The cook continued. "She's staying with the Billingses right now, but she's in need of a permanent job, and I thought. . ."

"This is highly unconventional, Mrs. Dermott. This sort of conversation is usually done in private."

"I know. But it seems this young girl's entire life has been unconventional."

A door had been opened. *God? Is this Your doing?* Yes or no, Annie wanted to walk through it. Run. "I could give you references from Miss Pin and Dr. Jonathan, ma'am. And perhaps Mrs. Billings." She thought of the mercantile and the bakery. "Mrs. Hayward knows me, and Mrs. Keening, and in this household, Miss Henrietta, and—"

Mrs. Halsing smiled. "It seems you have made the acquaintance of many fine people in Summerfield."

"I've delivered eggs daily, ma'am. I've enjoyed a chat now and then."

Miss Henrietta and Miss Pin came into the kitchen in a rush of chatter and friendship. Miss Henrietta adjusted her hat.

"Hello, Mrs. Halsing," Miss Pin said. She studied their faces. "Oh my. Has something happened?"

"We are having an interview with Miss Wood for a position," Mrs. Halsing said.

"For?"

"Housemaid."

Miss Henrietta's eyes grew bright. "We are in dire need since Mary moved on to help her ailing mother in London."

"So you approve of Miss Wood?" Mrs. Halsing asked.

"Of course." She looked at Annie. "Pin has filled me in on your horrible, exceptional day yesterday, Annie."

"She says she knows you, Miss Henrietta?" Mrs. Halsing said.

Oh dear. I've met her. I don't know her. Have I overstated?

With a smile Miss Henrietta pointed toward Annie's shoes. "Are you keeping your boots shined?"

"I wasn't, ma'am. My parents didn't like them shiny. They thought I was acting better than them."

The four women exchanged a glance. "You are better than them, Annie," Miss Pin said.

Annie was warmed by their words. She lifted her skirt an inch to show her boots. "But this morning I found them all shiny, like new. I have Miss Pin to thank for that."

"Then we thank Miss Pin," Mrs. Halsing said. "All this begs the main question: Do we want you to be a housemaid here at Crompton Hall?"

They all looked at Mrs. Halsing, waiting. *Please, Father, please. . .*

The woman smiled. "I think we do. If you are willing, Miss Wood."

Annie walked through the door God had opened, her heart overflowing. "I would be honored."

"It's hard work," Mrs. Halsing said. "Dusting, scrubbing,

making beds. You'll actually be an under-housemaid to start."

"I'll do whatever it takes to work here. And I'll make you proud. I promise."

"Then you have the position," Mrs. Halsing said.

Annie began to laugh, and slapped a hand over her mouth. Then suddenly, a rush of joy brought the threat of tears. "I. . .I don't know what to say."

" 'Thank you' will suffice."

She wanted to hug them but knew that would never do. "Thank you. Thank all of you!"

"Very well then," Mrs. Halsing said. "There is one stipulation. You need to provide your own uniforms. The mercantile has the sewing patterns, and stocks both gray and black fabric. If you can't sew, Miss Billings and some of the other women in the village can make them for you."

"I'm learning to sew right now," Annie said.

Miss Pin smiled. "With her parents contained, she now has the time to fully learn. I will oversee the project myself."

"Very good," Mrs. Halsing said. "It never hurts to have an extra skill in one's pocket. Who knows where it could lead you."

"Yes, ma'am." Who knew?

"Go on then. Uniform ready or not, come back tomorrow morning at nine and we'll begin."

"Yes, ma'am."

"Let's go then," Miss Pin said. "Mother will be so surprised."

No one was more surprised than Annie.

Annie's pending job required uniforms. It was a task Pin was excited to conquer. "You secure the pattern to the fabric so the pins aren't in the way of the cutting."

Annie held the sewing shears but only stared at the fabric. "I'm nervous. Cutting. . .it's so final."

"You'll be fine," Pin said. "We've taken the time to measure the pattern on you and placed it just-so on the fabric. You've done your due diligence. Just begin."

Annie took a deep breath, as if she were pondering stepping off a precipice.

Pin's cousin Etta laughed from her seat near the window, where she looked at fashion magazines. "You can't sew until you cut—or so I've been told."

Pin didn't appreciate her input. "Spoken from someone who's never even tried to learn."

Etta shrugged and turned a page.

Pin turned her attention back to Annie. "Come now. Just do it."

Annie began to cut along the edge of the pattern. With each snip her confidence seemed to increase until she was finished with the front of the bodice.

She stood upright. "I did it!"

"You did. Now keep going. Move around the table so you get the best angle to finish cutting all the pieces."

Annie tackled the rest of the task with intense concentration.

She'd make a good seamstress. She cared and was careful.

When the cutting was finished, they removed the pins and stacked the pieces according to groups: bodice, skirt, and sleeves.

"Now then. On to the sewing machine," Pin said. "We'll sew the shoulder seams of the bodice together then the side seams. Just like you practiced on scraps earlier."

Annie sat at the machine as though it were a world to conquer.

Yet conquer it she did. There were a few rip-outs when the stitching got away from her, but on the whole, she did very well.

"You have a natural ability for this," Pin told her.

Etta moved from the magazines to oversee the fitting. She nodded approvingly. "Keep this up, and you can help our lady's maids with the mending and alterations for Mother and me."

Annie's eyes lit up. "I'd like that." She turned to Pin. "Help me get good enough to do *that*."

Pin laughed. "You've come a long way in a very short time. This is a new life for you."

Annie stopped her pinning and looked up. "Speaking of. . ."

Pin could tell something serious was on her mind. "Go ahead."

Annie looked hesitant but began. "Begging your pardon, but I overheard you speaking with your mother this morning. About how you've been focused on me."

Pin thought back to the conversation in the parlor. Had she said something to offend the girl?

"You and Dr. Jonathan have done so much for me."

"We are glad to do—"

Annie held up a hand, stopping her words. "I can never thank you enough. But I overheard. . . I can see how that attention has kept the two of you from focusing on each other."

Pin felt her face grow hot. "You are a perceptive girl."

Etta chimed in. "She's right, you know."

Pin nodded. "We argued. Or rather I argued. I yelled at him and didn't give him a chance to say a word."

"Argued about what?" Etta asked.

Pin hated to say it aloud.

"About me, yes?" Annie said.

Pin nodded. "I didn't think he cared about you since he didn't come to the funeral. But now I see that he cared very much and was working to get justice for your brother *and* working to get you to a safe place."

Etta put her hands on her hips. "You didn't tell me about the argument."

"Because it was awful. I was utterly wrong."

"Have you apologized to him?" Etta asked.

"Not yet."

"Then go to him," Annie said. "Please. I don't want to come between you."

Pin glanced toward the door. "I know I should."

Annie retrieved Pin's coat and helped her on with it. Then she said, "Can I ask you a question?"

"Of course."

"What do you want the most regarding you and him?"

"Gracious, Annie," Etta said. "You get to the heart of things."

The question remained. Pin wanted to say she wanted marriage the most—and she did want it a lot. But things had changed since Jonathan had returned home and she'd rushed to find them a place to rent. *She'd* changed.

"I. . .I think what I want the most is for Jonathan to be happy. If he's happy, I'll be happy."

Annie beamed. "That's lovely."

Etta agreed. "That's the most romantic sentiment I've ever heard from you. Perhaps the only romantic sentiment I've heard from you."

Pin was shocked by this. "I'm romantic."

"You're driven."

Pin stopped buttoning her coat. She was right. Her focus had been on marriage, not Jonathan. The goal, not the man.

Etta finished buttoning her coat for her and spun her toward the door. "On you go then. Go find Jonathan and make him happy."

Walking the short distance to Jonathan's house, Pin wished she had another pie or something special to bring to him as a peace offering.

You're bringing yourself. That's enough.

She embraced the thought. Yet it made her remember the demanding, selfish Pin of late, the Pin who'd done little more than demand her way like a petulant child.

She wasn't a child. She was a twenty-one-year-old woman. It was time she started acting like one. *Help me say the right things, Lord—and stop me from saying the wrong ones.*

She knocked on the door and was surprised when Jonathan answered. "Pin." His eyes were wary.

"May we talk?" She felt the need to add, "*We* talk, not just *me* talk?"

His smile gave her courage. "That sounds acceptable. Would you like to come in?"

"Are your parents home?" She didn't need an audience for her apology.

He shook his head. "They went to check on a patient. Come in."

She stepped inside and took comfort from the warmth of the fire and the fact that it would be just the two of them.

"Please, sit," he said.

She was glad he led them to a settee where they could sit side by side. Pin angled her body toward his, needing to see his face. "First off, I need to handle some business for my mother that I have totally neglected. Your parents have long come to our house on Christmas Eve, so once again, you are all invited."

"Of course. We look forward to it."

She sighed deeply. "That taken care of, I need to get to the crux of my visit. The core of it."

"All right."

"I've come to apologize for my outburst. It was very wrong of me to jump to conclusions without letting you get a word in."

"You didn't give me a chance to defend myself."

"I did not. And that was wrong. You *were* helping Annie in far-reaching ways. You've totally changed her life."

"How is she?"

Pin was happy to tell the story of Annie's new position at Crompton Hall.

"She has initiative," he said. "I commend her for that."

"She has skill as a seamstress too. We've started lessons because she needs two uniforms. Actually, she is nearly done with both."

"With your help."

"Of course. But she's doing most of the work."

His eyebrows rose. "From beleaguered daughter to a determined worker."

Pin shook her head. "I think the ambition and desire to better herself were always there. She just didn't know how to escape the confines of her situation." She put a hand on his knee. "Until you shattered the situation, setting her free."

He took her hand and brought it to his lips. "I have my own apology to make."

"No need."

"Let me say this, please."

She gave him an encouraging nod.

"I came home to Summerfield riding a white horse, wanting to save the village with my medical prowess and education. I quickly discovered how much I need to learn." He looked to the floor. "I was humbled. It was hard to face my shortcomings."

"No one blames you for—"

"I know. And Father says I did all I could have done for Alfie."

"And now you've made up for any lack by stopping the Woods from causing more harm."

He nodded. "The constable says they *will* be punished. They will not hurt Annie again."

"She truly has a new life at Crompton Hall. That couldn't have happened without you."

"Without us," he said quietly.

Pin moved close and found her place beneath his arm.

Chapter Seven

Pin rubbed her neck and arched her back. It was two in the morning. She'd come straight to the workshop after making up with Jonathan and had helped Annie finish her uniforms. Then she had spent all night sewing him a new shirt for Christmas.

Now finished, she smoothed it against the cutting table, carefully folded it, placed it in the middle of a piece of pretty calico, and tied a ribbon around it.

There now. All is as it should be.

That accomplished, she went home to get some sleep.

Pin was awakened by a knock on her bedroom door. "Yes?" she managed.

"Miss Pin, it's me, Annie. I'm leaving now."

Pin noticed the time was half past eight. "Just a moment."

She got out of bed and wrapped a shawl around herself against the morning chill. She opened the door and found Annie standing there, wearing her new gray uniform. She carried a small bag and had one of Pin's old skirts and blouses on a hanger, along with her new black uniform.

She handed the skirt and blouse back to Pin. "Thank you for letting me use these."

"You're welcome, but consider them a gift. You'll need something to wear on your day off."

"A day without work?" Annie shook her head. "And thank you for finding someone to handle the eggs and deliveries for me."

"You'll be busy enough at the Hall."

"Whoever takes over the eggs can keep the money they earn."

"Perhaps we could donate it to the church?"

"I'd like that."

Pin took a long look at her. "You look ready for a new job."

"I am ready," Annie said.

"Mrs. Halsing will approve of your uniforms, and of you."

"Do you think so?"

Amid her doubt, Annie looked younger than her fourteen years. Pin drew her into an embrace. "I know you'll do well. For I know you will always seek to do more than is asked."

Annie drew back and looked into Pin's eyes. "I want them to know how much I appreciate this opportunity. And I want you to know how much I appreciate all you've done for me. You saved me, Miss Pin. You and Dr. Jonathan."

Pin experienced a sudden thought. "You saved us."

"How did I do that?"

"By giving us a way to see beyond ourselves. Helping you helped us."

Annie laughed and bobbed a curtsy. "Always glad to be of service, miss."

Pin was sad to see her go. "I'll come and visit, and when you have a free day, come to the workshop and we'll have more lessons."

"I'd like that."

Annie squeezed Pin's hand and was gone, down the stairs.

Pin heard Annie accost her mother with another round of gratitude. Then she leaned against the doorjamb and offered her own thanks to the Almighty who definitely worked in mysterious ways.

Annie stood before Mrs. Halsing, feeling quite natty in her new gray uniform.

The housekeeper nodded in appreciation. "I am impressed. You made that yesterday?"

"With Miss Billings's help. Yes, I did. And this black one too."

The woman took hold of the edge of the sleeve, checking the stitches. "So you are handy with needle and thread?"

"I want to be. I have much to learn."

Mrs. Halsing let go of the sleeve. "A commendable mind-set. Perhaps as time passes we can find some sewing work for you."

"I'd like that very much. . . . Ma'am or Mrs. Halsing?"

"Mrs. Halsing. Put your things over there. Then come with me and I'll introduce you to Watkins. She will be your direct superior. She reports to me, and I report directly to Lady Newley. Please her and you please me and our mistress. Understand?"

"I do, Mrs. Halsing."

"Come along then. There is always work to be done in such a great house as Crompton Hall. Especially since Christmas Eve is but four days away."

"I will help in any way I can."

Christmas at the Hall. No matter what work needed to be done, Annie would do it with a grateful and expectant heart.

A thought hit Jonathan in the middle of the night, rousing him: *Pin apologized yesterday, but she never mentioned marriage. That's all she used to talk about. Does she even want to get married anymore?*

He sat up in bed, shaken. With his thoughts stirred, a new fact moved front and center: he was to blame. He had been preoccupied with his career, Alfie's death, and himself.

The revelation led to an idea, a way to make up for all his shortcomings. . . .

Jonathan knocked on the door of Crompton Hall. The butler answered.

"Is Lady Newley available for a visit, please?"

"I will check, Mr. Evers. Dr. Evers. Excuse me."

Jonathan was led into the drawing room. It was not his first time, for Crompton Hall was known for its hospitality to residents of Summerfield. But he had never spoken to Lady Newley privately.

He admired the portrait above the fireplace of a beautiful woman wearing an extravagant gown.

"That's my mother-in-law," Lady Newley said as she entered the room. "She died soon after my husband was born."

"She's very beautiful."

"In all ways, from what I've heard. I try to do her proud." She nodded to a chair. When they were both settled, she said, "How can I help you, Dr. Evers?"

"I understand you have a cottage to let. The Horton place?"

She smiled. "You are not the first to show interest. Pin asked to see it not long ago."

"I know," he said. "Is it still available?"

She studied him a moment, her eyes wise. "It is. But I don't believe you've seen it."

"I haven't."

"And you wish to rent it, sight unseen?"

"Pin told me all about it. She loved it. If it makes her happy, it makes me happy."

"With that kind of attitude you will have a strong marriage."

"I hope so."

"Don't hope. Make it a strong marriage by working at it every day."

"I will." He left off the word *try*.

"All this talk of marriage... I was sure Etta would have told me about your engagement."

"She hasn't mentioned it because I haven't proposed yet. I was hoping to do so on Christmas Eve. My family spends the evening at the Billingses' home."

"What a marvelous present that will be. You will make Pin very happy."

"And she me. If she accepts."

"You doubt she will?"

He didn't want to go into it. "I pray she will. That is why I want to secure the cottage for us."

She scrutinized him a moment. "You and Pin have been close since childhood, have you not?"

"Forever and always."

"It's nice when friendship turns into love. My husband and I were friends before we promised ourselves to each other."

Promise. Suddenly Jonathan remembered one very special promise he and Pin had made years before. And with that memory came an idea, a perfect idea that would please Pin immensely.

"Jonathan?"

"Yes. Sorry. So, may we let the cottage, Lady Newley?"

With a nod she confirmed their business. "You may."

They spoke of money, and Jonathan agreed to bring the payment by.

"Let me get you the key. I'm sure you have much planning to do."

Jonathan hoped he wouldn't run into Pin during this next part of his mission—or anyone, for that matter. Luckily, the day was brisk and windy, meaning the old men who usually gathered in the square were cozily at home. Other than a few people walking to and fro, the square was quiet.

He sat on the low stone wall that formed a circle around the pump and felt for the one special rock that—when removed—would reveal their childhood hiding place. He wasn't sure there would still be anything in it, as the last time he'd put something inside was on New Year's Eve, 1899. The day of Pin's promise that one day they would wed.

With relief, he felt a handkerchief wrapped around the other item and placed them in his pocket without looking at them. He returned the rock to its place. Then he walked toward home but detoured to a copse of trees so he'd have privacy. He unwrapped the handkerchief to reveal the whittled figure of Pin that had been his gift to her. That once again *could* be his gift to her with a little work.

He took time to look at the handkerchief where Pin had embroidered: *Penelope and Jonathan Forever. 1900.* He smiled as another idea came to him.

He needed to work fast. He only had a few days.

Jonathan sat at the kitchen table and awkwardly held a needle and thread.

His mother looked on. "As a doctor you're going to have to get better at that."

"I can stitch up a wound better than I can stitch fabric." He stopped, took a new breath, and bent his fingers to get their circulation going again. The straight letters were easy, but the circular ones required many more stitches.

"I'd be willing to do that for you," Mother said.

"I have to do it myself."

She put a hand on his shoulder. "I didn't know you were a romantic."

He chuckled. "Neither did I."

Annie leaned on the railing as she walked to the top floor of the Hall for the last time that day. Her legs hurt. Her feet hurt. Her back hurt. Just a few more steps and she could fall into bed.

She straightened up when she heard steps behind her. She glanced back and saw it was one of the lady's maids. She moved to the side to let her pass. "Good evening, Miss Miller."

The woman stopped a step below Annie. "I hear you can sew."

"Some. Yes. I'm still learning, ma'am."

"Miss Dougard and I may have some mending for you to do. Do you have time for that?"

"I will make time."

She crooked a finger and Annie followed her to a bedroom at the far end of the hall. It was large enough for a table and chair, and a comfy cushioned chair near the fireplace. Miss Miller handed a skirt, needle, scissors, and thread to Annie. "The hem is coming out. Miss Henrietta wishes to wear it for Christmas Eve."

So much for falling into bed. "I will get it done, Miss Miller."

Annie carried the supplies to her tiny room. She lit the lantern and got undressed, carefully putting her uniform on its hanger, hung on a nail. She pulled the satchel from under the bed—which contained her undergarments, a toothbrush, paste, and comb—and retrieved her nightgown—or Miss Pin's nightgown. Everything she owned was a gift from Miss Pin.

Annie desperately wanted to remove her shoes but didn't dare because of the chill. There was no heat, and she noticed frost forming on the inside of the small window. She pulled the quilt off the bed, wrapped it around herself, sat on the chair, and mended the hem.

Although she felt like complaining, she resisted. This is what she wanted—to be utilized for her sewing ability. Yes, her body ached and begged for sleep, but she had her own room, her own bed with plentiful covers and a pillow, indoor plumbing down the hall, and a purpose to her days. With her attitude properly adjusted, the task was accomplished, and her first day was at its end.

Chapter Eight

Annie's stomach knotted as she knocked on the door of the housekeeper's rooms. She knew what she was about to ask was presumptuous—especially since she'd only been on the job two days—but she felt compelled to try.

She almost hoped Mrs. Halsing would say no.

"Come in."

Annie slipped inside a cozy parlor where Mrs. Halsing sat at a table making a list. "Miss Wood. How are you faring?"

"Quite well, ma'am. I am happy to be working here."

Mrs. Halsing set her pen down and cocked her head. "Is there a problem?"

"No, ma'am. Not at all. I was just. . .just wanting. . ."

"Out with it, girl."

"I would like to go visit my parents in the jail to see how *they* are faring. I would go quickly, just an hour at the most. I would get all my work done first, and—"

The woman clasped her hands on the table. "We are all sorry

about your previous situation. It is very magnanimous of you to want to see them."

Annie wasn't sure what magnanimous meant, and her face must have revealed the same, for Mrs. Halsing said, "It's very kind and generous of you."

Annie shrugged. She wasn't sure what her motives were.

"You may go after the bedrooms are cleaned. But you need to be quick about it. There is much to do to make ready for Christmas."

Annie smiled.

"You smile at hard work?"

"I smile at the thought of Christmas and any sort of festivity. It's all so new to me."

"You've never celebrated Christmas?"

She thought back, wanting to tell the truth. She remembered her parents grousing about not having enough of this or that. They'd drink themselves into a stupor on both the Eve and the Day while Annie played some sort of quiet game with Alfie. One time, Annie had secretly shared a few slices of fruitcake from the bakery with him. But none of those things counted toward a true celebration, and so Annie said, "No."

"You will certainly witness celebration aplenty at the Hall. And a moving service at the church too. And on the day after, on Boxing Day, you'll find a little gift from the master and mistress."

"A gift? Really?"

Mrs. Halsing's forehead tightened, and she looked away. "Go on, girl. Get your work done so you can have your visit."

This was not the first time Annie had been to the jail. She'd visited her father when he'd been caught stealing, and once for poaching on the earl's grounds. Until now her mother had always managed to avoid the place.

Life was always better during the few days Pa was contained. But Annie and Alfie knew that the better would turn to worse when he came home. He never learned from his mistakes because they weren't his mistakes at all. The constable was to blame, or the farmer who'd hired him, or King Edward, and especially his own children. It did no good to argue the logic of it either. No good at all.

The constable looked up from his desk when Annie entered. "Morning, Annie."

"Can I see them?"

He gave her an incredulous look. "You really want to?"

She didn't answer.

He stood. "I'm used to having your father in here, but to have the two of them. . ." He took up his keys, shaking his head. "Do they always argue so much?"

"All the time."

Before he opened the door to lead her to the cells, he paused. "I hear you got a position at the Hall. Do you like it?"

"Very much. They are nice people."

"That they are." He put a hand on her shoulder. "I'm glad you're safe now, Annie. I'm just sorry I didn't see the truth sooner."

To finally have people understand was worth the world to her.

He unlocked the door and they went into a larger room with a narrow aisle separating two cells that had iron bars from floor to ceiling.

"When do we eat, Hawkins, you manky prat? Yer treating us like animals. We're starving in—" Pa saw Annie. "Well, I'll be. It's about time you come. Get us outta here, girl."

"There's no getting out until you're tried," the constable said. "And punished."

Ma reached between the bars to touch Annie's shoulder, but Annie stepped back. "Ah, there now, girl. Be a good one and see what yous can do fer us."

Although Annie wanted to leave, she needed to say her piece. "If I could speak to them alone, Constable?"

He hesitated but said, "I'll be right outside." He pointed at his prisoners. "Behave."

As soon as he left they began prattling on about wanting this or that.

She had to interrupt to be heard. "I got a j—" She stopped herself before saying "job," realizing it might be best they didn't know where she was staying lest they cause trouble for Lord and Lady Newley.

"What you say?"

She shook her head. They'd never been interested in her before. Why would they be now? She got to the point. "You hurt me. You hurt Alfie to the point of his death, and I—"

"Don't you dare blame 'is death on us," Pa said. "The brat never would behave and—"

"It's that doctor's fault. He coulda saved 'im but didn't," Ma said.

"And yer fault for not getting 'im there quicker," Pa added.

Annie sighed deeply, letting all the could-have-saids fall away. "I'm going now."

"No!" Pa said. "You can't leave us here!"

"It's nearly Christmas," Ma said.

Now you acknowledge the day? Annie turned to leave.

"Wait! Do something to get us out, girl," Pa said. "You's pretty enough. See if you can beguile old Hawkins into. . .you know. . ."

Annie couldn't believe what she was hearing. "You want me to. . . ?" It was so despicable she couldn't say it out loud. Instead she left the room and headed directly for the door leading outside.

"That was short. You all right, Annie?" the constable asked.

She paused at the door, turned toward him, and said words she'd never expected to say. "Actually, I am quite well, thank you."

With that, she hurried back to the Hall and to her new life.

It was a tradition in the Billings family for Pin and her father to go into the woods to find and cut a tree they would decorate Christmas Eve. If Jonathan was in Summerfield, he came along.

As he did, this year. They'd found a nice fir about six feet in height, and made quick work of the cutting. Now the men were carrying it back to the house. "At least there's no snow on the ground," Papa said. "Your mother doesn't like us to drag in snow."

Pin looked skyward. "I like snow on Christmas. It's not a real Christmas without it."

"Actually, it is," Jonathan said.

He could be so literal. "You know what I mean."

"Actually, I do."

She'd missed his smile.

The men got the tree through the door with a flurry of pine needles and attached it to the wooden stand that Papa had made many trees ago. They set it upright, ready for the decorating on Christmas Eve.

Mama studied its tilt. "A little to the left."

"You just said to the right," Papa said.

"You went too far."

With another adjustment it was just right. Pin noticed there were sheets of pretty paper, scissors, and a glue pot on the dining table.

"Get to it, you two," Mama said. "I'm bringing some sweets 'round to friends. I leave the task of paper chains to you."

"And I have a few Christmas orders to attend to," Papa said.

Pin was glad for their absence. She had something important to tell Jonathan, and it could only be shared alone.

"I'll cut the strips," he said, taking a seat.

"You always leave me the pasting."

"Because you always tell me I make a mess with it."

She shrugged. "I'll do the pasting."

They found a rhythm between them. Someday they'd do everything together.

Someday.

Which led to her gift. "I have two gifts for you," she said as she created another paper link.

"I like gifts. But shouldn't we wait until Christmas?"

She shook her head, not wanting interruptions. "I need to give them to you today. The first one is this." She retrieved the shirt bundle. "I made it for you. Twice, actually."

"What does that mean?"

"Open it."

He untied the ribbon, parted the calico, and smiled. He held it up by the shoulders. "It's beautiful." He leaned over and kissed her. "Thank you so much. I will wear it on Christmas Eve."

"I cut up the first shirt I made you for Alfie."

He touched her hand. "How nice of you to think of him."

She shrugged. "Which meant I had to start over. I stayed at the workshop until two in the morning finishing this one."

"I'm sure it will fit perfectly."

Pin couldn't worry about that. In the scheme of things, the shirt was nearly inconsequential. This second gift was the important one. She sighed deeply. "Now, for gift number two."

"You look very serious."

"I am." She made herself smile. She didn't want him to think it was a bad gift. "This gift can't be unwrapped or even held in your hands."

"Is this a riddle?"

Perhaps it could be. She pointed to the clock on the mantel. "What does a clock measure?"

"Time."

She pushed aside the paper chain. "My gift to you is the gift of time. Our love has never been in question, but since your return I have pushed you toward marriage in a way that was not very ladylike."

"I didn't mind."

"Yes, you did. Admit it."

He shrugged. "Just a little. Perhaps."

She nodded at his admission and took his hands. "And so, Jonathan, I give you the gift of time. I will not push or prod or harass you. Perhaps you are right when you say we aren't quite ready for marriage." She studied him, gauging his reaction.

He didn't have any. He just stared at the table.

"Say something. Please."

It still took a moment for him to respond. "I appreciate your gift very much." His smile was tenuous. "Though I will say it's not what I expected."

"Me neither. Patience is not my virtue."

He drew her hand to his lips. "Thank you."

She accepted his thanks but was rather disappointed he didn't argue with her.

Jonathan hurried home amid blowing winds. Snow was coming. He could smell it.

His thoughts were consumed with Pin's gift: time. Pin, who had been pushing for marriage for the past six years, wanted to wait? He hadn't known how to respond when she'd agreed with him: that they might not be ready for marriage.

Had he said that?

To ease her mind he'd wanted to tell her about his gifts right then, but patience had prevailed. Just a few more days and he could fully show her his heart.

Once home he slipped inside, not wanting the door open any longer than it had to be in the cold.

His parents sat by the fire, reading. "Did you find a tree?"

"We did. And made paper chains."

"A tradition you've missed a few times over the years," Father said.

"Are you finished with your gift for Pin, Jonathan?" Mother asked.

"Not yet."

"What gift?" Father asked.

"A secret gift," Mother teased.

He needed a favor. "Mother? If you please?"

"Another secret?" Father asked.

"I need a woman's advice."

He waved them away, and they stepped into Jonathan's bedroom. "I have rented the Horton place for Pin and me."

Her eyes sparkled. "So you are proposing?"

"On Christmas Eve."

"She'll be so happy."

"As will I. But. . .I would like to bring her there and show her the cottage, and have it be nice inside. It needs some cleaning. Perhaps a fire going? Something festive inside?"

"Get her a tabletop tree."

"But her family has a large one at home."

Mother shook her head. "You don't understand. She won't care about the size of it beyond the fact it is hers. Yours." She squeezed his hand. "I'm so proud of you—of your heart. You'll make a good husband. You are a good man."

"So I'm a man now?"

She grinned. "I believe you are."

"There's so much to do. I still have work left on her gift, and with the cleaning and such. . ."

"You finish the gift and I'll help you with the cottage. If she comes calling here, I'll have your father say you are working on a surprise."

"Which is true."

"Such a surprise!" His mother actually giggled.

Chapter Nine

Christmas Eve

Annie and another housemaid, Bessie, worked together to tie garland to the walnut balusters on the stairs at Crompton Hall. The heady smell of pine tickled her nostrils.

Bessie began to sing softly. "Deck the halls with boughs of holly, fa la la la la, la la la la. . ."

Annie wasn't sure of the words but tried to hum along.

Bessie paused. "You can get the fa-la parts even if you don't know the words."

Yes, she could.

After many verses Miss Henrietta appeared at the top of the stairs and joined in. "Fast away the old year passes, fa la la la la, la la la la. Hail the new, ye lads and lasses, fa la la la la, la la la la. . ."

Annie felt as though the words were written for her. Indeed the old had passed and she was ready to hail the new. The three of them finished the song with gusto and much laughter.

Miss Henrietta walked halfway down the stairs, stopping near Annie. She was wearing the skirt Annie had mended.

Annie stopped her work and placed her back to the wall. She bobbed a curtsy.

"I'm glad you're here, Annie."

"As am I, Miss Henrietta."

After she moved on, Bessie said, "She's a nice one, she is. Always a kind word."

Until recently Annie hadn't realized how many kind people there were in the world.

Fa la la la la.

Jonathan's stomach was aflutter as he and his parents helped decorate the Christmas tree at the Billingses'. Warm wassail was served, along with fruitcake, stained-glass biscuits to hang from the tree, smoked salmon on toast, and other menu items he failed to notice because he couldn't imagine eating very much with his stomach in such a state.

"Are you feeling all right?" Pin asked as they draped their paper chain on the tree.

"I'm just excited for Christmas."

"You certainly look handsome in your new shirt. The seamstress is very talented."

He snuck a kiss to her cheek. "So I've heard." He was glad when they finished the task. "I have a surprise for you."

She grinned. "When I stopped by yesterday, your father said

you were up to something."

He took both her hands in his. "I need to take you somewhere."

"Where?"

"You can't know. In fact. . ." He pulled a scarf out of his jacket pocket that he'd borrowed from his mother. "I need to blindfold you once we get in the carriage."

"Well now," Pin's mother said. "This is secretive."

He was disappointed the parents had overheard. "We'll be back soon."

He saw his mother confer with Mrs. Billings who nodded and smiled. Jonathan hoped Pin didn't notice the conspiratorial looks and quickly helped her on with her coat and hat.

They stepped outside to his parents' carriage. He helped her in and tucked a blanket around her legs. Next, the blindfold.

"This is very mysterious," she said.

He took up the reins. "Indeed it is."

She linked her arm in his and off they drove until. . .he pulled in front of the Horton cottage and lifted her down.

"Can I remove it yet?" she asked.

"Just a minute. . ." He positioned her just-so on the walk to the front door. Then, with a prayer for God's blessings, he said, "You can remove your blindfold."

She did so and blinked to get her eyes seeing again. And then. . .

Pin couldn't believe her eyes. She stifled a gasp and her throat tightened.

"This is the Horton cottage."

Jonathan held out a key. "It's now the Evers cottage." Then he got down on one knee. "Penelope Billings, would you do me the honor of being my wife?"

The perfection of the moment was nearly too much. "Of course I will." She drew him to standing and kissed him.

More than once.

He lured her out of the embrace by dangling a key close. "Would you like to do the honors?"

Her hand shook as she used the key in the lock. She remembered seeing the cottage—after all, she had chosen it to be theirs a few weeks ago. And yet when she opened the door she saw a cottage transformed.

Her eyes were immediately drawn to the fire in the fireplace. The upholstered chair she'd chosen for Jonathan on her first visit sat before it, while another chair for herself—adorned with a cushion—sat nearby. She was drawn forward and put her hand on what would be *her* chair. "It's perfect," she whispered.

"Mother and I spent all of yesterday cleaning it up and making it nice for you. There's still much to do to make it our own, but—"

Pin turned and saw a small Christmas tree set on the middle of the kitchen table. It was decorated with holly swigs, red ribbon, and a small paper chain.

She began to cry and sought his shoulder. "It's glorious."

He comforted her then stood apart and handed her a handkerchief. But as she was going to use it she saw that it was embroidered. She looked at it more closely. "It's the handkerchief

I made six years ago."

"But with a new embellishment." He pointed to the shakily embroidered numbers under the "1900." "1907," he said. "At the turn of the century we made our first promise of a promise to be wed someday, and we *will* be, next year."

"You sewed this?"

He sighed. "From now on I will leave the fabric stitching to you."

She held the handkerchief to her chest. "I will treasure it always." Then she realized where he'd gotten it. "Our hiding place in the stone wall. I haven't thought of it in years."

"Remember what else was in it?"

"Of course. You'd whittled a little figurine of me."

He stepped to the tree, retrieved something from beneath it, and gave it to her.

She recognized the wood carving of herself, but there was another figure now. "This is you," she said.

"It is," he said. "And look. I carved it so my arm fits around your shoulders." He manipulated the two figures in a side embrace.

Pin stepped beside him, and together they mimicked the carvings. "We hid them as we hid the depth of our love. But now we will find a place of honor for them in our home. Now our love is for the whole world to see!"

He kissed her passionately then led her to their chairs by the fire. "This feels utterly right, doesn't it?"

"It's everything I've ever dreamed of." She needed to touch him, but his chair was too far away. She stood and scooted her chair closer so they could hold hands, side by side, in their own home.

Suddenly, she thought of a question. "When did you rent this place?"

"Last Thursday."

She nodded. "I gave it up last Monday."

"Gave up what?"

"Gave up the thought that this cottage would ever be ours. Mother told me I had to be patient. And so, I gave it up."

"And God gave it back."

Her heart swelled with gratitude. "He most certainly did."

Jonathan nodded with understanding. "So that's why you gave me the gift of time?"

"I was trying to do the right thing."

He squeezed her hand. "*This* is the right thing. *We* are the right thing."

A thought came to her. "I do believe God always planned for us to be together."

"As do I."

"But He wanted *this* Pin and Jonathan to be together, not who we were but who we are now." She had another thought. "I do believe we've kept our promise but also fulfilled our promise—our potential to be better people."

He smiled and drew her to his lap where she snuggled against him. "Do you want to hear what's really exciting?"

"Of course."

"The Pin and Jonathan we are now, are not the Pin and Jonathan we will be."

She nuzzled into his neck, loving the scent of him. "I promise we'll get even better."

"Indeed we will."

They sealed Pin's promise with a kiss. Or two.

Nancy Moser is an award-winning Kansas author of thirty novels that share a common message: we each have a unique purpose—the trick is to find out what it is. Her genres include contemporary and historical novels including *The Pattern Artist*, *The Fashion Designer, Love of the Summerfields*, *The Invitation*, and the Christy Award–winning *Time Lottery*. She is a fan of anything antique—humans included. Visit her website at www.nancymoser.com.

Mended Hearts

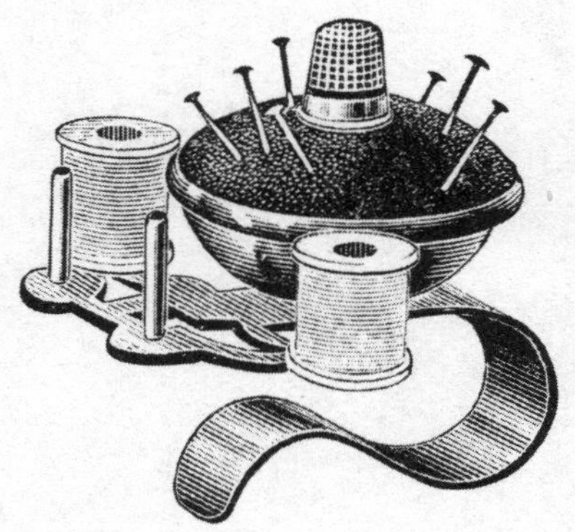

by Stephanie Grace Whitson

Patchwork? Ah, no! It was memory, imagination, history, biography, joy, sorrow, philosophy, religion, romance, realism, life, love, and death: and over all, like a halo, the love of the artist for his work and soul's longing for earthly immortality.

—Aunt Jane of Kentucky

Chapter One

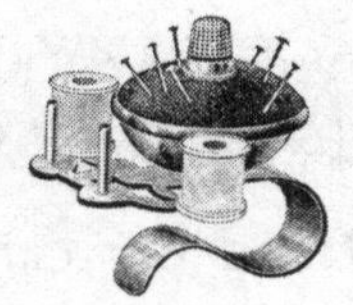

York County, Nebraska
January 1890

When the far-off dot on the road finally transformed itself into a bay mare with a splash of white between her eyes, a surge of hope lapped at the edges of Adam Friesen's fear. He turned away from the bedroom window, forcing a smile as he spoke to his wife. "The storm's staying to the west. And I see Aunt Jennie's buggy. She's almost here."

Esther's knuckles went white. She clutched the top of the patchwork quilt covering her pregnant body. Terror shone in her dark eyes as she gasped, "I cannot be having a baby today. It's too soon."

"Aunt Jennie will know what to do." Adam hoped that was true. Esther had suffered horribly bringing four-year-old Anna into the world. Things had to be different this time.

"Go," Esther said. "Tell her—" She bit the words off as she moaned, "Tell her to hurry."

Adam fled the room. He rushed through the kitchen, grabbed his coat off the hook by the door, and loped toward the drive, pulling on his coat as he went. The moment Aunt Jennie pulled the horse to a halt, Adam rushed forward. "It's too soon," he said.

Aunt Jennie didn't reply right away. Instead, she handed her bag and cane over and climbed down. Once she'd shaken her heavy cape into place and recaptured her cane and bag, she said, "You were right to send Anna with Wyatt to fetch me. Lizzie will keep her occupied." She paused. "Wyatt has gone after Molly and Mrs. Rhodes. They'll be here soon enough." She glanced toward the dark clouds gathering in the west. "I only hope they get here before that storm." Clucking her tongue as if to scold the weather into obedience, she hurried across the yard toward the house, turning back just long enough to call out, "You must pray, Adam."

Adam nodded. Only when the plump old woman had disappeared inside and closed the door behind her did he lead Aunt Jennie's fine little mare toward the barn, grateful to be out of the cold wind, grateful for the work of unhitching her and turning her into a stall, thankful Anna was safe with Aunt Lizzie, glad he'd hired Wyatt Dahl last fall. Thanks to that, he hadn't had to leave Esther alone to go for the midwife.

Esther had had a hard time bringing Anna into the world. As he leaned against a stall door, Adam obeyed Aunt Jennie and prayed, thankful the devout midwife couldn't know what he was saying. *Lord God in heaven, I ask forgiveness. I have not loved her as I should.*

At the sound of approaching hoofbeats, Adam went to stand

just inside the open barn door. Snow had begun to fall. Wyatt was returning with Molly and Mrs. Rhodes. *Thanks be to God.* Before Adam reached the buggy, the women had climbed down and run for the house.

Wyatt worked quickly to unhitch the buggy horse and lead it inside, encouraging Adam to leave the chores to him. But Adam shook his head. Esther was in good hands, he said. And yet, the moment his sturdy mare was in its stall, Adam hurried to the house. Oddly, Molly was donning her coat when he stepped inside.

At sight of Adam, she pulled her coat off and hung it up. She gestured toward the empty bucket sitting on the table. "Aunt Jennie says we need more water. When you get back inside, put it on to heat. I'll stoke the fire before I go back to—"

An unearthly wail interrupted her. Adam took a step toward the bedroom, but Molly stopped him. "Water first. And more firewood." She nodded toward the kitchen window. "It seems the snow will last."

Adam looked outside. Clumps of white gathered at the base of the tall grass growing alongside the corral fence. Esther's flower garden was little more than a plot of uneven lumps hidden beneath a layer of white. Another wail sounded from the bedroom, and Molly hurried away. The wail ascended to new heights.

I have not loved her as I should. Please, Lord. Esther screamed. His mouth went dry, and he headed into the swirling snow. *Please—if only You will help her, I will*—he broke off. He supposed it was a sin to bargain with the Almighty. Surely Deacon Lynch, who spoke of a God who was a consuming fire, would say so. *A consuming fire.*

He pondered the concept as he lowered the bucket into the well.

As he drew the bucket up, he prayed. *Please do not consume us. She is a good wife, strong and true. We have come a long road, bound together by vows spoken out of duty. Give us time together, and I will praise You at every opportunity for the rest of my life. I will build the pews for the new church. And I will love her. I will.*

Returning to the house with the bucket of water, Adam poured it into a pot atop the stove. No sounds escaped from the bedroom. He went back outside for more wood. *I will prove my devotion. And give thanks.* He began to list blessings. *Anna*—not the child of his loins but surely the child of his heart. *Good friends*—not the least of them the women helping to usher Esther's second and Adam's first child into the world. *Esther—who loves me. At last, she loves me.*

It had not been an easy road for Adam and Esther Friesen. Nearly four years ago, a wicked stranger had taken Esther's innocence, leaving her bruised and alone. She would never say who had committed that horrible act. It didn't matter, she said, when she confided in Molly. It was done and he was gone. But Esther was with child. When she finally told her best friend, Molly—who was also Adam's sister—Esther also confided her plans to run away.

When his weeping sister told Adam what had happened, Adam offered a brash solution. "If she'll have me, I'll marry her. No one need ever know."

Esther resisted at first. After all, Adam was several years younger than she. But his hazel eyes were pools of caring, his deep voice convincing. "You don't want to be with strangers when—you know. You'll be wanting your mother when it's time. Molly too." He stopped short, his face burning with embarrassment at the mere mention of something so intimate as a birthing. Finally, he croaked. "I can provide for you. For both of you."

It was true. Adam Friesen had inherited his parents' farm. He was hardworking. A solid member of the community. Dependable. Finally, Esther murmured, "You—you'd do that? For me?"

There was disbelief in her voice, but just beneath the disbelief Adam detected the faintest note of hope. And relief. The import of what he'd said clutched at his midsection, but Adam Friesen was not one to back down. Besides that, he'd be a hero to Molly and Esther, an attractive prospect.

"I would," Adam said. "I will."

Tears came to Esther's eyes. She put her hand on his arm and murmured, "God bless you, Adam Friesen."

Seven months later, Anna tore her way into the world. By then, Adam had learned to be Esther's friend. It was quite some time before the rest came. But it did. Eventually. And so, as he carried an armful of wood through the falling snow toward the house, Adam Friesen prayed. *God in heaven, save my wife. Our child. Our love.*

April 1890

St. Louis, Missouri

Mere words shouldn't have the power to suck the air out of a room. Seventeen-year-old Rachel Ellsworth knew that. And yet, all she could manage was a little gasp. Pressing one gloved hand to her corseted midsection, she concentrated. *In. . .out. In. . .out.*

Paying the undertaker had emptied Papa's account—his *only* account. The pastor assigned to take Papa's place would arrive in ten days, and Rachel must vacate her home. She'd expected that, of course. The church owned the parsonage and its furnishings. What she did not realize was that there was no money. None.

She clutched the arms of the upholstered chair. *In. . .out. In. . .out.*

The middle-aged woman seated to her right put a comforting hand on Rachel's arm. Next, she scowled at the young man standing behind them and scolded, "Don't just *stand* there, Landis. Get the dear girl a glass of water."

Landis Grove obeyed his mother, striding across the room to a side table. Everything seemed to slow down. Rachel watched as he lifted a crystal pitcher, poured water into one of the half-dozen tumblers arranged on a silver tray, and then crossed back to where she sat.

"Just a sip, dear," Landis's mother said. "I know it's a shock, but you're going to be all right."

Rachel took the glass and gulped water. She drew an almost normal breath before murmuring, "Thank you."

"You must listen to Mother," Landis said. He was still standing behind her, and his voice came as if from on high. "You're going to be all right. We'll take care of you. In fact, we've already taken steps to do just that."

Rachel's pulse quickened. *The Groves have made plans.* Landis was going to propose! She'd promised Father she wouldn't marry until she was eighteen, but he would understand. Crisis sometimes forced adjustments, and Rachel could think of no greater crisis than the news the attorney had just delivered. Reverend John Ellsworth had left his only child both homeless and penniless.

"Mother's taken everything in hand," Landis said. "You won't have to worry about a thing."

Mrs. Grove leaned forward and spoke to her husband, seated on Rachel's left. At his wife's encouragement, Mr. Grove reached inside his suit coat, withdrew an envelope, and handed it over. "It's addressed to Mrs. Grove and me because Mrs. Grove made the contact. But the note is to you."

"It will warm your heart, dear," Mrs. Grove said. "Your aunts sound delightful."

My aunts? Rachel took the envelope. Pulling out a single sheet of notepaper, she read.

April 10, 1890
Lost Creek, Nebraska

Dearest Rachel,

Please forgive us for not coming to you the moment we heard the news. A late spring storm laid down a sheet of ice last week, and one night after attending a particularly difficult lying-in, I slipped and fell. While no bones were broken, I currently need a cane to navigate. Lizzie finally convinced me that our attending John's service would only complicate matters for you.

It has pained us greatly to leave you alone to bear the burden of your beloved father's passing. Please know that while we have not been with you in person, your name has been on our hearts and in our prayers several times a day since we received the news.

Mr. and Mrs. Grove have kindly informed us of the difficulties arising regarding your father's earthly estate. Remember that such things are mere trifles in light of the eternal treasures John and Katie laid up in heaven. Do not forget that your heavenly Father knows what you have need of. Lizzie and I both hope that you will see His provision in this letter.

Please, Rachel, come to us at your first opportunity. Our way of life is simple, but we have prepared a room for you—both in our home and in our hearts. We hope soon to receive word that you have accepted our invitation.

In the Love of the Lamb,
Your aunts Lizzie & Jennie Meeker

The moment Rachel lowered the letter, Mrs. Grove reached over and squeezed her arm. "Now isn't that wonderful? Such a sure testimony to the heavenly Father's promise to provide for His own." She paused. "I can't say I'd have the kind of faith Reverend Ellsworth did in that regard. I'd never be able to leave my own child penniless, but—"

"Martha!" Mr. Grove scolded.

"Rachel knows I don't mean to criticize," Mrs. Grove retorted. "No one supported Reverend Ellsworth more faithfully than I. I'm just saying—"

"Yes," Mr. Grove said quickly. "We know." His voice was warm when he spoke to Rachel. "Your father was one of the best men I've ever known. And he raised a fine daughter."

"Indeed," Mrs. Grove said. With a forced little laugh, she added, "I wouldn't be surprised if we have to do battle with your aunts when the time comes for you to return to us. But it's obvious they are very keen on having you accept their invitation. Now, we've discussed it with Landis, and while he's reluctant to let you go, he understands how important it is for us to honor your father's wishes regarding your future plans." She looked up at Landis again. "Don't you, dear?"

Landis cleared his throat. "We did promise to wait until you're eighteen. And it's less than a year away."

He wasn't going to propose, after all. Feeling numb, Rachel nodded. *Never mind. He will soon enough. You'll be eighteen in November.* She glanced down at the letter again. The invitation did sound sincere. *Jennie and Lizzie.* Rachel had only faint memories of the two spinsters. She'd never met them before they arrived on the Ellsworths' doorstep soon after Papa sent the telegram informing them of their sister Katie's death—a terrible shock, for Mama hadn't been ill. She simply did not wake up one morning.

In the days following their arrival in St. Louis, Jennie and Lizzie moved quietly in the background, cleaning, arranging things for Mama's wake, managing the kitchen with amazing efficiency—essentially doing everything they could to help Rachel and her father navigate the first few days. Then, one morning a week after Mama's funeral, Aunt Lizzie said it was time for them to be going home.

Regret coursed through Rachel for not making the effort to stay in touch with her aunts since then. She'd been too lost in a fog of grief and too overwhelmed by the effort to keep Papa going to maintain a correspondence. Letters arrived weekly for the first year and then less often as time went on. After all, she didn't really know Mama's family.

The Meekers of Pennsylvania had been headed west when Mama met and fell in love with a young minister named John Ellsworth. Mama married and the rest of her family left her behind in Missouri. Rachel knew very little of what had happened to the family after that, beyond the fact that they'd finally settled in some far-off Nebraska town. She skimmed her aunts' letter again. *We have prepared a room for you—both in our home and in our hearts.*

Rachel remembered Aunt Jennie's round smiling face and kind voice. Tall, willowy Aunt Lizzie resembled Mama more—except where Mama's voice was mellow, Aunt Lizzie's was terse in a way that bordered on stern. Still, the invitation seemed sincere. And the Groves, Landis included, were clearly not going to invite Rachel into their family. Yet. What choice did she have?

"It's for the best," Mrs. Grove said.

"It's just for a little while," Landis croaked.

"But—my paintings." Just hearing the words made Rachel feel

small-minded. With everything that had happened, surely she must sound foolish asking about her paintings. Her cheeks grew warm as she blushed with embarrassment.

But Landis understood. He reassured her. "Mother says we'll have them wrapped for safekeeping and stored at the bank."

"In the vault," Mrs. Grove said. "We know how much they mean to you."

Leave them? All of them? Rachel protested. "But I can't just—leave them." She looked up at Landis. "You understand—don't you?" He had to understand. After all, wasn't the Grand Tour part of their wedding trip plans? He was going to take her to the Louvre in Paris. They were going to attend the next Exhibition.

"Of course we understand," Mrs. Grove said. "Which is why you must select two or three pieces to take with you. To help you feel at home." She paused. "Now, I know it's been a lot to digest, dear, but with the subject of your paintings, I believe we've found a pleasant way to conclude an unpleasant meeting. Shall we give Mr. Carpenter his office back?" She didn't wait for Rachel to respond before rising from her chair.

Rachel tucked her aunts' letter in the beaded bag at her wrist and took Landis's arm. As they left Mr. Carpenter's office and stepped into the midmorning sunlight, Mrs. Grove suggested they all proceed to the parsonage so that Rachel could choose the paintings she wanted to take with her on the train. "That will give the movers plenty of time to properly wrap the rest of your things for their removal." She gave a deep sigh. "I know it seems that everything is happening very quickly, but it is an unfortunate fact of life that the world continues to revolve and we are expected to spin with it."

Rachel fought back tears as Landis helped her into the Groves' carriage. It was only right to accept her aunts' invitation. Papa wouldn't have wanted the church he loved to go without a shepherd for long. Still, as the carriage pulled away from the curb and Landis's mother chattered away about the building of crates to protect her art and the packing of her easel and canvases, Rachel's sense of foreboding grew.

What was it Mrs. Grove had just said? Something about the world continuing to revolve. . .*and we are expected to spin with it.* Spinning, indeed. Her world was spinning out of control.

Chapter Two

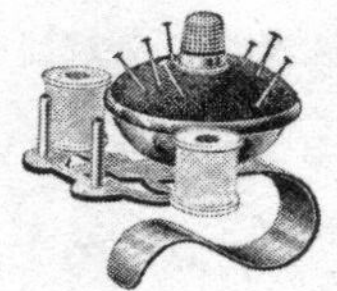

As the train car slowed, black letters on a faded board sign appeared just beyond the windows across from Rachel's seat. LOST CREEK. The name of the town only emphasized how Rachel felt after looking out at miles and miles of bleak, open prairie where the remnants of snowdrifts still clung to the edges of creek beds. As far as Rachel could see, Nebraska was vast, colorless, and empty—save for the people who lived in Omaha and a couple of other towns where the train had stopped along the way. But those small towns were mere dots of humanity on an empty canvas of land and sky, and the farther west she'd come, the more lost Rachel felt.

She leaned forward, hoping to catch a glimpse of her aunts. Had it really been less than two days since she'd boarded the train to her new home? Two days since she'd folded her wool cape and settled it into the rack above her seat back? After helping her board, Landis had walked along the platform until he found her car. He'd walked up to the window and pressed his open hand against the glass. She'd done the same even as tears streamed down her cheeks. *Only seven months.* Landis mouthed the words, touching the edges of his own mouth to encourage Rachel to force hers to curve upward.

Pushing down a wave of homesickness, Rachel stood to retrieve her cape. An elderly gentleman with a mane of white hair had been making his way up the aisle, but when Rachel picked up her carpetbag, he motioned for her to go before him. With a nod, she bustled through the door and down the iron steps leading to the depot platform. But there was no sign of the aunts. There was, in fact, not much of anything happening at the small clapboard depot.

She hesitated, looking toward the pathetic little town clustered just across the tracks. Finally, Aunts Jennie and Lizzie rounded the far corner of the depot. Short, round Aunt Jennie was still walking with a cane. Tall, slim Aunt Lizzie had a ruddy-cheeked, blue-eyed little girl in tow.

Aunt Jennie drew Rachel into a hug. "I am sorry we made you wait even one second. I am so slow these days. We're delighted you've come to us." She spoke to the little girl clinging to Aunt Lizzie. "This is her, Anna—Rachel, our niece."

The child gave Rachel a quick glance before thrusting the thumb of her free hand into her mouth and hiding her face in the folds of Aunt Lizzie's black cape. With a disapproving cluck of her tongue, Aunt Lizzie tugged on the child's hand, forcing her to stop sucking her thumb. "Say hello to Rachel," she demanded. The little girl turned her head just enough to peek at Rachel, but she did not speak. With a sigh, Aunt Lizzie crouched down to settle the bonnet dangling about the child's shoulders back on her head and tie it securely in place.

While Aunt Lizzie fussed with the bonnet, Aunt Jennie leaned close and murmured, "I delivered Anna's baby brother back in January. Sadly, her mother—" Jennie's voice wavered. She shook her head. "We've been helping their poor father with the children."

With the bonnet tied, Aunt Lizzie stood and handed the child off to Aunt Jennie. "I'll fetch the baby home from Molly's after I arrange for someone to bring Rachel's trunk to the house."

"Trunks," Rachel said. "And three bandboxes. For my hats." Landis's mother might have been willing to store paintings, but she had insisted Rachel would want every other earthly thing she owned with her. "And a crate protecting my easel and two of my paintings. Landis had it specially constructed to protect them." She paused. "Landis is my. . ."

"Yes," Aunt Lizzie said. "We remember Landis." She paused. "Two trunks, one crate, and three bandboxes. Do I have that right?"

"Actually, it's three trunks."

"Three."

Aunt Lizzie sounded incredulous, and Rachel rushed to explain. "I—I know it's a lot. It's just—I couldn't bear to leave Papa's books behind. And Mama's quilts. Only two, but—" Rachel's voice wavered. She swallowed. "Papa donated nearly everything to the poor."

When Aunt Lizzie next spoke, her tone was gentler. "Three trunks, three bandboxes, and one crate."

Rachel nodded.

"I'll see to it." Aunt Lizzie hurried into the depot.

Rachel watched her go, newly reminded of Aunt Lizzie's abrupt nature. She should have begged Landis to intervene with his parents. Surely they could have found room in that mansion of theirs for the books. She'd just assumed the aunts would have room. But they were already sheltering two children. Again, she apologized. "I hope I won't be in the way."

"In the way?" Aunt Jennie protested. "Dear child, we're delighted to have you. The truth is, we can use the help. We have plenty of room, and we've had great fun preparing for you." She looked down at the little girl. "Anna's helped us get your room ready. Wait until you see it!" Aunt Jennie led the way toward the road separating the train tracks from the edge of town, chattering as she walked. "Your room faces west. Lost Creek may not be much compared to St. Louis, but no one can match our sunsets!" They crossed the road while Aunt Jennie talked, making their way along a street lined with clapboard houses, most of them only one level.

Rachel was admiring the green shutters and window boxes on one when a young woman burst out the front door and trotted toward the street, leaving the screen door to slam shut behind her. "Aunt Jennie! Hello! Is this her?" The girl didn't wait for a reply before introducing herself. "I'm Nel. Nel Berkey. I've been watching for you! Welcome. I hope you quilt. You should come to Mama's quilting bee tomorrow. It's the perfect place to meet everyone—well, not everyone exactly, but at least ten someones—if everyone comes. Goodness but you're tall." She looked back at Aunt Jennie. "You were right. She's tall." Again, she smiled up at Rachel. "Aunt

call it joy, but he did feel something that didn't seem to come from the pit of despair. Two reasons to keep going. Anna. The baby.

The baby. Nameless, so far, because he didn't know what Esther wanted. The easiest thing was to just name the little mite for his two grandfathers, but Adam did not relish the idea of the constant reminder of either man, for neither he nor Esther had had a good relationship with their fathers. Growing up in families where faith was only pretense had been one of the first things to bring Adam and Esther together. Their home would not be that way.

Home. Would it ever feel like home again? Adam scolded himself at the thought. How it *felt* didn't matter. He had children to raise. Crops to plant. Livestock to tend. Esther's chickens. Esther's garden. All of it fell to him, now. All the work.

Thank God for Aunts Jennie and Lizzie. What would he have done without their kindness these last weeks? Anna was only four, and the baby—he had to name the baby. He glanced upward. *What was the name, Esther? The name you wanted?* With a shuddering sob, Adam reined the horses in just long enough to regain control of his emotions. When he felt he could face the dear women caring for his children, he clucked his tongue against the roof of his mouth to get the team moving again. Nearing the Meeker house, he heard Anna's voice before he saw her.

"There he is! That's my papa!"

How could another's joy cause a fresh stab of pain? And yet, it did. Still, when Anna came bouncing down the front steps, Adam hurried to pull up and climb down. When he crouched low and opened his arms, Anna flung herself at him, circling his neck with her thin arms and snuggling close. Adam closed his eyes and inhaled the scent of her, a mixture of clean clothes dried in the sun and sweaty blond hair.

"You've been playing hard," he croaked and reached up to push her hair away from her moist temples.

Anna nodded. "I hided from Rachel, but she found me and I ran fast so she couldn't tag me."

"And who is Rachel?"

A mellow voice answered from the top of the porch steps. "I'm Rachel. Rachel Ellsworth."

Adam looked up to where the stranger stood. Rising, he swung Anna onto one hip and snatched his hat off his head. "Adam Friesen. Anna's papa." Another wagon rumbled up.

Wyatt Dahl jumped down. "On the days you don't need me at the farm, I've been helping handle freight over at the depot. Any chance you could help me take the lady's things inside?"

Adam nodded. When he set Anna down, she hurried back up the stairs to stand beside Miss Ellsworth. To take her hand, Adam noted. He and Wyatt wrestled the first trunk off the wagon and began to carry it up the stairs.

Aunt Jennie came to the door. As she held it open for the men, she said, "I see you've met Rachel. She's come to stay with us for a while." She waved them into the house. "Upstairs. The room to the right." She invited Adam to stay for supper. "Lizzie's got an apple pie in the oven."

"That sounds so good," Adam said, "but I promised Molly I'd bring the children there for supper."

"The baby's already there. Molly agreed to watch him so we could meet Rachel's train, and we've yet to collect him."

Adam nodded. He and Dahl hoisted the trunk up the stairs and set it down inside the door to a huge room with a door opening onto the porch on the west side of the house. The aunts were certainly treating their niece well. Giving her the largest room in the largest house in town. Then again, no one was kinder than the Meeker sisters, no one more hardworking or generous.

Adam remembered how suspicious his own mother and her friends had been when the two spinster daughters of the widowed Dr. Fred Meeker first walked into First Church. It was the very first Sunday after their father—a notorious agnostic with a reputation for hard drinking—was laid to rest. As far as anyone knew, no Meeker had ever set foot inside a church until that day. But by living humbly, practicing mercy, and serving others, the sisters won their way into hearts. Adam didn't know what he would have done without them.

Aunt Lizzie stepped into the hallway from the kitchen just as Adam and Dahl descended the steep stairs to retrieve the second trunk. She put a few coins in Dahl's hand as she spoke. He tried to refuse, but she insisted, saying something about the evening train and a crate. Apparently the railroad had failed to transport something of Miss Ellsworth's. Something important, to hear Aunt Lizzie's tone of voice. Dahl reassured her that if the crate was on the next train, he'd find it and deliver it right away. The two men finished hauling trunks upstairs and then, with a tap to the brim of his cap by way of salute, Dahl left.

Anna giggled when Miss Ellsworth handed her the smallest of three bandboxes and asked if she'd carry it up the stairs. She did so, following the tall, slender newcomer who held the other two boxes aloft as if they held priceless treasure. Once back downstairs, Anna launched herself at Adam again, this time looping her fingers through his suspenders and stepping onto the toes of his boots while demanding they dance.

"Papa doesn't feel much like dancing tonight, little one," he said. Prying her fingers out of his suspenders, he lifted her into his arms again. "Oof," he grunted. "What are the aunts feeding you? You're heavier than a sack of potatoes."

"Too heavy for you to hold?"

"Never too heavy for that," Adam said, carrying Anna with him toward the front door.

Miss Ellsworth spoke as she descended the stairs, offering her condolences for his loss.

Anna spoke up. "Rachel's mama died too. And her papa. She didn't have anywhere to live, so now she lives here, just like Brother and me."

Miss Ellsworth smiled. "I suppose it does look like I'm moving in, but the truth is I'm just visiting for a few months. I'm to be married next year."

Adam barely heard what she said. *She lives here, just like Brother and me.* Did Anna think he'd given her up? Given the baby up? A new wave of sorrow threatened. "We must not keep Molly waiting," he croaked. "Let's be on our way."

"We'll have pie wrapped for you to take home with you later,"

Aunt Lizzie called from the kitchen doorway.

Adam thanked her before carrying Anna out the door and down the steps. Setting her on the wagon seat, he climbed up beside her. As he guided the team back out onto the road, the now-familiar sensation of helplessness washed over him. *She lives here, just like Brother and me.*

With all his heart, Adam wanted to bring his children home. With all his mind, he knew it was impossible.

Chapter Three

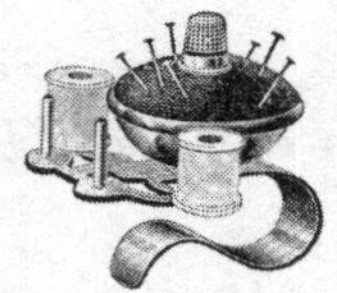

Rachel ducked down to see herself in the small mirror hanging on the back of the bedroom door. Perching her hat at just the right angle, she secured it with the elegant pin Landis had given her for Christmas. She closed her eyes briefly, thankful for the distraction of Nel Berkey's quilting bee. Her paintings and easel had not been on the evening train yesterday, after all. What if they were lost? Turning away from the mirror, she looked over at Mama's quilt, smiling at the memory of how pleased Aunt Lizzie had seemed when Rachel lifted it from her trunk and spread it out upon the bed.

"I remember Katie working on that," Aunt Lizzie said, tracing one of the pyramids made up of small triangles. "No one thought she'd be able to execute such a complex pattern, but she did it beautifully."

Rachel hadn't really thought about the difficulty of the piecing until that moment. Now, as she looked at the quilt more carefully, she realized that Mama had used dozens of different fabrics, and yet they blended together. Soft golds and pinks scattered across the surface like spring flowers popping up in a mostly dormant field of brown. Rachel couldn't remember ever thinking of Mama as artistic, and yet she'd transformed dress scraps into a balanced composition for a quilt. *Maybe my talent came from Mama.*

A soft knock sounded at the door. "Rachel? Aunt Lizzie doesn't want to be late."

Oh dear. She'd lost track of the time.

When Rachel opened the door, Anna's eyes opened wide. "You look pretty."

"Thank you." Rachel grabbed her beaded bag and nodded toward the stairs. "Let's go." Aunt Lizzie was waiting by the front door. One look at her simple calico dress and bonnet, and Rachel realized she was overdressed. She paused halfway down the stairs. "I should have asked what to wear." She dropped Anna's hand and prepared to retreat. "I'll change."

"Don't," Aunt Lizzie said. "We're already late." She opened the door and waved Rachel and Anna out onto the porch. Once outside, she took Anna's hand and led the way down the steps and toward the street.

Rachel glanced back toward the house. "What about Aunt Jennie?"

"Jennie doesn't quilt. She's trying a new bread recipe and tending the baby."

Aunt Lizzie kept walking. Rachel hurried to catch up and they walked in silence. From the row of farm wagons and buggies hitched in front of Berkeys', Rachel assumed a full complement of quilters had already gathered. She took a deep breath in a vain attempt to calm her nerves.

Aunt Lizzie pointed toward the Berkeys' and smiled down at Anna. "Someone's watching for you."

Rachel looked ahead. Blond hair and a pair of blue eyes were barely visible above the top of the picket fence bordering the Berkeys' front lawn.

"May I?" Anna asked.

Aunt Lizzie released her hand. "You may."

Anna tore off like a runaway filly.

Aunt Lizzie answered Rachel's unspoken question. "Ezra Dahl. Younger brother to the boy who delivered your freight yesterday. A 'little surprise' to his mother. You'd likely think her Ezra's grandmother if you didn't know."

The children disappeared around the side of the house and Aunt Lizzie opened the gate. Rachel could hear the buzz of conversation wafting through a window that opened onto the front porch. She apologized. "I'm sorry I made you late."

"You're forgiven. Just don't make it a habit."

The moment Rachel stepped through the Berkeys' front door, conversation stopped. If Aunt Lizzie hadn't been right behind her, she would have taken a step back. Instead, she stammered an apology for making Aunt Lizzie late.

Nel Berkey rushed in—from the kitchen, Rachel assumed. "Oh my goodness," she gushed and made a show of inspecting the nosegay of silk ribbon flowers arranged around the crown of

Rachel's broad-brimmed hat. "That's the most beautiful hat I've ever seen." She looped her arm through Rachel's, drew her into the room, and waved Rachel toward an empty chair. "Let me introduce everyone."

Rachel perched on the edge of the oak chair, clasping her beaded bag in her gloved hands and nodding at each woman Nel introduced. Other than Mrs. Berkey and Mrs. Dahl, little Ezra's mother, she despaired of ever remembering names, in spite of the little trick she'd learned from Mama long ago. Mrs. *Black* always carried a *b*lack *b*eaded *b*ag. Mrs. *Graystone* lived next door to a gray stone house. Robert *Grainger* was thin as a stalk of grain. But by the time Nel had pronounced the eighth name, Rachel had already forgotten the first.

In the momentary lull after introductions, Rachel sat looking down at her beaded bag and feeling ridiculous for wearing her most stylish ensemble to a gathering of women dressed in simple cotton day dresses. They probably thought the girl from the big city was uppity.

"You look like you just stepped out of the latest *Harper's Bazaar*," Mrs. Dahl said. She chuckled. "My George would give anything if I'd dress up on occasion. Then again, I'd give anything if he'd knock the mud off his shoes before he comes into my kitchen."

Soft laughter circled the room. Conversation ebbed and flowed, eventually landing on the topic of "poor Adam Friesen all alone out there on the farm."

"Does anyone know who's taking care of Esther's chickens?" one woman asked. "She always took such pride in that flock. Not in a sinful selfish way, mind you. But in the way that she'd brought them up herself and weren't they the best layers hereabouts."

As the women talked, Rachel deposited the beaded bag beneath her chair and began to thread a needle. Aunt Lizzie handed her a thimble. She put it on the middle finger of her right hand then hesitated, watching the other ladies quilt. One pushed the needle with the underside of her thumbnail. Another used the tip of a thimble, inserting the needle so it was perpendicular to the fabric and then, in a rocking motion, feeding stitches onto the needle before drawing the thread through the fabric. Nel used the side of her thimble and only took a couple of stitches at a time. Rachel decided to try that and hoped no one would realize she was a novice. She knew the basics, but once she'd learned to draw and paint, she'd had little interest in needlework.

"Look at those tiny stitches," Nel said, and nudged Rachel with her shoulder.

Rachel shrugged. "I didn't know if I'd remember how."

"It appears you do," Aunt Lizzie said with a smile.

The woman sitting next to Mrs. Dahl spoke up. "I was so sorry to hear about your recent loss, my dear."

Another said, "We've been praying the Lord would give you comfort. And make the journey here an easy one."

Rachel croaked her thanks. A wave of homesickness washed over her. She blinked tears away and concentrated on her stitching.

"It's good to have someone Nel's age join us," another woman said. "You'll meet more young people on Sunday. In fact"—she looked around the room at the others—"why don't we have a welcome picnic after church Sunday?"

Aunt Lizzie spoke immediately. "Jennie and I will host."

While the ladies planned, Rachel concentrated on stitching along the chalked line marching across the surface of the dark blue fabric. Friendly conversation and no small amount of good-natured teasing filled the room with a cloud of friendship and fellowship.

And the knot in Rachel's midsection relaxed.

Adam Friesen pulled out of the cemetery and headed for town, bent on fetching a load of lumber from the sawmill to continue working on pews for the new church. The promise to do the work hadn't saved Esther, but a promise was a promise. Besides that, the work kept his mind off all the things that were wrong in his world. He was nearly past the train depot when Wyatt Dahl flagged him down.

"You going to the Meekers' today?"

Adam shook his head. "Wasn't planning on it. Anna's with Aunt Lizzie at the Berkeys' quilting. I'll stop there to see her on my way out of town."

Dahl grimaced. "Miss Ellsworth's crate came on this morning's train. Aunt Lizzie asked me to check on it, but—I was hoping you'd take it over. When Pa learned I wasn't working for you today, he wanted me to see to the shoeing of one of the teams. He's not much for waiting once his mind's set on a thing." He shrugged. "No matter. I'll see to it."

Adam grunted softly. To say Wyatt's father "wasn't much for waiting" was a mild way to put it. "I'll do it," Adam said. The relief on Wyatt's face made him glad he'd set aside his own plans. He reined the farm wagon close to the railway loading dock. When he prepared to jump down to help, Wyatt waved him off.

"I can bring it out," he said. "I could almost carry it to the house. Almost." He retreated into the depot. When he returned, he was lugging a small crate, which he eased into place behind Adam's wagon seat. Adam shrugged out of his lightweight coat and draped it over the crate, lest dust sift inside. He spoke to the team and reined them about in the direction of the quilting bee. It was near on to noon. The ladies would be taking their lunch break, and his stomach was rumbling.

Ouch. Rachel pulled her left hand from beneath the quilt and inspected her middle finger. A morning's worth of miniscule pinpricks had taken its toll, and that last overzealous prick had drawn blood. Rachel looked over at Nel who glanced at the tiny drop of red.

Leaving her own needle in place atop the quilt, Nel rose. "I'm volunteering Rachel and me to get the food out for luncheon."

In the small kitchen, Nel pulled a stack of plates off a shelf while Rachel lifted away the napkins covering the contents of several baskets lined up on the kitchen table. A shout of joy in the backyard called her attention to Anna who was dashing toward a wagon pulling up to the back fence. "Looks like Anna's papa."

Nel peered through the kitchen window before snatching up a plate. "I bet Adam hasn't had a decent meal all day." She loaded the plate with food and hurried out the back door.

Rachel prepared plates for Anna and Ezra. Balancing a plate on each open hand, she backed her way through the screen door and out onto the porch. She hadn't expected a large dog to be sprawled just outside the door. With a loud "whoops!" she staggered, almost saved the plates and then failed. Both plates landed with a clatter, and the dog began to gobble food. Rachel ducked back inside for a broom, just as Aunt Lizzie and Mrs. Berkey hurried into the kitchen.

Rachel hurried to explain. "Nel took lunch to Anna's papa. I was taking food for Anna and Ezra. I didn't know there was a dog. I stumbled." She looked past Aunt Lizzie to Nel's mother. "I'm so sorry. I–I'll clean it up. Where's the broom, please? I feel terrible. The plates are in pieces."

"Goodness, child," Mrs. Berkey said. "It was an accident." As the quilters filtered into the kitchen to fill their plates and then moved into the dining room to eat, Mrs. Berkey produced a broom and dustpan. She chuckled as she glanced toward the back porch. "Give Buster a few more seconds and he'll have most of it cleaned up for you."

Broom in hand, Rachel went back outside. Aunt Lizzie followed with more food for the children. When Mr. Friesen caught sight of Rachel he left Nel with the children and crossed the lawn to the porch. "Wyatt Dahl loaded your crate into the back of my wagon just now. I'll be taking it on to the house after Anna and I have some lunch."

"Oh, thank you!" Rachel set the broom down and hurried to peer over the fence, surprised to see a coat draped over the crate.

Mr. Friesen went through the gate and climbed into the wagon bed. "I'd have had a packing blanket if I'd known I would be hauling precious cargo." Smiling, he lifted the coat. "See? None the worse for the delay."

Rachel nodded. "Thank you for taking extra care."

They walked back to the picnic table together, with Friesen sitting down beside Anna and Rachel continuing on to the house. Nel lingered at the table, but then Mrs. Berkey called for her. Rachel finished sweeping up and went back inside, where Nel was busy slicing pie.

"Cherry is Adam's favorite," she said, sliding a huge slice onto a pie plate. She'd headed for the door when her mother stopped her.

"Let me do that. You pour coffee for the ladies." She turned to Rachel. "Would you mind bringing dessert to the children?"

"Happy to," Rachel said.

"But—" Nel protested.

Mrs. Berkey cocked an eyebrow.

"Fine." Nel handed the plate over and spun away. She lifted the coffeepot off the stove and began pouring coffee with such energy it sloshed over the rims of more than one cup.

What'd I do? Why's she so upset? Rachel cut two small slices of pie for the children. "I'm sorry, Nel. I didn't mean—"

"Oh, it's all right," Nel said. "It's not your fault. Mother's just being. . .Mother." She sighed. "She thinks I was flirting. Goodness, I know better than that. It's only been four months. It's far too soon for Adam to be thinking of anyone else." She took a deep breath. "I was just offering to help with Esther's chickens. To find someone willing to take them until things get back to normal." She finished pouring coffee, muttering as she worked to mop up the spills. "It's not like he needs the eggs, all alone out there on the farm."

Rachel said nothing. Nel might not have been flirting, but there was something about the way she'd sprung to action when the man drove up, something about the way she said the name *Adam*. And did she really think his life would get "back to normal"? *Normal* didn't exist for a widower with two children. It probably never would—*unless*. *Ah.* So that was it. Nel wanted to help Adam Friesen find a new *normal*.

Rachel took the pie to the children. She saw Adam Friesen with new eyes. A girl could do much worse than the broad-shouldered, russet-haired farmer whose hazel eyes sparkled when he teased his daughter. Whose strong hands revealed a man who knew the meaning of hard work.

And Anna adored her papa. There was something very attractive about a man who took time for his children.

As Rachel returned to the house, she smiled to herself. How wonderful it would be one day to see her own daughter fly into

Landis's arms. They were both looking forward to having children. In fact, they'd discussed the matter extensively. They hoped to wait a few years before starting a family. After all, Landis needed time to settle into his position at the bank—but once they were ready, they would have three children. Hopefully at least one boy. Landis would be a good father. Rachel was certain of it.

Chapter Four

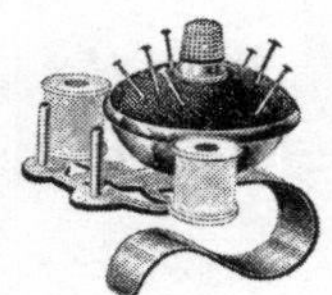

Rachel had just finished her own lunch and taken her seat at the quilting frame across from Hazel Mitchell (of the hazel eyes)—when a screech and a thud, followed by a cry for *Mama* summoned Mrs. Dahl. But she didn't even go outside before calling, "It's Anna."

Aunt Lizzie was quick to respond, followed by Rachel and Nel. They found Anna sitting on the ground near the swing, staring down at a jagged cut as blood dripped onto her dress.

"Oh. . .my." Nel went pale and stopped in her tracks.

Aunt Lizzie knelt to inspect the cut. "We need to take her inside."

Rachel scooped up the child, and they all hurried into the house. Rachel sat at the kitchen table with Anna in her lap. Finally, she convinced the child to move the hand she'd clamped over the wound so Aunt Lizzie could see it. It was a nasty cut. Mrs. Berkey retrieved some muslin, and she and Aunt Lizzie began to tear it into strips.

Nel's voice wavered. "Oh, that's awful. I'll get the doctor. And find Adam."

Aunt Lizzie shook her head. "Jennie can see to the cut. There's absolutely no need to bother Adam." Her voice softened as she said to Anna, "At least not until you have an impressive bandage to show him. You'll want to tell him how brave you were." She smiled. "Did you know that Aunt Jennie gives a special treat to brave little girls?"

Anna swiped at the tears spilling down her cheeks. "Wh–what is it?"

"All in due time, little one," Aunt Lizzie said. She cleansed the wound and wrapped Anna's thin forearm.

"It's too tight," Anna whimpered.

"It has to be tight for now," Rachel said.

"That will help it stop bleeding," Nel explained from across the room. "And it'll be quite all right once Aunt Jennie sews it up."

"She–she's gonna sew my arm?" Anna began to cry again. "She'll poke me. It'll hurt."

Rachel unbuttoned the cuff of her left sleeve and pulled it away from her wrist. "Look here," she said and pointed to a small scar. "When I was just your age, I was trying to climb a tree. I fell and this is where the doctor stitched me up. Once yours heals, we'll match."

"I wasn't trying to climb," Anna sniffed. "I fell off the swing and bumped the table."

"I knew that table was too close to the swing," Nel muttered. "I should have asked Adam to help me move it when he was here."

Anna traced the scar. "They sewed you up?"

"They did."

"Did it hurt?"

Rachel hesitated. "It did. But only for a little while." She paused. "And then I got three pieces of my favorite candy and when I went to bed that night, and my mama read to me until I fell asleep."

Anna said nothing for a moment and then asked, "It only hurt a little while?"

Rachel nodded.

"Can I sit in your lap when Aunt Jennie sews it?"

"Absolutely."

Anna spoke to Aunt Lizzie. "And if I'm brave I get a special treat."

Aunt Lizzie nodded.

Anna looked back at Rachel. "And you'll read me a story until I fall asleep?"

"I will. In fact, I brought a book of children's stories with me. I'll find it before bedtime so I can read you my favorite."

"And now we should take our leave," Aunt Lizzie said.

One of the quilters called from the doorway. "I've got us all packed up. I'll drive you. It will be my joy to help."

Joy. Rachel remembered. The woman's name was Etta Joy. Hazel Mitchell had hazel eyes. Mrs. Dahl was Ezra's mother. Of the eight women who'd come to quilting today, Rachel had only three more names to learn.

With Miss Ellsworth's crate beside him on the wagon seat and his wagon bed filled with newly sawn lumber, Adam Friesen pulled his team up to the Meekers' well, intent on watering the team before going inside. He expected Anna to hear his arrival and trip down the back stairs and to the well. When she didn't materialize, he wondered if quilting might have gone longer than expected. He could hear the baby crying—loudly. The child had strong lungs. Thanks be to God—and the Meeker sisters.

By the time Adam's second gray finished drinking, the baby had quieted. But there was still no sign of Anna. He set the bucket down and headed for the back door. When he knocked, Aunt Lizzie admitted him to a scene that wrenched his heart: Anna, her left forearm bandaged, sitting on Miss Ellsworth's lap at a table that had obviously been used to sew up a wound.

When she saw Adam, Anna held up a bandaged arm and blubbered her way through the telling of a fall and bleeding and stitches. "But I get a treat and a bedtime story," she sniffed, " 'cause I was brave." She looked up at Miss Ellsworth. "Wasn't I brave?"

"Very." Miss Ellsworth hugged her.

Aunt Jennie spoke up. "I'd have sent for you right away if it had been any more serious, but it only took a couple of stitches."

"And I was brave," Anna repeated.

Adam chucked her beneath the chin. "Can you be brave a while longer while Papa brings in Miss Ellsworth's crate?"

Anna nodded.

Miss Ellsworth looked down at her. "Is it all right if I help your papa?"

"You can help me set out some cookies," Aunt Jennie said. "If your arm doesn't hurt too much."

"It's better." Anna hopped down.

Back at the wagon, Adam maneuvered the crate to the edge of the wagon seat. "It isn't heavy," he said. "Just awkward." Miss Ellsworth steadied the crate while Adam balanced it on his shoulder. She held the door open while he carried it inside. All evidence of Aunt Jennie's doctoring had disappeared, and Anna was setting a plate of cookies on the table.

"We're making coffee," she said, in her best imitation of a grown-up voice.

Adam was heading toward the hallway to take the crate upstairs, when Aunt Lizzie spoke up. "If you don't mind, Rachel, Jennie and I would love to see your paintings."

Miss Ellsworth said she'd love that too, and so Adam set it down. Aunt Lizzie opened a drawer and produced two screwdrivers and a hammer. Aunt Jennie thrust the baby into Adam's arms.

The baby's blue eyes were wide open, and as he stared at Adam's face, his russet brows drew together. Thinking he was about to cry, Adam said, "It's all right, little one. Papa is here." When he caressed the tiny hand, the baby clutched his index finger. Adam wondered anew at the perfection of the round cheeks and dimpled chin. So taken was he with his boy, he didn't look away until he heard Aunt Jennie exclaim over one of the paintings.

"My dear, I had no idea you were so gifted."

"It's—" Aunt Lizzie paused, as if searching for a word. "It's marvelous. How did you ever manage to capture the light so perfectly? A magnificent sunrise in all its glory."

Adam looked up at the painting. *Magnificent* was a good word for it.

"I painted it for Papa," Miss Ellsworth said. "After Mama died. We were both so. . ." Her voice wavered. "We were struggling." She cleared her throat. "Papa took to reading the Bible aloud at the breakfast table every morning. He started with Psalm 139—about the day of death being decided before birth. That reminded us that God had never lost sight of Mama." She stared at the painting. "And he loved the book of Job. He said it was all right to tell God we didn't understand why Mama had to die. After all, God said Job was a blameless man, and Job asked plenty of questions. Which God didn't really answer. Still, one of the things God did say inspired this painting." She quoted from the Bible. " 'Where wast thou when I laid the foundations of the earth. . . . Hast thou commanded the morning. . . ?' " She shrugged. "I painted a sunrise to remind Papa—and me—that God commands the dawn and everything else. I love thinking about Mama there, just on the other side of that beautiful sky. Waiting." She choked out the words, "And now Papa's there too."

She set the painting down abruptly and fled out of the kitchen, up the stairs, and to her room.

Rachel stayed in her room until she heard the back door slam shut in the wake of Adam Friesen's departure. After she'd dried her eyes, she went through her trunk of books and found the storybook she'd mentioned to Anna. Finally, she descended the stairs and rejoined her aunts and the children in the kitchen. The baby was sleeping soundly in the coffee-crate-turned-cradle nestled in one corner near the stove. Anna was struggling to change the dress on a china-headed doll while the aunts washed supper dishes.

"Thank you for understanding my not wanting to come down for supper," Rachel said. Aunt Jennie had knocked softly once and retreated when Rachel pleaded for some time alone. She laid the book on the table and spoke to Anna. "Would you like some help with that?" Anna handed the doll over. Rachel admired its curly blond hair and painted blue eyes as she worked. "She's very pretty."

"Aunt Lizzie gived her to me to play with. Long as Papa can't have me at home. And after that, I'll still be able to come play with her. Whenever I want. Even if I'm grown up."

Rachel finished changing the doll's dress. Laying her aside, she reached for the book. "There's a story in here about a little girl and her doll. Shall we read that one when it's bedtime?"

"You remembered!"

Rachel nodded. She turned to look at the shipping crate and its contents, still sitting where she'd left them. Setting the book down, she rose and went first to the paintings. The dawn portrait was leaning against the still life, obscuring it.

"If you'd like, we can hang them in your room," Aunt Lizzie offered. "Unless they bring more sorrow than comfort."

"I'd like to hang them. Very much."

Aunt Lizzie inspected the still life. "This is excellent composition. The way you've set the goblet off to the side. Things are balanced but not overly so."

"You know. . .art?"

Aunt Lizzie shrugged. "Enough to be a bit of a snob about it."

"A *bit* of a snob?" Aunt Jennie chided, albeit with humor in her voice.

Aunt Lizzie explained. "Before we came west, our father was friends with some of the artists who eventually became part of the Hudson River School. Do you know it?"

"Know it?" Rachel exclaimed. "I adore their work!"

"Follow me," Aunt Lizzie said.

Moments later, Rachel gasped with delight when she saw the three oils hanging in Aunt Lizzie's room.

"Thomas Cole," Aunt Lizzie said, pointing at the first before moving on. "Edward Church. And that one's only a study, so it's not signed. But I do love it."

"I never would have expected—" Rachel broke off.

"To find *real* art in Lost Creek?" Aunt Lizzie chuckled. "Your pieces are very good. I hope you get to continue your studies."

"Landis promised that I could." As she and Aunt Lizzie went back downstairs, Rachel described the wedding trip she and Landis would take. "He understands how important my painting is to me. His father's banking interests often take the Groves abroad, and Landis is expected to follow in his father's footsteps. I may even get the chance to take some lessons in Paris."

The moment they returned to the kitchen, Anna demanded the promised story.

"As soon as I get my mess out of the way," Rachel said. She lifted the disassembled easel out of the crate before sweeping up packing straw and replacing the lid. Next, with her aunts' help, she carried the easel and paintings up to her room. Anna stayed behind, leafing carefully through Rachel's storybook, entranced by the color illustrations.

"It's good your two pieces are already framed and ready to hang," Aunt Lizzie said.

"You don't need to go to the trouble," Rachel said. "I can just set up the easel and use it for display." She looked doubtfully at the little space left after her three trunks had been lined up against one wall. "I'd like to store the shipping crate, though—in the barn, I suppose."

Aunt Lizzie shook her head. "Not in the barn. We'll ask Adam to take it up to the attic next time he's here.

Every morning began the same way. In the seconds after Adam woke, it was as if the past few months hadn't happened. And then he remembered. He always sat up abruptly and nearly jumped out of bed, trying to ward off the pain. He dressed in the dark and hurried outside to the well to splash water in his face and get a drink before heading for the barn, where the sweet aroma of hay and warm animals helped him battle the yawning hole in his life.

Most mornings, he pretended the children were at the house with their mother. Sometimes he even caught himself listening for Esther to call him to breakfast.

Today was different, though. Instead of fleeing the house like a frightened colt running from a storm, Adam stood peering into the small bedroom where his children should be sleeping. He closed his eyes, listening to the silence. *I have to bring them home. Somehow.* He looked up. *You command the dawn. Can You not help me to find a way to bring my children home?*

For the first time in a while, Adam wished either his parents or Esther's were still in Lost Creek. Their relationship hadn't been a good one, but surely the arrival of grandchildren would have helped cross the divide. Esther's had moved farther west and Adam's parents lay at rest in the same cemetery as Esther. The only family left in Lost Creek was Molly, Adam's older sister. She'd offered to raise them as her own, bless her. But Molly and Walter Bingham already had six children. Adam could not bear the thought of Anna and her brother being taken in out of duty—and eventually becoming a burden, which they surely would be to an already overworked mother. No, Adam thought. He must bring his children home and raise them up as a father should.

Fresh sorrow sent a pang through him. He'd had enough of sobbing, and so he raked his fingers through his hair and went out into the predawn light. He went first to Esther's chickens. As he opened the coop and then began to scatter grain for the emerging hens, he thought on Nel Berkey's suggestion yesterday that he let her arrange to "board them out." Nel meant well, of course. She could not know that Adam needed Esther's chickens right where they were, clucking and pecking at him when he gathered eggs. They connected him to the way life should be.

I've been thinking, Adam, Nel had said as she handed him a plate mounded high with food, *thinking of how I might help you and the children.* She hemmed and hawed for a moment before bringing up the notion of his giving up Esther's chickens. She'd even offered to drive out to the farm and tend them a few mornings a week—if it would help, she said. With Anna along, of course. And therein lay the seed of an idea.

Adam looked toward the east where the sun was just now beginning to peer over the horizon. Was it possible God would answer his prayer so quickly? Nel Berkey was willing to drive out to the farm. What if others could? It would be asking too much of Molly, of course, with all the children already hanging on to her apron strings. But Aunt Lizzie might do it. And what if Wyatt could bring Ezra with him one morning. Ezra, Anna, and Wyatt could see to the planting of the garden. Wyatt might be glad for an excuse to work out here more often. If he'd agree to take the gardening on for a share of the produce—old man Dahl might even like that idea. So. Nel Berkey, Aunt Lizzie, and Wyatt. If each of them could bring Anna to the farm one morning a week, she would know the farm was still home. That could be the beginning of mending the canyon that ripped through their lives when Esther died.

Adam hurried to finish morning chores, finishing by picking a small bunch of Esther's daffodils to take to the cemetery on his way to town. By the time Wyatt arrived, he was waiting, the buggy hitched. He shared his idea, and Wyatt responded with enthusiasm, "I'd love to bring Ezra out here. It's something we could do together."

"You'll be doing me a favor."

"Maybe. But you're returning it, giving me an excuse to avoid Pa. He might even like the idea when he hears you'll pay in produce."

Adam talked to the Almighty all the way to the cemetery. When he nestled the daffodils against the gravestone, he realized something felt different. He still didn't understand why God had allowed Esther to die, but he felt less rage. More. . .something. Not exactly acceptance. He didn't want to accept life without Esther. And yet he realized that he needed to do just that—God willing, without bitterness. After all, not once in all his life had Adam Michael Friesen commanded the dawn.

Chapter Five

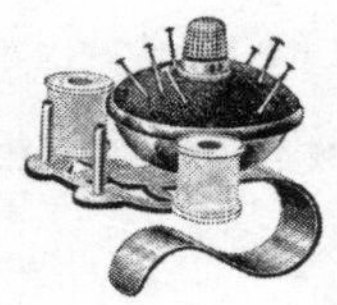

Rachel woke and lay still for a few minutes, listening to the steady drum of rain on the roof of the little porch off her room. Last evening, she'd left the door to the porch open to let the June breeze waft into her room while she reread Landis's letters. He'd kept his promise to write often—for a while. From April and all through May, Rachel received a letter almost every other day—and answered it immediately.

She described her room and how the aunts had helped to hang her paintings. She spoke of Aunt Lizzie's knowledge of the Hudson River School and Aunt Jennie's skill as a midwife. She recounted amusing little stories about Anna and a prank Ezra Dahl had played on the quilters, sneaking into the house while they picnicked outside and sprinkling flour over one corner of the quilt to obscure the chalked quilting design.

That earned him a spanking from his mother, even though I found it a simple task to brush the flour off and redraw the feathered design. You would have thought I'd sketched the Mona Lisa. At the end of the day, Nel recruited me to help her with a quilt she's planning for her hope chest.

She told Landis about the children staying with the aunts and how they had wheedled a place into her heart.

I didn't realize how much I would miss teaching the children's Sunday school class at home. It makes me especially grateful for the two little people residing beneath the Meeker roof. I do what I can to help their days pass happily—poor little motherless things.

She described how the deceased Mrs. Friesen's friends had banded together to take Anna to the farm several mornings a week. It enabled Anna to feed her mother's chickens and gather eggs. The child had even planted the garden with Wyatt Dahl, Mr. Friesen's farmhand.

I've gone with Aunt Lizzie and Anna a couple of times. It's a short and pleasant drive into the countryside. The Friesen place isn't anything like the impressive estate your father purchased last year, and yet there is something about it that says home—something that resonates deep within my heart and inspires daydreams of our future together.

In one of his May letters, Landis wrote that he was proud of her for making the best of the situation. He spoke of the new minister who had none of Reverend Ellsworth's oratorical skill. Even so, the church was enjoying a growth spurt with the arrival of three families attached to Washington University. Rachel would be pleased to know that two of the professors' families included people Landis and Rachel's age. They'd added a lively element to the annual spring picnic. Rachel would like them.

Rachel responded to each letter the day she received it. When the frequency of Landis's missives waned, she did her best not to complain. She said she missed hearing from him when he couldn't write, but she understood. He was busy learning at his father's side—an investment of time that would bear fruit for their future together. Keeping busy here in Lost Creek helped the time pass. They had only six more months to wait. She would be home for Christmas.

Rachel did not write about her dreams of a Christmas marriage proposal, although she expected Landis was even now making plans for it. At least she hoped he was. She'd offered enough hints. Often in the evenings after she slipped beneath the quilts, she held her left hand up, envisioning the ring Landis would place on her finger. She imagined standing in the glow of the fireplace in the private family parlor, the scent of the evergreen boughs adorning the mantle, the comforting warmth kindled by a cup of eggnog. Would he have hidden the ring box among the packages beneath the tree—or might he have kept it in his pocket for weeks, wanting to keep it near while she was far away? Either way, when Landis guided her around the dance floor at his parents' annual Christmas ball, an engagement ring would adorn her finger. It would make future Christmases pale by comparison. *The Christmas of our engagement.*

But an entire week had just passed without a letter from home, and as she lay in bed listening to the rain, Rachel could not shake the sense of foreboding. Rereading all those letters hadn't helped one bit. If nothing, she was more worried than ever. Landis must be ill. If there was no letter today, she would ask the aunts if she might send a telegram.

The storm raged. Rain poured. Thunder rolled. When a flash of lightning chased across the sky, Anna bolted into Rachel's room. She clutched the edge of the bed as she said, "Aunt Lizzie's already downstairs. She said she wouldn't let a little rain stop us from going to see Papa. She said not to be worried." The child cringed when thunder sounded again. "But that's *loud*."

Rachel held up the covers. Anna dove into the bed and Rachel pulled her close. "My mama used to tell me that loud thunder was the angels marching in heaven."

Another rumble. Anna looked over the edge of the quilt toward the porch. "That's lots of marching."

Rachel chuckled. "It is, but it's nothing to fear." She slipped away from Anna and put a pillow in her place. "Hug the pillow if you feel afraid again. I won't leave the room, but I do need to get dressed. I'm meeting Nel at the mercantile today to help her plan a quilt."

Anna clutched the pillow and ducked back beneath the covers. Rachel moved quickly to dress. By the time she'd wound her long hair into a bun at the back of her head, the storm had abated. She had the telegram wording planned. She'd retrieve the mail while at the mercantile with Nel, and if there was no letter from St. Louis. . .

Anna pulled the covers down just enough to watch as Rachel gathered Landis's letters and tied them together with a bit of ribbon. "Are those Landy's letters?"

"It's Lan*dis*, and yes, these are from him."

"Papa says people in heaven don't get to write. We just got to know they love us without any letters."

Rachel set the letters in the top tray of an open trunk. "He's absolutely right," she said and went to the bedside and sat down. "They can't write letters, but they still love us. And someday, we'll see them again."

"When we go to heaven. They can't come back here. They're in heaven with Jesus forever. Papa said so."

Rachel nodded.

"I wish Mama could come back for a visit."

"Sometimes I wish for the same thing."

Anna sat up. "I got a quilt Mama made. But Brother doesn't. Mama went to heaven before it got finished. If she could come visit, I bet she'd finish it."

Poor child. "Maybe we can ask Aunt Lizzie to bring it back to town with her after you visit today. If your papa doesn't mind. I'm certain the quilting ladies would love to finish it for the baby."

Anna hopped out of bed. "I bet the pieces are still in Mama's sewing basket. I better get dressed so we can fetch it!" She skittered out of the room and across the hall.

From her bedroom doorway, Rachel saw a nightgown flutter to the floor. When thunder rolled again, Anna shot back out of Aunt Lizzie's room. She'd managed to pull her dress on and was clutching shoes and stockings to her body. "Marching," she said to Rachel as she stepped across the landing and onto the top stair. "Marching. Marching. Marching." She was halfway down when lightning flashed. She flinched but kept going.

The rain stopped, Aunt Lizzie and Anna drove off to the farm, and Rachel picked her way through the puddles to the mercantile. The train hadn't pulled in yet, so the matter of a letter from Landis would have to wait. Rachel was thinking how sweet Anna would look in a dress made from the double pink calico when Nel stepped through the door.

"You'd think the mills would know there's enough double pink calico in the world," Nel groused.

"It'd make a darling new dress for Anna."

"I wasn't aware Anna needed new clothes." Nel sighed. "I do wish Adam would have said something. I've told him and told him I'll help in any way I can."

"It may not be a need. But it'd be something nice to do for her. Or with her, if she catches on easily."

"You're going to teach a four-year-old to sew?"

"Maybe. This morning Anna mentioned a baby quilt her mother

didn't finish. Aunt Lizzie's going to see about bringing it back with them today. Anna's excited about helping finish it."

"I remember it, and believe me, Anna won't be helping. It's a sunburst with a ridiculous number of pieces in each block." Nel paused. "You should just give it to me. I'll finish the piecing, and the quilters can take on the quilting as a group—maybe as a surprise for Adam, if Anna hasn't already ruined that idea."

Rachel directed the conversation away from the Friesens and back to the reason she'd come to the mercantile in the first place. "That pink I was admiring is part of a new shipment Mr. Sutter just got in. The latest colors, he says."

Nel scanned the bolts of cloth, frowning. "I'm so tired of brown and pink. And that green makes me positively dyspeptic." She reached into her bag, drew out a piece of paper, unfolded it, and handed it over. Nine blocks featured appliquéd hearts created with a narrow band of cloth, as if the strip were a broad line of ink. Each heart was dotted with red berries—or perhaps cherries, from the size—and green leaves. Alternating blocks between the hearts featured a wreath of appliquéd leaves. And more tiny red circles.

Rachel gasped with admiration. "I had no idea you could design quilts. This is stunning."

"Oh, I didn't design it. I just copied a quilt like it that was on display at the county fair a few years ago. I've never forgotten it." Nel smiled. "With all those hearts, it's a perfect wedding quilt."

Rachel teased, "I hope you're not already secretly engaged, because this is going to take a very long time to make. Even with help."

"I have time. At least I think it'll be a while." Her cheeks reddened.

Rachel looked around to make sure no one was within earshot before asking, "Anyone I know?"

The blush deepened. Nel tapped the edge of the paper. "I want it to be a masterpiece."

"It will be. All those tiny circles. . ." Rachel counted the dots around the heart. "Fifty-eight to a block and nine blocks—plus more for the wreaths? That's—a lot of tiny circles." Rachel looked up from the drawing. "Are you sure you want to take it on?"

"Positive. I can do the appliqué, but I'm no artist. And the shapes have to be just right. Do you think you could draw a pattern? And can you think of something that would make it unique?"

Rachel studied the sketch. "Those hearts and wreaths and berries really should be red and green. I don't think you'd be happy with another color. It wouldn't seem right." She looked past Nel to the fabric again. "However—"

"However?" Nel followed Rachel's gaze to the bolts of cloth.

"The original quilt you admired. Was the appliqué on a white ground?"

"Of course. Just like every other red and green quilt I've ever seen."

Rachel moved down the shelves of fabric and ran her palm across a vibrant orange. "Mr. Sutter said they're calling this *cheddar*. Or *California gold*. Using this for the ground instead of white or muslin would certainly make it unique."

Nel frowned. "An entire quilt out of that? Are you sure?"

Rachel pulled the bolt of gold cloth out and set it on the counter then added a rich green and a Turkey red. Taking a pencil in hand, she sketched a swag border. "Red swags with green sprouts here, at the place where the swags join. That would provide a vibrant frame to the blocks—an element the original didn't have."

"*Vibrant.* I suppose that's one word for it." Nel cocked her head to one side and studied the fabrics Rachel had selected. "I don't know. It's. . .loud."

"Cheerful," Rachel corrected. "Bold. Artistic, even."

"I'm not sure *artistic* would appeal to Ad—" Nel stopped abruptly. "To someone from Lost Creek. Not that there's anything wrong with artistic. *Your* young man would probably love it."

Rachel smiled. "*My* young man thinks quilts are unhealthful. Or at least his mother does. She actually quoted something out of a magazine on the topic not long ago. An article that touted new blankets over 'old-fashioned, outdated quilts.'"

Nel made a face. "I'd wager—if it weren't a sin to gamble—she's never attended a quilting bee. If she had, she'd know they're about a lot more than quilts."

Rachel laughed. "You don't need to wager. Mrs. Grove wouldn't be caught dead with a needle and thread in hand. She has servants for that kind of thing." She stopped abruptly. "I'm making her sound horrible. She's not. She's just. . .not like the ladies here." She patted the bolt of orange cloth and changed the subject back to Nel's project. "Buy enough to make a sample block. See what you think."

Nel shook her head. "If I'm going to do it, I'd better buy enough for the whole thing. Ida Joy ran into trouble last year when she did a sample block and by the time she got back to the mercantile, an entire bolt of blue was gone." She pondered the fabric. "Are you sure I'll like it?"

"I'm sure *I'd* like it," Rachel said. "But I'm not the one who's going to live with it." She handed the drawing back to Nel. "Think about it for a couple of days. If you want to come back to the house with me, I can draw up the pattern for the blocks. At least we'll get that accomplished."

Nel agreed and tucked the drawing in her bag just as Wyatt Dahl stepped into the store, the mailbag perched on his shoulder. Rachel tried—and failed—to be patient while Mr. Sutter sorted mail and Nel struck up a conversation with Wyatt about Adam's plans for the farm and how good it was of Wyatt to agree to managing the garden.

Finally, the kindly storekeeper/postmaster handed Rachel a small stack of mail, atop which rested an envelope from St. Louis. But it wasn't from Landis. Rachel recognized the flowery script at once.

Mrs. Grove.

Chapter Six

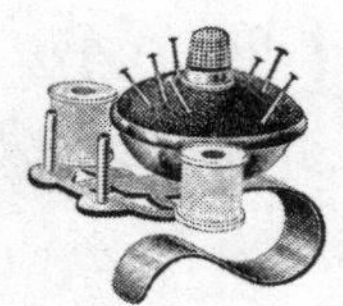

Nel broke off her conversation with Wyatt and hurried over. "What is it? You're white as a sheet." Grasping Rachel by the arm, she pulled her behind the counter and toward a tall stool. "Sit. Breathe. Shall I get you some water?"

Rachel shook her head. "It's just—Landis hasn't written for some time. I've tried not to worry, but—" She pointed to the flowing script. "This is from his mother." She blinked away gathering tears. "If Mrs. Grove is writing, something's happened." She turned the envelope over, but Nel stayed her hand.

"You should wait to read it. Until you get home."

Home. If Landis was ill, she must go home. There would be so much to do. Her heart raced just thinking of it. "I can't wait. I have to know." She reached for Nel's hand and gave it a squeeze. "But—stay?"

"Of course."

Trembling, Rachel opened the envelope.

June 19, 1890
St. Louis, Missouri

Dearest Rachel,

Do you remember that day in Mr. Carpenter's office when we agreed that the earth spins and we must continue to spin with it, even when it brings us sorrow? You were so brave, sitting in that opulent office hearing such terrible news. I admired you then and I know that should I see you in the future, I would have opportunity to admire you yet again. You are stronger than you know. We all saw it during the aftermath of your mother's passing and again when our dear Reverend Ellsworth passed on. You must be strong now. And brave.

The knot in Rachel's stomach grew. This was bad. Very bad. What if Landis—*no. Don't jump to conclusions.* She kept reading.

It is one of the burdens of motherhood to accept the task of sparing their children pain. We do it out of love. I hope that one day you will believe that love is the reason I have taken on this task. I want to spare Landis—and you—more pain than is necessary; Landis, so that he doesn't have to write words that wound one he has loved, and you, because hearing our news from me instead of Landis will hopefully cushion the blow.

At a soiree we hosted at Mr. Grove's social club last evening, Landis and Miss Daisy Marcom announced their engagement.

Rachel gave a soft cry of disbelief. Nel put a hand on her arm. Rachel reread the last sentence. Landis. . .engaged? Who was Miss Daisy Marcom? Rachel read on.

Daisy is the daughter of a Washington University professor. The family are relatively new residents in St. Louis who joined the congregation of First Church not long after you departed the city.

Huh. Landis had written about newcomers to the church. "People our age," he'd said. Something about how they'd "livened up the spring picnic." *I'll just bet they did.* Rachel clenched her jaw. Anger welled up. She almost crumpled the letter. Instead, she took a deep breath and finished reading.

You must know that Landis was devoted to the plans the two of you had made until—well. Until God brought Daisy into his life.

God did that? Rachel snorted with disbelief.

We must all accept God's direction, even when it demands that we walk a path heretofore unknown. May

He guide you through the sorrow this letter will undoubtedly bring. It has pained me greatly to write it.

Cherishing the good memories,
Wishing you the best,
Martha Grove

Wishing you the best. Rachel stared at the words in stunned silence for a moment before reading the post script.

I have personally seen to the packing of the paintings you left in our care. Rest assured that I have taken every precaution to see that they are well protected for the journey to Lost Creek. You may expect them to arrive at the depot within a couple of days of receiving this letter.

"What's happened?" Nel asked. "Are you going back? I can help you pack. If we hurry, you can meet the afternoon train. Tell me what to do."

"I'm not going anywhere," Rachel said. Blinking away her tears, she held the letter out. "Read it."

"Are you sure?"

Rachel nodded. Nel took it, and Rachel watched her friend's expression transform as she read. Concern. Confusion. Shock. Disbelief. And, finally, anger.

Finished reading, Nel held up the letter and practically hissed, "Who *is* this person?"

"Until recently, she was my future mother-in-law."

"*Was.* There's always something to be thankful for." Nel spit it out and then apologized. "I'm sorry. I shouldn't have said that." Again, she put her hand on Rachel's arm. "Let's walk. My house. Your house. Around town. Or I'll leave you alone. Just—tell me what you want."

Rachel stood on wobbly legs. "I don't—know." She stared down at the fabric still lying on the counter. *A masterpiece.* Nel wanted to make a masterpiece. Rachel pointed at the letter. "Put that in your bag." She reached for the other mail. "Let's go—" She shook her head and led the way out of the mercantile. She'd almost said, "Let's go *home.*" Would she ever have a home again?

Adam grunted with dismay as he set yet another mousetrap in the pantry. He'd been doing battle for over a week now and lost count of how many critters he'd carried out of the house. Had the varmints sent out some kind of announcement? *No one living at Friesens. Come party.*

With the trap set, he stood up, bumped a shelf, and upset a tin of something. It toppled off the shelf, and when he went to put it back, he noticed a small notebook tucked between a couple of empty crocks. He opened it. *Biscuits.* A recipe written in Esther's neat handwriting. Swallowing the lump that rose in his throat, he flipped through the pages.

And I thought she just instinctively knew how to make those biscuits. And flapjacks. Here was the recipe for the corn bread he loved. For Anna's favorite cinnamon rolls. And piecrust. His mouth watered at the thought of biscuits fresh from the oven, slathered in butter and topped with Esther's elderberry jelly. He flipped back to the first page and read through the instructions. How hard could it be?

A few minutes later, Adam slid a pan of biscuits into the oven. He cleaned up the mess and settled at the table to wait, sipping coffee and listening to the consistent drum of rain on the porch roof. After a peek at the biscuits—they needed more time—he sat back down and opened the Bible he'd taken to leaving on the kitchen table.

The book fell open to Esther's favorite, the Psalms, but Adam backed up to the beginning of Job. He'd been reading it since the day Rachel Ellsworth quoted it—choking back tears as she did so. The power the words had in Rachel Ellsworth's life intrigued him. He remembered her saying, *Papa said it was all right to tell God we don't understand.* There was plenty about his life right now that Adam didn't understand. Still, reading God's Word seemed to help quiet the turmoil.

Today, with the sound of rainfall and the aroma of freshly turned earth blowing in through the open window, as Adam read the book, he felt comforted. Rachel Ellsworth had been right about Psalm 139 too. Adam had taken to praying the last of it. *"Search me, O God, and know my heart: try me, and know my thoughts: And see if there be any wicked way in me, and lead me in the way everlasting."*

Most of the book of Job remained a mystery—except for the

last part, which definitely had the power to put a man in his place. This morning, as he thought on Job's "*what shall I answer thee? I will lay mine hand upon my mouth*," Adam nodded. He thought back over all the man had lost—his possessions, his family, and, finally, his own health. But not his faith. Never his faith. A man could learn a lot from Job's example.

When the biscuits were ready, he pulled the pan out of the oven and inverted it over the counter. He slit a biscuit open with a bread knife and slathered it with butter. The aroma of warm bread made his mouth water. He wasn't sure he needed jelly. He took a tentative bite. Then another. And, finally, he smiled. *What-d-ya know.* Adam Michael Friesen, making biscuits. Good biscuits.

Wrapping the warm biscuits in a towel, he set them near the stove and headed out to the barn. As he milked the cow, he muttered names. "Ethan John Friesen. Asher Friesen. William Friesen. George Washington Friesen. Benjamin Franklin Friesen." Favorite uncles. Distant relatives. Famous Americans. Nothing resonated. Nothing seemed to be a proper fit for the russet-haired blue-eyed boy who increasingly dominated his thoughts. "Esther," he finally said aloud. "If you don't find a way to speak up, I'm just going to toss some names I like in a hat and hope for the best." He chuckled. "Or I could let Anna name him. Although I don't relish the thought of Mordecai Azalea."

He heard Aunt Lizzie's buggy turn in the drive. Milk pail in hand, he made his way to the barn door and then across the drive to wait by the path leading to the house. The minute the buggy stopped, he set the milk pail down. "I wondered if the rain would keep my butter churner in town," he teased. Lifting Anna out of the buggy, he set her down and then held out his hand for Aunt Lizzie.

"I'm sorry we're late," Aunt Lizzie said as she climbed down.

"You aren't. I was only teasing." Adam tapped the tip of Anna's nose. "Go on inside, little one. You can have a glass of milk before the churning. And a biscuit."

Anna looked up at him with a small frown. "You don't know how to make biscuits."

"I learned. You and Aunt Lizzie go on inside. I'll see to the buggy and be along." He led the little mare across to the barn, unhitched her, and turned her into a small corral before returning to the house. The moment he stepped into the kitchen, Anna spoke—around a mouthful of biscuit.

"These are good."

Aunt Lizzie echoed Anna's sentiment. "And I'll admit I'm surprised."

"I found Esther's recipe notebook this morning." He allowed a little smile. "It seems I can follow directions—at least when it comes to biscuits." He paused. "I've been thinking. If I start soup in the morning, it can cook all day to be eaten for supper. That would work, yes?"

"It would," Aunt Lizzie agreed. "But you'd need to check on it. To make certain it wasn't burning. Or that the fire hadn't gone out."

Adam nodded. "Between Wyatt and me, we could manage. Do you think?"

"I think two strapping men should be able to figure out a kitchen. I can bring soup makings with me next time I come and give you a brief cooking lesson."

"We have quarts and quarts of tomatoes in the root cellar. Potatoes and carrots too. Maybe more. Why not use what's already here?"

"Why not indeed," Aunt Lizzie said, and reached for the apron hanging on a hook by the stove.

"Beyond salt and pepper," Adam said, "I don't know anything about spices."

"You will when I'm finished with you," Aunt Lizzie said. "And speaking of finishing. . .Anna mentioned a baby quilt Esther had started."

Anna spoke up. "Rachel said if you say it's all right she'll show me how to sew and we can finish it. Together. And then Brother will have a quilt Mama made, just like me."

Adam nodded. "If Miss Ellsworth wishes to help you finish it, I will be very grateful." He went into the small parlor. Esther's sewing basket was still on the table beside her rocking chair. A stack of completed quilt blocks, a spool of thread, assorted fabric pieces, a pincushion, and scissors were positioned just as they had been the last time Esther sewed. Adam gathered it all up and tucked it into the sewing basket. He picked up a piece of paper that had been hidden by the quilt blocks. Going to the one window in the room, he parted the curtains just enough to see. . .a list of names, all of them crossed out, save one.

Barrett Michael Friesen. Tears gathered as he looked up toward heaven. "So. You found a way." He carried the piece of paper and the sewing basket to the kitchen. He handed the basket to Aunt Lizzie, and then he swept Anna up into his arms. "Baby brother has a name."

Chapter Seven

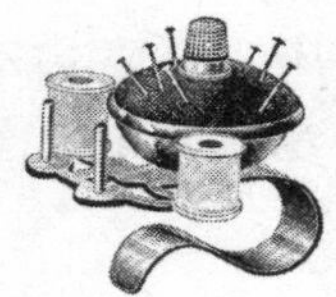

Feeling numb, Rachel sat at Aunt Jennie's kitchen table, her hands folded, her back straight. Nel stood behind her, one hand on the back of the chair, both of them waiting while Aunt Jennie read Mrs. Grove's letter.

"Can you believe it?" an impatient Nel finally said. "Of all the nerve."

The baby had been asleep, but at the sound of Nel's strident voice, he woke and began to cry. When Aunt Jennie moved toward the cradle, Nel waved her away. "I'll see to him. Rachel needs you."

Aunt Jennie came to sit beside Rachel. She reached for her gloved hand. "My dear, sweet niece. I am so very sorry."

The older woman's sympathy broke the dam of self-control. Rachel began to cry. Meaning to retrieve a handkerchief from the bag at her wrist, she managed only to tangle the strap and close it tighter. Frustrated, she began to yank on the strap. Aunt Jennie put a hand over hers. Rachel stilled.

"One lace-edged handkerchief isn't going to be enough, anyway,"

Aunt Jennie said and handed over a napkin. When Rachel began to sob, Aunt Jennie pulled her into her arms.

"How *could* he? Why didn't I guess? But no, I lost sleep over him. Envisioning poor brave Landis, wasting away but not wanting to worry me." She sat back and blew her nose. "I thought he was so—perfect. He was going to take me to Paris. He understood my art." Tears flowed again. Rachel leaned into Aunt Jennie's hug. And the baby cried louder.

Nel was standing at the sink, the screaming baby in her arms, a look of frustration on her face. "Is he hungry?"

"I'm all right, Aunt Jennie," Rachel said. "Help the poor little man."

Aunt Jennie rose and crossed to where Nel stood, taking the baby in her arms. In no time, the child was lying on a blanket near the stove, kicking happily.

"I'll make tea," Aunt Jennie said. "It's an herbal remedy." She nodded at Rachel. "It'll make you feel calmer." She'd just set the kettle on to heat when someone pounded on the back door.

"Jennie Meeker! It's Val Brooks. Lena says to come right away. Pains are getting close together."

Rachel spoke up. "You have to go. I'll be all right."

"I can stay," Nel offered.

"Thank you, dear," Aunt Jennie said. "I hate to leave, but I must." She began gathering supplies and tucking them into the carpetbag she took to every birthing.

Rachel forced more confidence into her voice than she felt. "It'll be all right, Aunt Jennie. Truly."

"Lizzie and Anna shouldn't be gone much longer," Aunt Jennie said. She looked over at Nel. "And you're sure you can stay? I don't want Rachel to be alone."

Nel promised.

Aunt Jennie pulled a small green tin down from the shelf above the stove. She handed it to Nel. "Steep two tablespoons of this in two cups of hot water. Wait until it's a very rich green color then strain the herbs out." She looked at Rachel. "Drink every drop." Taking the carpetbag in hand, she headed for the back door then hesitated at the threshold. "I'm not one for platitudes, Rachel, and I won't minimize the hurt you've been caused. But the woman who wrote that horrible letter was right about something. You're strong. And a man who lets his mother do his dirty work is not the right man for a strong woman." She paused. "You're going to be all right, dear. It will take time, but Lizzie and I will help you. And what you said a moment ago when you were crying on my shoulder—about not having a home to go to? Nothing could be further from the truth. You have a home right here in Lost Creek with people who truly love you."

In the aftermath of Aunt Jennie's departure, Rachel scooped up the baby while Nel made the tea. When Rachel looked into his face, the baby watched her intently for a moment then gave her a toothless grin. Rachel smiled back. "Aren't you a darling boy." She touched the dimple in his chin. "Let's see another. Yes, that's it, little man."

Nel set the cup of tea on the table, and Rachel handed the baby over. She took a sip and made a face. "That's—awful." She rose to get the sugar, and the baby began to cry.

"Probably needs changing," Nel said. "I'll see to the diaper if you'll tell me where you keep the clean ones."

By the time Rachel had drunk the tea, the baby had a clean, dry diaper, but he'd added flailing and kicking to the cry. Nothing Nel tried worked. Finally, a frustrated Nel handed him back. It was as if a knob had been turned from *sad* to *happy*. Instant smiles.

"Well, I never." Nel frowned.

"It's just that he knows me better," Rachel said. "He's getting to the age."

"And what 'age' is that?"

"The one where babies tend to cling to what they know and be wary of those they don't know as well."

"Is that what it is?" Nel sat down next to Rachel and tickled the baby beneath the chin. "Well, we're just going to have to fix that, aren't we?" She cooed, but the baby boy sat staring, his lower lip jutted out just enough to ward off any new attempts at removing him from Rachel's arms.

"Why don't you get out the drawing of your quilt," Rachel suggested. "I'll get some fresh paper and pencils and see what I can do about creating a pattern."

"Are you sure?"

"I am." Rachel rose, settled the baby on her left hip, and went into the parlor to retrieve yesterday's newspaper. Back in the kitchen, she laid it out on the table. "We can trim that down to the block size, and then I'll play with outlining the appliqué pieces. We'll work on that until we have the right balance. Once that's done, we can move on to leaf shapes and circles."

With a smile and a soft sound of affection, she laid the baby atop the pallet and wrapped him in a blanket. He closed his eyes and fell asleep.

"If I didn't know better, Rachel Ellsworth," Nel said in wonder, "I'd think you knew some magic that casts spells over babies."

"Don't be silly. I'm just—I've always had a knack with children."

"Well, I wouldn't mind if it were contagious," Nel said wistfully. "Especially when it comes to two particular children."

"Now that we're going to work on your masterpiece together," Rachel said, "he'll get to know you better." She looked down at the spot of spit-up on her dress. "And be spitting up on you in no time."

Nel grimaced. "Delightful."

"You don't get the smiles without the drool and spit-up," Rachel said. "And speaking of spit-up, he's going to be hungry when he wakes up, so if we're going to make any progress at all, now's the time." She reached for Nel's drawing.

Rachel was spooning the last bit of milky grits into the baby's mouth when she heard the rattle of a harness as Aunt Lizzie and Anna drove past the house and toward the small barn at the back of the lot. They were back. Aunt Lizzie would have to hear the news about Landis.

Nel looked up from tracing a leaf. "Do you want me to go? So you can—talk about it?"

Rachel sat back. "Would you mind if I took the letter out to the barn and sent Anna inside? She can amuse her brother for a few minutes."

"Of course," Nel said. "Go. The children and I will be fine."

Rachel went outside. Anna saw her and came charging across the lawn, spouting news. "Papa named the baby. Mama wrote it down, but Papa didn't know, and when he put the quilt blocks in Mama's basket he found the paper and now the baby has a name! And Papa found Mama's recipes, and he made biscuits. I didn't even know he could do that, but they were good. And Aunt Lizzie is going to teach him to make soup. Do you want to know it?"

"Know. . . ?"

"My brother's name, silly."

"Of course," Rachel said.

"Barrett Michael Friesen. Mama's name was Barrett before she was Friesen, and Aunt Lizzie says ladies do that sometimes so their family name doesn't get lost. Someday when I grow up and have a baby boy I'm going to name him Friesen." She stopped, frowning. "Although that isn't a very pretty name. Maybe I'll put it in the middle." Anna was still rambling on about names when Aunt Lizzie caught up to them.

"I need to speak with you for a moment," Rachel said then spoke to Anna. "Nel and I have been working on a project. You can give her all the news while I talk to Aunt Lizzie."

"Take this in with you," Aunt Lizzie said and handed Anna a lovely handled basket. "You can help Nel sort the quilt blocks."

Rachel watched Anna go and then held out the letter. "I've had word from St. Louis."

Aunt Lizzie read quickly then engulfed Rachel in a hug. "You'll stay here, of course. It will be a great blessing to us. I'm only sorry for the way it happened."

"Aunt Jennie said the same thing. About my staying here." Rachel took in a ragged breath. "I'd like that."

"It's settled then." Aunt Lizzie paused before saying, "This will be hard for you to believe, but in time you may come to realize that God allowed your heart to be broken in order to save you far greater pain later."

Rachel didn't want to think about that. Pondering the *why* of tragedy had never done her a bit of good. She'd heard Papa say the same thing dozens of times. "Instead of floundering in the Sea of Why, we must anchor ourselves in the Land of What Now." She would resist wallowing in *why* and do her best to focus on *what now*. At least part of the answer to the latter question lay right inside the back door of the house. *Help your aunts with Anna and the baby. Help Nel make her masterpiece. Finish Barrett's baby quilt. Think beyond yourself.*

Taking a deep breath, Rachel folded up the letter and led the way inside.

"Rachel! Come look!" Anna was kneeling on a kitchen chair, looking over the quilt blocks from Esther Friesen's sewing basket. She held up a round bit of cloth. "It's a sunrise."

"Sun*burst*," Nel corrected then addressed Rachel and Aunt Lizzie. "Now you can see what I meant when I said Anna wouldn't be able to work on them."

"But I *want* to," Anna insisted.

"The pieces are far too small."

Rachel looked down at the intricately pieced block, a circle surrounded by a dozen triangles interspersed with as many diamonds and then finished into a larger circle with wedge-shaped pieces. Nel was right. It wasn't a simple block. Still, she smiled at Anna. "We'll find a way."

"It's impossible," Nel said firmly. "We'll find something else for Anna to make." She picked up a circle of cloth.

Anna snatched it away. "It's *my* Mama's quilt and it's for *my* brother, and I'll sew it if I want to! Papa and Rachel said I could!" Anna grabbed a pile of pieces and charged out of the room.

Nel was fuming. "That child needs someone to take her in hand."

"She's been through a great deal for one so young," Aunt Lizzie said gently.

Nel's voice calmed. "Her poor papa must be overwhelmed. Even with folks doing everything they can to help. . .it just isn't enough." She paused. "Mother's said as much, and she's right. The poor man needs a wife. No one can expect him to manage alone."

No one does. Rachel thought it, but she didn't say it. Aunt Lizzie went after Anna who came back presently and choked out an apology. Together, they sorted the fabric pieces, triangles atop triangles, wedges atop wedges, circles atop circles.

Aunt Lizzie tucked them back into Esther's sewing basket. "I'll keep them here until the next quilting. I'll ask each of the ladies to complete one block." She smiled at Anna. "While the ladies are finishing the blocks, Rachel and I will teach you to stitch a perfect seam. Then you'll be able to help set them together."

"See, little one?" Rachel tugged on one of Anna's blond braids. "We found a way."

Anna shot an *I told you so* look Nel's way before retrieving the china-headed doll and sitting down beside her napping brother.

Aunt Lizzie continued to stack pieces back in the sewing basket. Then she noticed Rachel's sketch of Nel's masterpiece. She leaned closer, inspecting the drawing. "Wh–what's this?"

"It's from a quilt I saw years ago at the county fair," Nel said. "I've always planned to make it for my hope chest. I'm not certain I remembered it exactly, but—"

Aunt Lizzie traced a heart with the tip of her index finger. "You remembered very well. But it didn't have a border." She grabbed Esther's sewing basket. "I'll just put this in the parlor for safekeeping." She called to Anna. "And if you'd like to get started with a sewing lesson, you can come with me while Rachel and Nel work here at the table."

"I should be going," Nel said. She looked at Rachel. "I'm going to trust you and buy the gold fabric. If I hurry, I can get to the mercantile before it closes. Then I can work on cutting blocks and pieces this evening." She tucked her own sketch, Rachel's drawing, and the patterns for leaves and berries in her bag. Then she reached over and squeezed Rachel's arm. "I'm very sorry for what's happened to you. But I'll admit to being glad you won't be leaving Lost Creek. I've longed for a best friend. Now I have one."

Chapter Eight

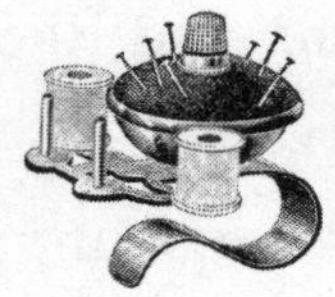

For the first month after receiving Mrs. Grove's letter, Rachel did well avoiding what her father had called the Land of Why. When the promised crate of her paintings arrived from St. Louis and Wyatt Dahl hauled it to the house, Rachel had him take it directly up to the attic. Just seeing the crate sent a pang of regret through her. She didn't need any reminders of what she'd lost. Best to put the paintings out of sight for now so she could focus on What Now.

An abundance of worthy tasks occupied her time. She pieced her assigned block for Barrett's baby quilt, advised a couple of quilters on new projects, and helped tend the garden. She even went along a few times when it was Aunt Lizzie's turn to take Anna to the farm. Once, she took the baby with them. When he reached for his son, Adam's hazel eyes sparkled with joy. *Hazel, with flecks of green.*

The brief flicker of attraction reminded Rachel of the promises Landis had made and would never keep, the future he'd abandoned in favor of one with someone else. A powerful sense of rejection constricted her throat and made her turn away from Adam and Barrett. She strode across the road to the garden where Wyatt Dahl was taking a hoe to the weeds. Anna ran after her, taking her hand as they walked. It was an innocent gesture, but it too reminded Rachel of Landis. She had so wanted children.

On the drive back to town, Aunt Lizzie tried to strike up a conversation. Rachel didn't have the energy for it. She knew Papa would not approve of her retreating into the Land of Why, and yet she couldn't seem to resist. Why would Landis throw her away so easily? Why didn't he at least write to her himself? Why didn't he give her a chance to fight for him? Why did good men like Adam Friesen lose the women they loved and men like Landis simply give them up?

The weather didn't help her mood. High temperatures and scorching winds sapped her energy and made her feel sluggish. By early August, Aunt Jennie was busy answering calls from mothers worried about losing babies to "summer complaint." Rachel and her aunts ate mostly cold food—boiled eggs and sliced ham, raw tomatoes and cucumbers. Anything that didn't require standing over a hot stove. Any baking happened either very late at night or very early in the morning. Windows were raised and stayed that way. Rachel took to sleeping on the little porch just outside her room, thankful not only for the screens that frustrated mosquitoes but also the chance to feel the slightest breeze.

Whys and regrets continued to roll in like waves, even as Rachel witnessed Adam's coming to terms with his loss. The quilters—who set up their frame beneath the shade tree in the Berkeys' backyard these days—spoke of how pleased Esther would be with the way Adam doted on his children. Wasn't it wonderful he'd followed Lizzie's advice in the kitchen? Husbands said the man's crops were in good shape. And he was making steady progress on the new church pews.

Rachel thought of Mr. Friesen simply as *Adam* now—probably because Nel mentioned him at every opportunity. Rachel didn't honestly know why, but she found Nel's assumed ownership of the details of Adam's life more than a little annoying. As if she had a special claim on it. Adam this and Adam that. It was enough to give a girl a headache.

In the predawn light of what promised to be another scorching summer day, Adam descended to the root cellar by lamplight. Setting the lamp on a shelf, he counted out three quarts of tomatoes. Two potatoes. A bunch of carrots. An onion. A piece of the dried herb hanging nearest the stairs. He couldn't remember the name of it, but Aunt Lizzie said it was good in soup. He'd soaked the beans overnight like she said. Today, he would put soup on to cook and be thankful he didn't have to stay in the kitchen with the hot stove. He and Wyatt would check on it periodically, and when they came in tonight, they'd find supper ready to eat.

Back in the kitchen, Adam added ingredients to the Dutch oven and set it over a low fire. He was drinking his second cup of coffee when Wyatt drove in—not alone, though. Nel Berkey hopped down and reached into the wagon bed for a basket.

"Surprise!" she called as she stepped into the house. "The quilters wanted to make sure there isn't any more of the fabric Esther was using for Barrett's quilt before they put the blocks together. I offered to check."

Adam said he didn't know.

"I didn't expect you would," Nel laughed. "Rachel has an idea for the finishing, but I told her we should keep it as close to what Esther wanted as possible. If there's more fabric, we should use it."

Adam motioned toward the parlor. "If Esther had more fabric, she'd have put it in the cupboard next to the sewing machine."

"I'll look." Nel plopped the basket on the table. "I've brought you boys a hearty lunch. I'll just spread a picnic under the cottonwood by the house."

"You're going to stay out here. All day?"

"Of course not." Nel giggled. "We wouldn't want to start any rumors, now would we? Aunt Jennie's driving by right after lunch. On her way to the Mitchells' to check on Blanche. She had their seventh last week. You didn't hear?"

Adam shook his head. He stood there, feeling awkward and wishing Nel hadn't invited herself to the farm. He resented the idea of her pawing through Esther's fabric. It was for a good reason, but still—truth was, there was something about Nel that just didn't sit well with him.

"You go on to work now," Nel said. "Don't let me keep you. I'll look for the fabric, and then I've brought handwork to keep me busy until it's time for our picnic." She flitted into the parlor.

Adam left the house, wondering why he resented the sight of a picnic basket brought by a friend. Maybe it was because Nel hadn't asked if he and Wyatt needed lunch. She'd just assumed. Hadn't even noticed—or had ignored—the soup pot on the stove. Nel was like that sometimes. Pushy. Had been since they were young. It hadn't mattered when they were all growing up, because Adam just kept his distance. It mattered now, though. He glanced toward the house. She was going through Esther's cabinet. Helping herself to fabric. Assuming. Too much.

As for a picnic lunch, he and Wyatt had corn bread and freshly churned butter and molasses, and that would be plenty for the both of them until the workday was over and they sat down to soup. With a soft grunt of displeasure, Adam made his way to the open work area on the north side of the barn where he'd set up an outdoor workshop beneath an overhang. The pews he was making were a simple design and he enjoyed the process. Making pews was predictable. If he did things right, they'd turn out right. Being able to depend on an outcome was a good thing.

He was so deep in thought that when Nel's voice sounded from the far corner of the barn, it startled him.

"I didn't know you were a master carpenter," she said, coming over to run her hand along the top edge of a finished pew. "These are beautiful."

He didn't look up. "I'm not a master carpenter, but they're sturdy and will likely last longer than any of us. Did you need something?"

"No. I just wanted to tell you I found the fabric. Now we can finish Barrett's quilt—just the way Esther wanted it."

Adam nodded. "Anna's excited about helping with it."

"Yes. Well, it's a fairly complex design. But we'll find something for little Anna to do."

He glanced her way, frowning. "Did I misunderstand, then? I'm certain Anna said Rachel—Miss Ellsworth—had promised she could help with it. It means a lot to Anna." He held Nel's gaze, willing her to give in.

Nel glanced down at the piece of cloth in her hands. "Then of course we'll find a way for that to happen." She forced a smile and looked back up at him. "Rachel's a dear, but she doesn't know quite as much about quiltmaking as I do. She might not understand how difficult it can be for a four-year-old to learn to stitch." She brandished the gold-colored square. "But when it comes to drawing, her talent really shines. Take this for example. It's my design, but as soon as I described it, Rachel drew it up as easy as pie."

Adam glanced at the square of cloth. *A heart.* What was he supposed to say? He gave a noncommittal grunt and concentrated on the sanding.

"What do we have here?" Wyatt came up behind Nel and

reached for the square of cloth. She snatched it away.

"Keep your grubby hands off it."

Wyatt made a show of holding his hands up and waggling them about. "Not grubby. Just washed them. Thought you were out here telling Adam to come to lunch." He pointed at the square of gold cloth. "Hearts, eh? Must be for someone special."

Nel drew it to herself so Wyatt couldn't touch it. "It's for my hope chest, if you must know."

"That mean you're hoping to get hitched?" Wyatt asked.

"It means I'll be prepared to make a home for—someone."

Wyatt's tone changed. "Well, *someone*'s going to be real lucky."

"Thank you. That's a very nice thing to say."

"Wasn't being nice. Just saying what is." Wyatt offered Nel his arm. "What say I help you set out that picnic you were bragging about. Adam can join us whenever he's a mind to."

Thank goodness. Nel allowed Wyatt to lead her away. Adam glanced up from his work a few times to check on the progress of the picnic. Not until things were set out and Nel and Wyatt were settled on the checkered cloth did he venture to join the party. He declined to sit down, ate while standing, and excused himself as soon as he could.

He didn't want to believe it, but it felt like there was a bit of flirtation going on from Nel's direction. Toward him. He hoped he was wrong. Nel was nice enough. She just wasn't the kind of person he'd ever want to marry. If he ever did marry again. *Huh.* He'd resisted the idea, but the truth was, Anna and Barrett deserved to have a mama. Someone to care for them right here at home. While the idea didn't horrify him, it did make him feel guilty. That was probably only normal. But Nel Berkey? There was not one tiny little spark in that direction.

It was quilting day, but Rachel wasn't going. She'd decided that in the middle of the night. Now, well after time to be up and about, she descended the stairs to the kitchen. "I'm sorry," she said to her aunts and Anna, "but I don't feel well enough to go to quilting today." She crossed to the stove to pour a cup of tea.

"Not well enough?" A concerned Aunt Jennie rose from the table. She put her palm to Rachel's forehead. "You don't feel feverish. Your appetite's been off, though. Any other symptoms?"

None I can say in front of Anna. Rachel shook her head. "I'm sure it's nothing serious. Just a headache. And I'm tired. That's all." *And sick to death of hearing Nel go on and on about Adam.* Ever since Nel had invited herself to accompany Wyatt Dahl to the farm under the guise of finding fabric for Barrett's baby quilt, it seemed that every time they were together, Nel had another anecdote to share about the wonders of Adam Friesen. Rachel had heard more than her share of anecdotes. The final blow had fallen only yesterday afternoon.

They'd been sitting on the screened porch at the back of the property, each one stitching away, when Nel lowered her voice and confided her secret. Adam Friesen needed a wife and she, Nel Berkey, was going to see to it that he got a good one. Her. It was only a matter of time. Adam probably wouldn't propose for a while yet. Although some men did. Goodness, Vernon Carter had barely managed six months before remarrying. But then Vernon had married the first woman who would take him, just to get out from under managing his four children. Adam was a devoted father. He would need more time. Nel blushed when she confided, "I'm hoping for a proposal at Christmas."

A proposal at Christmas. The phrase reminded Rachel of what she'd lost when Landis met that other girl, and it sent a barb straight to her heart. While Nel rattled on, Rachel fought back tears. Nel was oblivious until finally, Rachel claimed a headache and fled up to her room. She'd spent much of last night rereading Landis's letters—and Mrs. Grove's cruel missive. She could face neither the quilters nor Nel's barrage of Adam-anecdotes today.

"Nel will be so disappointed," Aunt Lizzie said. "She loves it that you're helping with her quilt."

"I've had quite enough of that infernal quilt," Rachel snapped. And then brought her hand to her mouth in horror. "I'm so sorry. I just—" A sob escaped. "Nel means well, but—"

Aunt Lizzie looked at her with concern. "You've been holding something in for weeks now, dear girl. Out with it."

Rachel looked over at Anna. She shook her head. "I can't talk about it. Not now."

Aunt Jennie caught on immediately. "Take your tea upstairs and rest. Perhaps you'll feel more like talking later."

Rachel obeyed. From her perch on the little porch, she saw Aunt Lizzie and Anna leave for quilting. And then. . .Aunt Lizzie returning a few minutes later. Alone. The expected knock at her door came moments later.

Aunt Jennie opened the door just a crack. "Even if we can't fix whatever's bothering you, it might help if you had someone to listen. Anna's with the quilters, and Barrett's taking his morning nap. I've made a fresh pot of tea, and I just brought some of my corn-bread muffins out of the oven. Please, Rachel. Let us help."

Rachel spun about in her chair. "You baked? In this heat?"

"Well. . .yes. You love my corn-bread muffins. I hoped it would tempt you to come downstairs."

It had been a very long while since Rachel had confided in another woman. Since Mama died. She'd learned to keep things in. To soldier on. Goodness, hadn't she been soldiering on all these months in Lost Creek? First, ticking the weeks off until she would leave. And now. . .just soldiering on. And all the while listening to Nel blather about her rosy future.

"Rachel?" Aunt Jennie pleaded.

Rachel rose from the chair and went to her bedroom door. "Yes," she said, her voice wavering with emotion. "I think—maybe—maybe it would help." Once downstairs, she joined her aunts at the kitchen table. She took a sip of the tea Aunt Jennie had just poured and tried to collect her thoughts. "I can't seem to get past losing Landis. I'm beginning to wonder if I ever will." Tears threatened. She forced them back and choked out a little more. "I know you both said I would. Goodness, even Landis's mother said I was *strong*. But I don't feel strong and I'm not sure I *am* going to be all right. My future was all planned out. And so beautiful. Paris. . .art lessons. . .Landis. Children." She allowed a little sob. "Now it's. . . bleak. Blank."

"Blank?" Aunt Jennie chided. "You may wish you could erase us, dear child, but that's never going to happen. You're stuck with us. And with Nel and the quilters and Adam and the children and even Wyatt Dahl. All of those people care about you."

Rachel sighed. "I'm grateful, but it doesn't help. I feel adrift."

"Of course you do," Aunt Lizzie said. "You've had a terrible shock. It will take time to find your way. But you will. In time."

"How much time?" Rachel spoke through her tears. "It's been nearly a month since that letter came, and I feel worse than ever. Adam lost his *wife*, but he's managing. He's even beginning to smile again. What kind of weakling am I that I can't get over losing a man who didn't even have the courage to write his own letter saying he'd found somebody else?"

Aunts Lizzie and Jennie were quiet for a few minutes. Finally Aunt Lizzie asked, "What does any of this have to do with going to quilting? Or with Nel and her quilt? Spending time with friends is a way to move toward healing."

Rachel sighed. "I'm sure it comes as no surprise to the two of you that Nel has set her cap for Adam. Which is fine. Who could blame her? He's kind and strong and hardworking—and very handsome. But Nel's obsessed. Lately it's all she talks about. And yesterday—yesterday she was daydreaming about how she hoped he'll propose. At Christmas."

"She—what?" the aunts said in chorus.

"I've tried not to resent her. Really, I have." Rachel's tears started to flow again. "But Christmas was going to be *my* engagement to Landis. I want to be happy for Nel—but every word she says reminds me of everything I've lost." She dabbed at her tears. "I just can't listen anymore."

Aunt Lizzie spoke up. "Adam Friesen is no more going to propose to Nel Berkey than a man is going to walk on the moon. They're totally unsuited for each other. Anyone who knows them can see that. And I'm quite certain Adam sees it even if Nel can't." She paused. "But that's neither here nor there at the moment. Right now, our concern is for you." Aunt Lizzie reached over and took both Rachel's hands in her own. "It may take longer than you want it to, but trust me, dear. One day you will wake up and realize the dark clouds have parted. The sky is blue again, and you are looking forward to what the day has for you. I know it beyond a shadow of a doubt."

Rachel wanted to believe Aunt Lizzie. Truly, she did, but what could a spinster know of broken hearts and lost dreams?

Aunt Lizzie let go of Rachel's hands and sat back. "Then again," she said, "what could an old maid like me know of such things?"

Rachel looked up in horror. "I would never say such a thing!"

"Of course not. But you'd think it. What beautiful young woman wouldn't, having an old hag like me spinning tales of blue skies ahead?"

Rachel started to protest, but Aunt Lizzie held up a hand. "I don't blame you." She reached for a muffin, plopped it on a plate, and handed it to Rachel. "Eat. I'll be back in a moment." She left the room.

Rachel looked over at Aunt Jennie who only shrugged and passed the butter and jam. She heard Aunt Lizzie go up the stairs. She heard a door creak. *The attic?* "Is she going to the attic? It'll be like an oven up there."

"If she's after what I think she is, she won't be up there long."

Aunt Jennie was right. Rachel had taken one tiny bite of muffin when Aunt Lizzie returned. Rachel's jaw dropped. Aunt Lizzie had retrieved a quilt from the attic. Hearts appliquéd onto a white ground. Leaves and berries. And the quilting! My goodness. . . the quilting.

Aunt Lizzie draped the quilt over the back of a chair and sat down. "Nel was too young to remember who made the quilt she admired at the fair all those years ago." She swept her palm across the surface. "It was to be my wedding quilt."

"Wedding." Rachel echoed the word, trying to absorb the idea of Aunt Lizzie in love.

The old woman's eyes filled with tears. "You see, dear niece. I *do* know what you're going through. Only my young man didn't write a letter. He died. At Gettysburg." She reached over and took Rachel's hand. "We do find a way to go on, a way to happiness. My life has not been the life I dreamed of, but it's been very, very good. And I *am* happy."

Rachel sniffed and wiped at the last of her tears. "I'm so sorry you had to go through that. Sorry I doubted that you could understand."

Aunt Lizzie touched the quilt again. "I kept it on my bed for a while, but in the end, even though it is exquisite, I just couldn't bear it anymore. I felt smothered beneath it, and I knew I had to put it away. I couldn't let my loss define the rest of my life. I had to look to the future. I begged God to help me find my way back to hope and joy. And He did. Not all at once. But He did."

Aunt Jennie spoke up. "You must not give up hope, Rachel. Don't deny how much it hurts. Cry the tears. Grieve. And know that on the other side there's the wonder of dawn and a new beginning—just as you painted in that sunrise for your father." She smiled. "Maybe that painting can remind you of another verse. The one about joy coming in the morning."

"And until joy comes," Aunt Lizzie said, "you simply do the next thing. Have the muffin. Drink the tea. Get dressed. Take a walk. You do the next thing and the next and the next. And one day, after countless 'next things,' you'll realize you're feeling better and finding your way."

What treasures these women were. What storehouses of wisdom. Rachel took a deep breath. "I know you're right." She offered a wry smile and muttered, "But I still don't want to hear Nel go on about a Christmas engagement."

"And who could blame you?" Aunt Lizzie rose from her chair. "I'm going back to quilting right now, and while I'm there I'll let everyone know that you're feeling a bit better, but Jennie's insisting you take it easy for the next day or so."

Aunt Jennie nodded. "And if you need more time, I'll ask for extra help with the children for the next few days. Or longer." She reached for the quilt and spoke to Aunt Lizzie. "I'll take it back up for you."

"I can do it," Rachel said. "Just tell me where it goes." She took a deep breath. "And then. . .there's a 'next thing' I need to do. It's time I unpacked my trunks." *And time I burned some old letters.*

Chapter Nine

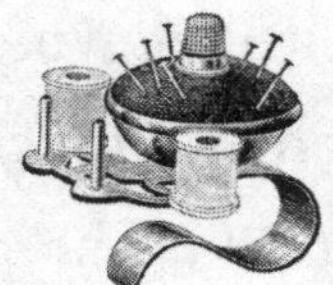

As August gave way to September and harvest neared its conclusion, Adam found a new way to see his children nearly every day. He began to spend more time with the crew building the new church, arriving late in the afternoon and lingering until he had to get back home for evening chores.

It was especially nice that he could count on one of the three women at the Meekers' being part of the group of ladies who served an afternoon snack at the building site. Once they realized Adam might be there, they began to bring Anna along—and Barrett, if he'd wakened from his nap. It was another precious few moments he could spend with his children.

It was on a perfect afternoon in late September, when Adam suddenly realized that on the afternoons when he was at the building site, he'd begun to watch the road for the arrival of the "basket brigade," as the men were wont to call the ladies. And not because he was hungry, although he always was. No, he was watching for a tall, slim young woman wearing an outlandish straw hat. Outlandish for Lost Creek, anyway. But probably very much in style in St. Louis.

One day, when the men were gathered around the table created with an old door and sawhorses, a breeze caught Rachel's hat and sent it flying. Adam chased it down. When he brought it back and she reached for it, their hands touched. It was only the briefest contact, and yet that night when he retired, Adam replayed the moment in his mind. It was as if he'd seen Rachel Ellsworth for the first time. Those dark eyes. The way the corners of her mouth turned up when she thanked him. And later in the afternoon, her laughter when she plopped a chain of woven clover on Anna's head and swung the child about.

He tried to resist the attraction. Tried to focus on friendship. With appreciation for what she was doing to help the Meeker sisters. After all, it was going on eight months since Esther died. It had to be hard for them. No doubt Rachel lightened the load. Anyone could see she delighted in children—and Anna and Barrett delighted in her.

"That one"—his sister Molly said one day when she was at the building site—"is going to be a wonderful mother."

Adam pretended not to hear.

Molly stepped close and spoke quietly. "Esther was my best friend. You made her very happy. And she'd want you to be happy. She'd also want her children to have a flesh-and-blood mama."

"Can't think on that," Adam groused. "I'm not ready."

"But when you are?" Molly nodded toward Rachel who was

busily serving up slices of pie to a gaggle of men. "Just don't take too long. You're not the only man in Lost Creek in need of a wife."

It might be a coincidence, but at that very moment Adam saw Rachel smile at Zeb Gruber. And then laugh at something Zeb said. *Huh.*

"And one more thing," Molly said. "In case you haven't noticed, your children favor Rachel over someone who shall remain nameless, but who has definitely set her cap for you. Initials *N.B.*"

Adam frowned. *N.B.* So. He wasn't imagining things when it came to Nel. "As to what Esther would want, when it comes down to it, isn't what *I* want what really matters? In that matter."

"You mean the matter you aren't ready to discuss?"

"Yes. That one."

Molly chuckled. "Agreed. In that matter, what really matters is what matters to you. I just thought I'd let you know that when it comes to that matter you aren't ready to discuss, what matters to me is that you're happy. And that's what would matter to Esther too." She shifted the baby in her arms to the other hip. "Glad we had this little chat." With a laugh, she hollered for the twins to round up their siblings and stepped back to the table where Rachel was serving pie.

And still talking to Zeb Gruber, Adam noted. *Huh.*

Rachel stood on the front porch looking east, where the sky blazed with pinks and peaches and oranges beyond anything she had ever painted. *"Weeping may endure for a night, but joy cometh in the morning."* Remembering that scripture made her smile even as she crossed her arms and hugged herself against the chill of the crisp, cool air.

Just as Aunt Lizzie had predicted, after many days of just "doing the next thing," it had happened. She'd begun to look forward instead of dwelling in the past. Most of the time. It had taken a new kind of "soldiering on" to move from the Sea of Why to the Land of What Now. She'd cried more tears and read more scripture and finally. . .finally, the pall of sadness over her life had lifted. Hope had begun to glimmer—especially in light of the day ahead.

The instant the neighbor's rooster crowed, she'd thrown back the covers and hopped out of bed, dressing quickly and hurrying downstairs and out onto the front porch so she could watch the dawn. And it was glorious.

"Thank You, Lord, for eyes to see," she whispered. "Thank You for Aunt Jennie. Aunt Lizzie. Their welcome. Thank You for new friends." She allowed a low chuckle. "Yes, Lord. Thank You for Nel. Help me be a good friend to her and a help with that 'infernal quilt.'"

If being able to smile about Nel's determination to capture Adam's heart wasn't proof that Rachel was going to be all right, nothing was. "Oh God, You are so good. Thank You for hope."

Behind her, the front door opened with a creak. Still in her nightgown, Anna came to Rachel's side. "What you doing out here?"

"Look," Rachel said, gesturing toward the sky. "Isn't it beautiful?"

Anna yawned. Rubbed her eyes. "It's all pink and purply."

"And orange and peach." Rachel moved to sit on the front step and motioned for Anna to come sit in her lap and snuggle close against the morning chill. "I've never been to a county fair before. I'm excited!" Anna's stomach rumbled. Rachel laughed and hugged the child. "Guess we'd better feed that growly bear."

Back inside, Rachel put her finger to her lips, signaling they should be quiet. Together, she and Anna tiptoed into the kitchen. Anna set the table while Rachel stirred up the fire, made coffee, and mixed a batch of flapjacks. They'd both eaten half their stacks when the aunts bustled into the kitchen with exclamations over how late they'd slept and how good breakfast smelled.

Rachel rose from the table and waved the aunts into their chairs. "I want to wait on you this morning." She poured batter into a skillet and coffee into mugs. She'd just set the coffee before the aunts when Barrett woke and began to cry.

Rachel changed his diaper, talking as she worked. "I've got grits cooking for you, little man." She picked him up, settled him on her left hip, and went to flip the flapjacks.

Aunt Lizzie leaned toward Aunt Jennie. "It would appear, sister, that we have become obsolete." She made a show of snapping her napkin and spreading it across her lap. "And if this is what it looks like, I'm all for it."

Once Rachel had set a plate of flapjacks before her aunts, she settled Barrett in his high chair. Tying a towel about his midsection for extra stability, she dished up grits, added milk from the icebox, and sat down to feed him. When she realized the aunts were both smiling at her, she cocked her head. "What?"

"It's good to see you doing 'the next thing' with a real smile on your face," Aunt Jennie said.

Anna asked for more flapjacks. Rachel fed Barrett and refilled the aunts' coffee cups between pouring and flipping more flapjacks. Finally, she poured herself a cup of tea and sat down.

"Rachel's never been to a fair before," Anna said.

"A *county* fair," Rachel corrected. "Papa and I went to the Centennial with a group of church members."

"If you went to the Centennial," Aunt Lizzie warned, "don't get your hopes up for today."

"The Centennial was overwhelming. There was too much to see and too much to do, especially when we only had one day there."

"Well, you won't be overwhelmed today," Aunt Lizzie said.

"But you will have fun," Aunt Jennie added quickly. "Last year's quilt exhibit was quite fine. There's to be a baseball game in the afternoon and a dance this evening—if we last that long."

Aunt Lizzie glanced Anna's way. "I don't suppose anyone here will care about it, but I have it on good authority there will be pony rides for the children."

Rachel wiped the baby's face and set him on the pallet. "Anna, could you entertain your brother for just a few minutes while I do the dishes?"

Aunt Lizzie rose to help. When Rachel tried to protest,

she waved her off. "Breakfast was lovely, and I am sufficiently impressed with your homemaking skills. But now I want to help so we can get going. Get the big picnic basket out of the pantry, won't you?"

A knock sounded at the back door. Rachel went to answer it. *Adam?*

"Papa!" Anna squeezed past Rachel and practically climbed him as if he were a tree.

Rachel waved him into the kitchen. "We weren't expecting company."

"What a nice surprise!" Aunt Lizzie exclaimed. "We didn't hear you arrive." She looked past him, obviously expecting to see his buggy.

"I pulled up out front," Adam said. "Over chores, Wyatt asked to borrow the buggy. He's hoping to surprise Nel Berkey and squire her about for the day." He glanced Rachel's way. "Wyatt's idea gave me an idea. What better way to spend a day than to gather up a passel of kids and friends?" He looked to the aunts. "If you don't mind riding in the bed of a farm wagon, I'd be pleased to drive you all. I must get home this evening to do chores, but if you decide to linger, Wyatt can bring you home. He was set on staying for the dance." He put Anna down. "I'm hoping to keep the children with me overnight. I've been wanting to see how that would go."

Aunt Jennie spoke for them all by asking Rachel to fetch some quilts to make a pallet in the back of Adam's wagon. "We can make the wagon bed comfortable for the drive, and then we'll be able to rig up a nice little napping spot beneath the wagon when it's nap time."

"I won't need a nap today," Anna declared firmly. "We're going to have *fun* all day."

Adam tweaked her nose. "We'll have fun before and after your nap."

Anna made a face, but she didn't challenge him. "Me and Ezra will want to ride the ponies. I hope we can find him."

"Oh, we'll find him," Adam said. "Ezra's riding with Wyatt and Nel. Whoever gets there first will save a spot for the other and set up camp as close to the entrance as they can get, claiming some shade near that little creek that runs through the fairgrounds." He crouched down to Anna's level. "Think we can be first?"

"Yes!" Anna said.

"You wearing your nightgown?"

"No!" Anna shot out of the room and up the stairs to dress.

Rachel called after her to be sure to bring her bonnet. "And speaking of bonnets," she said, "I'd best be getting mine."

Upstairs in her room, Rachel opened the bandbox holding her straw sailor hat. Settling it on her head just above the rather loose bun she'd created on rising, she reached for a hat pin. Instead of the elegant pin Landis had given her, she chose Mama's. Simple. Serviceable. And an excellent choice for a girl from Lost Creek, Nebraska.

Chapter Ten

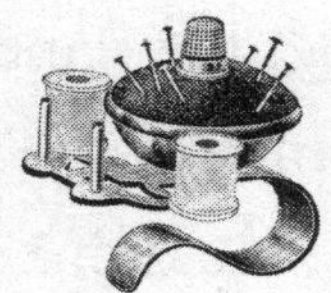

When Adam drove the wagon through the county fair entrance, he caught sight of Wyatt and Nel right away, settled exactly where they'd all hoped to locate in a spot of shade near the creek running along the edge of the fairgrounds. The couple sat on a blanket, with Wyatt pointing at something on a gold square of cloth spread across Nel's knee and listening to what she was saying with rapt attention.

As the morning progressed, Adam was surprised by many things. While Nel was holding her nose and trying to pull them all away from a livestock exhibit, Rachel Ellsworth seemed genuinely interested in learning the differences between a Hereford and a Shorthorn. Adam would not have expected that from a big-city girl.

After being excited about pony rides, Anna hesitated when confronted with a shaggy little beast that kept stomping one of its hind feet and tossing its head. Adam had never realized his daughter could be tentative about trying new things. She steadfastly refused to climb aboard, until Adam promised to walk alongside with his hand on the saddle, all the way around the temporary corral.

And then, as he walked alongside Anna's pony, Adam saw Rachel smiling up at Zeb Gruber and it made him feel—surely not jealousy, but something. He remembered Molly's comment that day at the church building site about him not being the only man in need of a wife. He didn't like seeing Rachel smile at another man.

And then there was the surprise over what he didn't feel when he took Barrett in his arms and let the ladies lead the way to the quilt exhibit. The quilters had finished Barrett's baby quilt. There it hung, pinned to a clothesline above the blue ribbon winner that was spread out across a stack of hay bales. Even he could appreciate the skill it had taken for Esther and her friends to wrangle all those tiny pieces into place. Dark blues, light blues—scraps of Esther's dresses, probably. The surprise was the absence of the awful sense of loss at the pit of his stomach. He felt. . .proud. And thankful. Proud of Esther. Thankful for the friends who'd completed the quilt. Thankful for the healthy baby boy in his arms.

When Anna took his hand, Adam looked down with a smile. "It's beautiful, little one."

"And I helped."

"She certainly did," Rachel said. "She sewed that last border on all by herself."

"I didn't think she could do it," Nel Berkey said. "But Anna proved me wrong. She did a fine job. We only had to re-stitch a very little bit."

Adam nodded. There were no tears to hold back. Only a gentle kind of sadness and a whisper of regret. He'd finally escaped the darkest part of grieving. He looked from Rachel to Nel and back again. "Thank you for making this happen." He pulled Anna to his side and gave her a one-armed hug.

After the quilt exhibit, the group meandered around the fairgrounds without a specific aim. Until Wyatt came trotting up to recruit Adam for a tug-of-war.

Adam shook his head. He jostled Barrett. "I'm busy."

"You aren't going to get out of it that easily," Nel said and pulled the baby right out of his hands.

Barrett protested. One of the aunts took him and settled him down.

"It's First Church against Lake Street," Nel said. "We can't let Lake Street win two years in a row." She tucked her hand beneath Adam's arm and tugged.

Adam looked over at Rachel in dismay, but she only shrugged. "Don't look at me. From what I know of church rivalries, they're not to be trifled with. Besides, I've seen you wield a hammer. Why not use those brawny forearms for something fun?"

"Rachel's right," Nel said. "The boys need your muscles."

Adam allowed himself to be pulled back toward the creek. On the opposite bank, half-a-dozen men he recognized as members of Lake Street had already assembled. First Church was definitely underrepresented.

"Those guys haven't been building a new church in their free time," Wyatt said. He raised his arms and flexed his biceps.

Someone on the other side of the creek jeered. "That all you got? Let's show 'em, boys." He strutted about like a circus performer preparing to lift a heavy barbell.

Wyatt took the challenge. "Come on, men. Let's do this!" He marched to the edge of the creek and grabbed the rope just this side of the white flag that marked its center.

The small crowd of onlookers began to shout encouragement, some to one team and some to the other. In a lull, Adam heard Anna cry out. "Yay, Papa!" He glanced over to where she stood beside Ezra Dahl, both of them jumping up and down with excitement.

Adam bent down and dusted his palms. Seeing the move, Wyatt let go of the rope and followed suit. Zeb Gruber showed up. He paused to say something to Rachel before joining the men. He tried to shoulder Wyatt out of the way.

"Strongest should be the front man," he said.

"Actually"—Wyatt said and let Zeb have the spot—"now that you mention it, the strongest men should be last in line." He moved back to join Adam at the end of the rope.

The front man on the opposite team shouted, "Ready for your baptism, First Church? Full immersion is the only way, you know."

The rope was stretched, the white handkerchief at its center poised mid-creek. Clutching a red kerchief, the official raised his hand high. The crowd quieted. Waited. And boom. The hand came down. The other team was strong. So strong, in fact, that for all of a couple of minutes, Adam thought surely Zeb was going to get that full baptism Lake Street had threatened.

"Hold!" someone cried from the crowd. "Come on, First Church. Hold!"

Adam didn't want to just hold. He wanted to win. Planting his feet, he collected himself, and then, with a shout and a mighty surge, he and his teammates pulled. Together, they dragged the Lake Street team into and across the creek.

Cheers went up even before Adam lost his footing and fell backward. He landed atop a clump of tall grass. Wyatt fell on top of him and rolled away, and the two men lay on their backs, looking at each other and laughing.

And for Adam, that was the biggest surprise of all. He was having fun. That odd feeling he hadn't been unable to identify this morning? *Happiness.* He'd forgotten how it felt.

After the men's tug-of-war victory, everyone accompanied the aunts back to the picnic spot. Adam lowered the wagon tailgate and the ladies set out a spread—fried chicken, canned peaches, sliced tomatoes, boiled eggs, fresh bread, and pie.

Barrett was already asleep in Aunt Jennie's arms. Aunt Lizzie and Rachel spread a quilt in the shade beneath the wagon. When lunch was over and it was time for the baseball game, Barrett was still asleep.

"You go on," Rachel said to Nel, Adam, and Wyatt. "Anna and I will stay here and mind the baby." She reached for Anna's hand and jiggled it. "We may even take a nap ourselves." Anna sank down and stretched out, with Rachel's lap for a pillow.

"It would appear, gentlemen"—Nel said, looking from Wyatt to Adam—"that I have you all to myself for the afternoon." Linking arms with Wyatt on her right, she wound her left arm around Adam's and proceeded to lead the men away.

Rachel reached over to stroke Anna's blond curls, smiling at the expression of happy exhaustion on the child's face. Whatever happened for the rest of the day, the county fair had been wonderful. She closed her eyes, listening to the murmur of the crowd, the swishing of horse's tails as the animals grazed nearby, a distant cheer as something wonderful happened in the baseball game. She was dozing when she sensed rather than heard a presence. She opened her eyes just enough to see a scarred boot.

"Looks like it wasn't just Anna who needed a nap." Adam settled on the blanket.

"And what of the baseball game?"

"Not a good one. Lake Street was ahead by five runs over the Country Boys in the second inning."

"Faulty pitching or a slow shortstop?" Rachel opened her eyes, satisfied to see surprise on Adam's face.

"You know baseball?"

"My father was a huge fan. The St. Louis Brown Stockings. We went to as many games as possible. And I learned a little in spite of the fact I was more interested in the fresh roasted peanuts than the game."

"There's a peanut vendor on the far side of the grounds. Say the word and I'll deliver to this very spot. It's the least I could do after you volunteered to stay here while we went off to have fun."

"And did you?" Rachel asked. "Have fun?"

"Surprisingly, yes."

"I'm so glad," Rachel said. She moved to get up.

"Please stay," Adam said, touching her arm. "I'd like it if we could—talk."

A pleasant little sensation rippled up Rachel's backbone. She felt herself blushing even as she settled back down.

Adam crossed his legs and leaned forward, elbows on knees, fingers laced and cradling his chin. "I know you grew up in St. Louis. Your mother passed a few years back. Your father was a pastor. That first day I met you, you made it clear you wouldn't be staying in Lost Creek. But now. . .some fool didn't have the sense to keep you, and here you are." He gestured about them. "Experiencing the glories of the York County Fair." He studied her. "How about it, Rachel Ellsworth, are *you* having fun?"

"I am." She said it without hesitation, and then she grinned. "Although I'm still not clear on the advantages of the Hereford over the Shorthorn. Or vice versa."

He laughed. "That's quite all right. I didn't know the difference between patchwork and appliqué until you explained it at the quilt exhibit."

"I guess we're even then."

He nodded. Studied her. Seemed about to say something more and then looked away abruptly. "It's time I made my way home. Evening chores are calling. Do you mind gathering Barrett out from under the wagon?"

Rachel slipped out from beneath a sleeping Anna and reached for the baby. She stood up with Barrett in her arms. "He's going to want to eat the minute he wakes."

Adam nodded. "I'd still like to take them both with me, but if you think it's crazy, I won't do it."

"Let me see if I can get him awake enough to give him his supper before you drive out. If you have cold biscuits or crackers at home, that'll do for a snack later—or breakfast tomorrow. And it's messy, but he can drink from a cup now."

Adam nodded. "We'll manage."

In the next few moments, Adam hitched the team, Anna woke, and Rachel fed the baby. She'd just settled him on the pallet in the wagon bed, braced between a couple of rolled-up quilts, when Nel and Wyatt returned.

When Nel realized Adam was leaving, she protested. "But there's to be a dance tonight."

"I'm no dancer." Adam nodded over at Wyatt. "But Wyatt will keep you spinning till dawn if you let him."

Nel peeked into the wagon bed. "You're taking Barrett?"

"I am. I want to see if I can handle the little man overnight." Adam lifted Anna up onto the wagon seat then turned to speak to Rachel. "I'll likely drive them back to town right after morning chores tomorrow. Maybe deliver a couple of church pews in the mix. After that, Wyatt and I have to get to the corn shucking." He climbed up beside Anna. "Wyatt, thanks for driving the ladies home. And ladies, thank you for a nice day." He touched the brim of his hat, chirped to the team, and drove away.

"We should plan a shucking bee," Nel said as she watched Adam drive off. She grabbed Wyatt's arm. "A shucking bee for the men, a quilting bee for the ladies, a community supper, and a dance to finish it off."

Rachel listened in stunned silence. What presumption. What gall!

Wyatt shrugged. "If you're going to take the Friesen place over, it's Adam you should be talking to, not me."

"Adam won't mind. He just said he'd welcome help."

Wyatt looked doubtful. "Far as I remember, he said he and I had a lot of work to do. Didn't say anything about asking for help."

"What farmer doesn't welcome help from his neighbors?"

Nel chattered away about where they'd set up the supper and whether or not they should clear out the barn or Adam's workspace to make way for a dance. All the while she talked, Rachel was watching Adam drive away, little Anna at his side. She put her hand to the place on her arm Adam had touched a few moments ago. She remembered the look of surprise on his face when she revealed a knowledge of baseball. And his calling Landis a fool for not keeping her. She thought about how easy it had been to say yes to his question about whether she was having fun. And she wondered what it would be like to be filling the empty space on the wagon seat.

Chapter Eleven

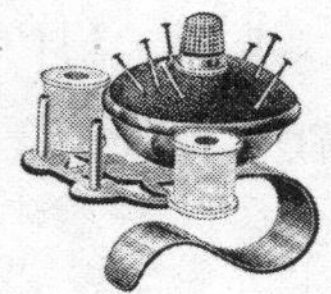

She. . .what?" Adam kept stirring the grits he was making for Barrett as he looked over to where Wyatt sat at the table, drinking coffee. The two had agreed that Wyatt would take care of morning chores—no matter his being gone half the night dancing and then driving the women home.

"You heard me," Wyatt said. "Nel's got the idea you'd welcome her planning a shucking bee for Saturday. And you know how Nel is. A shucking bee became a party—a quilting bee for the ladies, a community supper, and then a dance. I wouldn't be surprised if she comes out sometime today to ask where you want the dance—in the barn or under the overhang where you've been building those church pews."

Adam slid the bubbling grits off to the side and put another pan on, preparing to scramble eggs. He plopped a dollop of butter in the pan and cracked nearly a dozen eggs before saying anything.

"Help with the shucking wouldn't be so bad. Would it?"

"Of course not. But the rest of it?" Adam slid the iron skillet to the back of the stove beside the pan of grits before serving himself. "Help yourself," he said to Wyatt and sat down to eat. He waited for Wyatt to join him before asking, "How was the dance?"

Wyatt took a swig of coffee. "I surprised her. She didn't know I could dance."

Adam nodded. He took a bite of the biscuit, chewed, and swallowed before taking on the real topic at hand. "I need to have a talk with Nel."

"About?"

Adam gestured with his fork. "Bee this and bee that. And a dance." He shook his head. "Don't want it." He looked over at Wyatt who seemed to be studying him.

"You don't want Nel either. Do ya?"

"Nel and I have always been friends."

"That's not what I meant."

Adam sighed. Barrett was awake. Anna would be too before long. Rising from his place at the table, Adam went into the children's room. When he bent over the baby's crib, Barrett looked up at him and smiled. Reached for him. Adam lifted him into his arms, soppy diaper and all.

"Papa? I'm hungry."

Anna peered at him from beneath the covers, only the top of her blond head and her eyes visible.

"Go on out to the kitchen," Adam said. "Wyatt will help you get something to eat while I change Barrett's diaper. *Diapers. Do they get boiled with the rest of the wash. . .no. That'd be a different pot entirely, wouldn't it?* He pondered laundry for the two children while he readied Barrett for the drive back to town. When he returned to the kitchen, Anna was at the table eating.

"Thanks for helping," he said to Wyatt. He put grits in a bowl and poured milk with his free hand then settled Barrett on his knee at the table. *Oops. Need a bib.* He retrieved a dish towel, setting Barrett on the table just long enough to tie it around the baby's neck.

Wyatt sat back with a big smile on his face.

"Enjoying yourself?" Adam asked as he sat back down and spooned grits into the baby's mouth.

"You do all right," Wyatt said. "Can't say as I'm all that surprised. Nel has plenty to say about what a wonderful father you've turned out to be."

Nel again. Adam caught Wyatt's attention and nodded toward Anna. They'd need to measure their words carefully now that four-year-old ears were listening. "As to that matter," Adam said, "I should probably settle it once and for all after I drop the children at the Meekers' this morning."

Wyatt grinned. "I hope that means what I think it does."

Adam caught a dribble of grits with the spoon and returned it to Barrett's mouth. "If you hope it means there's not going to be any planning of festivities without first checking with me, and if you hope it means there's not going to be any assumption of a future that might include a partnership of any kind between myself and a certain person, then your hope will not be disappointed."

Wyatt took a bite of biscuit. Chewed and swallowed. Finally, he nodded. "Then you wouldn't be opposed to my pursuing a. . . er. . .partnership."

"I'd encourage it."

Wyatt reached over and tousled Anna's gold curls. "You hear that, little one? Wyatt's gonna help your pa." He chuckled. "In fact, how about I help by doing the dishes so you can leave right away?"

Adam rapped on the Berkeys' front door midmorning. When Mrs. Berkey appeared at the door, he snatched his hat off his head and stepped back. "Good morning, ma'am. I was hoping to have a word with Nel."

"She'll be delighted to see you," Mrs. Berkey said. "Please come in."

"Thank you, but I'd just as soon speak to her out here on the porch."

Mrs. Berkey looked back into the house. "It's Adam, dear. He's asking to speak with you."

A flurry of words ensued, but Adam couldn't hear them clearly. He did, however, hear footsteps ascend the stairs just inside the door as Nel hurried up to her room.

"Can I get you a cup of coffee while you wait?" Mrs. Berkey asked.

Adam shook his head. "No, ma'am. Thank you. I had coffee at the Meekers' just now when I dropped the children off."

Mrs. Berkey smiled. "And how did things go last night?"

"Fine. Just fine. Wyatt did morning chores so I could mind the children and—"

"Adam!" Nel squeezed past her mother. "Thank you, Mother."

She pulled the door closed behind her.

Adam stepped back lest Nel brush into him in her eagerness to join him on the porch.

"I'm sorry I kept you waiting." Nel made a show of smoothing her already perfect hair. "I wasn't about to let you see me until I'd changed out of my morning wrapper."

"Wyatt told me about your plans for the bee."

Nel smiled brightly. "I hope you're pleased."

This was going to be harder than he'd expected. "I'd be a fool not to be pleased when friends want to help."

"There's no reason to think *my* willingness to help will ever end. I care too deeply about you—and the children, of course—to ever—"

He'd practiced this speech all the way to town. He had to get Nel to hush long enough for him to deliver it, so he blurted out, "Nel. Stop."

"Stop. . .what?" She looked sincerely surprised. And confused.

Just deliver the speech. Adam took a deep breath. "You planned a party without talking to me first." Nel opened her mouth to say something, but Adam held up his hand. "Just listen. I practiced this speech all the way to town. Let me talk."

Nel crossed her arms. "All right. Talk."

He nodded. "You were a good friend to Esther and you've been kind to my children and me. I hope that never changes. But you can't be planning quilting bees and the like at my place. It sends a message to folks about you and me that's not true." He paused. *Oh no. She's going to cry.* "I hope those tears mean you're understanding what I'm trying to say."

Nel nodded. She looked away.

"I appreciate you as a close friend. But that's all we are ever going to be." He waited for the words to sink in. "Do you need me to say any more? Because I need this to be settled between us, once and for all." He waited. It felt like he waited a long time.

Finally, Nel took a deep, wavering breath. She sniffed and cleared her throat. "What—what did I do wrong? I mean. . .for you to change your mind about me. About us."

"I didn't change my mind. My thoughts never went beyond friendship. So. If you've talked to anyone about this shucking bee, you need to tell them it's canceled."

She pursed her lips. "Well, goodness, Adam. It's only ten o'clock in the morning. I haven't said a word about it to anyone. Except Wyatt."

Wyatt. The name landed in the middle of the conversation like a gift, and Adam grabbed it. "Now there's a good man." He watched Nel's reaction to the hint. It took a minute or so, but finally she uncrossed her arms and relaxed against the railing. He relaxed a little too.

"A good man—and a good dancer." With a little nod, she crossed the porch to the front door. Opening it, she stepped inside. And she did not look back.

A week after the county fair, Rachel was playing hide-and-seek with Anna in the backyard when Nel stopped by. After all the work the quilters had done to help with the county fair, they'd decided to take a brief hiatus from their weekly meetings at the Berkeys, and so Nel and Rachel hadn't seen each other. "I've missed you!" she said, when Nel came within earshot.

"Bet you haven't missed my big mouth," Nel said.

"What?"

"All that talk about marrying—making you listen. When the only reason you moved to Lost Creek was because of *not* marrying. Why didn't you just tell me to shut up?"

"It wasn't that bad."

"It was awful for me to do that without a thought of how it must have made you feel. I am so sorry."

"You didn't mean to hurt me. I know that." She changed the subject. "How's the quilt coming?"

"Only five hundred and forty of those infernal circles to go. That's actually what I came about."

A little voice sounded from the barn. "Rachel! You gonna find me or not?"

"Oh my goodness." Rachel wheeled about. "Excuse me. I forgot I was supposed to be 'seeking.'" She raised her voice. "I'm coming!" She hurried to the barn and made a show of not finding Anna who always hid in the same spot. After an appropriate delay and a few *where-is-that-child-now?* mutterings, Rachel peered behind the stack of hay bales in the corner. "There you are!"

Anna squealed with delight and tore out of the barn and toward the outhouse.

"Looks like it's a good thing you found her," Nel laughed.

"Can you stay? I'll make us some tea and we can catch up."

"I'd like that. If you have time."

"I have all the time in the world. Aunt Jennie's been called to a lying-in, and Aunt Lizzie is delivering supper to a family over on the west side of town." As she talked, Rachel retrieved Barrett and the quilt he'd been lying on. Anna exited the outhouse and they all headed inside.

Nel exclaimed over the fall bouquet in the center of the kitchen table.

"Papa picked them," Anna said. "He said Rachel likes sunflowers."

Rachel hurried to add, "Everyone loves sunflowers. After all, they're the last wildflowers we'll be able to enjoy before winter sets in."

"But Papa said *you* like them," Anna insisted.

"Anna, why don't you go get your sewing basket? You could show Nel what you're working on." After Anna left, Rachel explained. "We made up a little sewing kit that could be just hers. She's been doing a very nice job stitching a little four-patch doll quilt."

Nel was uncharacteristically silent. Finally, she said, "Did you know Wyatt Dahl was such a good dancer? I had no idea until the county fair."

Relieved that *Adam* wasn't the first name out of Nel's mouth, Rachel said, "No. . .I. . .I didn't. Know. Until then."

Anna came back with her sewing.

"I think he's probably the best dancer in the county. And strong? Oh my goodness! When he won that tug-of-war—"

"My *daddy* won the tug-of-war," Anna said, as she placed her sewing basket on the table and sat down.

"Well, yes, of course your papa helped. All the men on the First Church team helped." Nel shot a look that said *but we both know the truth* Rachel's way before peering into the sewing basket. "Is this what you're making?" She held up four rows of little quilt blocks.

Anna nodded. She pointed to one of the fabrics. "There was just a tiny piece left from when Mama made Barrett's quilt, and Rachel said we should put it in there, so one day when I have my own little girl and she sees it, it'll be a remember of my mama."

"A *remember*," Nel murmured. "That's beautiful."

Anna set the project out on the table, took up the next row of blocks, and settled down to pin them in place.

"Don't you want to do that for her?" Nel asked. "She'll never get it straight."

Rachel smiled. "*Straight* isn't the most important thing right now."

Nel pondered that for a moment before saying, "Anyway. Where was I?"

"Wyatt. Dancing."

"Oh. Yes. Well, there's more I'd like to talk about but another time. What I really came about was to see if you'd be willing to help with my quilt again. If I promise not to fill the air with a bunch of nonsense."

"I didn't think it was nonsense." *But I'd like it very much if that were true.*

"It was. And it probably hurt you. And I'm sorry." Nel took another sip of tea and stood up. "I should go now. Wyatt's mother invited me to supper with the family and I can't wear this old thing to meet the parents, even if I do already know them. So. About sewing together. What day is good for you?"

She's meeting the parents? Wyatt's parents? Rachel stammered a reply. "How's M–Monday afternoon? But it'll have to be here, unless I can bring Anna and Barrett with me if the aunts are busy."

"Monday." Nel nodded. "Thank you." She reached out to touch one of the sunflowers and murmured, "I hope you appreciate what these mean."

Rachel didn't know what to say to that. Nel was probably reading far too much into a bunch of wildflowers. On the other hand, a girl could hope.

Chapter Twelve

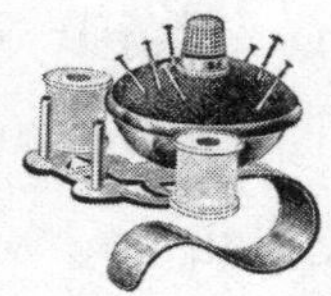

Adam stirred the fire in the stove and then went to peer out the kitchen window at the dormant landscape. Wyatt was late. Again. He'd agreed to come early a couple of mornings a week so Adam could have the children at home overnight, but Adam's attempt at establishing a regular routine wasn't working. At least it was for a good reason. Wyatt was spending a lot of time with Nel, which alternately relieved one problem and created another. Nel was no longer forcing her way into Adam's life. But Wyatt wasn't as reliable now that he had a reason to spend more time in town. *Ah, well.* Winter would be here soon, and once snow was drifting over the roads, the children would probably have to stay in town anyway. Best not to make an issue of it.

Turning away from the window, Adam prepared breakfast. As expected, a half-awake Anna stumbled into the room moments before Barrett woke. The children were almost finished with breakfast when Wyatt came inside with a troubled look on his face.

"What's wrong?"

"I don't like the looks of that cut on Bo's pastern. Took me a minute to even get him to settle enough to let me check it. There's heat running up the cannon almost to his knee."

Adam frowned. The horse had caught his hind foot in the fence the day before, but he'd remained calm and pulled it back. The injury hadn't seemed that bad. But it wasn't like Bo to be hard to handle.

"I'll stay here with the kids if you want to check it yourself."

"Anna," Adam said, "you help Wyatt with Barrett if he needs it, all right? Papa's just going to check on Bo. I won't be long."

Wyatt had been right about the big gray's unusual restlessness. When Adam tried to check the injury, the horse tossed his head and backed away. When he finally succeeded in checking the wound, what he discovered wasn't good. The cut was worse than he thought.

Back inside, he rummaged in Esther's fabric bin for something he could use for bandages. He'd ripped a mound of strips when Anna came into the little parlor. "Bo cut his foot. Papa's going to have to take care of it. I'll ask Wyatt to take you back into town."

"But *you* always do that."

"And I want to do it today, but I can't. You'll be fine with Wyatt."

Wyatt was more than willing to return to town. And was it all right if he took time to surprise Nel and stop by the Berkeys'?

Anna stomped her foot. "I don't *want* to ride with Wyatt. We'll be good, Papa. You can even take us out to the barn."

"It's too cold for that today," Adam said. He looked over at Wyatt. "After you drop the children, you can take lunch before driving back out here."

Anna thrust her lower lip out. "I want to stay home."

"You love it at the Meekers'."

"I love it better at home."

Adam knelt down. "I'm glad you do, little one. And I like it better when you're here with me too. But with Mama gone. . ."

"You said Mama's not coming back. You could get us a new one."

"Where'd you get an idea like that?" If Nel had been putting ideas in Anna's head—if she'd only been pretending to give up the ridiculous notion—

"From Aunt Molly."

"Molly?"

Anna nodded. "Aunt Molly said maybe someday you'd get us a new mama. She said our mama in heaven would prob'ly think that was a good idea. And I think so too. So Barrett and me can come home."

Well. That was a little better. Molly was interfering, but only because she loved Anna and Barrett and wanted the best for them.

"I'm sure Aunt Molly means well, but new mamas aren't something you just order up from the catalog." He forced a little laugh.

"I know that," Anna said. "Besides, Rachel's already here. Me and Barrett like her just fine. And you like her too. Else why'd you bring her sunflowers?"

Adam was suddenly aware of Wyatt, leaning against the door, his arms folded, a knowing smile on his face. The man was enjoying this entirely too much.

"We'll talk about this another time," Adam said. "Right now, you need to get dressed so Wyatt can take you back to town." After hesitating a moment, Anna trotted out of the kitchen and into her room. Adam glared at Wyatt. "Not a word."

"Did I say anything?"

"No, and you'd better not." Soon, Wyatt was headed back into town with the children and Adam had turned his attention to Bo. Mostly. *Rachel's already here. Me and Barrett like her just fine.*

The image of Rachel Ellsworth hovered on the fringes of the rest of his day. And while Adam could not quite envision her in Esther's house, he had no trouble at all envisioning her in his arms.

After Wyatt brought the children back to town—along with news of Bo's injury—Rachel could not seem to keep from worrying. Adam needed those horses. What if Bo didn't recover? When a couple of days went by and there was still no word, Rachel worried more. Thoughts of Adam seemed to hover over nearly everything she did. When nearly a week went by without his coming to town, even the aunts began to worry. And then cold, dreary weather settled in.

Anna was nearly inconsolable. "Will Papa visit today?"

"We don't know, little one."

"Why can't he come?"

"Because he has to take very good care of Bo. You know how important the horses are to the farm. They do so much work for your papa. But he'll come as soon as he can."

When Adam missed church on Sunday, the aunts and Rachel

planned to drive out together right after lunch. But then a storm moved in, bringing cold winds and sleet that coated the road.

"I'm sorry, little one," Aunt Lizzie said to Anna, "but if the wind picks up any more, the buggy could slide right off the road. It's too dangerous for us to go today."

Anna burst into tears. Aunt Lizzie eventually managed to convince her to join in a game of jackstraws.

Rachel mixed up a batch of bread dough. She was kneading—furiously—when Aunt Jennie joined her. "I hate it when winter announces itself with an ice storm."

Rachel gave the dough a punch. "Poor Anna was really counting on a drive out to the farm today."

"I don't think you have to worry about Adam," Aunt Jennie said.

"I'm sure you're right. I just can't seem to think of anything else." She shook her head. "It's strange."

Aunt Jennie chuckled.

"What's so funny?"

"I wouldn't call it strange at all."

"What would you call it?"

"I'd call it falling in love," Aunt Jennie said.

Rachel protested. "That's not it. I've been in love and this—this isn't the same."

"Are you sure you've been in love?"

"Of course I am. His name was Landis. Landis Grove."

Aunt Jennie nodded. "I remember the name. What I'm asking is. . .was that love or a habit? Everyone assumed you would marry, so you assumed it too."

Rachel pondered the comment. "I don't. . .know," she finally said. "I suppose I'm afraid to find out. Afraid he doesn't feel the same way."

"He does."

"How do you know? How will *I* know?"

Aunt Jennie smiled. "Have patience. When he finally decides to speak his mind, Adam won't leave any room for doubt. And in the meantime. . .enjoy every breathless moment."

Freezing rain coated the world in a glimmering sheet of ice. Tree branches broken by the weight crashed to the earth. More than once in the night, Rachel was awakened by a sound like cannon fire. Trees splitting, Aunt Jennie said. At last, warm air moved into the area and the ice began to melt.

"Papa will come!" Anna clasped her hands and hopped up and down with joy.

"Or," Aunt Lizzie said, "we could go to him. Would you like that?"

In less than an hour, the aunts, Rachel, Anna, and Barrett were in the buggy, sloshing along the muddy road. Anna could barely contain her joy. The moment Aunt Lizzie pulled the buggy to a halt, Anna dashed for the house, flung open the door, and went inside. She returned just as quickly, announcing that Papa wasn't inside.

Rachel hurried into the barn ahead of the others. She found

Adam, sound asleep atop a row of hay bales just outside a stall. When she put her hand on his shoulder, he started awake and sat up, blinking against the sunlight shining in through the door.

He squinted up at her. "What's the matter?" He lurched to his feet. "The children—"

"—are fine. It's you we're worried about."

Anna skittered up the aisle. The aunts peered inside. Seeing Adam and Rachel, they retreated after saying they'd see to getting a meal started in the house.

"We were so worried, Papa," Anna said. "Why didn't you come to church Sunday?"

"The ice," Adam said. He looked toward the stall. "And Bo." He stepped to the stall door. "No–no–no—" He jerked the stall door open and knelt beside the giant gray horse, lying on its side in the straw.

When Anna took a step toward him, Adam held up his hand to ward her off. Rachel reached for Anna's hand, and together they backed out of the stall. *Poor Adam.* The man was clearly exhausted. Losing one of his team would be—but wait. At Adam's touch, the horse flicked an ear. Lifted its head.

"Hey, boy," Adam murmured, his voice low and gentle. He grasped the halter and encouraged the horse to rise. With a mighty surge, the huge animal was on his feet. He shook from head to tail, tossed his head, and moved to the corner of the stall where a bucket waited, wedged into a corner shelf. He lowered his great head, snuffled, snorted, and turned his head to look at Adam.

Rachel burst out laughing. "I don't know a lot about horses, but

I know disappointment when I see it."

Adam looked up toward heaven. "Thank you!" He looked at Rachel. "He's hungry. He hasn't eaten in two days. I've been nursing him day and night. . .nothing I could do. . .I'd nearly lost hope." He looked back over at the giant horse. At Rachel. Down at Anna. "It's good to see you. So good." He scooped Anna up and gave her a hug. "He's going to be all right! Bo's going to be all right!" And suddenly he was including Rachel in the hug, whirling about and lifting her off the ground.

He set her down quickly and apologized. "I'm sorry." His face turned red. "I smell like a horse." He took the bucket out of Bo's stall and strode away, returning with grain.

The bell that hung just outside the farmhouse door rang. Aunt Lizzie shouted, "Breakfast in twenty minutes!"

"That's just time for me to get the rest of the stock fed."

Anna spoke up. "Rachel and me can feed the chickens."

Adam looked doubtful, but before he could speak, Rachel agreed. "We certainly can." She motioned for Anna to lead the way. At the doorway, she glanced back at Adam. His hair was a mess. And he *did* smell a bit like a horse. And she loved him.